The Little Gymnast

Anda Barnes is headstrong and impatient. She is always getting into trouble for climbing things and her hot temper doesn't help. Her parents are in despair. One day she watches the Olympic gymnastics on television and as she sits entranced by the acrobatic twists and twirls, Gran has a brainwave. She enrols Anda in the Ferndale Olympic Gymnastic Club!

At first, everything is perfect—Anda is a natural gymnast and she makes rapid progress. But Anda's parents are hard up and it becomes more and more difficult for them to keep up with the expense of her intensive training. When Anda hears about a scholarship to help young gymnasts she's determined to win it, for without the money the award would bring, Anda will have to abandon her hopes of ever becoming an Olympic Gymnast.

The Little Gymnast

Sheila Haigh

Hippo Books
Scholastic Book Services
London

To the little gymnasts
of Meare School, Somerset

Scholastic Book Services Inc.,
10 Earlham Street, London WC2H 9LN

Scholastic Inc.,
730 Broadway, New York, NY 10003, USA

Scholastic Tab Publications Ltd.,
123 Newkirk Road, Richmond Hill,
Ontario L4C 3G5, Canada

Ashton Scholastic Pty Ltd., PO Box 579, Gosford,
New South Wales, Australia

Ashton Scholastic Ltd., 165 Marua Road,
Panmure, Auckland, New Zealand

First published by Blackie and Son Limited, 1982

Published in paperback by Scholastic Book Services, Inc., 1985

Contents

1

Child on the roof

Anda Barnes rubbed her hands on the back of her jeans. There was only one way up to the church roof. Up the drainpipe. She shook it, feeling its age and its rust. A man's weight might have torn it from the wall, but it was strong enough for a girl as small as Anda.

Leaning back and pressing her sneakers into the wall she went up like a spiderman. She put her arms round a stone gargoyle that looked down at her. With a heave and a wriggle she was on the roof, her heart beating against the mossed tiles.

Above her the branch of a tall beech tree swept and dipped in the wind. Earlier that day a tiny black and white kitten had climbed the tree and made its way along the branch, looking for a way down. The thin twigs had bent, tipping the kitten on to the roof, leaving it stranded.

Now it clung, black-eyed and loud-voiced, on

the apex of the roof. Its miaows had filled the village and someone had called the fire brigade.

But it seemed to Anda that the fire brigade were not going to turn out for one tiny ball of miaowing fluff on the church roof. So she decided to rescue it herself.

There was the roof going steeply up towards the sky. Anda had lost sight of the kitten, which was on the other side of the bell tower. She lay on her stomach and crawled up the roof bit by bit.

The watching crowd saw a head appear over the crest of the roof. They cheered. Someone must have got a ladder! Then they fell silent. The blonde head with its twirl of hair and bird-like face belonged to a child in blue jeans and a blue track suit top.

"My God, there's a child up there!"

"Go back, you silly little girl!" bellowed a big round man, waving fat hands at Anda. "No one in their right mind would get up there!"

"Don't tell her to go back! She'll fall. Keep still!" shrieked an old lady.

"Who is it? Whose little girl is that?"

"It's the child from that tumble-down cottage out at Hootycombe," said the old lady. "I'll bet her parents don't know where she is!"

"They keep goats," said a little boy. "And chickens. I seen 'em."

Anda kept crawling, ignoring their shouts. A rush of rain pelted the leafy churchyard. The wet roof shone bright and slippery. Carefully Anda stood up. The next bit was easy. A narrow

2

ledge ran along the top, straight to the bell tower. She stepped down and balance-walked quickly along it.

"Anda, come down!"

"Anda, don't go any further."

Shouts like that echoed all through her life! For Anda had always loved to climb things. Trees, rocks, buildings. She was forever getting into trouble for it.

The bell tower was more difficult. It involved going down the roof, and along, then up again. She slid down, making the seat of her jeans wet, then flattened herself against the lichened stones of the tower and began to creep sideways. Her feet were at the most impossible angle, and there was nothing to hold on to. What a long way to the ground! Just a slide, a roll and down, down, down on to the hard flag stones.

The siren of the fire engine was blasting down the steep twisting hill into Elmsford. Anda hesitated, her legs aching with the effort of staying upright. Would she make it?

There was the kitten! A scrap of fluff at the other end of the roof.

"I'll get you. Don't worry, little cat!" whispered Anda. "Little baby cat!"

Thankfully she made it to the corner of the tower and was soon crawling up again. Getting back, with the kitten, would be worse, unless there was another way down.

The kitten saw Anda, and opened its little pink mouth in a silent miaow! It had cried itself hoarse.

On wobbly legs it walked along the roof towards her. Incredibly the point of its tail was up and the little face bright.

"That's right! Come on. Come to me, baby cat!" she crooned. And the kitten came straight to her. Sitting astride the roof, Anda picked it up. It weighed nothing! Just a handful of fur, four clinging thistledown paws, and a heart beating under Anda's thumb. Its face was like a pansy. Black and white, and velvety and wistful. As soon as Anda had it snuggled in her arms she wanted it.

"Bella, I'll call you! After the church bells!" she whispered. "And you're going to stay with me! You *dear* little thing."

She tucked the kitten inside her track suit top and did the zip up.

"Who do you think you are? Wonder Woman?"

The man's voice startled Anda. She swung round, and there was a fireman on a long ladder coming up the roof.

Down below was the fire engine, throbbing away in the road, its blue light twisting through the trees. More and more people had gathered, some of them people Anda knew. And kids she knew from the village school. She was surprised. She waved and shouted.

"Got the kitten!"

But nobody cheered. Probably they were all cross with her. The grown-ups would be, anyway!

"Hang on to me. We'll soon get you down!"

4

said the fireman.

"But I can climb down! I'm quite all right!" said Anda. She stared at his helmet. "Why have you got that on? There isn't a fire!"

The man shrugged.

"Regulations," he said.

To Anda's annoyance he reached out and picked her up, kitten and all.

"Put your arms round my neck and hold tight!"

"But I can climb down!"

The fireman wouldn't listen. He held Anda tightly as he climbed down the ladder. She had no choice but to hold on! Inside her track suit the kitten was crawling about. She could feel it trying to burrow its head out through her collar.

Within minutes they were on the ground.

"You silly, silly little girl! You might have been killed!"

Anda looked up at the man from the village Post Office. His face was the colour of a dish of rhubarb.

"What are your parents doing, letting you up there?" he thundered. "Don't they care?"

Anda's brown eyes sparkled angrily.

"They *do* care!" she said, looking him straight in the eye. "And they know where I am. I went to post a letter for Dad!"

She looked round at all the faces. They were all staring at her and Anda hated that.

The fireman patted Anda on the head. "I think she's a brave little girl! Now, where's that kitten?"

Anda grinned. She undid her zip and a little face appeared.

"Aw!" said everyone.

Someone reached out to pick up the kitten, but it clung to Anda furiously, its needle-like claws entangled in her shirt. She put a hand over it protectively. Little Bella. Bella would be her kitten now!

"It comes from Holly Cottage. Mrs Wood. She's got kittens."

"Bet you'd like to keep him, wouldn't you?" said the fireman kindly.

Anda nodded. She swallowed. To knock on Mrs Wood's door was worse than climbing the roof. Anda didn't like Mrs Wood. Once she had caught Anda balance-walking along her garden wall and given her a ticking off that had echoed all down the village street, and Anda had walked away with a very red face. Mrs Wood was not likely to give Anda one of her kittens after that!

"Come on, I'll take you," said the kind fireman.

Anda and the fireman and the kitten knocked on the door of Holly Cottage. And to Anda's surprise Mrs Wood actually smiled.

She reached out a bony hand and plucked Bella away from the girl's shoulder.

"We've had a litter of six. They're all over the place! Come and see!" She opened a door and led them into a dark room full of plants and heavy curtains. "This is the Mum cat," she said, pointing to a basket in the corner.

She put Bella down and the kitten scampered

6

across to its mother. There was much miaowing and nuzzling and licking.

"Do you want homes for them?" asked the fireman.

"Oh yes. Some of them are booked already. Of course I can't go out much, you see. My arthritis."

They chatted on about cats and dogs and geraniums, while Anda tried to find a moment to ask if Bella had a home. But suddenly she found herself walking back down the path and the fireman was saying goodbye. She hadn't found the courage to ask about Bella!

Anda was brave enough for anything, except knocking on Mrs Wood's door! And now beautiful little Bella was shut away inside Holly Cottage.

2

Olympic gymnasts

Home was a mile out of the village, up a steep lane that got stonier and stonier as it climbed between high banks. The track branched off, one path going up to the heather covered moor where sheep and ponies grazed, the other dipping down along the hillside to some birch trees. There stood Hooty Cottage. A right shambles, Anda's gran called it. Old sheds and bits of tin and chickens everywhere!

She didn't bother opening the gate but shinned up the chicken house, rolled across the roof and landed with a mighty leap in the garden.

"Anda!" Her dad was standing right there, tying up the bean canes. "Can't you arrive home in a civilised manner?"

He wasn't really cross. If he was cross his beard would bristle and his eyes would go pebbly. Most of the time he was peaceful and

8

twinkly. Anda adored him. At school she would fight anyone who said, "Your dad's a hippie."

"I posted your letter!" she said, hanging round his waist.

"Good girl!"

He went on tying string round the bean canes. He was a tall man with a wild frizz of sandy-coloured hair and a gingery beard. He wore denim shorts and sandals and a tartan shirt.

"See anyone?" he asked Anda.

"Dad, there was this kitten. And it couldn't get down, so ..."

"So you rescued it!" he said, laughing. "Trust you. Where was it? Up a tree?"

"It was only on the church roof, Daddy. I went up the pipe and across and round the bell tower and then this fireman came and carried me down. It was a darling little kitten and it belongs ..."

"What?" Her dad gave a roar loud enough to rock the chicken house. "You WHAT?"

"Went up the pipe and ..."

"You climbed on the church roof? And the fire brigade got you down?"

"Well, no. Well, they came to get the kitten really, but I got to it first. I thought it would get wet. I could have climbed down OK but ..."

Bill squatted down and put his two bean-stained hands on Anda's shoulders. His face was serious.

"Tell me that again, slowly," he said. "Tell me exactly what you did."

9

Anda began to feel that she'd done something dreadful from the look on his face. She explained as slowly as she could.

Bill seemed caught between grinning and being angry. In the end he roared with laughter. Then he frowned again.

"But you mustn't do things like that, Anda."

"What's she done now?"

Anda's mum was coming down the path with two buckets, on her way to milk the goats. She was small and pretty, with a face exactly like Anda's, except for its long, stringy hair. She never wore a dress. Always jeans. Sometimes Anda wished she would wear a pretty dress. Her mum was sweet and gentle sometimes, but more often tired and dishevelled. She was stricter with Anda than Bill.

"Oh no! Anda! You might have been killed!" she cried when she heard what Anda had done.

"It was OK, Mum. Why does everyone make such a fuss?" said Anda. "Everyone was shouting at me to get down."

"I don't care about *them*! It's *you* I'm concerned about," stormed her mother, her voice building up to a squeak. "Anda! You *are not* to climb things!"

"Oh, don't go on at her, Lynne!" said Bill, seeing Anda's face going pale. "It's the way she is!"

"Well, I can't cope with her!" raved her mother. "She knows she shouldn't do it! And you don't stop her! Well if you don't, I will. Go indoors, Anda."

Anda went, dragging her feet, leaving her parents arguing in the beans. No chance of her having Bella now! It really wasn't fair! Why couldn't people be pleased because she had climbed the church roof to rescue a kitten?

"Look what she's done in the first week of the holidays!" her mum was screeching in the beans. "She's written off a pair of shoes in the stream, she's broken the barn door swinging on it, split the corn sacks jumping on them, and countless other things. I mean, how can one child be so destructive?"

"She's got too much energy, I guess. She doesn't mean to be destructive, Lynne." Good old dad. He was defending her again!

"And look at the seat of your jeans!" exclaimed her mother, coming in at the door.

Anda twisted to look at the blackened seat of her jeans.

"That's from sliding down the church roof," she explained, and without warning the tears came burning and boiling down her cheeks. "Why can't you be pleased with me, Mum? I climbed all up the church roof to get Bella and the fireman said I was brave anyway. You're cross with me all the time. You don't like me. You don't like me. You don't!"

"Oh Anda!" Lynne held out her arms and held the stormy little girl tightly. "Of course we like you, darling! It's just that you get yourself into so much mischief."

"But I don't mean to," Anda sobbed. She didn't cry often. When she did she couldn't stop.

Her mother sighed. "I don't know what to do with you. I really don't."

"You won't really shut me indoors?"

"No, of course not! But just do try not to be always climbing things and breaking things!"

That made Anda cry even more. She blurted it all out, about wanting the kitten and being afraid to knock on Mrs Wood's door!

Lynne was not very hopeful. "I don't think we'd dare have a cat, not with all the chickens!" she said. "Anyway, we'll see. I'll talk to Daddy. You go and do something positive, Anda, for goodness sake. Do you want to do the pots or milk the goats?"

Anda looked at the pile of dishes in the sink.

"I'll milk the goats," she said.

She dried her face on her sleeve and took the two buckets awkwardly, one on each arm. She loved the two goats, Millie and Mollie. She put her arms round Millie's black and white neck and told the goat her troubles. Millie listened attentively, flicking her curved ears backwards and forwards, and blinking her gold eyes.

Milking the goats was easy, once you got the hang of it. She watched the jets of creamy milk filling the bucket, and tried to stop crying. It was her tenth birthday in two weeks. Maybe her parents would let her have Bella then!

But before that something happened that changed Anda's life completely!

She was having tea at Gran's when it happened. It was a Saturday and Gran had taken her shopping and bought some cream cakes for tea. She'd bought Anda an adventure book.

"To keep you quiet," Gran said.

Gran lived in a bungalow on the new housing estate in Elmsford. The big attraction at Gran's for Anda was the colour telly which was always switched on. Anda didn't have a television at all, so she always wanted to watch it, no matter what was on; the bright colours fascinated her.

Anda knew she had to sit still at Gran's. No swinging from doors or rolling on the floor! Today she tried extra hard to sit and read her new book.

But suddenly something on the television caught her attention. A girl was flying through the air, like a swallow! She landed and stood with her arms stretched high. Then she smiled, waved with both hands and ran off to the sound of cheering. Anda sat up straight, her eyes glued to the screen.

Next they showed another girl dancing and tumbling to music on a huge square mat. She danced and leaped and did the fastest hand-springs. She turned somersaults in the air. Things Anda thought only circus acrobats did!

"A marvellous performance," raved the commentator. "And this little girl is only fifteen years old!"

The girl waved to the cheering crowds in the Olympic stadium. She wore a white leotard and ballet-type shoes, and her hair was tied in a pony tail with a white ribbon.

Anda caught her breath. A spark of an idea

13

burned in her mind.

Other girls from different countries came on the screen. All of them were graceful and agile. They performed on a balance beam and swung on some high bars.

Anda jumped up and ran into the kitchen.

"Gran! Gran!"

"For goodness sake, Anda!" Gran rattled the tea cups.

"Gran, look! Look at these girls. Quick! Quick!"

Gran bustled into the lounge, surprised at the look of intensity on Anda's face. Together they watched a little Russian girl on the beam.

"Oh yes," said Gran. "I love to watch the gymnastics!"

"Gymnastics?" repeated Anda, tasting the word for the first time. At school they did PE or Music and Movement, both of which she enjoyed, but never anything quite like that! In herself Anda knew that she could do some of the things the Olympic girls were doing!

"I could do that!" she said excitedly.

"Go on!" teased Gran. "You'd tie yourself in a knot!"

"But I could, Gran! If I practised and practised, and then I could go in the Olympics when I'm older!"

"No, Anda ... You don't understand," said Gran. "Those girls are specially trained with special facilities. You couldn't do that in Elmsford!"

Anda's face fell.

"But I can do handstands and ..."

"No, don't show me!" said Gran, restraining her. "We're going to have tea now. Anyway, I've seen you doing handstands before."

"But I can do something else too. I could do it on the lawn!"

"No," said Gran. "It's teatime. And I don't think the neighbours would like a display of your knickers, thank you."

Anda sighed. She had a dress on today, white socks and pretty sandals, all of which were kept just for visiting Gran. She couldn't wait to get home now and put on her jeans and do gymnastics on the lawn. So she ate as fast as she could, and Gran looked at her disapprovingly.

"You're very quiet, Anda!" she remarked as she drove her home in her neat blue car.

But Anda's mind was miles away. In her head she was seeing again the girl in the white leotard, and the Russian girl on the beam. And she was seeing herself doing it.

"She's got her head full of those Olympic gymnasts!" warned Gran when they got to the cottage. "I can't get any sense out of her! Or into her!"

"I'm going to change into my PE things from school," said Anda and she charged upstairs, leaving her parents podding a mountain of peas.

Her PE things—red shorts and a T-shirt and black daps—were still in their bag in the corner where she had chucked them on the last day of term.

She changed quickly, throwing her dress and

her posh sandals up to hit the ceiling. At the top of the stairs she stopped. An interesting conversation was going on, and she could hear bits of it.

"Perhaps there's a gymnastics club! There's bound to be one in town—at the Sports Centre."

"I'll enquire."

"Shh," said Anda's dad, and after that she only heard whispers. She though she heard the word *birthday* and *gymnastics*. Then she heard the word *kitten* quite distinctly! Her birthday was next Friday. She would be ten. What were they planning?

She chose that moment to run downstairs and jump the last three steps.

"No, no, Anda! You're not to wear those in the holidays. You'll have nothing for school!" moaned Lynne. "Go and change. And I'll bet you've left your dress in a heap. Go and hang it up. Then you can help pod the peas!"

Anda turned on her heel. She didn't dare groan in front of Gran! She raced upstairs and did an angry somersault on her bed. She fell off on the floor and it shook the whole cottage.

"What on earth are you doing?"

Anda stood rubbing her elbow where she'd banged it. It seemed she couldn't do anything right!

3

Handstands

"Boots off and happy birthday in that order!" said Gran.

Mud was not allowed in Gran's house. Bill and Anda stepped out of their wellingtons. Bill winked at Anda.

"My socks are horrible," he said.

"I don't wish to know that, thank you!" said Gran brightly. "Have you got the ..."

"Shh! No. Not yet!" Bill put his finger to his lips.

"Doesn't she know?" mouthed Gran.

"I heard you!" giggled Anda.

"You mean about the thousand-and-one-piece jigsaw we're giving her?" said Bill in a loud voice. Anda couldn't bear jigsaws.

"He's been teasing me all the way!" cried Anda, looking expectantly at Gran. Gran had a beautiful bluey-green dress on and a big silver pendant. Her ash-blonde hair was swept into elaborate waves. It was difficult to believe she was Bill's mum!

She took Anda into the kitchen.

"Oh Gran!"

"Hey, that's really wow!" exclaimed Bill.

A fantastic cake stood on the table. In the middle Gran had done a picture in coloured icing of a girl gymnast. Her leotard was pink icing and it had ANDA written across it.

"That has to be a good luck cake!" said Bill.

"It's wonderful, Gran. How did you do it?"

Gran swelled with pride. "Look underneath, Anda. There's something else!"

She lifted the silver dish revealing an envelope.

"A card! Oh thanks, Gran."

Inside the card was a green ticket. It said *Ferndale Olympic Gymnastics Club. Membership Card. Anda Barnes.*

"Gymnastics Club?" squealed Anda.

"It's at Ferndale School. And you can go on Monday at four o'clock," explained Gran. "I joined you up for six months to see if you like it. They train all through the holidays. It looked well organised. I went and had a look. There's children there even younger than you!"

"Wow!" Anda's eyes were sparkling. Monday at four o'clock. Mentally she worked it out. Four whole days and three nights to wait!

"But the instructor—a lady it was I spoke to, said it was hard work!" warned Gran. "You have to work really hard, and do what you're told."

18

"Hoorah!" cheered Bill.

"How did you know about the club, Gran?" asked Anda, thinking that Gran had probably never turned a somersault in her life.

"I didn't know, dear," Gran explained, plugging in the kettle. "I went to the library and asked."

"The library!"

"Oh yes. You can find out anything you want to know if you ask!" said Gran.

Gran and Bill sat chatting over coffee. Anda sat and gazed at the cake and dreamed about being a gymnast while the rain lashed savagely at the window and Gran's garden whirled and tossed.

"Come on then, Anda. Surprise number two!" said Bill.

They left in wellies and rain coats. The old van, Murgatroyd, wouldn't start. Bill sat there turning the key again and again. "Blast the thing!"

Anda was used to Murgatroyd's not-starting music. She sat curled up on its front seat, reading the blurb on the back of her club card. She had another card with it. It said *British Amateur Gymastics Association. Personal Achievement card. Award 4.* Inside was a list of ten things you were supposed to be able to do. She didn't understand what all of them were exactly, but she knew one or two that they had done at school. Bridge—she could do that! Handstand—yes, she could even walk on her hands. Headstand—she could do that!

"What's a forward roll, Daddy?" she asked.

Murgatroyd started at last and they rattled away.

"A fifty mile an hour jet propelled sausage!" Bill said. Surprise number two was not going to be much, he added, when she had stopped giggling. "We can't give you things that cost a lot of money, Anda," he said, glancing at her. "We're trying to be self-sufficient, you know that, don't you?"

"Yes."

Bill only worked part-time as a brickie. That paid for the essentials. But apart from that, they tried to grow all their own food and manage without posh furniture. Anda knew that because it had been explained to her many times. It was the only way they could stay in the cottage.

Her parents loved Hootycombe very much. And so did Anda. She loved the primroses in spring, the long-haired sheep that ran wild with their baby lambs, the grey squirrels in the wood, and the great silver gulls that blew in from the sea. She loved the winter when the snow blew sideways, and the summer when she played for hours by the stream and went to bed to the sound of the hooting owls that gave Hootycombe its name.

When Murgatroyd stopped outside Holly Cottage she couldn't believe it. She stared at Bill over a big smile. "Are we having Bella? Are we?"

Bill ruffled the tuft of hair that stuck up over Anda's forehead. "It might be one of the other

20

kittens. It depends whether Bella's already booked or not. You won't mind terribly, will you?"

"No," said Anda dubiously.

Mrs Wood led them into the room with the heavy curtains. "It's a little she-cat, you know. That's why she wasn't chosen. They all want tomcats."

Bella was nowhere to be seen. Mrs Wood looked under the chairs and behind the curtains and on the bookshelves.

"She's not been outside much. Not since that day she climbed the roof! Now wherever is she?"

"I can see her!" squealed Anda, pointing to one of the chairs. A moving bump was going up the back of the chair, under the cover.

Mrs Wood grumbled while she extracted Bella from the chair. The kitten emerged flat-eared and wild-eyed in her hand. "Wretched animals!" she said. "Here you are. Hold on to her."

She dumped the wild black and white bundle in Anda's lap. The kitten was a big bigger, but she still weighed hardly anything. Suddenly the tiny face looked up at Anda with eyes like blue jewels.

"Hello!" said Anda. Bella stared at her, head on one side. Then she crawled up Anda's chest, right up to her face. She touched noses with Anda. White whiskers tickled her face, and the kitten drew back and sat looking. Then she put out a paw and dabbed at the string from Anda's anorak.

"Oh, isn't she darling! Isn't she tiny!" breathed Anda. In her arms the kitten began to purr as if she knew she had found a home.

"Cats know," said Mrs Wood. "She picked you out!"

"Won't she miss her mother?" asked Anda.

"She's eight weeks. She can lap all right. But only give her tiny meals," said Mrs Wood.

"What do we owe you?" Bill asked, putting out a finger to rub Bella's ear. "Isn't she beautiful!"

"Nothing. I'm glad to find homes for them. Anyway, it'll cost you enough to have her injected against cat 'flu and all that."

"Injected?" said Anda, horrified.

"There you are!" said Bill. "I said you were getting an injection for your birthday!"

"And the price of cat food!"

"Anyway, thanks a lot, Mrs Wood. We must be going."

"Thanks," said Anda.

They left Mrs Wood grumbling about the price of everything. Murgatroyd's noisy engine had no effect on Bella, and she curled up happily on Anda's lap, patting and playing. Anda couldn't stop gazing at her, and kept up a stream of exclamations.

"Oh look, Daddy! She's got pink feet! Her paws are pink on the bottom. Like pink beads!"

"Look at her white whiskers! Oh, she's got little white eyelashes!"

"Why are her eyes blue?"

"They'll change," said Bill, steering Murgatroyd carefully round a group of moorland sheep. "They'll go green as she gets older. Or yellow. Oh, she's magic, isn't she!"

"This is the superest birthday ever!" said Anda with a happy sigh.

"Make the most of it," said Bill.

All that weekend the rain poured and the wind blew. Bill and Lynne rushed about in macs and wellies, tying and staking their precious plants against the wind. Anda sat podding peas for hours, and Bella had a marvellous time chasing the stray ones around the floor. When the kitten finally climbed into her cardboard box to sleep, Anda went to the barn to practise gymnastics.

The barn floor was cold and gritty, but it didn't matter! As long as she kept away from the corn sacks! She spread some of the empty ones out on the floor for mats, and made one nice thick pile to practise headstands on.

Anda had always been able to stand on her head. And do cartwheels. Her teacher said she did lovely cartwheels. So she practised those too. But mostly she practised handstands. She could lean over backwards and make a bridge. That was something she was always being asked to do at school!

She felt sure she would surprise everyone at the gymnastics club!

4

To be a gymnast

Anda stood miserably at the door of the gymnasium, watching the track-suited children who were running about putting out mats and benches. She wasn't frightened of the gymnastics, but paralysed by an illogical fear of walking into a crowd of strangers.

At the last minute she'd pleaded with Lynne. "Please take me in. I can't go on my own."

"Rubbish. It'll be good for you." And Lynne had driven determinedly away in Murgatroyd.

Two girls swept past her, through the swing doors, laughing and talking. They ignored Anda. Her throat full of panicky tears, she crept back to the changing room.

And then she saw Julienne.

Julienne was struggling into a blue leotard, her clothes spread around her on the floor.

"Oh, I hate this horrible leotard!" she was grumbling. "It makes me prickle. The trouble is ..."

Anda stood, wondering how anyone could find so much to say to a complete stranger! For a gymnast Julienne was heavily built. Her moon-pale face between two chunky brown plaits had a worried look. It was not a happy face, but when she smiled at Anda her eyes were blueberry blue and friendly.

"Are you just starting today?" she asked.

"Yes," said Anda.

"Haven't you got a leotard?"

"No."

"It doesn't matter. But you'll have to take those off," advised Julienne, pointing to Anda's black plimsolls. "I'm Julienne Wellington. Hello!"

"Hello. I'm Anda Barnes."

"How old?"

"Ten."

"Me too. Where are you from?"

"Elmsford." Anda took off her plimsolls and socks.

"I'll look after you."

Julienne talked incessantly. Anda followed her about wide-eyed and silent.

The enormous gymnasium was well equipped. Wall bars. Ropes. Benches and beams. Asymetric bars. And a huge trampoline!

"We aren't allowed on that!" said Julienne, seeing Anda's eyes light up. "We have to have spotters!"

Before Anda could ask what spotters were, Julienne had sprinted over to a trolley piled high with blue mats.

"Tumbling mats," she explained. "We have to put them all out."

As more and more children arrived, Anda felt painfully aware that she was the only one in shorts and a T-shirt.

"Julienne," she said as they undid the straps from one of the blue mats, "what's a forward roll?"

Julienne and another girl looked at each other and laughed.

"Don't you even know that?" shrieked the other girl, a blonde, pony-tailed, pixie-faced child. "That's the easiest thing!" Anda took an instant dislike to her. She came and undid the strap Anda was undoing, impatiently with pink efficient fingers. "Not like that! Like this!"

"That's Lena," Julienne said. "And that's Christie over there. She's our instructor. And that's John. He's her husband."

Bewildered, Anda followed Julienne to where a track-suited woman was sitting, surrounded by piles of paper, little heaps of money, and a tangle of wires coming from a tape recorder. A group of girls stood round her saying "Where's my ..." and "Can I ...." Christie was coping patiently, her wavy grey-haired head bent over a chart.

Despite the grey hair her face was young, and when she saw Anda it broke into a magical smile. Straightaway Anda felt welcome.

"You must be Anda!"

Christie didn't say Anda Barnes, like they did at school.

26

"You can call me Christie, OK?"

"OK," Anda smiled. "I couldn't wait for today! I want to go to the Olympics!"

The other girls giggled, and Julienne rolled her eyes comically. But Christie looked at her solemnly.

"Right! We'd better get you started then, hadn't we. Got your card? Lovely. Good girl," she said, taking it. "You can go with Group D, that's our beginners group, and stay with them."

"OK," said Anda.

Christie put a hand on Anda's shoulder.

"I'll just say this to you, Anda, before we begin. Don't go on any apparatus unless you've been told to, and don't do anything until after the warm up. You don't understand what that is, do you?"

"No."

"Well, it's very important. Even Olympic gymnasts still have to do it. Try to copy the exercises the others are doing. The secret is to practise every day at home."

"Oh I do," said Anda, and Christie laughed softly.

The group consisted of two five-year-olds, one fragile dark-skinned girl called Elizabeth, and several who looked about ten. One of them with a pale freckled face looked scruffier than the others, in faded training tights and a tatty sweater. She looked tough and alone. Anda stood by her, and asked her name.

"Kerry."

Christie started the tape recorder. In three groups the forty girls in the gym began to move. Anda stood for a moment, fascinated.

Left behind, and seeing Christie looking at her, she joined in. First they were running on their toes. Then leaping sideways. Bending and stretching followed, touching the floor and swinging.

Next it was bridges. Down flat, then up, with backs arched.

"Try to get your legs straight!"

Christie went round helping. She passed Anda who looked at her anxiously, upside down.

"Good," she said. "You're all right."

More exercises followed. Anda thought she would never remember them all! Some were difficult, especially one that involved sitting with legs wide apart and getting your chest on the floor. And the splits was difficult. Nobody in her group could do it. Except for Kerry.

"It takes months!" Christie said. "Don't force it. Let your muscles get used to it!"

By the time the warm-up was finished, Anda felt friends with the group.

"We're beginning with floor," Christie said. "Start with forward rolls!"

At last she was to discover what those were! Anda positioned herself at the back of the queue to watch.

"Oh, somersaults!" she thought when she saw the others rolling over and over. "I can do *those*!"

So she rolled at speed along the mat, three times, hoping to impress Christie. The girl in front turned round angrily as Anda crashed into her. "Mind out."

"Come here, Anda."

She went to Christie.

"Watch," said Christie. "Watch Lena."

She called Lena over and asked her to do a forward roll. With a contemptuous glance at Anda, Lena stretched tall, stood poised and then sprang into a graceful roll.

"Did her head touch the floor?" asked Christie.

"No."

"What did her legs do?"

"I don't know."

"Watch again."

Patiently she made Lena repeat the roll several times so that Anda could watch.

"Now you try."

Anda suddenly found she didn't know how to begin! Christie showed her how to squat and spring. Remembering to tuck her head in and to get up without using her hands was more difficult than she'd thought! Christie wanted her to keep her ankles and knees together as well. Over and over again she tried.

Backward rolls were even more complicated! Anda decided to practise the two rolls at home. She hadn't expected to fail at something so easy.

Handstands next. Then headstands. She wasn't doing those right either!

"It's our turn for beam now," said Christie.

There were three beams, one at floor level, one at knee height and the high full-sized "Continental Sports" beam. Anda couldn't wait. She bounded and skipped.

"Can I go on the big one?" she asked Christie.

"Yes, OK," said Christie. "Just try it out. Get the feel of it. Walk about on it and sit on it. We'll teach you some things to do when you're used to it! No, Kerry, let Anda have a minute to herself first. You work on the benches."

Kerry got down, her face expressionless.

"What are you staring at?" she said to Anda.

"Nothing."

Kerry turned her back. Something was wrong with her, Anda thought, puzzled.

At shoulder height, the big beam was no higher for Anda than many of the gates and walls she had climbed! Under her bare feet it was hard, velvety and high in the air! It felt marvellous. She walked straight to the other end, turned and ran back. Christie was standing close, her face anxious and surprised.

From watching the Olympic girls on television, Anda thought she had to dance on the beam. So she danced, stretching and twisting. It took concentration, and a lot of inelegant wobbling.

"John!" Christie was shouting.

John came quickly and stood beside Christie.

"Look at this child!" said Christie.

Together they watched Anda as she danced, with her bird-like face and flexible toes. Her balance was steady, her movements, though untrained, were graceful as she moved through a fantasy world of her own, small and strong and sunbrowned. She decided recklessly to try a cartwheel.

"No, Anda!"

Too late!

Simultaneously Christie and John ran sideways and caught Anda as she came flying off the end of the beam.

"Can I go back up?" she laughed.

John and Christie stared at each other. They didn't tell Anda that most children on the beam for the first time just walked gingerly along it. Some found it scary.

"Have you been on an Olympic beam before? Or any beam?" asked John curiously.

"No. Only an old fence post in the garden," said Anda. "Can I go back up?"

"Yes, for a few minutes. But *no* cartwheels or handstands. Just dance, OK?"

"OK," said Anda. But later on she got a quiet lecture from Christie about safety. And Julienne told her in no uncertain terms as well.

"You're potty! You must be potty! Fancy doing a cartwheel your first time on the beam! You're mad! You'll get chucked out of the gym club if you take silly risks! Christie won't have that!"

"But I didn't know. I thought I could do one!" protested Anda.

The vault was strange to Anda.

Watching Julienne's group finish their turn

at vaulting, she thought it looked easy, especially with a spring board, or reuther board, as it was called. Open-mouthed, she watched Lena sprinting past. Bang, off the reuther board, up into a handstand and over.

"Have I got to do that?" asked Anda, looking at Christie.

"No way!" said Christie. "You'll just be squatting your feet on and jumping off to start with!"

Julienne came next. But she chickened, running then stopping with her arms over the vaulting buck.

"We haven't got time for chickening!" John said to her.

Julienne rolled her eyes comically and returned for a second go. Her last chance, John said.

Julienne didn't do a handspring vault like Lena. She managed a sort of scramble, caught her foot on the buck and fell.

"Don't *worry* about it, Julienne," said Christie kindly.

Julienne managed a smile, but her distress was obvious.

"You have to be tough to be a gymnast!" said Christie. Then she looked at Kerry. "You aren't vaulting, Kerry, are you?"

"No," said Kerry in her quiet voice.

"You go and do floor work," said Christie. "Gently. No somies."

Kerry turned on her heel. She looked upset too! That was one major thing Anda learned in her first lesson. That gymnastics was not all laughter and cartwheels! There were tears there too, in the gym.

When her turn came, Anda ran confidently and bounced on to the reuther board. But it was not as springy as she'd expected! Slam, she hit the buck with her stomach and would have fallen back if Christie hadn't caught her.

"I could do it better than that!"

Cross with herself, she had another try.

"Really tuck your knees up high this time," advised Christie.

But it took several more crashes before Anda managed to get her feet on the buck and stand up.

John was watching her.

"Let me have her for five minutes," he said to Christie. "Can you watch my girls beam?"

John gave Anda so many instructions that her head felt like a computer! Chin up, knees up, run fast, run slow, push with your arms, land on the right bit of the spring board, stop when you land! John wanted her to do a through vault. She ran like a tiger, hurting her feet as she stamped on the reuther board.

The result was a breathtaking jump, through her arms and onto the crash mat.

"Stop when you land! Straight back!"

He steadied her.

"Great!" he said. "Now take it again!"

Anda ran back.

"Wow!" she said to Elizabeth. "I didn't know I could do that!"

"I'll bet you don't do it next time!" laughed Elizabeth.

Anda was thinking the same. John wagged a finger at her.

"Think, think, *think!*" he called.

She did. Focussing her attention on the buck and John's instructions, she ran, and flew over, this time with her feet tucked up neatly. Stopping took a lot of effort, but she managed it, and stood with a straight back and raised arms.

"Good girl!" said John, and again he asked her, "Have you done any vaulting before, Anda?"

"A bit. But our school box isn't so high."

"Oh," said John. "A little village school, is it?"

"Yes. Elmsford."

"I know," said John. He beamed down at Anda. Here at last was the talent he had dreamed of finding! For ten years he and Christie had run Ferndale Olympic Gymnastic Club. Their girls had entered competitions, gained a few medals, passed lots of grades. But Ferndale had never yet had a champion!

John kept his thoughts to himself. After all, Anda might not stick the rigorous training.

"Now don't go trying that at home, will you?" he said. "Only in the gym with proper equipment and someone to catch you! That's really important, Anda. Are you listening?"

"Yes."

"See you next week, then? Go on, your group is on the bars now!"

After the club Julienne was keen to talk to Anda.

"You did OK, didn't you? First time!" she said enthusiastically.

"I don't know," said Anda.

"Except for your nutty cartwheel on the beam!" cried Julienne. She turned to Lena who was putting her clothes away in a smart white bag. "Did you see what this mad fool did on the beam?" she shrieked. "She only did a cartwheel and went flying!"

Lena looked curiously at Anda.

"I'll bet you got a lecture from John!" she said.

"Yes. And one from Christie," said Anda, embarrassed.

Kerry was there with Lena, her face puffed and upset. The two girls were friends. Lena put her arm round Kerry and they walked off together.

"What's the matter with Kerry?" asked Anda.

"Oh, Kerry!" said Julienne. "She's not really like that. She used to train with the competition girls and then she got sick. She had an operation and she's been in hospital for months and months. Now she can't train properly for about a year. That's why she's upset all the time."

Anda felt sorry for Kerry.

She and Julienne wandered outside to wait for their mothers. Anda told Julienne about Bella, and Hooty Cottage and the stream.

"You lucky *thing*," said Julienne. "I'm not

allowed any pets. We live in a flat. Just Mum and me. She and my dad are divorced."

"You'll have to come up one day. We could do gymnastics on the lawn. And jump the Hooty Stream," said Anda generously.

"I'd love to. Could I?" Julienne's eyes shone.

Julienne's mum arrived in a gleaming car. She wore a smart suit, make-up, and had all the windows shut. She smiled icily at Anda.

A moment later Lynne drove up in muddy, spluttering Murgatroyd, her hair flying and all the door handles tied up with string.

"How was it?" she asked.

"Fabulous!" said Anda.

"You didn't make a fool of yourself then!"

"No!" Anda looked at Julienne and grinned. "Well—not quite!"

Julienne rolled her eyes and said teasingly, "Cartwheels?"

Anda grinned and waved as Julienne was whisked away in the sleek car. "See you next week!"

5

You can't go!

Anda flung herself on her bed and cried. The rough blankets burned her cheeks, and the walls shook with her sobs.

"You can't go. So accept it!" Lynne's voice called upstairs.

Outside, the autumn day was toasted and still. A thousand leaves fell silently in the Hooty glen. The four o'clock November sun was sinking. Through her tears pink light shone into her room with its muddly floor and white walls covered in posters of gymnasts. Five past four. Ten past four. Warm-up would be starting now! Where's Anda? Why isn't she here? And today she was due to complete her fourth BAGA award, Grade 1.

Determined to catch up with Julienne, she had worked every day at her exercises until she hurt. Horrified to hear of her using sacks in the barn, Christie had lent her a faded tumbling mat so that she could safely practise her agilities. When sunny, she worked on the level turf by the Hooty Stream, sometimes staying there until dark.

She had flown through Award 4 and 3. Award 2 had taken longer. The backroll to handstand was particularly difficult. Anda thought her arms would never be strong enough!

The four BAGA Awards, Christie told her, were only the first step. After that, she would be invited for extra training with the "competition squad". And that had become her burning ambition.

Gymnastics had given her something to work and dream for. She knew that John and Christie thought her talented and expected great things of her. But today was the second dreadful time she had missed going to the club!

"You'll get thrown out if you don't come every week!" Julienne had joked, but the words rang in Anda's head. She and Julienne had become close friends, although Julienne was a bit jealous of Anda's fast progress.

"Where were you last week?" Christie had said, while John looked at her coldly.

"We had a sick goat," explained Anda. "And Mummy had to wait in for the vet." She hadn't minded so much that time because of her concern for poor Millie. She'd stayed in the goat shed stroking, soothing the distressed goat until the vet had arrived.

Tonight it was different. Murgatroyd

wouldn't start. So there she was, stuck! And Lynne's casual attitude to it enraged Anda to the point of tears. She wanted to kick Murgatroyd to pieces! Anything to stop Lynne going on about her housework in her calm infuriating way!

Eventually Lynne came upstairs bringing tea and biscuits. Bella was on her shoulder.

"Come on, love. You can't stay like this for ever," she said, gently putting Bella down on the bed. Bella was almost a cat now, fluffy and adorable and very, very naughty! Butting her head against Anda's cheek, she purred loudly, walking round and round Anda's head until she sat up.

"Dear little cat!" murmured Anda, cuddling her. "She cares anyway!"

"That's not necessary, Anda," said Lynne, tight-faced. "You're a horrible child sometimes. You really are. I have feelings too! Do you think I liked it, Murgatroyd not starting? Do you?"

Anda shrugged.

"You aren't the only important person in the world!" said Lynne. "If Murgatroyd needs a new battery, it means that Daddy's got to take on extra work when he's already worn out keeping this place going! He's just as important as you! And what if you don't go to the blinking gym club for once?"

She leaned her arms on the window, staring out at the pink sky.

"Tonight was special, Mummy. You don't understand," snivelled Anda. She held the hot tea mug and sipped it noisily.

"Why don't I understand?" asked Lynne wearily. But when Anda tried to explain how Christie and John felt about her being talented and joining the competition girls, Lynne just said:

"Don't you think you're stretching it a bit, Anda? You're far too young for competitions! I know you're good at it, love, and I know you've practised, but it's only for fun, surely! You're too young to be taking it that seriously!"

This enraged Anda even more.

"But I'm *not*, Mummy! If anything I'm too old! John says I started a bit late, that's why I've had to work so hard! Honestly, Mummy, if you knew! Spider Girl's only *seven* and she trains with the competition girls!"

"Just what is it going to involve—this competition training?" asked Lynne.

"It means I can go on Thursday nights as well. And Saturday mornings if I want to. You don't have to pay!"

"But Anda we *can't* take you three times a week!" exploded Lynne. "The time, and the petrol, and the hanging about in town waiting for you! You can forget that! I'm telling you!"

There was a thunderous silence.

Bella went on relentlessly pouncing on bits of the bedspread.

One by one Anda's dreams flew out of the window. Hatred gripped her throat and she turned on Lynne who stood at the window blocking the light.

40

"You can't stop me going!" her voice came out squeaky and strange.

Lynne stood her ground. "Can't I?"

And of course she could!

"I'll run away then."

"There's the door!" said Lynne.

"You're horrid!" said Anda, turning in the open doorway. "And I *hate* you!"

Later she was to remember with guilt Lynne's shattered white face looking at her.

Down the stairs she thundered, through the cabbage-strewn kitchen, and out. Bella streaked after her, back arched, tail kinked.

Left alone in the cottage Lynne sat down on Anda's bed and covered her face with her long thin hands.

"Cool it, cool it," she kept telling herself. Anda had run away before. She would be back!

But Anda, as she ran along the banks of the Hooty Stream and up through the crunching bracken, was determined. She would never go back. Never. She climbed on and on up the twisting path, right to the top of the moors. The sky shone overhead like a china bowl, blue and pink at the edges.

A white obelisk stood on the summit. Anda sat on it, kicking it with her track shoes. Below her the lights of Elmsford twinkled through the trees. She could hear sheep baa-ing, and the distant bubbling of the Hooty Stream.

A loud wail reached her ears.

"Bella!"

Surely Bella hadn't followed her right up

there! The half-grown kitten crept out of the bracken, looking absolutely terrified. She had never been so far from the cottage before.

"Oh, poor Bella."

Although Anda picked her up, Bella would not be calmed.

"I'll have to take you home!"

Reluctantly she set off down the path. Bella wouldn't be carried but ran ahead of Anda in kink-tailed gallops. Within sight of home, the kitten relaxed and started to chase leaves. Anda sat up in the birch tree watching the cottage.

Drained of anger and energy, she sat limply. The stars came out like ice chips, chilling her, and the tinfoil stream sang into its ferns.

"You'll never be a gymnast," said a voice at the edge of her mind.

"I hate you," she said to the Hooty Combe. "For being so far away from Ferndale!"

She had never felt like that before! Shattered, she clung to the birch tree. Every happy thing in her life seemed suddenly to have gone—the summers, the squirrels in the wood, the primroses, the snow. Gone, leaving nothing but gymnastics. Even her parents whom she loved dearly now stood like enemies between her and her ambitions.

Listening to her dad's footsteps coming home up the lane, she felt worse and worse. Guiltily she saw him open the cottage door and take Lynne in his arms. She heard them talking. The birch tree held her in cold white arms.

Bill stood in the garden.

"Anda!"

The Hooty Combe went quiet.

"Anda!"

She froze.

"I can see you. Act your age and come on in. We've got some talking to do!"

She would have to face the music! Slowly she climbed down and walked back, heavily. Bella trotted beside her anxiously, sensing the crisis.

Little was said, however, and the week drifted by. School and tea, and school, and breakfast. Guy Fawkes night passed in a blaze of sparks. Rain fell, and the Hooty Stream roared and frothed. Soon it was Monday again and, for the first time, Anda had neglected her training.

To her surprise, Bill took the afternoon off and both her parents drove to Ferndale with her after school. They parked Murgatroyd and came right into the gym!

Christie looked reproachfully at Anda. She raised her eyebrows questioningly.

"Problems last week?"

Anda looked back. For once she didn't smile. Christie was alarmed. Anda's sparkle had gone, and there was a sad little girl in its place!

"Mum and Dad are here. Dad says he wants to watch. Can he?"

But Christie had gone! "Great! I want to see them a minute!"

"Hi, Anda! Where've you been?" cried Julienne. "Have you been ill?"

Anda shrugged.

43

"Kerry even trained when she was ill. And she had an operation!" said Lena.

"I wasn't ill. Murgatroyd wouldn't start."

"Murgatroyd?"

"Our van."

"It's a heap," said Lena. "No wonder!"

"Shut up, Lena. You're a snob!" said Julienne sharply. She took Anda to one side, her blue eyes concerned. "Christie was cross. I tried to make excuses for you. You might have phoned—oh, you haven't got a phone, have you? I forgot. You should have been here last week. We went on the trampoline!"

"Did you get your award?" asked Anda.

"Yes. But John says I've still got to learn the vaults." A frown crossed Julienne's face. "Then we can both train with the squad!"

Anda shrugged. She looked so miserable that even Kerry spoke kindly to her.

"You'll be OK. We've all had problems, honestly," she said. "I should know!"

Anda looked at Kerry's small freckled face and saw courage there. For the first time she began to like Kerry.

The girls finished putting out the equipment, and started warm-up. John and Christie were outside the glass doors talking to Anda's parents! She could see them nodding and gesticulating and she would have given anything to listen!

At last they all came back into the gym. Bill and Lynne sat down on its floor. Anda ran over anxiously.

"We aren't here," announced Bill. "Take no notice of us. Go on. Get on with it!"

His eyes were twinkling.

"Come on, Anda."

Christie whisked her away to work on the bars.

"You've got super parents!" she said. "They really do care and they are interested! We think we can work some transport out for you, Anda. So if you work hard you can come on Thursdays and Saturdays, with my competition girls!"

"Oh! Oh, Christie!"

Anda's energy came back like a ball of fire. She felt she could jump as high as the ceiling!

"But they want to watch, just this once, to see what you're up to! Try to forget they're there—OK?"

"OK!"

"What are they doing here?" Julienne wanted to know as the two girls rubbed chalk on their hands. "My mum would like to watch and Christie won't let her!"

Hardly surprising, Anda thought. Julienne's mother was bossy and pushy. But she kept her thoughts to herself.

"I'm joining the competition girls!" she whispered. "If I work hard tonight! So we both can!"

"Oh super!" Julienne's friendly smile came on. Then a frown. "Honestly, it's not fair! I've been coming here since I was six and I've only just made it! And you walk in and do it in six months!"

Anda shrugged. She felt awkward when Julienne got jealous.

Bars and beam were not part of the first four BAGA grades so their group concentrated on floor and vault for most of the lesson. Julienne's back flip was strong and sure.

But Anda made a mess of hers!

"Of course you've had no practice for a fortnight, have you?" said Christie. "Have you been doing the exercises?"

Anda bit her lip.

"Not properly. I was upset and I let it all go!"

"That's no excuse!" reproached Christie. "Well, come on, we'll work at it now!"

Again and again, with Christie supporting her, Anda flung herself backwards onto her hands. It was no good! Yet two weeks ago she had done one, almost without support. She tried and tried. Then her limbs began to shake.

"All right, leave it," said Christie kindly. "Have a breather!"

But Anda shook her head. She didn't want to leave it. Especially with her parents sitting there!

"Why can't I do it?" she said, fighting the tears hard, and managing to stop them.

"I couldn't do it for ages, Anda!" said Julienne comfortingly. "Ages and ages!"

"You're not kidding!" joked Christie.

But Anda still felt frustrated because she couldn't do a back flip. She watched enviously as Julienne did hers.

Eventually Christie put her on the beam.

"Go on. Show your mum and dad what you can do!" she encouraged. "Go on. I want them to see!"

So up she went. She had progressed on the beam but she was allowed to do only what she'd been taught. Anda Barnes Specials were banned, Christie said! Dance steps, leaps and arabesques, a forward roll, and the splits she could manage. Tonight she was aware of Bill's intense blue eyes staring up at her as she worked. She resisted the temptation to show off!

But it was her vaulting that really made Bill's jaw drop.

"God!" he said quietly. "She's a human dynamo! I see what they mean about her. Do you, Lynne?"

"She frightens me!" said Lynne. "But I think it's marvellous. We mustn't stand in her way, Bill, if she's got that kind of talent!"

6

The competition squad

Anda's first session with the Competition
Squad was a shock. She arrived at the
gymnasium with Julienne, her brain full of
dreams.

"I'll bet we learn a new vault!" she said.
"And we'll really be starting seriously on the
beam and bars! I can't wait!"

For once Julienne was uncannily silent.

"Aren't you well?" asked Anda, thinking that
Julienne's nose looked whiter than usual.

"No. I've got stomach ache."

Anda was about to sympathise when Lena's
piercing voice interrupted.

"You've got nerves!" she shrieked. "Anyone
can see that! Stomach ache!"

"That's not true!" Julienne growled back.
"Anyway I wasn't even talking to you!"

"You wait! John and Christie are really hard
on us this session."

"Oh, stop stirring it, Lena," said Anda angrily, sensing Julienne's distress.

"She's as hard as nails," muttered Julienne as they followed Lena into the gym.

Lena turned.

"Hard as nails makes a good gymnast!" she said smugly. She ran to chat with the older girls.

"She'll get her come-uppance! Don't worry!" said Anda.

There were fourteen girls in the squad, six teenagers and eight younger girls, including Kerry, Anda and Julienne.

Warm-up was much as usual, with a few harder exercises. The shock came afterwards.

"Right, Julienne, Anda, Elizabeth, Spider Girl, Kerry and Lena go next door to ballet."

"Ballet!"

"Yes, ballet!" Christie grinned at Anda's shocked face. "We're lucky. We've got a proper ballet teacher on Thursdays."

Anda looked sadly at the mats and bars. All that tumbling time wasted! Doing ballet! Her body felt warm and bursting with energy. She ran up to Christie.

"Do I have to?"

"Yes, you do have to. It's an essential part of your training. And so, I might add, is doing what you're told without question!"

Anda felt like arguing. Ballet! What a dirty trick!

But Christie had other people to think about besides Anda.

"Come on, Anda!" Julienne's eyes were

sparkling. Stomach ache gone! Ballet was what *she* had been looking forward to.

The dancing teacher was called Valerie. Anda thought she looked like a string puppet with elastic fingers and eyes like mint humbugs.

Fascinated and a bit resentful, she found herself a space.

"Let's see you stand first." Valerie had an unexpectedly earthy voice. She pounced on Anda straightaway.

"Look at you. With your bottom stuck out. Tuck it in. Pull your tummy in. Drop your shoulders."

She came and arranged Anda, patting her into place like a plasticine doll.

"Oh dear, you look crippled now. Drop your shoulders! What's your name?"

"Anda."

Walking was even worse.

"Pull your heads up! Tummy in, bottom in, toes pointed. No, not like that. For crying out loud! You can't even walk properly!"

Anda felt she must be the worst. She got angrier and angrier as she tried to co-operate.

"Pull your stomach in, Anda! You look like a banana walking along."

Anda stopped dead. A banana walking along, was she? She, Anda Barnes, who could do poetic cartwheels and fantastic back flips. Why should she be imprisoned with this Valerie and made to learn how to walk?

"Move on, you're in everyone's way!"

But Anda stood, looking at the floor, a

saucepan boiling inside her head.

"Oh, we're not going to sulk, are we?"

Julienne and Kerry were giggling. Unforgivable! But the sight of Julienne walking past like a majestic princess was comical. Giggling would destroy her silent protest, so she walked on after Julienne, with her mouth zipped tightly. Mercifully Valerie turned her attention to Lena. Apparently Lena was hopeless too! She got called everything from a tin soldier to a daddy long legs.

But Julienne didn't get "the treatment" at all.

"That's very good!" said Valerie. "You've got it. Walk round and we'll watch you!"

Begrudgingly, Anda thought Julienne did look elegant. She glanced at the clock. However much longer?

Next they learned some of the ballet positions, and then a step chassé.

Anda turned to Kerry.

"Don't we get to do any gymnastics this lesson?"

"Course we do. We've got another ten minutes with Valerie, that's all. Cheer up, Anda!" said Kerry kindly. "You'll like the next part. We have to do music and expression."

Valerie played some music, and asked them to dance to it, one by one.

"You can put in some cartwheels and things," she said. "If you want to. But nothing that needs support because I can't support you. The main thing is the music and the dancing. Listen to it and try to move with it. Who's going first?"

Anda shrank into the mat. She didn't want to dance with Valerie there criticising her!

"I'll go!" said Julienne.

What she lacked in gymnastics, Julienne made up for in her dancing. She wasn't afraid to express herself. Anda was amazed at how good she looked.

"Well done!" said Valerie and Julienne rolled her eyes happily.

Anda went last, feeling bad inside. She considered the ballet positions and steps they had learned. Valerie's insults jarred in her brain and she felt inhibited. Her dancing by the Hooty Stream and on the beam for Christie was forgotten. She felt unable to move! The music started. She did two cartwheels and stood wondering what to do next.

"No, you mustn't stand and think!" cried Valerie. "Keep going! Oh, take your finger out of your mouth for goodness sake, child!"

It was a nightmare. She moved, and stopped, and moved and stopped, and Valerie shouted at her, and the music escaped unnoticed across the ceiling. Her throat took over. She made for the door. The green and black corridor sped past and she was in the changing room, sobbing and sobbing, seeing people's shoes and bags gyrating through her tears.

No one rushed after her. She was alone, crying and ashamed of herself. How could she ever go back and face Valerie? Or Christie, after that?

Still sobbing she found her jeans and put

them on, and pulled her sweater over her head. Hands in pockets she walked slowly out of Ferndale.

An astonishing sight met her eyes. Snow! Twisting and twinkling. The air like a great fridge. Snow, weeks before Christmas, icing everything.

Anda gazed in a surge of excitement. She wanted to rush and scoop it up in handfuls, to walk home, kicking it and feeling it on her face. Then she remembered it was her first time at Ferndale as part of the squad! If it hadn't been for that ballet lesson!

"Anda!"

Julienne was beside her.

"Where are you going? Wow! It's snowing!"

Together they watched the snow falling.

"Why have you got your jeans on?" asked Julienne.

Anda glowered.

"That woman!"

"Who, Valerie?"

"Yes, *her*. If we're going to have *her* every week I'm not coming!"

"Oh, Anda! She isn't that bad! I like her."

"It's OK for you. You can do it."

Julienne bit her lip, hurt at her friend's anger.

"If you knew, Anda. The times I've been jealous of you. When you could do the vaults that I couldn't do. I mean, ballet's not difficult."

"It wasn't the ballet. It was *that woman*."

"Oh come on, Anda. We're in the gym now!"

Julienne's blue eyes looked anxious. "Forget about it."

So she replaced her clothes and returned to the gym with Julienne, only to be stopped by a cold-eyed Christie.

"You aren't coming in here, madam," she said, "until you've apologised to Valerie."

"I'm not apologising to *her*. *She* should apologise to me!" fired Anda, and the saucepan began bubbling again.

"If you are going to be a gymnast," said Christie coolly, "the first thing you will learn is discipline and respect for your coaches. Including Valerie."

"What do you mean?"

Anda stared at Christie, who had never before spoken to her so harshly.

"Exactly what I say. You go and apologise to Valerie. I don't care how hard it is or how much you hate it. And if you've got a discipline problem I don't want you in my squad."

Christie walked away. Anda opened her mouth to shout "Stuff your rotten squad", and shut it just in time to stop the words.

"I'll come with you," said Julienne kindly, but Christie called her away to practise walkovers. Anda hung at the door, torn between rushing out into the snow and being a child, or apologising to Valerie and being a gymnast. What hurt the most was Christie's sudden coldness.

She shivered at the door, her legs and feet getting colder and colder. She would have to warm up all over again! What a waste of time.

"Hello, Anda. Got problems?"

Anda swung round and there was Valerie, her mint humbug eyes looking straight into hers. The earthy voice sounded concerned, or was it mocking?

"No. I'm OK."

Valerie stood looking at her. "I'm sorry if I upset you," she said. "I've got a sharp tongue. You'll have to learn to laugh at me."

Anda couldn't believe her ears.

"But Christie said—I had to ..." she choked, "apologise to you."

"Apologising isn't being sorry. It's a mechanical act," said Valerie. "It's OK. Forget it. I expect I'm tougher than you!"

Her kindness was disarming.

"I am sorry, Valerie. Really."

"Forget it! We'll get along." Valerie patted her on the shoulder. "Go on. Go and do your flip-flans or whatever they are!"

"Flip-flans?"

"Flapjacks then!"

"Flic-flacs!" cried Anda and they both laughed.

She ran over to where Julienne was practising round-off back flips.

"Have you? You have!" said Christie briefly to Anda. "We're practising round off and two flips. Then we're going to learn a back somie on the trampoline, so get working!"

Anda made a dive for the mat and lunged into the tumbling sequence. But on the second back flip an excruciating pain in her leg made her cry out. She hopped away and sat down, catching her breath while the knot of pain tightened.

"What's the matter?" asked Julienne.

"I don't know."

"Your face has gone white! Christie! Anda's hurt herself!"

Christie came at once.

"It's not your day, is it?"

Anda shook her head, determined not to cry again! The pain eased. Christie made her lie face down.

"You've got cramp," she said. "At least I hope that's all it is. You're freezing cold, child! That's the worst thing for a gymnast. Put your track suit on and do some warm ups. You know you shouldn't work cold! You could have pulled a muscle!" She called to one of the older girls. "Carol, do Anda's leg, will you?"

"I haven't got a track suit," said Anda, but Julienne was there straight away with hers.

"Put mine on. Go on, it doesn't matter!"

With Carol massaging her leg, and Julienne's track suit round her, Anda soon recovered. After some warm-ups she felt normal again. But she'd missed most of the floor work and Christie refused to let her vault.

"Not until you're sure that leg is OK. You work on the bar."

So she spent the last half hour working on the single bar, enjoying it, but feeling left out! Across the gym Julienne was having a good day!

Sailing over the vault and getting praise from John.

The session finished with a lot of technical talk. The girls were given notebooks and told to write down everything they learned, and what exercises to do before Saturday. Then, to Anda's embarrassment, Christie said:

"Has anyone got an old track suit or some training tights they could lend or give to Anda?"

"I'll be getting one for Christmas," said Anda quickly. "And a leotard."

"Yes, but in the meantime," said Christie.

Surprisingly it was Lena who spoke up.

"I've got one you can have. It's only an old thing."

"Thanks," said Anda ungraciously. She didn't want to wear a track suit Lena had worn.

"By the way, you'll need competition leotards with the club badge eventually," Christie told them, pointing to a picture in a catalogue. "This is ours. This purple one."

"When can we enter something?" asked Lena.

"Well—there's the under elevens county championships next February. February 21st. You can enter if you want to, but don't expect to win anything. Just enter for experience and only expect a few marks each. We can enter a team or you can go as individuals," explained Christie.

Anda's eyes lit up. February 21st! Two months from now!

The snow was melting as they drove back to Elmsford.

"We get cut off if it gets really deep!" Anda told Julienne. "And I can't go to school!"

"You won't be able to get to gym club either," said Julienne. "What if it snows on the 21st February?"

"It won't" said Anda determinedly. "Or if it does, Dad will have to pull me there on a sledge!"

"What's the 21st February?" asked Julienne's mother.

"The under elevens County Championships!"

"Oh darling! Your first competition! How wonderful!" gushed Julienne's mother. "We must get you entered at once! I must go up to town and get you a silk leotard and we'll do your hair up with a coloured net pompon to match!"

Julienne didn't smile.

"Christie said we could enter if we want to, but not to expect high marks," explained Anda.

"I might not enter at all," said Julienne unexpectedly. She gave Anda a sharp nudge as if to warn her not to say anything.

Her mother's reaction was immediate. "Not enter! After all we've spent on your training! You most certainly will enter. And I shall be there to see you are fairly marked! Not enter indeed!"

7

You will not fall

"Oh Julienne, you *can't* be worried about that vault. You can do squats with your eyes shut now!" said John. "If there's one thing I'm sure about for Saturday it's you getting over the horse!"

Today was their last practice before the competition.

Julienne grinned and rolled her eyes.

"That's better!" said John. "You've got competition nerves. We all get them. Kerry's terrified!"

Kerry tried to look surprised. Her first competition since her illness was important to her.

"That's right, crack your freckles!" said John.

No one seemed to care about Kerry. Her parents weren't coming to watch her! She got herself to the club three times a week on an old

59

bicycle, and nobody ever came with her or fetched her.

"Are you scared, Anda?"

"A bit," she admitted. "Mostly of the people watching!"

"Well why do you do it then, if you don't want anyone to watch?" teased John.

"I just love doing it," said Anda frankly.

John ruffled her hair.

"That's it, isn't it, Christie? That's the soul of the sport!" he said. "What are these? Paint-brushes?"

Anda giggled and pulled at the two ridiculously small bunches she had put her hair into. She longed to grow it into a bouncing pony tail like Lena.

In bed that night she mentally rehearsed her floor routine and thought of the group who were entering. She was worried for Julienne and Kerry. For herself she was confident of doing her best, and knowing that Bill and Lynne and Gran would love her whatever she did.

Under the wind and the stars Hooty Cottage creaked cosily. Eventually Anda slept, excited, not dreaming that Saturday was to be the most dreadful day of her life!

When she arrived home from school on Friday Lynne met her with a bright happy face.

"Go and look on your bed," she said.

"I'll just give Bella her tea," said Anda. "What can she have?"

"Treato!" said Lynne, producing a surprise

60

tin of expensive cat food. Bella usually had scraps and goat's milk! Purring loudly she tucked into the plateful Anda put down for her.

"Go and look upstairs! Go on!"

On her bed was an amazing sight. Lynne had washed her track suit and laid it out. Beside it was a smart white sports bag, a pair of brand new track shoes, thick white socks and a purple competition leotard!

"Mum!" screamed Anda throwing herself at Lynne who had followed her upstairs.

She couldn't believe her eyes. She'd expected to compete in her training leotard when everyone else had a purple one. "It doesn't matter," Christie had said. "As long as you're clean and tidy."

"But *Mum*. This is incredible! Where did it all come from? From Gran?"

"No. From us. I ordered the leotard from Christie's catalogue ready for the competition. Then we decided your shoes were grotty and you needed a smart bag, so I went shopping!"

Anda felt knocked out. She'd never before had new things except for birthdays or Christmas. She couldn't think where the money had come from!

"We didn't want to let the side down," explained Lynne. "You've practised so hard, love, and Bill and I are so proud of you! We wanted you to have the best, and look as smart as the other girls!"

"Oh, *Mum*." Anda fingered the new things wonderingly. "That's incredible. But...."

"But what? Your eyes are out on stalks!" laughed Lynne.

"Well, I'm not going to win or anything!" said Anda anxiously, suddenly feeling she had to live up to the new clothes!

"No. We know that! But at least if you fall flat on your face you won't look scruffy."

"But I thought we were broke, Mum!"

Lynne sat down on the bed. "There is a 'but'," she said slowly. "I was going to tell you first."

"What?"

"Well—it's the goats."

"The goats? Oh, what have they eaten now?" laughed Anda. "Not Christie's tumbling mat?"

"No, love. They've gone."

"Gone?"

"We've had to sell them. A man came and took them away this morning."

Millie and Mollie gone? Taken from home, in a truck with a strange man who might not love them!

"Well, say something! said Lynne.

"I didn't want them to go." Anda stared at the floor. "They were born here. They'll feel—*lost!* Oh Mum! I didn't even say goodbye to them."

"Don't, Anda! They'll be OK. They've gone to kind people. I didn't want them to go either. Nor did Bill!"

Bill refused go be miserable.

"We can't sit moaning about them. They've gone and they'll survive. And we'll survive. We

62

can't have it all ways. So let's be positive! Where's tea? Shall I heat up a tin of Kittynosh?"

He bounded downstairs and started rummaging in the kitchen.

"He's wonderful," said Lynne. "He's upset and he's trying to be cheerful, and you've got to do the same."

So Millie and Mollie had been sold so that she, Anda Barnes, could look smart! Supposing she did everything wrong after that? Suddenly the competition loomed with a different face.

Bill's cheerful example was difficult to follow. But she tried. She ate tea and chatted about everything but goats. A year ago she would have cried and raged. She was unaware how much gymnastics had changed her, and how grateful her parents were for the change!

Later she ran out to the cold barn for a last practice, passing the silent goat shed. She wore two sweaters, thick tights and jeans. *Hard as nails,* she kept thinking. *Hard as nails makes a good gymnast.* Don't cry over Millie and Mollie. Work till you hurt and the two goat faces will go away.

She worked at perfecting her agilities. The tinsica, the back walkover with change of leg, trying to get smooth, stretched and flowing.

It wasn't until Bella came creeping under the door that she almost stopped for a cry over the goats. But Bella made her laugh. She whirled and climbed. She lay on her side and kicked the mat. She slid across the floor after chicken feathers.

After two hours she heard Bill's boots crunching down the path.

"Come on, Anda. It's eight o'clock. That's enough, surely?" he said. He stood watching her curl back to touch the floor and into a back walkover. "How can you *do* that?"

Anda was reluctant to stop.

"Have you looked outside?" said Bill. He took her arm and flung the door open. And there, in the yellow light from the barn, was a wild twisting snowstorm! A white crust clung to the door and drifts were forming triangles in the vegetables.

"A blizzard!" cried Anda.

In the swarming snow she danced and skated. Hundreds and thousands of snow dots sprayed her hot face and hands. The wind came in sneezes, almost knocking her over.

Bella was a hysterical snowball tearing in and out of the cabbages. Anda tried to scoop up enough snow for a ball to throw at her dad. Shaping its coldness in her hands she suddenly remembered the last time it had snowed.

"What if it snows on 21st February?" Julienne had said.

The snowball fell from her hand and smashed.

"Dad!" she began. "It's not going to last—is it?"

"Come on inside!" he urged, picking up Bella.

The lounge was oven hot. Anda tore off her sweaters and sat with her face pressed to the window.

"We've got to be there at ten in the morning," she said. "Gran's taking us, isn't she?"

"Yes."

"The snow will melt on the roads, won't it?"

Bill and Lynne looked at each other.

"Won't it, Dad?"

"Sometimes it does."

"They'll grit them, surely? Won't they?"

"If we're lucky."

"I wonder if Millie and Mollie are all right," said Anda, peering out at the speeding blizzard. "Do you think they've got a cosy shed? Do you think they'll be scared in a new place?"

Bill sighed.

"They had mountains of straw in the truck. And they've got each other," he said sadly. "It wasn't just your clothes, you know, Anda. It was, well—rates and Murgatroyd's battery and petrol, and chicken food. Things like that."

"Anyway, you'd better get a good night's sleep, Anda," advised Lynne briskly. "You need to be fit tomorrow!"

"I think we all will!" agreed Bill. "How's your ski-ing?"

"I'll never sleep," said Anda. "Can I take Bella to bed? Please! Just tonight! I want her with me."

"Oh, let her," said Bill. "Take her box up. She won't stay in it, but never mind."

So with a last look at the snow, and a hot water bottle, cocoa, and Bella, Anda went up to bed.

"Will Gran be scared?" she asked Lynne. "Of driving in snow on slippery roads?"

"Probably. But Bill can drive. Try not to worry. See what the morning brings."

Bella sat demurely washing in her box. But as soon as Lynne had gone, she jumped on the bed. She walked round Anda's head, then lay on her chest, purring and staring with her green jewel eyes.

Anda got up and tried on her purple leotard. It fitted beautifully. She tried the hairband and admired herself in the mirror. The purple made her hair look golden. If only it would grow! She stared at her pink cheeks and brown eyes in the mirror, surprised that she looked quite pretty.

"You're going to do OK tomorrow, Anda Barnes," she told her face silently. "You will not fall off the beam. You will do your upstart on the bars properly. And you will not cry if it goes wrong!"

"Miaow!" agreed Bella.

The purple leotard was hung up where she could see it. She leaned on the window sill watching. Peaks of snow growing up the glass. Whirling whiteness out across the moor. A difficult journey tomorrow! An early start. But it never once occurred to her that she would not make it to the competition.

8

What if it snows?

She awoke at six. Barely daylight but the room was full of strange white light from the snow. The wind had dropped and the sound of shovelling rang through the Hooty Combe.

Anda rolled out of bed. The day! The great day of the competition! She dressed at speed before peeping out of the window.

Snow, curved and whipped like meringue. No grass. Only stalks and broccoli tops and bracken curls. The birch trees stood sock deep and the Hooty Stream was a tinkling chasm of black.

Anda gazed in silence. Half of it was magic, and half of it was terrible.

"You up already?" said Bill as Anda shot out of the back door.

"Dad! We aren't cut off. Are we? Are we?"

"I don't know until we try. Lots of villages are, according to the news."

"The main road will be OK. Surely?"

"Not at the moment it isn't. There's abandoned cars everywhere. They've got the snow ploughs out," said Bill.

"We are going, Dad. Aren't we? We've got to. I've got to be there. I've got to!"

"All right, cool it, Anda," he said. "We'll try. That's all I can promise. We might not even get out of Elmsford. I can't perform miracles."

"I've got to get there. I've got to," repeated Anda desperately.

"Well, you pray and I'll drive!" said Bill a bit angrily. "There's more snow on the way!"

"I hate the snow!"

Bill shook his head.

"Oh man! A kid of mine, hating the snow!" she heard him say as she went inside. Determinedly she packed her gymnastics clothes in the new white bag and slung it over her shoulder.

Lynne was in the kitchen behind a tower of sandwiches.

"Survival kit!" she said. "And you know I'm staying here in case you don't make it back tonight."

"Oh, Mum!"

"I'm disappointed. Terribly disappointed. But supposing we all three got marooned? What about Bella, and the chickens? They'd starve."

"I know."

Disappointment number one. Her mum not being able to come.

"Gran might not go either. She's terrified of

slippery roads," warned Lynne. She filled two flasks, one with soup and one with coffee.

"You dress for the Arctic," she said. "Two sweaters. You might have to walk back here if you get stuck. I shall worry myself stupid!"

But for the competition, it would have been thrilling to set off on an expedition into the snow, kitted out for survival!

"We're mad!" said Bill as they bumped out of the gate in Murgatroyd.

Seven o'clock. Surely three hours was long enough for them to get there, Anda thought.

It took ages to negotiate the lane. Where the snow was thin, Murgatroyd slid from bank to bank. Where it was thick, they had to dig.

"A good thing she's old and battered!" said Bill.

To start with it was fun. But the hand of Bill's watch moved steadily. Half past seven. Twenty to eight. Thank goodness for the downhill run to Gran's.

"Of *course* I'm coming!" Gran said indignantly when Bill explained how bad the roads were. "I started Anda off. I'm coming! You put the snow chains on the car and I'll be ready."

"Good old Gran!" said Anda, thinking how brave she was. "Mum said you were terrified."

"Nonsense. I've been miles in the snow." Gran unlocked the garage with a flourish. Bill dug away the surplus snow and started to fix the chains, one on each wheel. Precious minutes were ticking away.

Gran reappeared dressed in a sheepskin coat,

trousers and thick boots. They finally left at half past eight.

"We'll never get up the hill. I'll try the toll road," said Bill. "And let's hope the main road will be cleared by now."

The toll road was a long detour round the foot of the moors. With Bill driving, Gran's car clicked along bravely like a little boat sailing out.

Nine o'clock, and the white road wound ahead completely deserted.

"If we keep this speed up, you might just make it for warm-up, Anda," Bill said optimistically. "What time's the actual competition start?"

"Eleven," said Anda, and her stomach started to rumble with nerves and hunger.

Wine-dark clouds loomed ahead. The wind rose, whipping dry snow off the hedges and across the road. Suddenly the air was full of hundreds and thousands again.

"That's done it," sighed Bill. "Another blizzard. Now we are in trouble."

"Keep going!" said Gran. "At least make it to the main road."

"Quite honestly it would be better to turn back. Look, the windscreen wipers are hardly coping. It's madness to go on!"

"Oh no, Dad!" cried Anda.

"Go on," said Gran. "We've got a chance."

"You'll wish you'd listened to me!" said Bill anxiously.

Reluctantly he kept driving and Anda sat

back in relief. She started worrying about missing warm-up and the shame of being late.

The blizzard got thicker, and Bill got angrier.

"Don't stop!" pleaded Gran. "Or we'll get stuck."

"I can't go any faster. It's deeper here. There's a dip in the road."

The car rolled into a patch of deep snow and stopped with its engine roaring.

"That's it!" said Bill grimly. He tried to reverse out of it but the car wouldn't move.

"Come on, Anda. We'll push," said Gran gamely.

They got out, into the blizzard.

"Push her back!" shouted Bill. "Not forward!"

While the wind was whisking snow along the ground, piling it against the wheels, they heaved at the bonnet. Gran wheezed and Anda giggled. She knew she shouldn't be giggling but it struck here as hilariously funny, pushing a car that wouldn't move.

At last Bill took the shovel from the boot.

"I'll have to dig her out. It's getting deeper by the minute."

He took one look at Gran's purple-red face through the whirling snow and said:

"You get back in. Go on. You'll make yourself ill."

But Gran wouldn't. She stood in the snow, wheezing, trying to scrape it away with her boots.

"Here you are, toughie. You shovel too." Bill

71

handed Anda the coal shovel. She started to dig furiously, getting hotter and hotter with the snow streaming past her face. Beside her Bill dug like a madman, blowing and swearing. The faster they worked, the more the wind flung snow over the car. Soon the windows and doors were plastered.

Bill had another go at revving the car. The engine whined and strained, but the wheels stayed locked. He got out again and threw his shovel as far as he could throw it. Anda was startled. Bill rarely lost his temper but he had now.

"Will you GET IN the car!" he hollered at Gran who was gasping for breath.

"I won't be spoken to like that!" she wheezed.

Bill took her arm and wrenched the car door open.

"You are to get in or you'll BE ILL," he shouted. "And then we'll need an ambulance. Now get in and stay in and do as you are told, woman!"

Gran got in, looking upset, and shut the door.

"You can rev her if you like, and we'll dig. If I can just get her turned round we can go back."

"But Dad. What about ..." began Anda, her dreams of the competition toppling.

"Don't you whine!" he snapped. "We've done our damnest to get you there and we can't. So that's it. Just don't grizzle!"

He fetched his shovel. Snow was driving thickly over the road, covering their wheel tracks.

"Oh please Dad. Can't we . . ." she tried to say as his red face and snow blotted beard loomed up in the snow.

He put a snowy arm round her.

"I'm sorry I got mad," he sighed defeatedly. "Look—just try and be brave, Anda. I'm sorry about the competition. Just for goodness sake don't cry."

Anda took a deep breath and pulled her shaking knees together.

"I wasn't," she said. "Come on, let's try digging again."

But with the car completely stuck, and the blizzard worsening, it was hopeless.

"Take your anorak off and shake it. We'll get in and decide what to do," said Bill wearily.

Inside, the car was a warm cocoon.

"Are you OK?" Bill asked Gran.

"Yes, I'm fine." Gran had recovered enough to sip coffee. "What's the best thing to do? You're the survival expert!"

Bill considered.

"There's no sign of it stopping," he said. "You realise the car could get completely buried?"

Gran nodded.

"I know."

"We could stick with it. Or walk back to Elmsford, about five miles. I doubt if we'll get any help. There'll be too many other people stuck!"

Anda sat in the back, silent, her thoughts in a corked up bottle. Bill had said "Don't grizzle" and so she didn't. She avoided looking at the white bag or at Bill's watch.

Soup and a sandwich were handed over to her.

"Eat it quickly. The sooner we go the better," said Bill.

They had decided Gran should stay in the car and keep warm, while Bill walked back into Elmsford for help.

"I should think you're fit enough to come with me, Anda, aren't you? Then Gran can have all the rugs and the food. She's got to keep warm."

Anda swallowed her soup and stuffed the sandwich down.

Reluctantly they left Gran, bundled up in rugs, alone in the car. She waved and smiled cheerfully.

"Come on, kid," said Bill. "Stick right behind me and walk in my tracks. We'll make it."

Anda had no words left. Numb-throated, she followed Bill's dark green mac and tall wellies along the silver white road.

On and on they walked in a strange rhythm, their backs to the wind. Images came into Anda's mind. Julienne dancing. Lena on the beam. Kerry's determined freckles. The high leather vaulting horse. Herself in the purple leotard. The audience clapping. The hours and hours of practice that nobody clapped. Black wellies and soaking jeans walking, walking through the powdery snow.

74

Bill turned to see if she was OK.

Her small face with its big shiny eyes looked up at him from the hood of her anorak and a halo of dripping wet hair.

"You all right?"

She shrugged inside her heavy wet clothes. "Yep."

"Don't be too sore over the competition. There'll be others. Christie will understand," he said, taking her hand.

Anda shrugged again. Two tears rolled down her face, but she didn't sob.

"There are other priorities right now," said Bill. "You realise Gran is in danger! Old people can be very ill from exposure. Or even die!"

"No. I didn't know!"

"She'll be OK for a few hours. But we must get someone out to her! That's why I'm walking as fast as I can. Are you keeping up all right?"

"Yes," said Anda, and added cheekily, "I'm fitter than you any day! Poor Gran! She didn't want to come really."

They walked on and Anda sank back into her gloom.

"There is a future after today, you know!" said Bill. "You can still train with the Squad. You've still got your talent, Anda. There'll be lots of competitions for you."

He scrubbed the snow from a signpost.

"Elmsford one mile!" he cried. "We're nearly there!"

One o'clock and they were trudging through the new estate like two snowmen. Gran's yellow front door had never looked so friendly to Anda. People could die in blizzards! Hours of wading through snow-drifts and her worries about the competition had faded. Staying alive was important now. Forcing her legs to keep walking, carrying the lead weight of wet clothes. Worrying about Gran left alone, perhaps scared, perhaps dying from cold.

Bill went straight to the 'phone.

"You get in the bath," he ordered Anda. "Go on."

He rang the police and told them where Gran was.

Anda stood in the bathroom looking at herself in the mirror. February 21st! Instead of dancing in a purple leotard, there she stood in a dripping brown anorak with hair like wet spaghetti. What a waste of a gymnast!

She lay in a steaming blue bath. Then she padded into Gran's bedroom and borrowed a big woolly jacket to wrap herself in. Was Gran dead? Gran, who had given her the chance to do gymnastics. And what about her mum, alone at Hooty Cottage in the blizzard? And Bella?

But Gran was very much alive! She was rescued by two policemen and carried through the snow to their Landrover. An hour later she arrived home in it, her eyes sparkling with excitement. She refused to sit down but bustled round getting tea and putting wet clothes in the tumble drier.

"For you two heroes," she said. "You both deserve a gold medal for walking all that way in

76

the snow. Especially Anda! It must have been up to your waist!"

Anda smiled. It was good to feel brave. Afterwards! And Gran had thoughtfully remembered to bring Anda's precious white bag with her in the Landrover.

"I'm really disappointed at not seeing you compete today," she said warmly. "Perhaps I can come to the club and watch you?"

"If Christie ever lets me in the door again!" said Anda.

"I'll ring her up," said Gran spiritedly. "And tell her what we've been through trying to get there!"

And she did. Later that evening when they had decided to stay the night with Gran rather than attempt the walk to Hooty Cottage in the dark.

"There you are. You talk to her!"

She waved the 'phone at Anda.

"No," mouthed Anda, thinking Christie would be angry.

Gran forced the 'phone into her hand.

"It's OK, Anda. I know you couldn't help it. You must have been shattered!" said Christie's voice kindly.

"I was," said Anda. "We tried. We left at seven o'clock."

"Lots of people didn't make it. Kerry didn't. Julienne was late—and she made a mess of it—oh dear!" went on Christie. "What a day! Lena fell flat on her face on the bar and got a nosebleed. She is human by the way!" she joked.

"Oh!"

So other people had had a bad day too!

"Anyway, so few kids turned up because of the snow that they've decided to hold it again—in April probably—so you'll still be able to enter!"

"Oh, great!" said Anda.

"And there's another one in March—a floor and vault competition at Ferndale," said Christie. "And there's a training weekend, and a trip to London, all sorts of things, so cheer up."

On Sunday morning she was at last able to enjoy the magic of the snow. Through diamond drifts she and Bill climbed the lane to Hooty Cottage. The cottage looked like a peppermint palace. Lynne stood at the door with Bella in her arms, relieved to see them.

Anda spent the morning skidding and rolling in the snow and cracking the ice around the Hooty Stream. She sat in the birch tree, sucking an icicle, thinking ahead to the floor and vault competition in March. This time nothing must go wrong! Nothing, nothing must go wrong!

9

Please let me enter

The train from the West Country pulled in at Paddington Station. The group of gymnasts from Ferndale jumped out, talking and laughing.

"Now we get the Underground to Wembley," said Christie.

Anda was completely bewildered. She hadn't been to London before.

Julienne was scornful. "I've been here heaps of times!" she yawned. "This is nothing, Anda. You should see the big shops. Mummy brings me every year Christmas shopping, and we get squashed to death. It's awful. Come *on!*"

Anda had stopped again to talk to the pigeons. She was sorry for them.

"Christie's *gone!*" cried Julienne, almost pulling her over. Giggling, they tore across Paddington Station, round people and over suitcases.

Next she was frightened to step on the escalator until Christie said, "What you! A gymnast! Frightened to step on that!"

Anda stepped on at once, her face red.

Downstairs she was even more terrified of the tube train taking her into a tunnel that roared and puffed like a dragon's nostril. She clung to Julienne, giggling to hide her nervousness, until they came out into the street at Wembley.

"She hasn't said a word since we got here!" laughed Julienne, intrigued to see Anda actually scared of something.

"You'll have to get used to travelling if you're going to be a gymnast!" John said. "What about International Competitions, Anda? We can't pack you in a parcel and have you delivered! One country mouse. If lost, please return to sender."

Anda grinned.

Once inside Wembley Arena, it was worth it. They had come to watch the finals of a national gymnastics competition.

The competition began with *March of the Champions*. While the audience clapped in time, in marched the teams and the arena was full of colour. Tiny gymnasts, each team in matching leotards, strutted in proudly with high chins and pointed toes. Watching them Anda realised why Valerie had fussed about her learning to walk!

"Why isn't there anyone from Ferndale?" asked Anda.

"Oh we tried!" said Christie. "We always enter!"

"Perhaps it'll be you down there one day!" said John leaning round to speak to Anda.

"I wish it was!" she answered.

How lovely to march around with everyone clapping, she thought. But when the actual competition started, she couldn't imagine how long it would take her to reach that standard!

"Can I enter next year?" she asked Christie.

"No, love," Christie smiled gently. "You aren't old enough or experienced enough."

"If I train extra, extra hard?"

"No. You can't push it, Anda! Superman wasn't built in a day. He took years!"

"I wish I could wake up in the morning and find I could do everything!" said Anda sadly.

"There'll be plenty of little local things you can enter. Cheer up!" said Christie kindly. "You walk before you can run!"

Anda sighed. She opened a bag of crisps and shared them with Julienne, munching and thinking as she watched the polished performances. Briefly she thought of Hooty Cottage and her parents. Her training was making things difficult for them. Lynne missed the goats, and Bill was doing long hours bricklaying instead of the gardening he loved. She felt guilty, but she couldn't give it up. What really worried her was something Bill had said about Murgatroyd. Murgatroyd only had another week before her MOT. She would fail, and there was no money to put her right. And without Murgatroyd she could not get to Ferndale on Saturdays!

But during the lunch break at Wembley, Anda made a fantastic discovery.

She and Julienne were browsing round the stands in the foyer. Julienne had bought herself a BAGA T-shirt and some badges. Anda had brought half her piggy bank to spend. She bought a can of fizzy drink which she wasn't allowed at home.

Suddenly a poster caught her eye. A young gymnast, and the words "South West Training Award" in large letters, and "Please take a leaflet".

She took one of the glossy folders and opened it.

What she read filled her with excitement.

"I've *got* to find Christie!" she said. "I've *got* to enter this. I've *got* to!"

She was jumping up and down.

"Have you gone mad?" asked Julienne.

"No. Look!"

"Oh that. Yes, I saw it. Good, isn't it?"

Julienne was still busy choosing badges. She already had a large collection sewn on her anorak. Anda searched for Christie. She and John were in the arena, talking to a man in a black track suit.

Too shy to walk across there, Anda waited impatiently at the steps, knowing she would get snubbed for interrupting. At last they came towards her.

"Christie!"

Anda thrust the leaflet into Christie's hand.

"Can I enter this? I've got to, Christie. Please

let me. Please. It's specially for people like me!"

"Hang on a minute. Cool it!"

"It's a training award! Two hundred pounds a year to cover things like clothes and transport and training weekends," said Anda, her eyes sparkling. "And it's for under twelves!"

Christie flicked through the leaflet.

"What a super idea!" she said. "This is something new!"

"But can I?"

"It looks hopeful," sighed Christie. "But I did *tell* you, Anda, you may not be able to *this* year. You just haven't got the experience."

"But it does say even beginners can enter!"

"I know. I know. But you don't realise what you'd be up against, Anda! The competition will be hot for this, I can tell you!"

"But I could *try*. Then Mum and Dad could have the goats back!"

"I'll discuss it with John," was all Christie would say.

Intensely disappointed, Anda returned to her seat. She read the leaflet through about six times. Christie hand't said no. And she hadn't said yes.

The day passed in a blur of medal ceremonies and train journeys. The training award suddenly became *thought number one* in Anda's head. She tried asking John, but he only said:

"We'll see. You haven't even entered a competition yet, Anda. *You* don't know how you're going to react. You might be a bag of nerves!"

"I won't be," she said stubbornly.

"Well—see how you get on next week. Then we'll decide. I'll discuss it with Christie," said John. "Don't get too intense over it. What's the big hurry? You're only ten!"

"It's not that I want to win medals or anything," sighed Anda. "It's Mum and Dad. They wanted to be self-sufficient and now they can't because of me."

"All parents make sacrifices for their kids," said John. "Some parents have even moved house for their kids to be near the gym club!"

The idea of leaving Hooty Cottage tore at Anda's thoughts. It only made her more determined to enter for the training award. See how you get on next week? Right, she'd show them! she thought. Next Sunday was the floor and vault competition at Ferndale.

10

The day of the purple leotard

Sunday dawned clear and crisp. Anda was awake early, dreading to see snow again. March lambs cried up on the moor and the Hooty Combe glittered with primroses. Bella was leaping and twisting after a butterfly. Anda watched her thoughtfully, thinking how she loved the little cat. It was almost a year since she had rescued her from the church roof—a year of gymnastics!

"Make the most of it, Anda!" said Bill as they set off. "This is Murgatroyd's last trip, probably."

"Is it her test tomorrow?"

"Yes. She won't pass. She needs about £200 of work. She'll have to go to the great garage in the sky."

"What's going to happen, Dad? Are we going to get a new one?"

Bill hit the ceiling.

"A new one! Of *course* not. You can't just *get* another car. Just click! Like that."

"But—what will we do for transport?" asked Anda, anxious about getting to Ferndale on Saturdays, and to competitions and weekend events Christie had planned.

"Wait and see. I might manage a moped," said Bill. "You could ride on the back."

"I'd love that!" cried Anda imagining herself arriving at Ferndale like a Hell's Angel.

"You might not," said Lynne. "Or Bill might get a saleman's job with a flash car to go with it."

Bill gripped Murgatroyd's wheel tighter.

"Just lay off, will you, Lynne," he snapped.

"I was only. ..."

"Well you *know* how I feel about it. There's no need to start on in front of Anda."

He changed gear with a roar. Lynne sulked.

Anda's first competition. The day of the purple leotard! And her parents were miserable!

"If I do OK today, Christie's going to let me enter for this training award, Dad."

"Great. You have a go. But don't feel you've got to."

"Fat chance!" growled Lynne. "We've never been awarded anything!"

In upset silence they travelled the rest of the way. Anda remembered hearing her parents up late arguing. About money, she imagined. Money, and transport, and having a child who was a gymnastics addict. Winning the training award would change that. So today was vital. Decision day. She was glad to see Gran's cheerful face when they reached Ferndale.

"I'll do her hair, dear. You sit down. You look awful!" she said. She hurried Anda into the changing room.

"What's it going to be? Bunches?" she asked.

"Yes."

Anda's hair had grown but not enough for the coveted pony tail. Gran had made her two purple pompons on elastic to match the leotard.

"There, you do look sweet!" she crowed, dapping round with the comb.

"Aw!" jeered Kerry mischievously.

Anda gave her a passing smack.

The changing room was full of gymnasts and fussing parents. Sixty children under eleven from clubs all over the county. Anda glanced at odd individuals, wondering how good they were. A cool, hard, experienced lot, she thought jealously. How she wished she had started younger. Seeing children smaller, calmer and apparently tougher than her was frightening. But she soon found out that others were as nervous as she was.

Julienne arrived looking white-faced.

"I don't need any help, Mummy. Really I don't!" she was saying. "My hair's OK like this."

She had her plaits in two loops, one each side, and a purple leotard like Anda's to show she belonged to Ferndale.

"Hi Anda! You look *wow!*" she cried. "Are you going in for warm-up now? Wait for me. Please wait. I'll be quick. I don't need you,

Mummy, really I don't."

"Oh, but you. ...."

"*Please*, Mummy. Leave me. Please!"

Gran took in the situation. She bustled Julienne's mother away like a long-lost friend.

There were four entries from Ferndale. Anda, Julienne, Lena and Kerry. No one was with Kerry. She looked smart, but was strangely quiet. She stayed close to Anda and Julienne.

Anda glanced briefly at the chattering audience sitting on chairs around the twelve metre floor area. During warm-up Anda was aware of Bill's blue eyes watching her. And Gran's surprised face. They couldn't take their eyes off her. They were proud of her. It felt good.

Warm-up was difficult, with such a crowd. Coloured bodies, flew past Anda doing flic-flacs and dive rolls, their coaches crab-walking beside them. Some of them looked fantastically good! She couldn't find a space to practise her own tumbling run, until Christie came to help her. She got a lecture as well.

"You watch your concentration, young lady! Your eyes are all over the hall. Never mind who is doing what! You concentrate on *you*. OK?"

"OK."

"And don't forget to present yourselves to the chief judge!" said Christie. "She's there. In that corner!"

Anda looked at the chief judge, who was just settling into her chair. She didn't look frightening.

The floor was cleared and the gymnasts lined up in the corridor outside, ready for march in.

"I've been looking forward to this part," whispered Anda.

"So have I" Julienne whispered back.

"Silence!" bellowed John.

They stood like Martians, waiting. The Ferndale group were third in the line with six gymnasts ahead of them, two in yellow and four in royal blue. Then came Lena, Julienne, Kerry and Anda, and a long line of gymnasts behind them.

The music started. A bolt of excitement ran through Anda. Then it was happening. She was marching in, head high, toes pointed, carefully leaving the right space between her and Kerry, and not looking to the right or left.

"You've got to be absolutely po-faced," Christie had said.

The audience rose to the occasion and clapped in time. And they clapped every group as it was presented. Anda was the smallest in her group. She stretched and waved. Straight ahead of her she glimpsed her parents and Gran, their hands going like drumsticks, and that made her smile.

The competitors were split into two groups. Group B marched out to do their vault which was set up in the hall. Group A, Anda's group, sat on benches to wait. Behind the benches were some mats for last minute warm-ups before their turn.

The girls who started weren't particularly

good! Certainly not up to Lena's standard. But probably better than her, Anda thought. None of them danced as well as Julienne!

Lena began to warm up behind her. Suddenly Anda was aware of Kerry sitting next to her. Kerry's whole body was trembling and she had pressed her hands over her temples.

"What's the matter?" Anda asked gently.

Kerry shook her head.

"I can't," she whispered. "I can't go on."

"Why?"

"Look at me! I want to and I can't. I don't know how to stop it."

Kerry shook even more violently. Julienne, who was getting keyed up for her own performance, put her arm round her.

"Don't, Kerry. You'll be OK!"

"Warm up," advised Anda. "Christie said to, if we got really nervous."

"I feel really sick and giddy!" whispered Kerry. She dropped her face into her hands. Anda looked round for Christie. But Christie was operating the tape recorder.

"I'll withdraw," said Kerry. "Tell Christie."

"You can't, Kerry. It's only nerves! Go on, warm up!"

But Kerry wouldn't move. Julienne and Anda looked at each other helplessly. Supposing Kerry really was ill?

Lena was walking out. Only two more! Then Anda! Her heart began to thrum and her hands were sweating.

"You're setting me off!" she whispered to

Kerry. "Look—Lena's going!"

White-faced, Julienne warmed up. An inner calm kept her together, even though she was as nervous as Kerry.

Kerry sat up, gripping the bench with both hands. She took deep breaths, watching Lena.

Lena's performance was fast, snappy and efficient. Anda watched enviously. If she could tumble like Lena and dance like Julienne! But she had hardly time to think about herself. Next to her Kerry had forced herself to action, her freckled face damp and tight. Anda took her own suit off. She did some stretches and walkovers, half-watching Julienne's poetic routine.

Julienne got a huge clap, and a cheer that sounded like Bill! She walked back, rolling her eyes, her face pink. And Kerry was going out, presenting herself to the judge, waiting for her music.

Kerry was elfin thin. She could do aerial cartwheels and high tucked somersaults. She danced with cobweb fingers and a deep frown.

"Don't frown, Kerry!" Christie had said many times, but Kerry always did.

Completing her routine in front of an audience was a devastating achievement. She walked back with a magical smile, almost giggling with delight. The audience clapped, but there was no one special to cheer her.

Now Anda's turn.

A rush of nerves, sudden determination. An explosive strength within her that must be perfectly controlled, perfectly guided into a perfect performance.

A haze of faces. A long moment as she waited like an unlit firework for the judge to nod at her.

"Absolute concentration," Christie had said. "Perform in your own little world. Concentrate all your energy within yourself and don't waste a drop!"

The judge nodded, pencil ready, glasses flashing.

Anda presented herself as elegantly as she could and walked to her starting point.

Her music had a bubbling rhythm with sudden stops and runs. She danced and ran into her first tumbling sequence, a round off two flic-flacs and a back straddle roll, putting speed and stretch into it.

Across the room Christie held her breath and sweated. Little Anda had put more amplitude into her opening sequence than Christie had expected. She was terrified Anda would get over-enthusiastic and crash or make a wild attempt at an agility that was not in her routine. But she didn't.

Synchronizing her ballet steps and arm movements with the music as Valerie had taught her, Anda curved and twisted, working in a tinsica, walkovers, handsprings, cartwheels. She knew the routine like clockwork, and she tried to give it extra grace and polish. Her dive roll was the highest she had ever done, her final pose well timed. The precious minute had passed! She walked off, trying to look dignified, hearing Bill whistling and cheering and everyone clapping.

Had she done OK? She thought she had. No mistakes, only a slight twist in landing from her handspring. And she had tried desperately hard. Bill looked across at her and pounded the air with his fist. He had a massive smile. Even Lynne looked happy now! But best of all was Christie's raised eyebrows and nod of approval.

"That was good, Anda!" said Lena, to her surprise.

"You were *wow!*" said Julienne.

"What about you then!"

"Shh!"

They were supposed to be quiet. It was difficult after they had performed. Anda glanced at Kerry.

"Are you OK now?" she mouthed.

Kerry nodded and beamed.

John came up behind them and put his arms round them both. Kerry started to chatter.

"Shh!"

Anxiously they waited for the marks which were read out in batches. Christie had told Anda and Julienne not to expect more than four or five.

Lena had eight point six, the highest mark so far in the competition. Then Julienne's mark.

"Julienne Wellington. Five point eight."

John gave Julienne a pat, but she looked gloomy. Anda knew it was because of her mother. "I'll get three," she was thinking. "I couldn't be as good as Julienne."

"Kerry Bartlett, seven point nine five."

Better than Kerry had expected. Her face broke into a smile.

"Anda Barnes, seven point two."

"What!"

That couldn't be right! She couldn't have scored all that! More than Julienne? Almost as much as Lena!

Bill let out a cheer. Anda was embarrassed. She could see Gran trying to shut him up. She ought to have told him that spectators had to behave!

She turned to John in amazement.

"They've made a *mistake!*" she whispered.

"Why?"

"I can't have scored all that. You said...."

"No. That's about right," he murmured. "Boy, did you rise to the occasion! Paintbrush!"

He gave one of her bunches a tug and walked off. He only called her "Paintbrush" when he was pleased with her! She sat in a daze. Happiness spread over her like sunshine.

After lunch Anda's group warmed up for the vault. Two tries each were allowed. Anda had badly wanted to do a handspring vault which she was quite good at, but John had said "No—not in your first competition!" so she was doing a straddle which carried a lower tariff.

This time Julienne was upset. Vaulting was not one of her strengths, and she knew it. She fell awkwardly, then chickened and missed her turn.

"I'll never get over. It's the timing. My run

up goes all wrong," she said to Anda. "John's cross with me. I know he is. He thinks it's psychological." Julienne was rubbing her ankle. "I think I twisted it when I fell."

"You ought to tell Christie!"

"It might be all right. I'll leave it."

"Christie's talking to your Mum," said Anda. "And Valerie is."

"Oh no. They're arguing!" sighed Julienne. "I hope Mum isn't complaining about my marks."

Certainly Julienn's mother looked ruffled, and so did Christie. But to everyone's surprise. Julienne managed a neat squat vault and scored three for it.

Soon it was Anda's turn. She took a deep breath and fixed the leather horse in her eye. Straight ahead. Speed. Power. Don't look at Gran! She was over, and walking back for her second vault.

John was standing by the horse.

"Straight legs," he had said as she finished. So she tried, but pitched forward on landing. She scored five. Not bad for a low tariff vault.

Now they were free to sit with their parents until the final march in and medal presentation.

"You were terrific!" said Bill, giving Anda a cuddle.

"I don't know how anyone your size can get over that great thing!" said Gran, waving a hand at the vaulting horse.

"I shut my eyes!" said Lynne.

"Mummy, you didn't!"

"I did!"

"But you never saw me vault!"

"No, but I opened my eyes in time to see you were still alive and not scattered all over the hall!"

Anda giggled. Her parents looked more cheerful now.

"I've chatted to Christie," Bill told her. "She's going to put you in for this South West Training Award thing—but she did say you only had the slimmest of chances. You aren't really experienced enough."

"Oh, great!" Anda's eyes sparkled.

"You did better than she expected today!"

"I know. I've just been lucky! It's been a perfect, perfect day for me!" smiled Anda. She wouldn't get a medal, but her marks and Christie's promise were enough to make her high. She felt like singing and dancing.

"We ought to celebrate!" said Bill. "Why don't we?"

"What with?" asked Lynne.

Bill dug in his jeans pocket and produced some silver.

"A bottle of plonk for us and pop for Anda."

"And Bella can have some cream!" said Anda.

At the end of the day, Lena had come second in the overall marking, and Kerry was third in the vaulting.

"We aren't too far down the list!" said Anda as she and Julienne stood looking at the marks after the final march in. Everyone was going home and the sound of chairs being stacked rang around the hall. Kerry cycled off by herself with her precious medal in her hand on a joyfully zig-zagging bike.

"Our first competition!" sighed Anda. "Wasn't it smashing! I wish we could do it all over again!"

"Your first. And my last probably."

"Julienne! What do you mean?"

Julienne had been oddly quiet ever since the vaulting. Now she dropped her bombshell.

"I might give it up."

"Give it up! What, give up gymnastics? You can't! You must be mad!"

Julienne silently stared at her toe drawing patterns on the floor. Her blue eyes had black clouds in them.

"Why?" persisted Anda, but her friend couldn't seem to answer. "Does Christie know?"

"Yes," said Julieene slowly. A tear rolled down her cheek.

"But why? Oh don't, Julienne!"

Suddenly Julienne was sobbing violently, her head against the wall.

"I can't—can't stop!" she choked, and shook Anda's hand away. "Leave me, just leave me."

"But ..."

"LEAVE ME!"

Anda stood, alarmed, wanting to help. Together they'd survived some tough training sessions. She had seen Julienne hurt and afraid, insulted by Lena, shouted at by John, but never had she seen her cry.

Lynne came up.

"Whatever is wrong with Julienne?"

But Julienne went on sniffing and gulping against the wall.

"Where's your mother?"

"She's in—in—in—the car." The words came in jumps. "She's wait—waiting for me. I don't want her."

"You can tell us, love!"

Julienne leaned against Lynne. Eventually the story came out, in bursts and sobs.

"Christie thinks I haven't—haven't. ..."

"All right, take your time!" crooned Lynne, stroking Julienne's hair.

"Christie said I haven't got the nerve for gymnastics."

"Oh you have!" cried Anda, wanting to comfort her friend, but even, as she said it, she knew Christie was right.

"No. It's true. It's—it's OK for people like you and Lena," wept Julienne. "You don't get scared—not scared of vaulting or bar work. I do. I'm scared all the time and Christie knows. There's no way I can hide it any more."

"Then it's best to give up, surely? After all you *are* a brilliant dancer!" said Lynne gently.

"It's my Mum really," went on Julienne in a torrent of words and tears. "She wanted me to be brilliant and I'm not. She pushed Christie into training me really and she's given a lot of money to the club and so Christie sort of had to, I suppose. It was OK while we were just doing our BAGA awards, but now it's got too difficult— Christie said I'd reached my limits and I couldn't get any better. She said did Mummy want me to be badly injured to prove the point, and that shut her up. She's been talking to Valerie about ballet."

"Oh, poor Julienne!" said Anda. "You're my best friend, Julienne, honestly. I don't know what I'll do at the club without you!"

Gradually Julienne was unwinding.

"I'll still come on Mondays. Christie said just to come and enjoy myself and I'd be welcome! She said perhaps I could help her start the little ones off."

"Well, you'd like that, wouldn't you?" asked Lynne.

"I suppose. I do like little kids."

"Perhaps you could be a coach when you get older!" suggested Gran. They were all standing there now, round poor Julienne.

"You can still come to tea and jump the Hooty Stream!" said Bill. "And I want free tickets for your first Swan Lake, mind!"

That produced a watery smile. Before long they had calmed Julienne down between them.

"Can't you come back with us to tea?" she asked. "Ask your Mum."

"OK."

They walked out to the car with Julienne. Her mother was waiting, drumming her fingers on the steering wheel.

"Well, no," she said when Lynne asked her about tea. Her usual bossy manner had softened. "I've been sitting here thinking. I was going to take Julienne out or something. She's had a hard time. I've been too ... well—it's difficult."

Lynne nodded.

"OK. Perhaps another day?"

"Of course. And we'll still take Anda on Mondays—don't worry."

The two women smiled at each other.

"Perhaps she has got a heart after all," said Lynne as Mrs Wellington drove off with Julienne, solemn-faced, in the front seat.

"She wants a kick up the ..."

"Bill!" said Gran sharply.

"Well! She does. I wouldn't want *my* kid going through that!" His blue eyes were angry.

"I don't. I love it!" said Anda anxiously.

"I know. There's no way Christie's going to throw you out!" said Bill. "But promise me, Anda, you won't get in a state like that! If ever you get too scared, or bored, you are to stop. I don't care if you never win anything. Just be happy. The training award doesn't matter!"

"It does!" said Anda. "And I am happy, Dad!"

Not even Julienne's upset could take away her own joy at having done well in her first competition. The happiness surrounded her in a golden cloud. She floated home in it, and floated to bed, and floated to school in the morning. Six months, six precious months, between now and September to float her way to the training award!

11

Nerves

In the warm September sun, a man stood at the front door of Hooty Cottage with a cat in his arms. The cat's head hung limply, its eyes shut tight, one leg crushed and bleeding. The man knocked again. He was a sheep farmer with thick brown arms that cradled the injured cat.

There was no answer. So he carried the cat back to his Landrover where his mate sat waiting.

"They've gone out with his mother, I reckon. Gone for the day. What shall we do?"

"It *is* their cat, isn't it?"

"Yes. It's little Anda's cat."

The farmer sighed heavily. Bella had streaked across the lane in front of him, and he hadn't been able to avoid her. He scribbled a note on an envelope and stuck it through the letterbox. Then away down the lane he drove, slowly, to avoid shaking the cat who lay in the back of the Landrover.

Half past six and a car full of happy people came bumping up the lane. Bill, driving Gran's car, with Lynne in the front and Anda and Julienne in the back singing and giggling.

The qualifying rounds for the training award had been held at a Sports Centre about a hundred miles from Elmsford. Despite a sort throat and headache, Anda had performed well. Perhaps well enough to qualify. Perhaps not. The eighteen finalists and their coaches would be informed by letter.

What worried Anda was her bar routine. Not yet capable of anything difficult, she'd felt her sequence was inadequate. At the last minute she'd refused to wear handguards, which she found awkward, and she'd torn the skin from an old blister on her left hand. It stung and smarted under the dressing, and Christie had been more cross than kind.

"You won't be able to train on bars for weeks if you don't look after your hands!" she'd threatened.

The pain didn't help. But Julienne did. She was kind and sparkly, not at all jealous. On the long trip home she'd giggled and played games, taking Anda's mind off the way she felt. Hot, headachy and certain that she hadn't qualified.

Julienne was staying the night at Hooty Cottage and they'd planned a happy Sunday, picking blackberries and playing with Bella.

"She's usually on the wall!" said Anda as they turned into the gate. "She always sits there waiting for us."

The two girls hunted for her. Anda stood in the yard calling. A cry came from the cottage.

"Oh no, Bill! Oh no!"

Lynne had found the envelope. It said:

"Very sorry. Hit cat with Landrover. Have taken it to vet next to Elmsford Stores."

Anda stood in the doorway, looking at Lynne's stricken face. With his arm tighly round her, Bill showed her the envelope in silence. Coldness rushed down her back and through her fingers.

"I wasn't there," said Anda in a tiny, tiny voice. "I left her here alone and she ..."

She couldn't bear to think of the little cat's pain and shock. She twisted out of Bill's arms and made for the stairs. He called her back.

"No. Come on. It's no good panicking. We get back in the car and go down to the vet. Now."

He led the way outside. Lynne and Anda were both in tears. Julienne followed them, wide eyed.

"She might be OK. Vets can do marvellous things these days!" Bill was saying.

But Anda's mind burned with thoughts of Bella suffering, her delicate bones broken.

She let Lynne take her into her bedroom and remove her shoes while she lay crying on the bed.

"I can't bear Bella to be hurt. Please don't let it be true, Mum."

First the goats. Now Bella. Bella was dead. Because of gymnastics.

"She's ill," she heard Lynne say quietly. "You go, Bill, you and Julienne. Go on. I'll stay."

"Poor Bella," wept Anda. "All the time I've been training and Bella was here by herself. This morning she came and miaowed and she didn't want me to go. And now she's been killed."

Lynne put a thin hand on Anda's forehead.

"You'd better try to get some sleep," she said. Anda slept deeply and could not be woken. When she did wake up it was two o'clock in the morning.

"Bella!" she thought instantly and got out of bed. Next door she could hear Bill snoring. She sneaked downstairs, surprised to see the glow of a light.

"Julienne?"

Julienne looked up in surprise. She was kneeling on the rug with a large cat basket in front of her.

"Come and look," she said. "You won't believe it, Anda. She's actually purring."

"Purring?"

Anda stood at the bottom of the stairs, too scared to look in the basket.

"It's OK," said Julienne. "You come and look. Come *on*. Don't be scared!"

"I wasn't!"

Anda crept to look.

"Oh!"

She hardly dared touch the silky fur.

"Don't pick her up," said Julienne. "She's

had an operation. The vet's put a steel pin in her leg. She's just coming round from the anaesthetic."

Dumbfounded, Anda saw Bella's front leg. The shaved fur. The row of stitches. There was no blood, and Bella looked clean and fluffy. Anda reached out and gently stoked the top of her head.

"She's lost two teeth, and she was badly stunned," went on Julienne. "But the vet says the rest of her is OK. He X-rayed her. She'll get better, Anda."

Anda gulped. With one finger she stroked Bella's ears.

"But—but her leg! How can she run about?"

"She will. The vet said he'd done lots of cats and dogs before and they can all walk about OK. She might limp for a bit. We've got to keep her warm because she's in shock."

"It's a miracle!" breathed Anda.

In the morning when Bella opened her yellow eyes and looked at Anda, it seemed even more a miracle. The cat stood up gingerly and stretched. She hopped out of the basket and staggered towards the kitchen.

"Oh, poor Bella!" Horrified to see her so wobbly and lame, Anda rushed to pick her up.

"No, leave her," said Bill. "She's got to learn to walk again. And she's still dopey from the anaesthetic."

Anda poured out a saucer of milk, and Bella's fluffy tail went up. She was starving!

"Cats have a remarkable recovery rate," said

Bill. "Oh look, she's washing. That's a good sign."

"And you, young lady, are having a quiet day!" Lynne said to Anda. "You've got a temperature! Look at her face, Bill."

"Hi, beetroot chops!" said Bill.

Overcome by an intense headache she returned to bed and Julienne played by herself in the Hooty Stream and picked blackberries for Lynne.

"I'll tell Christie you're sick if you don't make it tomorrow," she said when she came up to say goodbye. But Anda hardly cared. All day she got worse and worse. There was no question of her going to school tomorrow, or to Ferndale.

The doctor came, bouncing and grumbling up the lane in his car.

"She's got a nasty virus," he told Lynne. "Keep her in bed for a few days, and off school for at least a week. And she must rest. No gymnastics."

Anda had been training too hard, and worrying. Four hours a day, through the summer heat, and three times a week at Ferndale. Now that school had started again, intensive preparation for the training award had exhausted her.

The doctor prescribed some horrific pink and red capsules, and Lynne crept about with hot drinks.

Lynne carried Bella up and down stairs, and Anda, when she wasn't sleeping, spent hours leaning over her box talking and gently stroking. The cat's bright face and silky fur still seemed miraculous.

"I should be training, Mum," Anda kept worrying.

"You've *got* to rest."

"Tomorrow I'll be able to."

"Yes, tomorrow."

The black days chugged past. Wednesday. Thursday and no Ferndale. Gran bringing ice cream. Corngold sun outside.

Saturday. And the postman, with a long white envelope addressed to Miss Anda Barnes. Lynne stood fingering it, wondering whether to let Anda open it or not.

"Come on. Sit up. You've got an important letter!"

She drew back the curtains.

"Do you think this is *it*, Mum?" Anda took the letter.

"It might be a no," said Lynne. 'Don't be disappointed."

Slowly Anda peeled and unfolded the paper. Dear Miss Barnes, I am pleased to tell you....

"I don't believe it! Mum, I don't believe it! I've been selected for the final!"

Anda let out a scream and bounded up and down in bed. Her head throbbed and she dropped back against the pillows. She and Lynne flung their arms round each other and laughed.

"Oh, Mum!"

But Lynne sobered down. "It's on October 18th. That's only a month!" she exclaimed.

"And look at you! Love, you'll never make it."

"Of course I will, Mum. Don't be silly."

But she was horribly afraid that Lynne was right. She had missed over a week of vital training. By Monday she could eat properly. She got up and dressed, horrified to find her legs like jellies.

Depressed, she sat wondering how she would ever vault again. All she wanted to do was sit on the cottage doorstep in the sunshine and watch Bella padding round in the garden.

"We don't mind about the award," Bill had said. "You get better and be happy."

But Anda cared desperately about the award. Without it her training was going to spoil her parents' life more and more. They had parted with the goats; Murgatroyd was scrapped; and Bill had sacrificed his dreams. The only thing left was to sell Hooty Cottage and move. She had to try!

In the end it was Bella who finally gave Anda the courage she needed. Bella led her, hobbling, right down to the Hooty Stream. She stood up on her hind legs and dabbed at a passing butterfly.

The turf was dry and warm in the autumn sun. Anda sat down. She stretched her legs and pointed her toes. As if drawing strength from the glittering stream and the sunshine, she began her warm-ups. The long haul back into training had started!

12

The final

On the eve of the 18th October she had a row with her parents. She had a terrible feeling she was going to fail and she didn't want them to watch.

"Christie will take me. She'll pick me up in Elmsford."

"But we'd arranged to borrow Gran's car, Anda! You *know* we want to go. We'll take you!"

"I just—would rather be on my own."

"I see!" said Lynne icily. "After all we've done for you and your gymnastics, you don't want us there! That's nice, isn't it!"

"It's not like that, Mummy!"

"Well, what is it then?" We've been to your other competitions! I thought you were glad of someone there to cheer you on!"

"I am but—well, this is special. I feel different about it. I need to be on my own so that I can really concentrate."

"Well, surely the other children's parents will be there?"

"Yes. Some of them. There's not really an audience—only the judges and promoters, I think."

"But we've arranged to have Gran's car! I just don't understand you, Anda! You shouldn't have arranged that with Christie!"

"I didn't. She offered to if I was stuck."

"Well she needn't. You can come with us, Anda. Gran would be so hurt. She wants to come. Don't you realise how much *she's* done for you?"

"Yes."

Anda sighed, and Lynne suddenly blew up.

"Honestly! You expect everything laid on for you and then throw it back in our faces!"

"No Mum, it's...."

"All we've given up for you, and then you tell us we aren't wanted! That really does take the biscuit!"

Shattered and confused, Anda looked at her silently.

"You don't know the half of it, Anda. What we've been through for you! Do you think we like having to borrow Gran's car?"

"I do, Mum. That's *why* I want the training award. And I'm scared of letting you all down."

Bill came to her rescue.

"You won't let us down! We're proud of what you can do, and the way you've fought back after that flu! I wish I could get it into your thick skull that we don't care about you winning!"

"But if I don't?"

"We'll find a way."

"What way?" asked Anda suspiciously.

"Well—we can't go on borrowing Gran's car.
That's a temporary measure. I'll have to repair
Murgatroyd myself and get her back on the
road."

"But if I won, you'd have the money for
petrol to take me there, Dad. And for my
training weekends and clothes and things."

"If you won—it would just be a bonus!" said
Bill.

"But would you get another goat if I did?"
persisted Anda who had never forgotten the
shock of the goats being sold to pay for her
clothes.

"Well—yes, I must admit I might do."

"He would," said Lynne.

That decided it. She had to win!

When they reached the Sports Centre in the
morning, the sheer size of it frightened her.
Around the arena were stacks of seats, quickly
filling up with spectators. Outside were huge
posters and a queue of people buying tickets.

Anda panicked. "Oh no! It's like Wembley! I
didn't know! I thought it was only going to be a
few people! Not all this lot! Oh no!"

"You'll be all right!" said Gran. "You
haven't got nerves!"

"I have."

Bill gave her a push.

"OK, we'll go home then," he teased.

"No, Dad!"

"Go on," he said. "And good luck!"

Suddenly glad they had come, Anda ran to find Christie in the warm-up room. Most of the competition squad were with her, including Lena.

"Whatever are you doing here?" asked Anda in surprise.

"Watching you, you twit!" said Lena.

"They've come to cheer you on!" said Christie. "So no coughing on the beam!"

Anda grinned. She still had a cough and was hoping it wouldn't interfere with her performance.

"You'd better get in your seats," said Christie and the squad moved off, unfamiliar in dresses and jeans. Kerry had even made a Ferndale flag to wave.

Completely overwhelmed, Anda sidled up to Christie. "Christie—I don't know if I can. I didn't know it would be so—so huge!"

Christie looked down at her. "Anda!" she said reproachfully. "You're not going to chicken out are you?"

"No, of course not."

With a chest full of hammering nerves, she got changed.

Julienne was there suddenly, full of chatter, doing Anda's hair for her. "There's a display after the competition!" she bubbled. "Christie thinks it's something I could do! Modern rhythmic gymnastics."

"You'd be good at it!" said Anda.

A glance into the stadium made her nerves worse. The beam and bars looked somehow ominous.

"What a crowd!"

"It's not *that* many people!" said Julienne. "It's not really like Wembley. You've been used to the little group of parents we usually get!"

"I'm even scared to go in for warm-up!" said Anda. "I wish you'd come in with me."

"I'm not allowed! Look, it says only coaches and competitors. I'll go and sit with your mum."

"All right. Tell her she's not to shut her eyes when I vault!" replied Anda, reluctant to let Julienne go. "And—don't tell them I'm scared."

"Why not?"

"'Cause Dad thinks—they all think I've got guts. Only I haven't really. Not today!"

Christie came sweeping in.

"Aren't you warming up yet? Come along!"

"See you. Good luck!"

Julienne disappeared round the corner. Anda looked up at Christie. Didn't Christie have any idea how terrified she was? Apparently she did, for she hurried Anda into the arena. Once she'd started warming up, she soon got used to the rumble of talking people. An hour's warm-up. Then march in and presentation.

"Anda Barnes. Age eleven. Ferndale Gymnastics Club."

Step forward. Stretch. Wave. Try to look happy! Somewhere in that beach of people sit

113

Bill and Lynne, and Gran. The Ferndale flag is waving. You've got to win!

"Penny Green. Age eleven. Park Gymnastics Club."

"Heidi Adam. Age eleven. Sandhaven Gymnastics Club."

Her two rivals! Penny, black-haired, ponytailed, full of bouncy confidence, and Heidi, solemn-faced, bobbed hair and bamboo legs. Next to them, three eleven year old boys. Then the ten and twelve year olds.

The hall pulsated with rhythmic clapping as they marched off to sit beside the performing area.

"You're first on bars, Anda!" Christie met her with a programme in her hand. "Come on. Back in."

"Oh no, Christie!"

The asymetric bars were her worst discipline. And she was to be first to stand alone in the huge stadium and begin! Christie was fixing her hand-guards, adjusting the bar for her. No backing out now!

"Anda Barnes, on bars," boomed the announcer, and a nerve-splitting hush fell on the audience. Gran's heart thudded across the hall. Lynne shut her eyes.

"Concentration," whispered Christie.

The bars. And only the bars. No hall. No people. No Dad. No Gran. Only bars.

With swift precision Anda found herself doing her bar routine, her limbs going like clockwork, straddling and catching, circling and swinging. Then her underswing dismount, arched and high from the top bar. A blur of Christie waiting to catch her if she needed it. Her feet bolted to the mat, her aching body forcing itself to stand swallow-like to finish.

"I don't know what I did," she said breathlessly to Christie. "I just sort of—went mechanically. What did I do?"

Christie gave her a hug. "You did OK. It was kind of—fast! But as good as you've ever done."

But when Anda saw Penny Green's performance, her hopes fell. Penny did far more difficult moves than her, and did them expertly. Anda could have wept with sudden, unreasonable disappointment.

Heidi was even better.

Overcome with gloom, Anda sat twiddling her hair, talking quietly to Christie.

"They weren't that good!" Christie said encouragingly. "And don't forget it's your overall score, not just the bars!"

Anda gritted her teeth and smiled at Penny and Heidi as they moved on to the beam.

The terrible nerves had calmed a little. Depression had set in. Her 5.80 on bars was pathetic compared with the sevens the other two had scored. Again she was to perform first on beam.

A pause while the judges argued on a score. She looked up, and suddenly spotted Gran, Bill and Lynne. Three tense faces, and Julienne's full moon smile. Kerry was holding the homemade flag high above her head. She thought how Kerry had fought back after her illness. She thought of Bella climbing the stairs with such courage. And her own courage flooded back.

"Don't you let this go, Anda Barnes!" she thought.

The judge was ready for her.

"Anda Barnes on beam."

A neat straddle mount. Forward roll. Still there! Arabesque, turn, cat-leap. Now her forward walkover. She was lucky! With a fifty:fifty chance of falling, this time she completed it and stayed upright. Dance, slide to splits, pose. She even felt steady enough to put extra style into her dancing. The time whistle blew and she quickly did her barani dismount. She heard Christie shout:

"Yes!"

Applause. Wolfwhistles from her dad. Julienne's plaits whirling.

Now for the marks.

Tensely she and Christie stared at the marks board while Penny warmed up.

"Seven point nine five."

It meant nothing until the other two had finished.

"She hasn't got as much amplitude as you!" whispered Christie as Penny began her beam exercise. It was no more advanced than Anda's, and she wobbled twice and fell once. Then Heidi made a complete mess of hers, falling three times and overrunning her time. Two low scores brought the three girls almost level.

"You've got a chance now, Anda! You really have!" said Christie, with her magical smile. "I never expected you to do this well! You could win, you know! You could!"

"I was lucky on the beam. My walkover!" smiled Anda, the excitement rising inside her.

"There's often an element of luck! But more often it's the way you respond to this kind of situation," said Christie. "Or you could lose by half a mark."

"No."

From that moment Anda believed she could win. Her handspring vault was strong and clean. But Penny, with a beautiful yamashita, finished one whole mark ahead.

"It's you or her. There's no way Heidi can catch up now!"

Now only the floor exercises lay between her and success or failure.

Tiredness was creeping into her. She still had a cough, and the stress of the long afternoon was taking its toll. Her leotard felt prickly and one of her wrists ached. Beads of pain shot up her arm when she put weight on it. To her annoyance Christie insisted on strapping it for her.

"I can't *dance* with a great bandage thing on!"

"Rubbish. Everyone does. You see Olympic girls with bandaged knees and things."

"But I'll look horrible!"

"You won't."

"I will, Christie, and it's too tight! I can't flex my fingers freely!"

"If it's not tight it won't help."

"But Christie!"

"Don't fuss!"

She had no choice but to wear the hot white wrist support.

"You must *not* let it put you off, Anda! Come on, you're getting tired. Where's that fire in your belly?" coaxed Christie.

"It's—still there!"

"Good girl. Warm up now. Five minutes."

Five precious minutes to limber and stretch, and hate the bandage on her wrist!

And then the little girl from Hooty Combe stood waiting at the corner of the mat. The mass of people looked down, and saw her bird-like face, big brown eyes and golden pony tail. No longer a child who cried and smashed things and ran away, but a gymnast, cool, disciplined and full of corked-up fire.

"Open your eyes!" hissed Bill up in the audience. "You are to watch this, Lynne!"

Lynne opened her eyes.

"Anda Barnes on floor."

Her music began. Space age music, full of power and sparkle.

Holding hands very tightly, Bill and Lynne watched the tiny figure in the purple leotard. Round off, flic-flacs, back somersault.

"Oh Heavens!" murmured Gran.

And Julienne sat with her plaits twisted round both hands, heart thudding for her friend.

Anger at wearing the wrist bandage helped to

118

give her extra height, extra stretch. She danced and flew like Thumbelina, while her parents clutched each other, not breathing.

Poetically she finished on the last twang of music.

Bill, Lynne, Gran and Julienne stood up and cheered. Even Gran behaved like a football supporter, dropping her glasses and clapping wildly.

Anda walked off with a weird feeling of finality. The cheers died away. She shook. Nothing mattered until Penny's score. Penny was leading by one mark.

"Just don't be disappointed," Christie kept saying, as they waited for the white numbers to appear.

Her own score: seven point nine five.

And Penny was walking out to begin.

In the longest minute of her life, Anda sat looking up at her parents and Gran, thinking of Bella and the Hooty Stream. Thinking of everything but Penny's performance. To lose by half a mark!

In a cocoon of gloom she sat. Whatever happened, she must smile, and congratulate Penny, and steel herself for the final march in.

Tension. Silence.

Then a roar from the crowd, and Christie suddenly swept Anda off the bench and hugged her.

"You've done it! You've done it! You HAVE!"

"What?"

"You've won it! By half a mark, Anda!"

She stood there. "I can't have!"

Christie laughed.

Anda looked across at Penny and saw a pale defeated face. Only then did she believe it. She'd been too uptight even to look at Penny's score.

"But she's better than me," she said to Christie.

"She wasn't today."

Impulsively Anda rushed up to Penny and took her hand. "I'm sorry," she said. "Was it important for you—the award?"

Penny shrugged. "Well—no, not that desperate. I'll get a medal. Was it for you?"

"Yes. Very desperate."

"I'm glad, then. Well done."

"Yes, well done!" added Penny's coach warmly.

"We'll meet again—at other competitions!" said Penny. "I'll beat you next time!"

Standing on the podium receiving her medal was a unique moment that would live forever. With her gold token medal was an envelope containing the precious details of the award. She waved it high and the applause pounded in her ears. Bill whistled, Lynne wept and Gran beamed with pride.

Then they were marching out. The boys in white. The girls in coloured leotards. The hall throbbing. The rhythmic display team ready to march in. Julienne rushing towards her. The moment of glory still bright in her heart.

Far away in the chill of autumn, Hooty Cottage twinkled expectantly. The stream sang and the birch trees danced with golden leaves.

On the gatepost a little black and white cat sat watching the lane, waiting for her saucer of cream.

Also by Anita Hughes

CHRISTMAS AT THE RANCH

A Novel

ANITA HUGHES

St. Martin's Paperbacks

Published in the United States by St. Martin's Paperbacks, an imprint of St. Martin's Publishing Group.

CHRISTMAS AT THE RANCH

Copyright © 2022 by Anita Hughes.
Excerpt from *Christmas at the Lake* copyright © 2023 by Anita Hughes.

All rights reserved.

For information, address St. Martin's Publishing Group, 120 Broadway, New York, NY 10271.

www.stmartins.com

Library of Congress Catalog Card Number: 2022013553

ISBN: 978-1-250-89645-2

Our books may be purchased in bulk for promotional, educational, or business use. Please contact your local bookseller or the Macmillan Corporate and Premium Sales Department at 1-800-221-7945, ext. 5442, or by email at MacmillanSpecialMarkets@macmillan.com.

Printed in the United States of America

St. Martin's Griffin edition published 2022
St. Martin's Paperbacks edition / October 2023

10 9 8 7 6 5 4 3 2 1

To My Mother

Chapter One

It was three days before Christmas and Samantha Morgan was putting the finishing touches on the manuscript she was due to send to her editor when the doorbell rang. Her heroine, Sloane Parker, had just called Phineas, her boss at British Intelligence, to tell him that she caught Miguel, the head of the diamond-smuggling cartel she had been assigned to shut down. Miguel was in a jail deep in the Guatemalan jungle while Sloane was back at her hacienda, rubbing antivenom ointment on her spider bites and popping the cork off a bottle of celebratory champagne.

For a moment, Samantha forgot where she was, and thought Miguel was at the door and the Guatemalan police had double-crossed her. Then she remembered she was in her Brooklyn apartment and that Miguel and the diamond cartel only existed in her imagination.

But she wasn't expecting anyone. And whoever it was should be pressing the outside buzzer, instead of standing at her door. How did they get in? The knocking sounded again and a familiar voice called her name. Her dog, Socks, hopped from his comfortable place on the sofa and waited by the door for Samantha to open it.

She unbolted the two dead bolts and removed the

fireplace poker she kept lodged under the doorknob. Her suspicions that she knew the mystery guest were confirmed when she saw the face of her editor. "Charlie, what are you doing here and how did you get in the building?" Samantha asked.

"Aren't you going to let me inside?" Charlie dusted snow from his overcoat. "It's freezing."

"I'm sorry, I was writing and didn't hear you." Samantha ushered him into the small living room. Samantha's slippers were wedged under an ottoman and there was an empty bowl of popcorn. "How did you get in?" Samantha asked again.

"You gave me the key a month ago." Charlie removed a dog's squeaky toy from the sofa. "You were afraid someone could slip in behind me when you buzzed me in."

"I can't remember anything when I'm in the middle of writing," Samantha conceded. "And I read that thirty percent of apartment robberies occur because the burglar enters a building by sneaking in behind someone who was buzzed in."

"You live in Park Slope. You should be more worried about getting run over by one of those giant strollers jamming the sidewalk."

Samantha glanced at the clock on the mantel. The living room had exposed brick walls and a bay window. Her favorite feature was the fireplace. She knew she had truly hit the New York real estate lottery with this apartment. She loved snuggling with her rescue mixed beagle, Socks, in front of the fireplace at Christmas while she sipped hot apple cider and Socks chewed on a bone in the shape of a gingerbread man.

"What are you doing here? Aren't you supposed to be on the way to Emily's parents' house in Vermont?" she asked.

Emily was Charlie's fiancée and they were going to spend Christmas week at Emily's parents' house in Vermont. It sounded magical: a village square with a skating rink and sleigh rides and free Christmas cookies. Samantha almost wished she had somewhere to go for Christmas. But she hated driving on icy roads and there was no one she wanted to spend a whole week with other than Socks.

"There's a work emergency and I need your help," Charlie replied.

"Everyone in publishing is off for the holidays. Don't you remember attending the Christmas party?" Samantha said, grinning. "You and Emily hit the eggnog a little too hard, you both forgot the lyrics of 'Jingle Bells.'"

"This is serious, Samantha. Arthur is having a house party and he wants you there."

"That's not serious, there are dozens of parties this time of year." She waved her hand. "I'll call and say I got food poisoning or I slipped on the ice and twisted my ankle. I'll send a Christmas ornament as a gift. He'll forget he invited me by the new year."

"This is different. It's for the whole Christmas week and Arthur specifically said he wants you there. Arthur's Christmas parties are legendary. You should be excited."

Last year, Arthur hosted a Christmas party at the Rainbow Room on the sixty-fifth floor of 30 Rockefeller Plaza. Samantha wasn't invited. Arthur's tradition was to invite only one author and a variety of other guests. But she'd heard about it. There was lobster trucked in that morning from Maine, and Moët & Chandon champagne and chocolate lava cake served with vanilla gelato for dessert. Each guest received a personalized gift. The author, Derek Houseman, wrote detective novels, and he received two tickets on the Orient Express plus airfare.

"No way," Samantha said with a gulp. "You know I hate to drive in the winter. And I couldn't survive a whole week with complete strangers. What if one of them is returning from a foreign country and I come down with the bird flu?"

"Bird flu isn't a thing anymore," Charlie grunted. "You have to leave the apartment, Samantha. It isn't healthy to spend all your time writing."

"I volunteer once a week at the humane society and I'm a member of the food co-op. And I've been tutoring Way Ling's daughter in English. She gives me free dumplings and we sit in the back of the restaurant."

"You named three places within five blocks of your apartment." His tone was gentler. "When was the last time you left Brooklyn?"

"I go into Manhattan all the time. I've never missed a team meeting," Samantha reminded him.

"That's because you're a professional and I appreciate it," Charlie said with a nod. "But this is a command performance. You have to go."

"It's not my fault that marketing created a social media campaign based around the fact that I'm just like Sloane Parker," Samantha said with a grimace. "So what if Sloane wears a Galliano gown and flirts with a Russian double agent at a hotel bar in Moscow? I can still be happy in sweatpants, curled up with Socks in my living room."

"That campaign helped make you a *New York Times* bestseller," Charlie reminded her. "Your readers love imagining you're just like Sloane and now isn't the time to ruin their fantasy. Sales of the last book were down. If Arthur asks you to do something, you say yes."

"How far down?" Samantha winced.

She knew sales on her latest Sloane Parker were lower

than the previous book. Charlie had sent her and her agent a sales report last quarter. But she hadn't asked Charlie about sales in over a month. If he had good news, it would come in an e-mail with GOOD NEWS in the subject line, followed by at least one exclamation mark. When there was bad news, Charlie didn't send e-mail updates at all.

"Down enough that Arthur sent an e-mail asking if I knew an author named Melody Minnow," Charlie said gravely.

"Melody Minnow isn't an author," Samantha growled. "She's an Instagram star who can barely splice three coherent sentences together."

"It doesn't matter. Her Instagram has four hundred thousand followers and they buy her books. We need to keep your image out there." Charlie studied Samantha's sweatpants and faded T-shirt. "And nineties grunge isn't going to cut it with your readers."

"These are new sweatpants, I bought them online," Samantha said. "And wait until you read the latest Sloane Parker. Sloane rappels through the Guatemalan jungle wearing stiletto heels that even I was jealous of."

This didn't sway Charlie. "Please, Samantha. I'm your editor. It's not just your job on the line, it's mine too."

Charlie had been her older brother Jake's college roommate and she had known him since she was sixteen. While Samantha was in high school, Jake often brought Charlie home to their parents' house in New Jersey on long weekends and spring break. Samantha had loved to write stories since she was a child, and she was flattered when Charlie asked her to look over his English essays. After Charlie and Jake graduated from college, Samantha was the first to congratulate Charlie when he got a job as an editorial assistant at a publishing house.

Four years ago, Samantha was at the lowest point in

her life and Charlie rescued her. She had a job at a PR firm in the city and a serious boyfriend, and lived in a loft in the East Village with a roommate. But then she was laid off, and soon after, her boyfriend, Roger, moved to California. Her roommate got engaged and left her with a rent that quickly depleted her savings.

She was about to move back to her parents' house in New Jersey when Charlie suggested she write a novel. Samantha thought he was crazy; just because she kept the stack of notebooks with all her childhood stories in a drawer under her bed didn't mean that she could write a three-hundred-page novel. But that night she was drowning her sorrows in a James Bond marathon and wondered why the woman always had to be the love interest or the sexy villain. Why couldn't there be a female James Bond who wore designer gowns, knew sixteen different ways to fix a martini, and also happened to be the most sought-after secret agent in the western hemisphere? When Samantha went to bed that night, Sloane Parker appeared to her fully formed, right down to her mass of auburn hair and almond-shaped hazel eyes, and was equally comfortable wearing stiletto heels as she was combat boots.

Charlie introduced her to a well-respected agent who sold the manuscript to the imprint where Charlie was an editor. The first Sloane Parker book sold 100,000 copies. Charlie was a thoughtful editor and they made a great team. With the money she made, Samantha was able to afford a new laptop and a one-bedroom apartment in Brooklyn. Writing the books was easy: she loved researching exotic locations online and inventing male characters who resembled a *GQ* magazine model with a heart of gold. But keeping up the social media persona the marketing department invented was harder. Samantha had an unhealthy fear of almost everything and it seemed to be getting worse. She was terrified of large insects and hated flying. She couldn't eat at a salad bar without worrying she contracted an intestinal disease. But she also didn't want to let Charlie down.

Samantha knew how publishing worked: Charlie had been promoted four times during his career, and his latest position as senior editor was somewhat dependent on her. If his star author failed to make the *New York Times* Best Sellers list again, then Charlie's own job was in danger. He was one of her best friends and she owed her career to him.

"I would, but what about Socks?" she asked Charlie. "I doubt I could find a dog sitter at Christmas and Arthur is allergic to dogs."

"I already thought about that," Charlie responded. "Emily and I will take him to Vermont. Emily's parents have two dogs with their own doghouse. The dogs even get their own Christmas dinner: beef tips and doggy Christmas pudding for dessert."

"You know I hate to drive in icy conditions," Samantha tried again. "It would be difficult to get a car service without advance notice. They're all booked ferrying people to holiday parties or the airport. And Arthur's country house is almost two hours out of the city. You know how Uber inflates their rates over the holidays. It would cost a fortune."

Samantha hadn't been to Arthur's house in Connecticut but she had heard about it. It sat on two acres, with tennis courts and an indoor swimming pool.

"There's a car waiting downstairs, paid for by the company." He smiled broadly. "All you have to do is pack a bag, sit back, and relax."

Samantha stood on one foot the way she sometimes did when she was trying to think of a new plot point. But no excuses came to mind. Charlie looked so hopeful, like Socks when he was eyeing take-out chicken she bought for dinner.

"A whole week." She wrinkled her forehead. "Can I come home early for good behavior?"

"You might actually enjoy yourself. Arthur is a wonderful host and he always has interesting guests," he offered. "Not to mention you're a twenty-seven-year-old woman living in New York and you haven't had a date in months. You're not going to meet someone tapping away on your laptop."

"Why aren't you and Emily going?" Samantha asked. "You are my editor."

"We weren't invited." Charlie shrugged. "The house party is even smaller than his party last year at the Rainbow Room. You and some of Arthur's personal friends and a few other guests. A critic for *The New York Times* will be there and buyers from the biggest bookstore chains. It's a real honor for you to receive an invitation," he prompted. "You can't turn it down."

"All right, you win," Samantha sighed. "You don't have to wait. I'm capable of carrying a bag down to the street."

"Of course I'll wait. I'm a gentleman." Charlie leaned against the cushions. "And I don't want to learn that you paid off the driver to leave. Take all the time you need."

Samantha had barely settled into the back of the town car when her phone rang. She took it out of her purse and saw an unfamiliar number.

"Samantha? It's your mother," a familiar voice said over the line. "I'm calling from the international phone your dad bought for the trip. We're in Amsterdam. Today we're going to visit the Christmas markets and tonight we're seeing the largest performance of *Swan Lake* in the world. Tomorrow we leave for Vienna to see the Christmas concert at the Schönbrunn Palace. I'm so glad we took this trip: the best eight European capitals to see at Christmas. I forgot to give you the itinerary. I'll send it from my phone. I had no idea you could send e-mails from your phone. The ticket lady at JFK Airport showed me how, it's so convenient!"

Before their recent retirement, Samantha's parents had both been teachers. During Samantha's childhood, they always celebrated Christmas at home. Samantha had loved the family traditions: Driving to the Christmas tree lot on Christmas Eve and picking out the perfect tree. Waking up on Christmas morning to Bing Crosby's "White Christmas" playing in the living room and the smell of maple syrup and pancakes wafting from the kitchen. Her father putting on whatever clothes he received as gifts: the reindeer sweater her mother knitted from a pattern coupled with the striped tie she and Jake bought with their pooled allowance.

Jake got married five years ago and moved to California. Every year, his wife's family rented a house in Palm Springs for December. Even Samantha's parents could see why Jake and Andrea preferred spending the month zipping around in a golf cart and sipping iced tea in the shade of their casita. Now Samantha and her family celebrated Christmas and Thanksgiving together during the same week in November, and her parents decided Christmastime was the perfect opportunity to visit the places on their retirement bucket list. Each year, they invited Samantha to join them but she refused. At first, it was because she and Roger were together and he had to spend part of Christmas with his own family. Since Roger had left and Samantha's fear of flying began, she was content cozying up in her apartment with Socks for company and a steady stream of Hallmark movies playing on her computer.

"It sounds wonderful." Samantha reclined against the headrest. It was snowing and she couldn't see out of the car's tinted windows. The driver had put on Christmas music and there was hot cocoa in the cup holder.

"I wish you had joined us. I feel guilty leaving you alone at Christmas," Samantha's mother added.

"I'm fine," Samantha answered. "I'm actually headed to Connecticut. Arthur Wentworth is having a house party and he invited me."

"That's wonderful news." Her mother's voice brightened. "I'm sure there will be some young people there. Maybe you'll meet someone . . ."

"Not you too," Samantha groaned. "I don't need a man, I'm happy on my own."

"We all need someone to share things with," her mother countered. "You should join us this summer when we go sailing in Portugal. I've heard Portuguese fishermen are very sexy."

"You know how I feel about flying," Samantha said, shuddering.

"Oh, Samantha, it's not that bad," her mother prompted. "Almost every airline has a bar in the terminal. And they give out those sleep masks and noise-canceling headphones. I drank two gin and tonics before we boarded and slept all the way to Heathrow."

"I'll think about it," Samantha agreed, knowing she wouldn't. She was happy swimming at the local YMCA in the summer or going out to Rockaway Beach.

"You were such a fearless child. You and your dad built that tree house and I couldn't get you down for days," her mother recalled. "Maybe you should keep seeing your therapist . . ."

"I didn't mind seeing a therapist, but she can't help with this," Samantha said.

Samantha's fears started a few months after Roger moved to California. Samantha's best friend from college, Whitney, saw a special promotion for eight days at an all-inclusive singles' resort in the Bahamas. It was geared to twenty-somethings and promised scuba diving lessons and happy hours and all-you-can-eat buffets. A week before they were scheduled to leave, Whitney came down with appendicitis and couldn't go. Samantha went alone and it was the most terrifying experience of her life. First, there was a fire in one engine of the plane and they had to make an emergency landing. Samantha sat in the back of the plane watching in horror as the ground came up too fast to meet them and was sure they were all going to die.

Then, three days into the trip there was a hurricane. It came up so quickly, there was no time to evacuate, so instead, the guests were forced to stay in their huts. One hut collapsed and two young women from Nebraska were seriously injured. The hurricane practically destroyed the resort, and for four days it devastated the island; they were without running water and electricity. Finally, planes were allowed to land at the tiny airport and Samantha had to brace herself for the flight home.

From there, her fears seemed to snowball. The next week, she read about a tourist boat that caught fire off the coast of California and a hiking accident in Maine. There was an avalanche at a ski resort in Utah that killed four people and a sixteen-car pileup on I-95 that left five people dead.

No matter how she tried, she couldn't stop clicking on links and scrolling through photos. One night, she was so upset about a thirtieth birthday party at a warehouse in Williamsburg where the roof collapsed that she called Roger just to hear his voice. They hadn't spoken in months. Instead of consoling her, Roger pointed out that Samantha didn't know any of these people and that she should stop going on the internet.

After that, she almost couldn't face leaving the apartment. She had hoped that writing the Sloane Parker books would help distract her and make her forget her own brush with disaster. But in some ways, it made it worse. Her imagination grew so vivid that it was easy to imagine all the bad things that could happen. Yet, she couldn't stop writing. She loved the character she'd created in Sloane Parker, and there was nothing else she'd rather do.

"When you come home," Samantha said now, "I'll take the train to New Jersey and climb up into the tree house."

"You don't have to do that, sweetie," her mother replied. "I have to go. Your father and I are hungry and planning on eating dumplings and *kerststol* at the Christmas markets: sweet bread stuffed with almond paste and dried fruit and covered with confectioners' sugar. I'll buy an extra loaf and bring it home for you."

Samantha hung up and her stomach rumbled. Maybe it wouldn't be so bad to spend a week at Arthur's place. Charlie said he had a private chef. There were bound to be breakfasts of omelets and homemade waffles.

The car slowed and Samantha frowned. It was too snowy to see outside the window but they couldn't have arrived.

The driver hopped out and opened her door, and she realized they were at the airport.

"I don't think we're in the right place." Samantha poked her head out. "We're supposed to be in Connecticut."

"I have my instructions right here." The driver grabbed a piece of paper from the passenger seat. "United Airlines terminal, JFK. Flight 255 to Jackson Hole, Wyoming, departing at four p.m."

"You must have mixed it up with another passenger," Samantha said easily. "Why don't you call your company and sort it out?"

The driver shook his head. "The instructions came from Mr. Green himself."

Charlie had told him to go to the airport? That was impossible. She dug out her phone and called him.

"Why am I in the departure terminal of JFK when I'm supposed to be winding my way through the country roads of Connecticut?" she demanded when Charlie answered.

"Did I say that the house party was at Arthur's place in Connecticut?" Charlie said innocently. "It's at his ranch in Jackson Hole, Wyoming. Fifty acres of winter wonderland perched at the foot of the Teton mountains. Arthur bought it last summer, it's his first Christmas there."

"Charlie." Her voice was unsteady. "Santa Claus couldn't drag me onto a plane to Wyoming."

"I've seen pictures and the ranch is more luxurious than a five-star resort: an indoor/outdoor Jacuzzi, home theater, horseback riding in the summer, and tobogganing in the winter. The bedrooms have heated floors and there's an intercom next to your bed so you can call anytime to request extra blankets."

"I don't need anyone to bring me extra blankets," she said, on the verge of tears. "Because if the party isn't in Connecticut, I'm going to be spending Christmas week in my bed in Brooklyn."

"It's an easy flight. Four hours nonstop to Jackson Hole. There's a United Club right inside the terminal. Order one of those sweet Christmas drinks that taste like a milkshake but knock you out and then watch *Sleepless in Seattle* on the plane. You'll be arriving before Tom Hanks and Meg Ryan find each other on top of the Empire State Building."

"Not happening." Samantha gripped the passenger door. "What if the plane slips on ice while taxiing or the pilot can't see because of the snow?"

"It's the pilot's job to get the passengers safely to their destination," Charlie assured her. "Just like it's your job to write Sloane Parker books. You're good at your job and they're good at theirs. Sometimes you have to have faith, Samantha."

"That was a low trick, Charlie," Samantha whispered, the icy air blowing into the car.

"Please, Samantha, I know you can do this and you might be surprised. Who wouldn't want to spend Christmas week in one of the most sought-after holiday destinations in America?" He paused. "And you don't really have a choice. I already told Arthur you were coming."

The pit in Samantha's stomach threatened to become a full-sized crater, but she was stuck. She needed to remain on Arthur's good side. And she couldn't disappoint Charlie. "All right, I'll go."

"Excellent! I packed you an extra suitcase with après-ski boots and warm sweaters and a down parka. The parka and sweaters are Emily's, she was happy to lend them to you. And I expensed the après-ski boots, they're top of the line. You're all set to go elk watching in Grand Teton National Park."

"I'm not going to trudge through the snow looking for elk," Samantha said, shivering. "I'm going to sit in front of the fire with a book and pretend I'm in my living room."

Samantha hung up and the driver took her bags out of the trunk. He checked them in and she entered the terminal.

There was a giant Christmas tree and flight attendants walked by, dressed in festive red-and-green uniforms. Samantha took a deep breath and made a beeline for the United Club. If she was going to survive this week, she was going to take her mother and Charlie's advice and start with a very stiff drink.

Chapter Two

Samantha fastened her seat belt and imagined she was Sloane Parker sitting in the first-class section of an Emirates flight from Frankfurt to Dubai. Sloane is trying to decide which fellow passenger is a Russian spy. At first, she is positive it's the priest in seat 3A. There's a telltale circle around his ring finger where a wedding ring used to be. Then a stunning blonde sits next to him and he drapes his hand over her thigh. Sloane decides he must not be a priest and guesses he's a businessman sneaking away for a hot weekend affair. Especially when he reaches up to the overhead bin and the priest's collar is actually a neck brace from some kind of injury.

Next, she's convinced it's the little old lady in seat 5B. The woman is wearing a sweater and boots, she obviously isn't dressed for Dubai's 104-degree temperatures. When she pulls out her laptop to FaceTime, Sloane is confident some Russian oligarch's face will appear on the screen. Instead the most adorable eighteen-month-old toddler comes into focus, waving furiously and saying, "Present, Grammy?" into the camera.

Sloane picks up the wineglass the flight attendant left on her tray table and sighs dejectedly. That's when it comes to her. Emirates boasted that their flight attendants trained as wine sommeliers at the finest sommelier school in Provence. Sloane had asked for a New Zealand wine with an oaky aroma but this wine doesn't smell oaky. A true Emirates flight attendant would never get it wrong; it could cost her her job.

The flight attendant is the Russian spy! Why hadn't Sloane realized right away? It's the perfect cover. Sloane closes her eyes and allows herself to get some sleep. After all, they're trapped on the same flight for the next seven hours. She'll call her boss, Phineas, at British Intelligence when they start their descent into Dubai.

Samantha zoned back in. "Excuse me," she said to the flight attendant. "I don't really feel like wine. Could I get a Diet Coke instead?"

The flight attendant approached Samantha's seat. She took Samantha's plastic cup and gave her a puzzled expression.

"This is Diet Coke; we don't serve alcohol on domestic flights."

Samantha smiled sheepishly and wished she could disappear into the seat cushion. Instead, she busied herself arranging her books on the seat beside her. She had to stop writing the current book she was working on in her head when she couldn't sit down at the computer. But the last hour of boarding the plane had been so stressful, she had to do something to shut it out.

First, there was the moment she arrived at the gate and saw the plane. It wasn't the big, solid plane Charlie had promised—the kind that flew from New York to London and was so large, you hardly noticed you were in the air. This plane seemed the same size as the planes her brother, Jake, built from Lego kits when they were children. Samantha asked the gate attendant if she was actually at the right gate; she assumed the plane would be bigger. The woman pointed meaningfully at the flight board and asked if Samantha had been to Jackson Hole. The airport was tiny, you could barely squeeze a commercial jet into the arrival gate.

Then there was boarding the plane itself. Samantha's seat was 12A and she expected to be near the front. But the plane was so small, it was in the last row, next to the bathroom and the flight staff's coffee maker. Samantha told the flight attendant she couldn't possibly sit in the back. Everyone knew if there was a crash, it was the first section to go up in flames. The flight attendant graciously moved Samantha to the second row and even gave her a spare seat. Samantha thanked her, but she guessed from her expression she only did it so Samantha didn't frighten the other passengers.

"Excuse me," a male voice said, interrupting her thoughts. He pointed to the books scattered on the seat. "That's my seat."

"I don't think so," Samantha replied, without looking up. "The flight attendant promised it to me."

"Here's my boarding pass." He waved it in front of her. "It's my fault. My connecting flight from Chiang Mai was late and I almost missed this flight. I hate to mess up your library, but there aren't any other seats."

Samantha blushed furiously. She had brought a lot of books. But she didn't trust using a Kindle. If it died mid-flight, she'd have nothing to read. Then she'd have to look out the window and see how high up they were. Or worse, if it was already dark, she'd be stuck staring straight ahead, counting how many times the plane hit turbulence, like a woman in labor timing her contractions.

"I'm sorry," she said, stuffing them into her carry-on.

The man sat down. He was very tall; his knees touched the tray table.

"That's quite a pile of books," he remarked. "You do realize it's only a four-hour flight?"

Samantha wasn't going to explain to a complete stranger.

"I'm a big reader. Not enough people read these days," she defended herself. "They flip through social media and listen to podcasts. Podcasts are fine; I learned how to sauté lamb from Thomas Keller's podcast, and now it's Socks's favorite food. I only give it to him on his birthday, of course. It's very expensive. But it's really good, I tried it myself."

"Your boyfriend is named Socks?" the man asked, puzzled.

"Socks is my dog. Thomas Keller has a dog and he only feeds him lamb and veal. That's doable if you own some of the priciest restaurants in America, but not practical if you live in a one-bedroom in Brooklyn and most of your income goes to paying rent."

"I lived in New York a few years ago," the stranger reflected. "From what I've heard, now you could buy the whole village where I've been living for the price of a rented garage in Carroll Gardens."

Samantha remembered him saying his connecting flight was from Chiang Mai. She was intrigued despite her anxiety. The mention of foreign, exotic locations always interested her. She never knew where the next story idea would come from. She'd found the inspiration for her book about Sloane uncovering a tequila-smuggling ring in Mexico after watching *The Love Boat Reunion* with her mother.

"The village was in Chiang Mai?" she asked.

"I flew into Chiang Mai, in the north of Thailand," he said, nodding. "The village was up in the mountains. I'll never forget driving through the countryside: rice paddies as far as the eye could see and fields as bright as emeralds. The sunsets were every color of the rainbow, and in the early morning, the mist covered everything like some sort of jeweled magic carpet."

For a moment, Samantha felt a slight twinge, like when she sat hunched over her computer for hours without taking a break. What would it be like to actually go somewhere magical instead of ogling it on the internet? To walk across fields so soft, it felt like floating? To experience a sunset that made her ache from its beauty?

When Samantha was a junior at Swarthmore, she planned on studying abroad. It was all set: a semester in Cambridge, England, followed by a summer learning Italian in Pisa, with weekend trips to Venice and Milan.

But the doctor found a suspicious lump in her mother's breast that was possibly cancer. Samantha couldn't leave her. By the time the succession of biopsies was completed and the results came back negative, it was too late—the semester had started. Then, Samantha won a summer internship at a New York PR firm that was too good to pass up.

After that came Roger, who was content traveling between the fridge and the television to watch his beloved Yankees games. Soon after Roger left, she started writing the Sloane Parker books and her fear of traveling began.

Sometimes she wondered how her life would have turned out if Roger hadn't moved to California. They'd be living together in one of those New York neighborhoods that were becoming so trendy: Crown Heights or Washington Heights. Samantha would have a new job at a better PR firm and Roger would be an associate at a sports law firm. They'd spend the weekends hiking in the Catskills and summers in the Hamptons.

Her therapist, Dr. Leanne Gruber, said she shouldn't take the breakup too personally. Obviously, Roger wasn't capable of loyalty. A true Yankees fan would never move to Los Angeles. Samantha thought that was easy for Dr. Gruber to say. Her office walls were covered with photos of her family vacationing in exotic destinations like Hanoi and Tokyo. Samantha had Socks and her computer, and a fear of pretty much everything else.

Now Samantha was about to reply when she heard a sound. It was the flight attendants locking the doors for takeoff. She remembered it from the last time she'd flown, three years ago on a book tour organized by her publicist. The tour had been a disaster. At every stop, Samantha was so nervous about the next day's flight, she couldn't get through the book signings without breaking into a sweat. And she refused to take Charlie's offered Xanax. Dr. Gruber warned her that pharmaceuticals were a rabbit hole Samantha didn't want to go down and Samantha agreed. What if somehow her brain chemistry was altered and Sloane Parker disappeared from her imagination?

Instead, her publicist released a statement that Samantha didn't want to disappoint her fans by not visiting their local bookstores. Since she couldn't visit all the bookstores in America and still write one Sloane book a year, she wasn't going to tour at all.

The plane's cabin went dark and Samantha clutched the seat divider.

She turned to the man next to her.

"Please tell me a story," she said.

"Excuse me?" He frowned.

"Tell me a story," she urged. "I need something to distract me during takeoff."

"I don't know you," he said. "We don't even know each other's names."

The plane was moving faster down the runway. It lumbered into the air, the whole undercarriage beginning to shake. Samantha pictured it as a giant stuffed holiday turkey before it goes into the oven.

"I'm Samantha," she tried again. "Please, anything. A Christmas story if you like."

"Let me try to think of something . . . ," he conceded. "The children in the village in Thailand had never celebrated Christmas. Most of them had never even heard of Santa Claus. I wanted to do something special so I took a little boy named Kaman to Chiang Mai to buy presents for everyone. The first thing we did was go to the zoo where the panda cubs were wearing Christmas costumes. Next we went to the Four Seasons Hotel for their holiday tea. Santa Claus always makes an appearance, and they serve the best afternoon tea in Chiang Mai. When we sat down, I'd never seen Kaman's eyes so big. He ordered one of everything on the menu: ham quiche and chicken puffs and smoked salmon crackers. I didn't think he'd have room for dessert but he ate two scones and a fruit tartlet, and a mango pudding so rich, he couldn't finish it. He couldn't stop talking about it the whole way back to the village. By the time we arrived, I wondered if I had done the wrong thing. If Kaman bragged to the other children, they might get jealous. And Kaman wouldn't be satisfied with what his mother usually prepared at meals.

"Instead he said nothing to the others. He ate his dinner and thanked his mother for cooking. That night, he appeared in my room. He said he understood now why I insisted he learn his lessons. One day, he'd be a successful businessman and he'd take his mother to a big fancy hotel for a holiday tea at Christmas."

The plane lifted higher and suddenly it did that thing planes do after takeoff: pausing in the air as if it wasn't certain if it wanted to go up or down. Samantha gripped the seat divider tighter. It was only when the plane leveled off that she opened her eyes and realized she hadn't been clutching the seat divider. Instead, her hand was firmly around the man's sleeve.

"I'm sorry." She removed her hand quickly. "I didn't mean to grab on to you."

He picked up his wrist and moved it around.

"That's all right. I'm guessing the feeling will come back soon," he replied. He glanced at Samantha curiously. "Are you going to be like that the whole flight?"

"No, of course not," she said, regaining her composure. The lights had come back on in the cabin and passengers rustled in their seats. Flight attendants moved confidently through the aisle and she could see the lights twinkling on the wings.

"Well, I am when there's turbulence, no one likes a bumpy flight," she began. "And if the pilot asks you to fasten your seat belt because there's bad weather ahead and the bad weather never comes. I mean, how can you relax if you know something terrible is going to happen? It's like pretending not to be scared in the first fifty pages of a romantic thriller. You know the score: the couple is madly in love and he gives her chocolate and roses— before she discovers he's the head of an Algerian diamond cartel and she has to poison his bowl of couscous to escape," she mused, remembering the plot of an early Sloane Parker book. "And during the plane's descent. Everyone knows the descent is the most dangerous part of the flight. It seems like a silly time to crash, after you've endured hours of foot cramps and eating nothing but salted peanuts."

"I hope you never date a guy who gives you roses and candy." He grinned. He turned to her encouragingly. "You do know that flying is the safest form of travel."

"I've read the statistics." She nodded. "There are five million car accidents for every eight plane crashes. But you see, I'm paid to have a vivid imagination. I can't just turn it off." She sighed. "I had a couple of drinks in the airport bar but it didn't really help. If only they served alcohol on the flight. I can understand why they don't, especially during the holidays. People get upset if the plane is late or if they get a last-minute text saying the toy store is out of this year's version of a Disney princess and their six-year-old is going to be devastated. Then a couple of scotches only makes it worse. But a cup of eggnog right now would be nice to take the edge off."

The man rummaged through his carry-on. He took out a small bottle of Kahlúa and placed it on the tray table.

"We can ask the flight attendant for cream," he suggested. "Kahlúa and cream is one of my favorite drinks."

"Where did you get this?" She studied the black bottle tied with a gold ribbon.

"I was going to give it as a Christmas present, but I can get another, and you need it more," he said smilingly.

"Well, you and my wrist. I do need to get the feeling back before we land."

The man introduced himself as Drew. He was about thirty and had dark hair and the bluest eyes Samantha had ever seen.

Drew asked the flight attendant for a cream and two cups, and she replied sharply that cream was reserved for coffee. Then she noticed Samantha sitting beside him and changed her mind. It was worth giving up a carton of cream so she didn't have to deal with Samantha's drink requests for the rest of the flight.

"Do you really get paid to use your imagination?" Drew asked after they both finished two Dixie cups of Kahlúa with 2 percent low-fat milk. It was the best the flight attendant could do; the cream was already gone.

Charlie had been right: those sweet milkshake-like cocktails did go down easily. Samantha already felt better. For a moment she wondered why she worried at all. The plane's cabin was warmly lit and outside the window, the sky was full of stars.

The man in front of them was eating something out of a paper bag. The scent reminded Samantha of the cinnamon rolls sold at her favorite bakery at Christmas.

"Doesn't that smell so good?" She inhaled deeply. "That's what people don't understand when they spend all their time on social media. You can't taste baked ham with mashed potatoes by looking at people's Instagram posts of Christmas dinner," she continued, bleakly recalling her rival, Melody Minnow. "And you can't fall in love with the hero of a book written by a pseudo-author who admits her writing influences are Harry Styles's songs. Harry Styles is a great performer, but no one listens to the words, it's all about Harry's hair.

"A reader has to feel the author practically gave her own kidney when she writes. Not dictated an entire chapter into her iPhone while she simultaneously got a pedicure and shopped on Etsy." She glanced at Drew hastily. "Not that I would give up my kidney easily. I want to save mine in case someone I'm close to ever needs a kidney transplant."

Drew studied her carefully.

"You're very interesting," he said, and sipped his cocktail. "But you didn't answer my question."

Samantha couldn't remember a man asking about her besides Charlie and the checkout person at the pet store where she bought Socks's dog food. But they rarely discussed their personal lives. The conversation usually focused on whether she should switch Socks to wet food because his kibble was giving him a toothache.

It was probably the warm buzz of the Kahlúa combined with the unexpected smoothness of the flight, but she ended up telling Drew everything: how writing the Sloane Parker books not only rescued her bank account, it allowed her to stop dwelling on Roger and introduced her to a whole new world.

She enjoyed everything about writing for a living: working from her apartment and not having to pay five dollars every morning for a Starbucks double macchiato on the way to the office. Samantha rolled out of bed at seven thirty, took Socks for a quick pee walk, came home, made her beloved Krups double espresso with foam, and was sitting at the keyboard by eight. The Krups coffee maker was her second favorite thing in her apartment behind Socks.

She loved it when she really understood the characters in a book: how Sloane could fall for the handsome Englishman with the Henry Cavill smile even though she suspected he was part of a fake-handbag manufacturing ring. Even Victoria Beckham couldn't resist a Hermès handbag; Sloane was no different. It was only when Sloane noticed the signature gold lock turned in the wrong direction that she was positive it was a fake. She immediately handed her new love over to the authorities and gave up the Hermès bag as evidence.

And she adored it when she typed "The End" and believed she had created something magical. A story that would now be distributed like Santa Claus delivering presents from his sled, for readers all over the world to enjoy.

Then she told Drew about the less wonderful parts of the job. How the marketing department created her online persona, and she was forced to pretend she regularly dived with sharks in the South Pacific. How Melody Minnow was stealing her readers even though Melody's books were written in 280-character paragraphs as if she learned how to write on Twitter.

And the worst part of all was that writing about Sloane's adventures made the risks in the world seem so real. After her brush with death in the Bahamas, using her imagination to come up with Sloane's predicaments made her afraid of everything.

"I can see how that would be difficult," he said with a grimace when she finished. "Have you told them that you don't want to pretend anymore? Hire a photographer to take a cozy photo of you with Socks in front of your fireplace instead?"

"Charlie won't even consider it," she sighed, shaking her head. "Even Danielle Steel understands how important author photos are. And she started writing when they still used typewriters. These days, Instagram sells more books than any other medium. That's why Melody is so popular."

"If it's any consolation I've never heard of Melody Minnow," he remarked. "I'm not even on Instagram. Lots of people aren't."

Samantha didn't know anyone without an Instagram account. The marketing manager assigned to her book even wanted Socks to have his own account. They showed her mock pictures of Socks sitting beside her in a 1940s-era fighter plane, flying over the coast of France. Samantha put her foot down. It was the same way certain celebrities felt about their children on social media. Samantha couldn't make Socks do something without his consent.

"How do you not have an Instagram account?" she wondered.

"I've been living out of the country for five years," Drew explained. "Building schools in underdeveloped countries. Many places don't have internet."

"I thought social media was everywhere," Samantha said glumly. "It will be in space as soon as Elon Musk's first flight goes to Mars." She sipped her drink. "Working with children sounds so satisfying, you must love what you do."

"Not always," Drew reflected. "I once ended up in a village in the Amazon jungle where families had lost their homes because of big industry. The children were so sad and there was no way for me to help them. I didn't have the resources to rebuild the entire village. And once, in a school in the Andes mountains, a little boy tried to swap his Choose Your Own Adventure books for another child's packet of Fruit by the Foot." He grinned at the memory. "From then on, I tried to keep a supply of fruit snacks in the school libraries. But mostly, I do love it. There's nothing like seeing a little girl's face when she takes a piece of chalk and figures out a math problem on the blackboard. As if that one piece of chalk were an airplane ticket to a better life."

A sudden sadness settled over Samantha. When she first started writing, her dream was to personally deliver her books to women's cancer wards. She hoped the patients would receive the courage to fight their medical battles from reading about Sloane's adventures. But then she developed a fear of hospitals that was so bad, she couldn't take Socks for his checkup at the vet without breaking into hives.

Perhaps her mother was right, she should ask Dr. Gruber to help with her phobias. It would be her New Year's resolution. Then she could do some of the meaningful things on her wish list: take holiday dinners to the homeless in Manhattan, go on a nationwide book tour of retirement homes.

Suddenly the plane began to shake. At first it was one jolt, just enough to make Samantha spill Kahlúa and milk on her blouse. She was mopping it up when the second bump came.

She sat back in her seat and closed her eyes.

"It's all right," Drew assured her. "Airplanes were designed to dip up and down. It's perfectly safe."

Samantha was about to protest when the mild shaking resembled a full-scale earthquake. She was reminded why she flatly refused a producer's invitation to come to Hollywood and talk about a movie option. Charlie had been furious. Samantha pointed out that Zoom worked just as well. In the end, the producer came to New York and they all had dinner at Sushi Yasuda in Midtown. The producer turned out to be just some twenty-year-old kid with unlimited access to his father's credit card. But it had been fun to hear him name-drop and Sushi Yasuda's fatty tuna was delicious.

Then the plane began to roll and even Drew was quiet. Samantha kept her eyes shut and counted the things she was grateful for: Her mother introducing her to Nancy Drew books; Nancy Drew was still the smartest private investigator ever. The episodes of *Gossip Girl* she watched in high school that provided tantalizing glimpses of Manhattan. Her fuzzy socks that she bought with her first royalty check. Charlie had encouraged her to buy something meaningful—jewelry or a piece of art. But there was nothing more important than having warm feet while she was writing her next book.

The plane did one final dip and Samantha let out a gasp. Suddenly they were on the ground, and the lights in the cabin flickered on.

"We landed," she gasped, peering out the window.

"That usually happens at the end of a flight," Drew said pleasantly. "Are you okay? You were mumbling something about Blair and Serena."

Samantha wasn't going to admit she was reliving the *Gossip Girl* Christmas episode.

"I was thinking up names for characters," she said instead. Relief flooded through her and she felt almost giddy. "I didn't know we were about to land."

"It always gets turbulent near the mountains," he offered. He handed her a napkin. "You made it all in one piece. Besides the Kahlúa moustache, but that's easily fixed."

Samantha dabbed her mouth. She pulled her carry-on from beneath the seat and waited for the doors to open.

It was one of those airports where you had to walk outside before you reached the terminal. For a moment, Samantha allowed herself to take it all in. The air was fresh and clean, like nothing she knew in New York. The whole mountain was alive with Christmas lights and the sky was such a dark velvet, it resembled the most luxurious black cocktail dress.

"Oh, it's beautiful," she said out loud.

"Wait until you see it during the daytime." Drew was standing behind her. "The Teton mountains are the most breathtaking in the American west."

Then someone pushed her and Samantha was afraid

she'd slip on the cement. She followed the other passengers into the terminal. It was surprisingly modern, with framed posters of men and women wearing cowboy hats and boots.

"Would you like a ride somewhere?" Drew offered.

She had to find a bathroom. The spot hadn't come out, and she couldn't arrive at Arthur's with a Kahlúa stain on her blouse. And Drew was very polite, but he was a stranger. Even Sloane Parker knew better than to accept a ride from a man who hadn't been vetted by British Intelligence.

"No, thank you." She shook her head and held out her hand. "You've been very kind. I wouldn't have survived the flight without your help."

He smiled and it resembled what she imagined Sloane's love interest in the book set in Australia smiled like. It was one of the few stories when Sloane's suitor didn't end up being the villain. Instead, he helped her capture a ring of illegal koala hunters. They had one glorious night of passion in a tent near Ayers Rock before Sloane flew back to British Intelligence headquarters.

"It's almost Christmas." Drew shook her hand. "Being kind is what the season is all about."

Samantha entered the bathroom and opened the suitcase Charlie had provided. Emily must have picked out the clothes; Emily worked for one of those trendy fashion brands that Samantha had never heard of before they started suddenly appearing on every celebrity's Instagram story. Emily insisted she received more sample clothes than she could wear, and Samantha and Emily were the same size. There were suede pants and a cashmere sweater so soft and fluffy, it reminded Samantha of a cat curled up in the morning sun. She chose an emerald-green V-neck sweater and a pretty red scarf. She touched up her makeup and walked back through the terminal to the sidewalk.

A driver in a black uniform was standing in front of an SUV. He was about sixty with weathered skin and silvery hair.

"Miss Morgan?" He approached her.

Samantha glanced around and realized he was talking to her.

"Yes?" she asked cautiously.

"Mr. Wentworth sent me, I'm Bruno." He pointed to her bags. "Can I take those for you?"

Samantha slipped into the passenger seat. The car was gloriously warm. The seats smelled of leather and there was a decanter of brandy in the side compartment.

"I didn't expect to be picked up, I planned on calling Charlie for the address and taking an Uber," Samantha said when Bruno started the car. "How did you know it was me?"

"Mr. Wentworth wants his guests to feel comfortable from the moment they arrive," Bruno replied. "And I could tell from your photo." He held up a Sloane Parker book that had been wedged between the seats. "My wife, Elaine, is a big fan. She asked if you wouldn't mind signing a book."

Samantha took out the fountain pen she kept in her purse for signing her books. She was almost enjoying herself. It felt good to be on solid ground, instead of being tossed around in the air. And she was flattered that Bruno's wife wanted her autograph.

They drove past the famous Jackson Hole antlers in the town square. There was a western-style saloon strung with Christmas lights and a life-sized gingerbread house.

Families milled around waiting to meet Santa Claus, and Samantha saw a bright red sled, stacked with presents.

"Jackson Hole at Christmastime is one of the best small towns in America," Bruno said. "There are sleigh rides and ice-skating, and people line up outside Persephone Bakery for their European hot chocolate."

Samantha peered out the window. Even the snow seemed different than at home. In Brooklyn when it snowed, it meant that she might slip when she took Socks for his walk. In Jackson Hole, it made the whole scene more inviting, like thick white icing on a holiday cake.

Then the SUV left town and they drove up a small incline. Samantha was beginning to get nervous again, when they turned on to a private road. Bruno pressed a button and they slipped through iron gates. It was hard to see in the dark, but Samantha took in a garage and a long barn. They drove a little farther and the main house was in front of them.

Not even Charlie's description had prepared her: it was like a proper ski lodge with huge windows and a great stone chimney. There was a small turret made of glass and inside she could see a spiral staircase and walls of bookshelves.

"I've never seen anything like it," Samantha gasped.

"It's Mr. Wentworth's library." Bruno followed her gaze. "You can see it from all over the valley."

Samantha thought it resembled the most amazing lighthouse, but with books.

Charlie had been right: the week wasn't going to be so bad after all. The town of Jackson Hole was as charming as a holiday postcard, and Arthur's ranch was something straight out of a movie.

She gathered her purse and followed Bruno inside.

"Samantha, you made it," Arthur said, coming to greet her. Arthur was in his fifties with salt-and-pepper hair and blue eyes. He wore a smoking jacket over corduroy slacks and he was holding a cocktail glass.

"I'm so glad you came," he said as he took her arm. "Let's get you a drink and I'll introduce you to everyone."

The entry led into a step-down living room. Floor-to-ceiling windows faced the mountains and one wall was taken up by a fireplace. The ceiling was made of timber and there were thick woven rugs and leather sofas.

Samantha was about to comment on the giant Christmas tree strung with blue and silver lights when she heard a familiar voice.

Arthur was leading her to the bar.

"What would you like to drink?" Arthur turned to her.

A man was standing behind the bar. He was very tall and wore a navy sweater. He turned around and Samantha's mouth dropped open.

"This is my son, Drew," Arthur introduced them. "Drew just arrived from New York. I'm surprised you didn't meet on the plane."

Samantha's knees went weak and she could feel the color drain from her cheeks.

She flashed on everything she told Drew on the plane. She wasn't anything like Sloane Parker, and everything the marketing department said about her was a lie. When the marketing department first came up with the idea, it was meant to be a one-time thing. Everyone on her marketing team was delighted and amazed when Sloane Parker's Instagram followers kept tripling and sales went through the roof. After that, it was too late to change things. The team decided the fewer people who knew the truth about Samantha the better. Arthur knew about the campaign; he oversaw everything at the publishing house. But he had no idea that Samantha wasn't like that in real life. That she would never dream of diving in a cage with sharks, and that her closet didn't contain a single Badgley Mischka evening gown.

Then she reminded herself what Charlie had told her about Arthur's invitation. Sales of her latest book were down, and the house party was her chance to impress Arthur with her commitment to her writing, and for Samantha to meet important critics and booksellers. If she had turned it down, next year Melody Minnow might have been the author on the guest list and Charlie might have had to find a job at another publisher.

Drew's eyes met hers. He smiled slowly.

"We did actually," he said to his father. "I know exactly what Samantha would like to drink. Kahlúa and cream."

She opened her mouth to answer but it came out as a squeak.

"Kahlúa and cream would be fine, thank you," she said, nodding.

Thank god for alcohol. It was the second time today she couldn't think of any other way she was going to survive.

Chapter Three

Samantha sat up in bed and groaned. She had dreamed that Sloane Parker was trapped in a ski cabin in the French Alps. Sloane had only herself to blame. She'd accepted a dinner invitation from her ski instructor, Jean-Claude. Jean-Claude had a sexy French accent and took her skiing off-piste in their first lesson. He must have drugged her Jägermeister, because one minute they were sharing fondue in a mountainside restaurant and the next she was strapped to a chair with a handkerchief stuffed in her mouth.

Sloane heard voices in the next room and wondered whether Jean-Claude was talking with her captors. She wiggled the chair but she couldn't see through the keyhole. In her pocket was a long-handled fondue fork she had saved as a souvenir. She used it now to cut through the rope that tied her wrists. Then she climbed out the window and grabbed the skis leaning against the wall.

It was only when she was sipping an après-ski drink in Val d'Isère that she allowed herself to relax. She had called the French ski patrol and alerted them to money launderers using the cabin as a hideout. Let them finish the job and arrest them. She preferred drinking mulled wine and flirting with a Swiss snow polo player. Phineas at British Intelligence would be pleased. Phineas was the opposite of a Francophile. He believed anyone who wore a beret and ate things that crawled couldn't be trusted.

Usually when Samantha dreamed about her books, she wrote the ideas down in a notepad she kept on her bedside table. This morning she couldn't concentrate. Every time she remembered her arrival last night at the ranch, there was a sick feeling in her stomach.

How could Drew not have mentioned that his father was Arthur Wentworth, CEO of her publishing house? And how could she not have guessed herself? She'd never met Drew but she had heard that Arthur had a grown son who was always traveling around the world. To be fair, Samantha didn't have much reason to know all of Arthur's family business. And on the plane, she never asked Drew why he was going to Jackson Hole. It was too late now. Drew could have told his father everything: That for the last four years, Charlie and the whole team had been lying about Samantha's social media profile. That she was only here because Charlie tricked her and she couldn't wait to leave.

She was tempted to find Bruno and ask him to drive her straight back to the airport. She could invent an emergency—there was a gas leak in her apartment, Socks needed a blood transfusion and the vet wouldn't give anyone access to his medical records. But Charlie would be furious and she'd be back where she started: with Melody Minnow threatening her readership and she and Charlie out of a job.

The only way she could think clearly was after some strong, dark coffee. She put on a robe and found a pair of slippers. It was 8:00 A.M.; hopefully no one else would be up. She'd bring a cup of coffee to her room. Then she'd figure out what to do.

Arthur's kitchen was straight from the pages of *Architectural Digest*, western edition. There was a ten-burner range that could easily cook up enough bacon to feed a dozen ranch hands. A center island took up the middle of the room and the appliances were hidden behind oak panels.

She was trying to figure out how to use the coffee maker when she heard footsteps.

Drew was standing in the doorway. He wore jeans and a thick jacket.

"Samantha," he greeted her. "I just went for a walk. I didn't know anyone was up."

"I wanted to make coffee, I hope that's all right," she said, feeling guilty. She should have asked if guests were allowed to use the kitchen.

"Of course, I was going to make a cup myself." He watched her furiously pushing buttons. "Would you like some help?"

Samantha was happy to turn it over to him. "I've been trying for fifteen minutes. It must be stuck."

Drew reached around and clicked a button in the back.

"My father loves high-tech gadgets." He grinned. "It's made by a Dutch company; they only manufacture four hundred a year. They didn't want to ruin the aerodynamic design by putting the switches in the front."

Suddenly she longed for her familiar Krups coffee maker. If she were at home, she'd be drinking her second cup of coffee while Socks curled up in his doggy bed and her favorite Christmas songs played on Spotify, and she'd have nothing to worry about except Sloane Parker's next adventure.

Drew made two coffees and handed one to Samantha. She took one sip and had to agree that the undoubtedly four-figure price tag for the coffee maker was worth it.

The coffee was incredibly smooth and just the right temperature: not too hot to burn her tongue, but not the least bit cool so she had to pop it in the microwave and heat it up.

She noticed that Drew was staring at her slippers.

"I didn't mean for anyone to see me in a robe and slippers," she said awkwardly. "I was going to take the coffee up to my room."

"I like your slippers. I've never seen anything like them," Drew remarked.

"Every year, Socks and I exchange Christmas presents," she offered. "I tried to think what Socks would buy for me if he could go shopping."

"You thought he would buy slippers with floppy ears and a dog's nose?"

"It was either that or a box of cereal shaped like dog bones," she answered. "But I prefer coffee and toast or oatmeal in the mornings."

Drew sipped his coffee thoughtfully.

"You're very attached to your dog, aren't you?"

"Dogs are loyal," Samantha said, nodding. "And Socks doesn't mind if I spend all day writing."

"I've never had a dog," Drew replied. "I grew up in a penthouse on the Upper East Side. My father's decorator furnished it all in white: white carpets, white sofas. Dogs weren't allowed."

"It doesn't sound as if little boys would be either," Samantha said doubtfully. "I've never even been inside a Manhattan penthouse. Well, except once for a book reading."

Charlie had promised it would be fine. The penthouse had a private elevator that was so fast and quiet, Samantha wouldn't even know it was moving. And the owner promised to keep the drapes in the living room closed.

But the elevator was broken, so she had to take the service elevator, which stopped at every floor. Ever since the engine fire on the airplane, Samantha was terrified of heights. When she arrived, one of the attendees wanted to see the view. Everyone else oohed and ahhed, but Samantha couldn't read from her book without experiencing vertigo.

"My childhood was quite boring. My parents were teachers. My mother made peanut butter sandwiches and we always had a dog," Samantha said, stirring her coffee. "A cocker spaniel and then a dachshund called Salty because he resembled a pretzel. After that a mix named Bucky. Bucky's personality changed more often than a mood ring." She paused. "I loved Bucky the most. I cried for weeks when he died."

Drew perched on a stool. His face took on a somber expression.

"I never had a mother to make peanut butter sandwiches. She left when I was four." He sipped his coffee. "My father kept buying houses as consolation prizes: the place in Connecticut, a beach house in the Bahamas. A kid doesn't care where he lives, all he cares about are the people inside the house."

"I'm sorry." Samantha stared down at her cup.

She couldn't imagine not having two parents. Samantha and her mother might not agree on everything, but Samantha knew her mother cared about her more than anyone in the world.

"I did get a pet eventually." Drew smiled as if he was determined to change the mood. "When I lived in Fiji, I had a pig. Porky was a good pet, though his morning breath was terrible."

"You did not call your pig Porky," Samantha said, laughing.

"Actually, I didn't," he admitted. "One of the children in the village named him, and it sort of stuck."

Samantha placed her cup on the counter.

"About the things I told you on the plane . . . ," she began.

"You mean that you're not the kind of woman who wears stilettos and evening gowns while rappelling off a cliff in Venezuela?" He grinned, glancing at her robe.

"If your father knew, Charlie and I could get into a lot of trouble."

"Don't worry, I didn't say anything," Drew assured her. "To be honest, I have my own problems with my father. I'd rather not talk to him in private."

"What kind of problems?" Samantha inquired.

"You have other things on your mind." He shrugged.

"You listened to me on the plane," she reminded him. "I'm happy to do the same."

"My father and I were very close growing up. He never put the publishing company before me," Drew began. "You could say he raised us both together. He loved taking me to the office, but he rarely missed my school plays and soccer matches. While I was in college, I spent a semester building a school in Thailand. Everything about it was different from New York: the thatched houses built on rivers, the people who were so grateful for small kindnesses. It was the children especially who I couldn't get out of my mind. When the Jeep pulled up at a village, they swarmed around me for a packet of raisins. And when the school was finished, the smiles on their faces were as big as if Santa Claus delivered the desks himself. I knew what I wanted to do after I graduated." He paused. "My father agreed to help me financially until I was thirty. Then I would come back to New York and work for him. I took a publishing course the summer before I graduated from college. It taught me the basics, and we agreed that when I joined the firm, I would work for three months in each department, learning the ropes," he finished. "I turned thirty a month ago."

"Can't you talk to him?" Samantha ventured. "Most parents want their children to be happy."

"I was planning to," Drew sighed. "That was before Beatrix put her foot down."

"Beatrix?" Samantha repeated.

"My fiancée. We've been together for three years," Drew replied. "Beatrix loved the idea of building schools in third world countries. She imagined herself as some kind of modern-day Amelia Earhart. Lately she's changed. She's tired of wearing the same clothes for weeks and she misses manicures and pedicures. Sometimes I find her scrolling through her photos of a favorite pair of loafers as if she's mourning the death of a friend. She was supposed to come to the ranch but she gave me an ultimatum: either we stay in New York or the engagement is off."

"That seems a little harsh if you love each other," Samantha said, wincing.

"I can't blame her," he remarked. "Few women would consider eating soggy noodles in a tent during a monsoon as the perfect birthday celebration. And having a snake slither into your sleeping bag is the fastest way to end a romantic moment."

At the mention of snakes, Beatrix had Samantha's sympathy. Snakes were high on the list of creatures Samantha was afraid of, ahead of spiders and those flying bugs they have in Florida that made Samantha want to retire somewhere colder like Alaska.

Even Sloane Parker inherited Samantha's fear of

snakes. In a recent book, José, the sexy casino owner, gives Sloane the gift of a ruby necklace shaped like a snake. After they make love, José removes the necklace and replaces it with a real snake. Sloane wakes in the morning to discover a snake sharing her bed and José and the ruby necklace gone. José stole the necklace from a Colombian drug lord and gave it to Sloane to get through customs.

"I can see her point." Samantha shuddered. "Didn't you discuss it before you got engaged?"

"Beatrix thought I'd change my mind."

"And you didn't?" Samantha wondered.

Drew leaned back on the stool. He rubbed his brow.

"I love Beatrix, but I love what I'm doing too," he said slowly. "I don't want to choose."

Samantha didn't say that sometimes life makes choices for you. Sometimes the person you think you're going to spend your life with decides he wants something completely different: An ocean warm enough to swim in year-round. An office where dress-down Friday means board shorts and sockless loafers.

Roger hadn't even asked Samantha if she wanted to join him in California. He simply packed his suitcases and left.

Someone else entered the kitchen. It was Arthur, dressed in a striped tracksuit.

"Drew, Samantha, you're both up early," he greeted them. "I was headed down to the gym for a morning workout."

Samantha stifled a yawn. Obviously neither Arthur nor Drew believed in sleeping in during vacation.

"I came down to get coffee," Samantha said. "Drew showed me how to use the coffee maker."

"After breakfast all the guests are going elk watching in Grand Teton National Park," Arthur said, pouring a glass of orange juice. "The car will leave at eleven a.m."

A lump formed in Samantha's throat. She tried to think of an excuse not to go.

"I'm afraid I'll have to miss it," she addressed Arthur. "I'm under deadline. I wouldn't want to be late with the next book."

Arthur turned to Drew. He smiled pleasantly.

"Tell Samantha how I feel about work and pleasure," Arthur prompted.

"My father believes the most successful people know how to take time off," Drew offered.

"The head of a rival publishing house taught me that early in my career," Arthur agreed. "He invited me and Drew to his beach house in Costa Rica. I asked how he could rationalize owning a second home that was so far away. He waved at the flickering torches and white sand beach and said there he didn't allow himself to think about business. When he returned to New York, he was ten times more productive. That's when I bought my first house in Connecticut." He beamed at Samantha. "You're officially on vacation, and I expect you to do all the things the ranch has to offer. I promise you won't be sorry."

Drew turned to Samantha. He smiled and his eyes were the color of the winter sky.

"Wait until you see the elk, they're the most magnificent animals in the world."

Samantha walked briskly around the grounds. It was easy for Drew to say that elk were spectacular, he didn't seem to be afraid of anything. A quick internet search revealed that elks weighed seven hundred pounds. The male elk's antlers weighed forty pounds alone and during the winter they let out a scream called bugling that could be heard for miles.

Samantha had been tempted to call Charlie. But when she took out her phone, there was a series of texts sent from Emily's parents' house in Vermont. Socks wore a red dog sweater and beside him was a dish of candy-cane-shaped dog bones. Samantha couldn't complain to Charlie when Socks was having a wonderful Christmas.

In front of her stood the barn. She opened the door and walked inside.

One of the few animals that Samantha wasn't afraid of was horses. She'd fallen in love with horses at the age of ten, when her mother gave her a copy of *Black Beauty*. Samantha read it every night and dreamed of owning her own black stallion. She spent hours reading about the brave horses of World War I. And she watched the movie *Seabiscuit* twice, each time using up a box of Kleenex.

On her third date with Roger, they took a horse-and-carriage ride through Central Park. It was her first Christmas in New York, and snuggling under the blanket, listening to the horses' hooves clomping on fresh snow, was the most romantic thing she'd ever done.

Even after Roger left, she still wasn't afraid of horses. There was something so calming about them. Sometimes when she had to go into Manhattan, she stopped at Clifton Stables just to feed sugar cubes to the horses.

Arthur's barn had a timbered ceiling and plaster walls. There was a tack room and a separate room filled with cowboy hats and leather boots. The whole place had that wonderful barn smell. It was a mix of hay and horse feed, and something Samantha couldn't name but was warm and inviting.

"You're smelling Froot Loops cereal," a male voice

said behind her. "I mix it in with the feed. The horses love it."

Samantha turned as an older man came out of a stall. He wore a flannel shirt and corduroy slacks.

"Bruno!" Samantha recognized the driver who brought her from the airport. "What are you doing here?"

"I look after Mr. Wentworth's horses." Bruno put down his bucket.

"I thought you were the chauffeur," she said, puzzled.

"Only when Mr. Wentworth needs extra help," he replied. "My main job is with the horses. Mr. Wentworth bought the barn and all the horses with the ranch." He stroked a chestnut horse. "This is Blixen. He was born on Christmas a few years ago."

"He's beautiful," Samantha commented. The horse had large brown eyes and a white patch on his nose.

"Go on, stroke his nose," Bruno encouraged her. "Blixen can spot a true horse lover."

Samantha brought her hand to the horse's nose. It was moist and smooth under her palm.

"I've always loved horses," Samantha confessed. "Though I only sat on ponies as a child." She grinned. "There isn't much horseback riding in Brooklyn."

"Horses are very intelligent," Bruno said thoughtfully. "The only time a horse throws its rider is if the horse or rider are in danger. If you listen to a horse, you'll never get into trouble." He smiled. "My wife, Elaine, says if people communicated as well as horses, the world would be a better place."

Samantha wondered what would have happened if Roger had talked to her about how he felt. Would he have listened to Samantha? Or was he too focused on the picture he had of himself: partner in a sports law firm by the age of thirty, invitations to parties in the Hamptons. Could she have convinced him that he could be happy with less? Associate instead of partner, weekends just the two of them, eating bagels and reading the sports pages of *The New York Times.*

Instead, Roger gave up everything they had for the promise of something shiny and new. A partner-track job and a beachside condo that happened to be three thousand miles away.

Samantha shook these thoughts off. She tried not to think about Roger. She was only nostalgic because she was away from her apartment and Socks at Christmas.

"Your wife sounds pretty intelligent too," Samantha said with a smile.

"Elaine and I have been married for forty years. Elaine helps out in the main house and we live in rooms above the barn." Bruno picked up the bucket. "Marriage is all about teamwork. A good marriage is the best thing life can offer."

Samantha decided to change the subject.

"Do you really feed the horses breakfast cereal?" she asked.

"Horses have a sweet tooth just like people," Bruno said with a grin. "And it's Christmas. They deserve a special treat."

A short time later, Samantha reached her room as her phone rang. It was her mother on FaceTime.

"Mom, you never use FaceTime," Samantha answered in surprise. Her mother wore a Nordic sweater and her graying hair was covered by a beanie. "You're holding the phone upside down."

The image changed and her mother smiled into the camera.

"The owner of the Airbnb said FaceTiming is cheaper," her mother said knowledgeably. "It uses Wi-Fi instead of minutes on your phone."

Samantha kept silent. She had been trying to explain that to her parents for ages.

"You should see the Airbnb," her mother was saying. "I thought staying in someone's home would be like staying at your aunt Phyllis's beach cottage during the summers. You know, when you and your cousins had to sleep in the attic, and your father and I got dishwashing duty every night. Inge serves the most delicious Scandinavian breakfast: pickled herring on crisp bread and poppy seed buns. And our room is delightful. We can see all the way to the fjords."

"The fjords!" Samantha said in alarm. She pictured her parents hiking with ice picks over frozen ice. The ice could crack and they'd be swallowed up by the cold, dark river. "The trip was supposed to be eight European capitals at Christmastime."

"It's an overnight excursion from Oslo. It wasn't on the itinerary but I saw it posted on Nigella Lawson's Instagram page. I convinced your father we had to do it. Nigella said it was a life-changing experience."

"Since when are you on Instagram?" Samantha inquired.

"We joined at the beginning of the trip. Marjorie and John couldn't come because John had a hip replacement. I promised I'd post photos. It's so much fun. Like those slide shows we used to show at the end of the summer. Enough about us," she said. "How is Connecticut?"

Samantha gazed out the window. The Teton mountains loomed in the distance and the fields were covered in snow.

"I'm not in Connecticut," she said bleakly. "The house party is at Arthur's ranch in Jackson Hole, Wyoming."

"Jackson Hole!" her mother exclaimed. "One of the tour guides mentioned Jackson Hole. It has more black diamond runs than almost any ski resort in America. And the bison meat is delicious. They serve it at every restaurant."

"What's bison?" Samantha asked.

"Samantha, really. Don't you remember your American geography?" her mother clucked, sounding more like a teacher than a mother. "Bison are members of the buffalo family. Only, bison have humps and their horns are sharper. Bison are everywhere in Wyoming. You'll see them walking along the side of the road."

"I'll watch out for them," Samantha said nervously. "And you should stay away from the fjords. It sounds dangerous. You're supposed to be treating yourself to nice hotels."

"Nice hotels can be boring, we want to see the real Norway." Her mother paused. "Please don't worry about us, Samantha. We're very careful, and remember your father was an Eagle Scout, he's prepared for anything."

Samantha was tempted to say that was decades ago but she didn't want to make her mother feel old. She couldn't help but worry. They were her parents and she didn't know what she'd do without them.

They finished talking and Samantha hung up.

Drew was wrong. Everyone was on Instagram. If Samantha's mother took travel advice from a cooking celebrity, why wouldn't readers snatch up Melody Minnow's books based purely on the lipstick Melody wore in her Instagram profile?

She absently typed "bison" into her computer search.

Bison weighed two thousand pounds and liked to move in herds.

She snapped the laptop shut and sank into the bed.

Not only did she have to worry about a seven-hundred-pound elk charging her when they went elk watching. Now she had to watch out for a whole family of bison when she simply walked down the street.

The worst part was it was only 8:00 A.M. Much too early for a drink.

Chapter Four

Samantha sat in the ranch's living room and waited for the other guests to come downstairs. She had skipped breakfast. Instead, she'd spent the last two hours in her room, tapping out a new plot for a Sloane Parker book.

Sloane Parker is at a weekend house party at a Scottish castle and she's certain someone is trying to get rid of her. At first, she thinks it's the host, Lord Percival. Only Sloane knows that the castle doesn't really belong to Percival, but to his half brother, Charles. At dinner, Percival announces he's going to share his inheritance with Charles; there's room in the castle for both of them. Then Sloane suspects the butler. In crime novels, the butler is often guilty. The butler turns out to be Charles's son, so he has no reason to dislike Sloane. A mysterious woman in a red dress appears and Sloane recognizes her old nemesis, Clarissa Cooper. Of course, it's Clarissa! She was Phineas's favorite agent at British Intelligence until she was accused of selling secrets to the Russians. She'll do anything to get back in Phineas's good graces, including rubbing out her competition.

"Samantha." Drew approached her. "You weren't at breakfast."

Samantha pulled her mind from her thoughts.

"I wasn't hungry," she admitted.

"Martha, the cook, was disappointed," Drew said with a smile. "She wants all the guests to experience her 'cowboy breakfast.' Eggs and sausage and johnnycakes like the pioneers used to make over a campfire stove."

Samantha didn't know what a johnnycake was, but the thought of eating sausages when her stomach was doing nervous flips made her feel sick.

"I'll make up for it tomorrow," she promised. "I don't want to hurt her feelings."

"I brought you something," Drew said, handing her a small package.

She unwrapped the brown paper. Inside was a pair of binoculars.

"They're for viewing the elk," Drew explained. "So you can feel like you're right next to them."

Samantha turned them over carefully. She had no desire to make the elk seem closer than she absolutely had to. Drew was only being kind. It wasn't his fault she was spending Christmas week at his father's ranch.

"Thank you." She took a deep breath. "I'm sure it will make it even more exciting."

Two cars drove the group to the National Elk Refuge at the foot of the Teton mountains. The air was fresh and the sky was the palest shade of blue. Even the sun seemed to be struggling to make a difference. It was almost noon, but the temperature on Samantha's phone read below zero.

Everyone piled out and Drew walked beside her.

"It's gorgeous, isn't it?" he said, his hand sweeping over the view. The refuge was completely flat and stretched for miles. There was only one fence separating it from the road. Above them, the mountains were sharp and immovable. The entire landscape was covered in a deep layer of snow.

"When I was in high school, I attended summer camp in Jackson Hole," Drew said. "At first, I wasn't sure I wanted to go. It was so far away from home. But my father had spent time in Jackson Hole during college and he wanted me to experience the same things. By the second summer, I was hooked. I loved the fishing and hiking, swimming in the glaciers, and rafting on the river. I'm so glad he bought this ranch. He had been looking for the right property for ages, and this one came available last summer. He's so happy here, he's like a kid. And as an adult, I understand his obsession more clearly." He paused and his eyes were thoughtful. "Everything is so big out here, sometimes it makes our own problems seem quite small."

Samantha glanced at the clusters of elk and felt the opposite. Her problems weren't small at all. They weighed seven hundred pounds and if she moved wrong, they could trample her.

Not even Sloane Parker could easily outrun a pack of stampeding elk. Sloane had enough trouble when she ended up in the middle of a bullfight in Barcelona. The bullfighter, Ricardo, was actually a fellow agent who had been badly gored by the bull. Thank god Sloane was wearing her red Valentino gown. She ripped it off to use as a cape and managed to avoid the bull and rescue Ricardo at the same time.

"I thought we were going to watch the elk from the car," Samantha said to Drew. Her heart pounded and there was a tightness in her chest.

"The car brought us to the refuge." Drew pointed to a red wooden box that resembled a child's wagon. "We see the elk from the sleighs. We can get closer that way, and the elk aren't afraid. They keep feeding as if we're not even there."

"We're going to watch the elk from that!" Samantha gulped. The sleigh hardly looked sturdy enough to hold ten adults. And it was completely open. Like one of those miniature cereal boxes with the top cut off.

"Let's get seats in the front." Drew motioned to her. "If we have to sit in the back, we might not see anything at all."

Samantha slipped in beside him. She was tempted to close her eyes but she didn't want the other guests to know she was frightened. Instead she tried to focus on something small and familiar. She wanted to quickly pull out her phone to look at her background photo of Socks. But the first thing the tour guide did when they climbed into the sleigh was instruct everyone to put away their phones. There was nothing to look at except twenty-four thousand acres of wild landscape that was home to six thousand elk.

The guide kept up a steady prattle of facts to entertain them. The elk refuge was started in the 1800s. The elk population had dwindled and it was difficult for the elk to keep up their yearly migration. These days, the elk arrived in early December and stayed until summer after the calves were born. They were allowed to roam freely and shared the refuge with other wild animals.

"If we're lucky, we'll see bison and foxes and even some wolves," the guide said so brightly that Samantha was tempted to slap her. If a wolf came near the sleigh, Samantha would scream. No one could blame her. Humans were supposed to be afraid of wolves, that's how one didn't get eaten.

"Is something wrong?" The guide had noticed Samantha's panicked expression.

Everyone turned to Samantha and her cheeks flushed.

"I was wondering what a wolf looks like," she said hurriedly.

"Like a coyote but larger," the guide said.

"I've never seen a coyote either," Samantha ventured.

"Oh, you'll see coyotes too. They love to come right up to the sleigh. Just make sure you don't feed them," the guide said cheerfully. "We don't want the coyotes to think they can have an easy lunch."

Samantha tried all her calming tricks: She counted to a hundred and imagined she was sitting in a warm bath of lavender-scented bubbles. She even visualized her goals: getting a movie deal, making enough money to support an animal shelter so all stray dogs would always have a home. Nothing worked. Reluctantly she picked up the binoculars and took in her surroundings.

Then it happened. An elk came into view. He was close enough for Samantha to admire him, but far enough for her not to be afraid. And he was the most beautiful animal she had ever seen.

For a moment, Samantha forgot everything. The voice of the tour guide was muted, and the other guests disappeared. It was just Samantha and the elk gazing at each other across the snowy field.

"Oh, he's amazing," Samantha said out loud.

"I told you." Drew's voice seemed to come from far away. "The elk are the kings of the plains. And they're so graceful. They can run forty miles per hour even though they have to carry their antlers."

At that moment, another animal came into view. Samantha recognized it from her mother's description. It was a bison and it was headed straight for the elk. The elk kept looking at Samantha as if it was asking what to do. Samantha opened her mouth as the elk reared on its hind legs. Its hooves stomped the ground and it hurtled toward the sleigh.

Her binoculars dropped onto the bench. The other passengers shifted in their seats but she was too terrified to move. She kept waiting for the elk to change direction. The closer it came, the more determined it seemed to reach the sleigh.

At the last minute, when she could practically smell the elk's fur, it stopped. Its ears pricked up and it tipped its head. Then it made a bugling sound and moved off to join the herd.

The hushed silence broke. Samantha heard the sound of a camera clicking and one guest nervously opened a bag of mints.

"Wasn't that exciting. You'd almost think it was staged. Don't worry, it was completely real," the guide said in her high-pitched voice. Her eyes shone as if they'd just witnessed the tennis finals at Wimbledon. "If that doesn't guarantee a five-star Yelp review, I don't know what would!"

The sleigh let them off at the entrance to the refuge. Samantha couldn't wait to climb back in the car. Her teeth chattered and she could feel her pulse racing.

They drove to the center of Jackson Hole, where they were all going to have lunch. The moment the car parked, she set off on her own.

"Samantha, wait," Drew called after her.

Samantha was already halfway down Main Street. She was so shaken; she didn't want to talk to anyone. Especially not Drew.

"What's wrong?" he said, catching up with her. "You haven't said anything since we left the refuge."

"You're asking what's wrong?" she demanded, turning around. Her cheeks were flushed and she couldn't stop trembling. "I told you that I'm afraid of everything. Then you gave me binoculars and made me sit up front."

"I thought you'd enjoy seeing the elk through binoculars," Drew said, perplexed. "It was perfectly safe. My father would never arrange an outing that put anyone in danger."

"Well, I didn't feel safe," Samantha retorted. "I felt as if any minute, I'd be skewered by the elk's horns like a roasted marshmallow. I thought you were listening to me on the plane, but you're just like everyone else. You don't really hear anything someone is saying to you."

Samantha didn't wait for Drew to reply. She strode down the sidewalk and ducked into a shop.

"Can I help you?" the woman behind the counter asked.

Samantha turned around. She hadn't even noticed what kind of store it was. The counter was strewn with souvenirs. There was a snow globe with a miniature version of Main Street, and a rack of postcards that read WELCOME TO JACKSON HOLE. Sweatshirts were decorated with pictures of bison and there was a row of après-ski boots and fake fur slippers.

"I'm just looking, thank you," Samantha answered.

"You'd be surprised how many people haven't finished their Christmas shopping," the woman said, smiling. "Some years, people bang on the door after we've closed, even on Christmas Eve. I don't mind. I'd rather stand in a warm shop during the Christmas holidays than sit home alone."

"Is this your store?" Samantha inquired.

The woman shook her head.

"I manage it during the winter. In the summer, I work at a horse ranch." She paused. "Everyone does that sort of thing in Jackson Hole. People who have lived here for years do anything so they don't have to leave."

"I'll be quite happy to leave," Samantha said with a grimace. "I was almost trampled by an elk at the elk refuge."

"That's why you darted in here like a fox outrunning a pack of dogs." The woman closed the cash register. She held out her hand. "I'm Marigold, let me know if I can help you find anything."

"What a pretty name," Samantha reflected, shaking her hand.

The woman was in her late forties. She was quite beautiful with light brown hair and blue eyes. She wore a turtleneck with a long skirt, and a stack of bangles dangled at her wrist.

"The marigold is my favorite flower. It grows all around Jackson Hole," Marigold said. "I never understood why we have to keep the names we were born with. I renamed myself when I was quite young."

"I never thought of it that way," Samantha said, smiling. "I'm a writer, I keep a notebook of names to use in my books."

"How clever, I've haven't met any writers here in the gift shop," Marigold mused. "Though we get a lot of celebrities in Jackson Hole. They buy fancy ranches and think they're all going to become cowboys."

"I wasn't cut out for life on the open range," Samantha admitted. "To be honest, I'd rather be sitting in front of the fireplace in my apartment with my laptop and my dog."

She didn't know why she couldn't stop rambling. It felt nice to talk to someone. She was beginning to regret the way she stormed off from Drew.

"Jackson Hole has a lot to offer," Marigold said. "You might be surprised to find how much you like it."

"I'm only here for Christmas week," Samantha answered. She suddenly felt guilty for taking up the woman's time. "I'll buy some souvenirs. What do you suggest?"

Samantha bought a cushion embroidered with the Teton mountains for her mother, and a fishing hat for her father. She picked out matching Christmas pajamas for Charlie and Emily, and a squeaky rubber bear for Socks. She would regret buying the squeaky toy. It drove her crazy when Socks made noise while she wrote. The only other choice was a dog bone shaped like antlers and even holding it made her shudder.

"You might like the huckleberry jam," Marigold offered, ringing up the purchases. "Huckleberry grows all around Jackson Hole, it's one of our most popular items. Persephone Bakery serves the best huckleberry pie, and in the summer the line outside Moo's for their huckleberry ice cream stretches around the block." She smiled at Samantha. "You have to be careful if you go huckleberry picking. It's the bears' favorite food."

Samantha put down the jar of jam she had been holding. Thank goodness it was December. One couldn't pick huckleberries in the snow.

A pendant of an arrowhead hung from the cash register. The arrowhead was made of turquoise and the chain was polished silver.

"Arrowheads hold great importance to Native Americans." Marigold had followed her gaze. "They believe if you wear an arrowhead around your neck, you're protected from harm. Warriors wore them into battle, and the women used them to keep their children safe from bears and other wild animals."

"You must sell tons of these," Samantha said, thinking about the bison that wandered down the street. "Every tourist should have one."

Marigold's brow furrowed.

"The shop supports local Native American artists, and many of them have become my friends. I don't sell anything Native Americans consider sacred." Marigold shook her head.

Samantha looked at Marigold curiously.

"It actually works?" she wondered.

"Native Americans wouldn't still carve them if it didn't," Marigold answered. "It's my pendant. It was carved for me by a good friend who is a member of the Arapaho Tribe. They live on a reservation not far from here and I often visit them. The Arapaho and the Shoshone are the only federally recognized tribes left in Wyoming, though many Native American communities still call it home."

"It's beautiful." Samantha gazed at it thoughtfully.

Marigold studied Samantha as if she was deciding something. She unsnapped the pendant and handed it to Samantha.

"Why don't you borrow it?" she offered. "You can return it to me when you leave Jackson Hole."

Samantha's eyes widened.

"You just met me," Samantha said. "Why would you lend me a precious necklace?"

"My Native American friends always say to rely on your intuition: to know where to make your home, and who to consider your friends," she said slowly. "Something tells me you need it."

Samantha turned it over in her palm. The turquoise glinted in the afternoon sun.

"You know a lot about Native Americans," Samantha reflected.

"They're a big part of the American west," Marigold agreed. "When I started working at the gift shop, I learned everything I could so I was well informed for the tourists. I ended up learning even more important things for myself. I've become quite close with some of the Native American communities, I attend their yearly powwows and sometimes go to their public dances. They have a lot to teach people who are open to listening."

"I'd love to borrow the pendant," Samantha decided. "Thank you for offering it to me."

Marigold nodded and smiled.

"The people here take care of each other," she said. "Maybe you'll fall in love with Jackson Hole and not want to leave at all."

Outside, the sidewalk teemed with tourists. Couples posed for photos under the famous elk antlers, and families sipped hot chocolate and ate gingerbread cookies. Santa Claus handed out presents from his sleigh, and carolers wearing cowboy hats sang Christmas carols in front of the Million Dollar Cowboy Bar.

Samantha couldn't remember the last time she'd strolled down the street on Christmas Eve. By this time last year, she had been safely in her apartment with the fireplace poker wedged under the door. The front door of the building was left open to receive last-minute packages and Samantha was afraid of who might enter the building.

She realized she was starving. She hadn't eaten any breakfast.

First, she stepped inside a restaurant called the Cowboy Steakhouse whose menu promised it served Old Western food in a new, healthy way.

After she read the descriptions—burgers so thick you couldn't cut them with a knife, mashed potatoes swimming in butter, and mince pies topped with extra-thick whipped cream that would take a week of running to work off—she hastily put back the menu and left.

Then she entered a restaurant named the Gun Barrel that served grilled rainbow trout and a selection of salads. Samantha took one look at the animal heads mounted on the wall and knew she couldn't eat with a stuffed moose staring down at her.

Finally, she entered a café named the Bunnery that had been a local favorite for decades. Samantha could see why. The smell wafting from the kitchen—golden-brown waffles with maple syrup and some kind of cinnamon pastry—was heavenly. And the décor was so cheerful. Poinsettias were scattered around the room and the tables were covered with blue-and-white-checkered tablecloths. A Christmas tree was decorated with horse-hoof-shaped ornaments and the fireplace was hung with stockings.

Samantha approached the hostess desk. "A table for one please."

"I'm sorry," the girl said, glancing up. "We're completely full."

Samantha's stomach rumbled. She didn't want to go back onto the street. And she didn't want to eat at one of the other restaurants with names like Snake River Grill and Snake River Brewing Company. Just seeing the word "snake" took away her appetite.

"How long will it be for a table?" she asked hopefully.

The girl tapped on her computer screen. "We're fully booked all afternoon. Like every restaurant in town." She frowned as if Samantha should know better. "It is two days before Christmas, all the hotels are booked all week."

Samantha opened her mouth to make some snappy reply: "Jackson Hole is a holiday destination. The restaurants should be able to handle all the tourists." But those were the kind of comments that made New Yorkers unpopular. And she refused to be unkind to anyone, especially at Christmas.

A man crossed the floor. It was Drew. He was holding a coffee mug and smiling.

"She's with me," he said to the hostess. "I'm sitting over there, next to the fireplace."

The hostess glanced at Drew. She shrugged and picked up a menu.

"Follow me," she said grudgingly to Samantha. "You're lucky. The kitchen is still serving bunny waffles with organic butter for the next hour."

Samantha waited until the hostess left. She turned to Drew.

"You didn't have to do that," she said stiffly. "I could have grabbed a sandwich at a deli."

"I didn't have to. But I wanted to," Drew remarked, sipping his coffee. "I couldn't let you be chastised like a child who came down too early on Christmas morning."

Samantha laughed. "The hostess was a bit mean. I was only asking for a table, not a ride on Santa's sleigh." She shifted uncomfortably. "I wasn't very nice to you earlier. I apologize."

"You mean when the elk charged our sleigh?" Drew said, with a twinkle in his eye. "You were a bit rough on me. Apology accepted."

"I've never been so frightened," she said honestly. "You were so calm and self-assured. I suppose it's different when you've spent time out here."

"You get used to it. The first summer I was in Jackson Hole, I couldn't believe that bears practically share the road with cars," Drew said. "But they're quite content to leave you alone." He grinned. "Unless you leave out the garbage, then the bears think you're inviting them to join you for dinner."

Samantha imagined bears peering through the windows at Arthur's ranch while they were seated at the dining table and her stomach dropped.

"Don't worry, my father keeps the ranch perfectly safe." Drew noticed her expression. "He walks around the property every evening checking for bears, and he's a stickler for always sealing the trash."

Samantha recalled the things she told Drew on the plane.

"Your father is a great person," she said guiltily. "Anyone would be thrilled to be invited to his ranch. It's my fault that I'm not enjoying it."

Drew took a pastry from the bread basket and offered one to Samantha.

"You said on the plane that you can't turn off your imagination." He pulled apart his muffin. "But it's more than that."

"What do you mean?" she asked.

"When you said that no one listens. Were you talking about anyone in particular?"

Samantha was about to protest when the waitress brought their plates. Drew had ordered Belgian waffles, and Samantha had French toast made with cinnamon bread and a white mocha with hazelnut flavor for her coffee.

Sitting across from Drew with the winter sun streaming through the window, she felt so far from New York and her life before Roger left. She used to love meeting Roger for Thai food after work, and she never minded taking the subway home alone. She looked forward to visiting thrift shops in the Catskills on the weekends, and going apple picking in the Hudson Valley during the fall.

Slowly Samantha started talking. She told Drew how she and Roger met the month after she moved to New

York. They were both picking out dogs at the animal shelter. Roger was about to adopt Socks. He handed Socks to Samantha and said he saw them looking at each other. Samantha and Socks belonged together.

The first year they were so happy. They both wanted the same things: satisfying careers, a family, and enough money to travel and give back to their community.

"Roger is three years older than me. He started keeping track of his friends from law school on social media: one was clerking for a judge; another was the youngest partner at an entertainment law firm. He made a list of goals for himself and stuck it on the fridge in his apartment. I didn't think there was anything wrong with that, I had my own goals," she said, toying with her spoon. "It started to interfere with his happiness. He worked late every night because he wanted to bill more hours than the other associates. He accepted invitations to parties even though he didn't like the host. When I asked him about it, he shrugged and said that's what lawyers did to get ahead.

"One morning, I was at his apartment after he left for work. A lease was sitting on his desk. I thought Roger was going to surprise me and ask me to move in with him." She looked up at Drew. "I only realized after he left for California that the lease was for an apartment in Manhattan Beach, not Manhattan." She finished, "You can't help someone if they don't admit something's wrong. If Roger had told me how he was feeling, if he'd listened to me, he might have stayed in New York."

Drew put down his coffee cup. He picked up his fork.

"And since then?" he wondered. "Who do you talk to now?"

"I talk to Socks," Samantha confessed. "And Charlie's girlfriend, Emily, when I need fashion advice. Sloane

Parker would be stuck wearing sweatpants and sloppy T-shirts instead of Galliano gowns if it weren't for Emily." She grinned. "And I talk to my mother. She calls in the evenings. She says it's because she misses talking around the dining room table. Really she's checking to make sure I eat a proper dinner instead of frozen pizza four times a week."

"Maybe that's the problem, maybe you should find someone to talk to," Drew suggested.

They reached for the syrup at the same time and for a moment their hands touched. Samantha felt a jolt of electricity. As if she'd picked up a blouse straight out of the dryer.

She took her hand away and concentrated on cutting her French toast.

"Tell me about Chiang Mai," she said, changing the subject. "I did a report on Thailand in high school. It has the most beautiful temples."

After lunch, they strolled along the sidewalk. Christmas music drifted from the pergola and a horse and carriage clopped around the town square.

"Do you mind if we do a little shopping before we go back to the car?" Drew asked. "I promised Kaman I'd send the children in the village some souvenirs."

They stepped into a gift shop filled with baskets of candy canes and Christmas toffees. Samantha helped Drew choose a child's bow and arrow set, and a selection of scarves and mittens.

"I should take a photo of you under the elk antlers," Drew said, carrying his packages outside.

"I don't need a photo," Samantha said.

The antlers were decked out with Christmas lights and a giant red bow.

"Everybody needs a photo under the Jackson Hole antlers," Drew insisted. "You can send it to Charlie and your parents."

Samantha hesitated. There wasn't any reason not to take a photo. And she could show Charlie she wasn't cooped up in her guest room, avoiding everyone. She was actually out trying to enjoy herself.

Samantha waited for a family to finish taking their photo. She moved under the antlers and Drew took out his phone.

"Wait, let me put down my packages," he said, crouching down on the sidewalk.

Suddenly there was a whooshing sound, followed by a heavy cracking. Samantha glanced up and a giant icicle teetered above her. She ducked and it narrowly missed her head.

Drew rushed over to her.

"Are you all right?" he asked. "That icicle was as sharp as a dagger. You could have been badly hurt."

Samantha reached up to unwrap her scarf. She was wearing the arrowhead pendant. She had forgotten all about it.

"I'm perfectly fine," she assured him. Her hair was damp and a smattering of ice dusted her shoulders.

"Why don't we take a photo another time," Drew said, his voice thick with concern. "Let's get back to the ranch. We could both use a hot toddy with extra bourbon."

Samantha sat in the window seat in her guest room. She had a view of the whole valley. Cross-country skiers glided across fresh powder and a snowmobile jumped over the snow.

She touched the pendant around her neck. For some reason, she hadn't been afraid when the icicle fell toward her. Could Marigold have been right? Had Samantha instinctively known the arrowhead would protect her?

Her phone rang and she answered.

"Samantha." Charlie's voice came over the line. "Just saying hi."

"You don't have to check up on me," Samantha chuckled. "I'm doing everything that Arthur suggests."

"I wasn't checking up on you exactly," Charlie returned. "I have some good news."

"What kind of good news?" Samantha inquired.

"I had a phone call from a producer in Hollywood. Zach is interested in the Sloane Parker books."

"You got a call on Christmas Eve?" Samantha frowned.

No one did business on Christmas Eve. She wondered if Charlie was trying to make her feel better, but he wouldn't do something like that. Charlie took his job too seriously.

"Zach says the only time he has to read is during the holidays," Charlie explained. "It's only a phone call, but you never know. Sloane would be perfect for Hollywood."

"I'll keep my fingers crossed," Samantha said. "I was about to take a bath. Arthur is serving a special dinner and then we're going to watch Santa Claus arrive by aerial tram."

Charlie's voice was warm.

"I'm glad you're there, Samantha," he said. "It means a lot to me and I'm sure you'll enjoy yourself. Arthur is a wonderful host."

Samantha hung up and entered the bathroom. Her reflection stared back at her and she fingered the pendant. She imagined walking down the red carpet in Hollywood at her movie premiere. She'd be wearing some fabulous couture gown and Socks would have a black tie around his neck and blue booties.

She took off the pendant and laid it on the counter. Perhaps her luck was changing. It was Christmas, and Christmas miracles happened all the time.

Chapter Five

Samantha flipped through the sweaters hanging in her closet. She'd have to thank Charlie for packing a suitcase. Emily had the best taste and Samantha felt so grateful that Emily had lent her so many clothes. There was a tie-dyed alpaca sweater with that wonderful vintage feel, and a white cable-knit turtleneck from H&M, and a Naadam sweater in the softest cashmere. Emily insisted a cashmere sweater was the essential fashion piece of the season. To Samantha, the only necessary clothing item was her writing sweatpants. Without her favorite sweatpants—navy flannel that she bought when she was let go from her old job at the PR company and wore for a month while watching James Bond movies and reading the novels her roommate left on the bookshelf—she may never have started writing the Sloane Parker books at all.

Emily was a wealth of fashion advice on Sloane's wardrobe. Just this morning, Samantha sent Emily a quick text about an idea she had when she woke up.

Sloane is dangling from a zip line in a jungle in northern Thailand. Beside her is Drake Halladay, the sexy British explorer she met at a temple in Bangkok. The rope that connected them to the zip line broke, and they were stuck thirty feet in the air. Sloane uses the ancient necklace given to her by a Buddhist monk to fasten herself to the zip line. Then she instructs Drake to hang on to her waist. Together, they inch along the zip line until they are safely on the ground.

Emily had texted back exactly what Sloane should be wearing: a Jenny Packham forest-green evening gown paired with Yves Saint Laurent stilettos. It was the perfect suggestion. The green blended in with the tropical foliage, so Sloane and Drake weren't spotted by the drug lords who had been trailing them from Bangkok. Plus, the Saint Laurent stilettos had spiky heels that were quite useful for trudging along the forest floor.

Samantha texted Emily six smile emojis and put away her phone. Martha, the cook and housekeeper, was preparing Christmas breakfast and Samantha didn't want to miss out.

Ever since she'd returned to the ranch yesterday afternoon, she'd felt better. Her appetite returned and she enjoyed Christmas Eve dinner with the other guests. The dining room looked so festive: the great oak table was set with red and gold china and flickering candelabras. A small Tiffany's box sat in front of each place setting. Samantha's held a gold pen engraved with her initials.

Charlie was right. Arthur was the most thoughtful host.

The meal had been delicious. Martha made rack of lamb and king crab legs, and platters of braised brussels sprouts and honey-glazed yams. For dessert there were three kinds of pies. The huckleberry pie was so sweet and tasty, she resolved to go back to the souvenir shop where Marigold worked and buy a jar of huckleberry jam.

At dinner, Samantha sat beside Drew and they talked about the year he celebrated Christmas in Fiji. The locals served spiced mutton wrapped in leaves and cooked in coconut cream over an open stove. Everyone gathered in community houses and there was traditional dancing. Samantha listened to Drew, her cheeks flushed from the wine, and thought Fiji was the perfect setting for a Sloane Parker book. She could already see Sloane trapped for days in the Fijian jungle, frying bananas over hot coals and drinking coconut milk to keep away the hunger.

The next morning, she selected the tie-dyed alpaca sweater and paired it with camel-colored slacks. First there was something she had to do, then she would join everyone at breakfast.

"Bruno!" she said when she entered the barn. "It's Christmas, I didn't think anyone would be here."

"I always spend Christmas morning with the horses," Bruno replied, turning to greet her. "When I was younger, I'd go for a ride before breakfast. Snow everywhere you turn, and not a person in sight." He smiled and his eyes crinkled at the corners. "It made me feel closer to God than attending Christmas services."

Samantha unwrapped a napkin. Inside were golden-brown sugar cubes.

"I brought the horses some sugar." She showed them to Bruno. "I hope that's all right."

"The horses will love them," Bruno said and smiled, filling a bucket with hay. "Though don't feed Blixen first. He's very greedy. He'll take everything in your hand and ask for more."

Samantha fed sugar cubes to a white palomino. Its jaw nuzzled her palm, and it tipped its head in a thank-you.

"My wife wanted me out of the apartment anyway," Bruno said conversationally. "We're FaceTiming our grandchildren in an hour and I was distracting her from getting ready."

"My parents are in Norway," Samantha remarked. "I'll FaceTime them later. It's the middle of the night there."

Samantha had checked her Instagram feed this morning. Her mother had posted a photo of them holding hands with strangers and dancing under a giant Christmas tree. There was a photo of them sitting at a café and holding mugs with pictures of reindeer.

The caption read, "Our first cups of glogg!"

Samantha wondered if her mother knew glogg was made with red wine. Her mother never drank red wine; it gave her a headache.

"Elaine thinks FaceTime is the most wonderful invention," Bruno was saying. "Our daughter and her family live in California. We never miss our grandchildren's birthdays, and we can spend holidays together without doing all the cleaning up."

"I suppose," Samantha sighed. "People spend so much of their lives online. My mother takes travel advice from a reality chef, and even the tour guide at the Elk Refuge only cares about Yelp reviews. And it's terrible for authors. Readers don't buy a book based on the writing. They buy it if they like the author's Instagram feed."

"I doubt that's always the case." Bruno frowned. He moved his bucket to the next stall. "*Black Beauty* was the first book we gave our daughter, and it's now our granddaughter's favorite."

"That might happen if I ever write a classic," Samantha said glumly. "But just because Sloane Parker knows her way around Saks's dress department as well as she does around the Sahara Desert, readers think I should be the same."

"Elaine was up half the night reading your new book," Bruno commented. "She wishes there'd been books like it when we were first married. Sloane Parker is a great role model. Years ago, Elaine wanted to get her pilot's license and learn to ride a motorcycle, but women didn't do those kinds of things."

Samantha would never have Sloane ride a motorcycle. You only had to read the statistics to know it was dangerous. And wearing a helmet did terrible things to Sloane's hair. But Sloane got her pilot's license in the first book. British Intelligence wouldn't hire her without it.

"I wish more readers felt that way," Samantha sighed, taking another sugar cube from the napkin. "Writers have always had odd habits but no one cared. Hemingway could only write standing up, and Victor Hugo wrote *The Hunchback of Notre-Dame* completely naked. He was on a tight deadline and didn't want to be tempted to leave the house."

"I'm sure you'll continue to be a success," Bruno said, stroking Blixen's nose. "I've always taught my daughter the same thing," he reflected. "The only limits we have in life are the ones we put on ourselves."

Samantha sat at a table in the ranch's dining room. The breakfast that Martha had prepared was delicious. The sausages were flavorful but not spicy, and the poached eggs were perfectly timed so that the yolks were runny and the whites were firm without being dry. Samantha had tried for a year to make poached eggs. She never seemed to get it right. Even Socks grew tired of eating her failed attempts.

Outside the window, a light snow was falling, and inside, a Christmas tree twinkled near the fireplace. All the guests were in a good mood. The sound of clinking cutlery mixing with the scent of warm pastries made Samantha feel as if she were at some exclusive resort.

The only thing missing was Drew. He wasn't at breakfast and Samantha wondered if he grabbed a cup of coffee and went for a walk. For some reason, she wished he was here beside her.

The door from the kitchen swung open and Drew appeared. He was wearing a snowflake-patterned sweater and there were circles under his eyes.

"Samantha," he greeted her. "Do you mind if I sit with you?"

"Please do." She made room for him. "Is something wrong? You look like you haven't slept."

Drew sprinkled salt on his omelet.

"I stayed up rehearsing how to tell my father that Beatrix isn't coming. It didn't go well," he said glumly. "Every time I came to the part where he might ask me why, I couldn't think of how to reply."

"You haven't told your father about her ultimatum?" Samantha questioned.

"My father and Beatrix are quite close." Drew reached for the pepper. "They both love books and fine wines and beautiful houses," he sighed. "She'd be the perfect daughter-in-law."

"Your father isn't the one getting married," Samantha reminded him.

"It's not my father's fault that he and I don't want the same things," Drew reflected. "I love books but I have as much interest in the production of them as I do in how this sausage got to the plate." He waved at Samantha's sausage. "What excites me is giving the books to children to read. But you can't buy a two-bedroom apartment in Manhattan with the kind of money I earn. And he isn't likely to see his grandchildren if I'm working halfway around the world." He put down his fork. "When I tell him about Beatrix's ultimatum, I'm putting an end to his dreams too."

"Maybe Beatrix will see your point of view," Samantha said hopefully. "Lots of women leave a life of luxury for love. Look at the heroine in *Lady Chatterley's Lover.* Lady Chatterley gives up being the lady of a grand estate to live with a gamekeeper."

Samantha suddenly felt awkward. Drew probably had never heard of *Lady Chatterley's Lover.* It had been one of her favorite books in college. She loved it so much, she included it in a Sloane Parker book.

Sloane goes to bed with Stavros, the young Greek fisherman she falls madly in love with. Stavros begs her to quit British Intelligence and work with him on his fishing boat. Sloane imagines their lives together—fishing all day and growing bronze from the sun, making love in secluded inlets and drinking ouzo at night—and is about to agree. Then she finds a copy of *Lady Chatterley's Lover* in Stavros's suitcase. All the paragraphs where Mellors seduces Lady Chatterley are underlined. Sloane realizes that Stavros is only trying to seduce her to gather information about British Intelligence. She tells Stavros she can't come and she takes the book with her when she leaves. Phineas is a big fan of D. H. Lawrence and she's going to give it to him as a birthday present.

"I haven't read that since high school," Drew said with a grin. "And to be honest, I never agreed with it. The only reason Lady Chatterley fell in love with Mellors was because her husband wouldn't talk to her. I tell Beatrix everything." His shoulders sagged. "She just doesn't want to hear it."

Samantha felt a pinprick of warmth toward Drew. Roger never read fiction. His stack of books only included the latest bestsellers that had similar titles: *The New York Times Guide to Being a Successful Entrepreneur. How to*

Become CEO of a Fortune 500 Company by the Age of Forty.

"Maybe you and Beatrix could talk to your father together," Samantha suggested.

"I tried calling but her phone goes straight to voice mail." He shook his head. "I should have told my father sooner. I feel like Santa Claus delivering coal to his stocking."

"Drew, Samantha," a male voice called.

Samantha looked up. Arthur had appeared in the hallway. He held a coffee cup in one hand and a plate of muffins in the other.

"I'm glad to see you at breakfast, Samantha," Arthur said, joining them. "Martha isn't happy unless all the guests try her pumpkin spice muffins." He set the plate on the table.

"I don't have room on my plate! And I think I'm still full from last night's dinner." Samantha smiled at Arthur. "It was a wonderful evening. Thank you for my present."

"Our star author needs a gold pen to sign her books. You must take some time to explore my library. Feel free to take any books you want to read," Arthur said, beaming. He turned to Drew. "I was disappointed that Beatrix didn't arrive in time for dinner." He glanced around the dining room. "Where is she? She must be here by now."

Drew busied himself cutting his omelet.

"Her plane must have been delayed," Drew said, looking up from his plate. "You know what it's like traveling on Christmas Eve. You leave New York and find yourself in Boston instead of Philadelphia. Then the airline reroutes you through Chicago and you don't arrive at your destination until midnight."

Arthur stirred his coffee. His brow wrinkled.

"I didn't know Beatrix was in New York. You said she was spending the week before Christmas with her parents in Atlanta."

"Atlanta is even worse," Drew said hastily. "The last time I flew from Atlanta, my luggage went to California and I ended up in Detroit."

"Well, I hope she makes it by this evening." Arthur bit into his muffin. His eyes twinkled. "I have a surprise for the two of you after Christmas dinner. I've been working on it for weeks, even Martha is sworn to secrecy."

Arthur drifted off and Drew pushed the hair from his forehead.

"My father shows up and I act like a seven-year-old with his first speaking part in the school play," Drew groaned. "Don't even repeat to me what I said. I don't want to remember."

Samantha tried to stop from smiling. Drew had resembled a child. His blue eyes seemed even larger and there was a sweet innocence about him.

"It's not your fault that Beatrix isn't here."

"It's my fault that I didn't warn him," he countered. "You'd think that someone who has no problem cutting through red tape to get a school finished before the monsoon season can mention to his father that his fiancée is skipping Christmas. I've never been a good liar and I hate to hurt people."

"Anyone would consider those to be good qualities," Samantha said, laughing.

Drew ate another bite of omelet.

"There's nothing I can do about it now." He shrugged. "Everyone is going snowmobiling at Togwotee Pass after breakfast. Would you like to ride together?"

Samantha was about to make up some excuse. But Arthur wouldn't approve if she stayed at the ranch.

"It's perfectly safe. You can sit in the front," Drew encouraged her. "It feels like riding a bumper car at the fair but without the tracks."

Samantha fingered the arrowhead necklace. Marigold said it protected the wearer from danger, and it had stopped the icicle from falling on her.

She didn't really have a choice.

"All right," she agreed with more confidence than she felt. She gulped her coffee. "You have to steer, in case I need to close my eyes."

The snowmobiles picked the guests up at the ranch. Samantha was afraid she'd be cold, but the guide outfitted everyone with thick parkas and gloves. The guide's name was Buck and he was the opposite of the brash tour guide at the Elk Refuge. Buck went over the safety instructions with the precision of an airline pilot before a flight. By the time everyone climbed aboard the sleek snowmobiles with their soft leather seats and duck-like feet, Samantha felt confident and secure.

Not even Buck's descriptions of what they were going to see prepared her for the breathtaking scenery. The snow had stopped falling and the air was crisp and bright. The sky was bluer than anything she had known in New York, and the snow was a blinding white.

First, they crossed miles of snow-blanketed fields. The Teton Valley fell beneath them and in the distance, Samantha could see the ski tram and skiers making wide circles in the snow.

Drew placed his hands lightly around her waist and something inside Samantha shifted. She had that feeling of not wanting the moment to end.

Then the fields stopped and they entered the forest. Icicles glittered in the trees and squirrels darted in front of them. Samantha noticed all kinds of animal foot-prints, and Buck allowed the group to stop and take photos of a family of deer. Samantha texted Charlie and Emily a picture of the deer and captioned it, "Santa's reindeers taking a break on Christmas day," and sent it with a meme of Santa Claus asleep in his sleigh.

There was one frightening moment when they reached the top of Togwotee Pass and a snowmobile skidded into a snowbank. Samantha waited, the mountains fierce and forbidding above them, and wondered whether they should turn back. What if there was an avalanche and they were all buried in snow?

But Buck calmly helped the snowmobile get back on the trail. He handed around flasks of hot coffee and chocolate bars he kept for such occasions. By the time they all started their engines, Samantha's fears had subsided.

On the way back, she let Drew drive the snowmo-bile. Her body curved into the familiar rhythm, and she couldn't remember having so much fun. When they left the snowmobiles at the entrance of Teton Village, she wanted to do it all again.

"That was wonderful," Samantha said, beaming.

The guests had dispersed to have a late lunch and buy souvenirs. Samantha and Drew sat at the coffee bar in the General Store. The store was like something out of the 1950s. It sold everything from vacuum cleaner bags to motor oil to Christmas cookies in heart-shaped tins. There was a section of packaged foods, and another of cowboy hats and leather boots.

"I knew you'd enjoy it," Drew replied. He had ordered hot chocolate with whipped cream for both of them. "It's even better than skiing. There's that feeling of just you and the mountains."

"Jackson Hole is like a scene in a midcentury sitcom." Samantha waved outside the window.

A red sleigh was parked in the square, and the Christmas tree was decorated with miniature skis and ski poles. A group of children was having a snowball fight, and adults warmed their hands in front of an outdoor fireplace.

"You know the TV shows I mean," Samantha continued. "Every family had two freckle-faced children and their biggest problem was when they mixed up the Christmas presents for their favorite teachers."

"Life doesn't always have to have problems," Drew said and sipped his hot chocolate thoughtfully. "Sometimes, you can stop and enjoy yourself."

Drew seemed more relaxed than he had been at the ranch. The circles under his eyes had disappeared and his cheeks were tan from the afternoon sun.

"It's hard to stop when my next book might not be signed up because of poor sales," Samantha sighed, poking her whipped cream with the straw. "I don't know what I'd do if I didn't write Sloane Parker books. It's what I look forward to when I get up in the morning."

Drew studied her curiously.

"You really love writing, don't you?"

"More than anything," Samantha acknowledged. "Even as a little girl, I can't remember a time when I wasn't writing. I filled so many notebooks with stories, my mother had to buy them in bulk from Costco. After college, I got a job at a PR company but I never thought I could write books as a career. Then I got laid off and at all my interviews, the human resources personnel only wanted to know if I was experienced at Snapchat and Instagram. When Charlie read a few chapters of my first

Sloane Parker book and said I might actually earn a living at it, I thought I'd won the New York lottery."

"You went snowmobiling today over some of the most challenging terrain in the west," Drew reminded her. "Maybe you could do some of the things you pretend to do on Instagram."

Samantha touched the arrowhead pendant. She hadn't mentioned it to Drew. She wasn't sure if he would think it was silly.

"Today was different," Samantha answered slowly. "Our guide told us exactly what to do. I couldn't get on a plane by myself and go somewhere new. What if I lose my passport and get stranded in a foreign country? Or my credit cards get stolen and I have no way to get home? That happened to Sloane when she was trailing an art thief through the Swiss Alps. He stole her credit cards and her phone, so there was no way for her to contact British Intelligence. Sloane had to work for a month at the local cheese shop to afford a new airplane ticket." Samantha smiled at the memory of the plot. "It was one of my favorite books to write. I bought a whole selection of cheeses to get the details right. My favorite was Edam cheese. Even Socks liked it, and he's not a big fan of dairy."

"You're afraid of being afraid," Drew said. He gazed at Samantha and there was something new in his eyes. "You're braver than you think."

"How do you know I'm brave?" she countered.

He placed his mug on the counter.

"When I was eight, I attended my first sleepover birthday party," he began. "I wasn't really friends with the kid but he invited the whole class. It was the typical kids' party where everyone eats too much sugar and starts throwing Nerf darts at each other instead of the dartboard." He grinned. "I was fine when we took out our sleeping bags, but in the middle of the night I couldn't sleep. The boy's mother noticed I was upset and asked if I wanted to call my mother. I said I didn't have a mother, she left when I was four. She looked at me and said I had nothing to be afraid of. I'd already survived the worst thing that could happen to a kid and I was perfectly fine."

Samantha was quiet. When Samantha was a little girl, her mother always picked her up from birthday parties. Often her mother would stay and chat with the other mothers.

"I'm sorry," she said finally.

"Most people are afraid to try to write a book. They think they're not good enough or their work will be criticized. You've written more than one book." He picked up his mug and his wrist brushed hers. "You don't have anything else to be afraid of."

Samantha and Drew finished their hot chocolates and walked into the square. It was late afternoon and the air was freezing. Skiers piled off the tram and there was the sound of ski boots crunching on hard snow.

"Tonight, after dinner, the ski patrol skis down the mountain carrying electric torches," Drew said as they walked toward the waiting car. "There's a parade and everyone sings Christmas carols around the Christmas tree. I was thinking of going. Would you like to join me?"

For a moment Samantha wondered if Drew was asking her out. Then she remembered he hadn't told his father about Beatrix. He probably just didn't want to be alone with Arthur.

She enjoyed Drew's company and it sounded like fun. Growing up in New Jersey, she never missed the Christmas sing-along with her parents.

"Yes." She nodded, tugging on her gloves. "I'd like that very much."

Samantha shook the snow off her boots and entered the ranch's living room. She was going to take a bath and then get dressed for Christmas dinner.

A beautiful blonde stood in front of the fireplace. Her hair was tied in the kind of ponytail that usually looked silly on most grown women, but on her was sophisticated. She wore a ski parka and après-ski boots that Samantha had seen in a magazine spread of European ski resorts: white moon boots that came up to her knees with faux-diamond buckles.

Samantha sighed, her self-confidence slipping. She had met women like that at industry events. She was probably some supermodel launching a series of beauty books. Over cocktails, she'd confide in Samantha that her book was going to be featured on *Good Morning America*.

Samantha's nose was red from the cold, and she hadn't brushed her hair since she took off the snowmobile helmet. She'd slip upstairs and meet her later when she was properly dressed.

"Samantha." Arthur appeared from the hallway. He wore a turtleneck and slacks and carried two cocktail glasses. "I'd like you to meet someone."

He handed a glass to the woman and turned to Samantha.

"This is Beatrix, Drew's fiancée," he introduced them. "Beatrix, this is Samantha Morgan, one of our star authors."

Beatrix looked at Samantha. Her smile was as dazzling as the large diamond on her left hand.

"I was just telling Arthur how thrilled I am to be here. I skied in Jackson Hole years ago, everyone knows it has some of the best powder in America. And Arthur is so clever with the mix of people he invites to his house parties," Beatrix said brightly. There was something false in her voice, like when Samantha gave Siri a different accent.

"It's nice to meet you." Samantha held out her hand.

"I just love writers, they're so interesting," Beatrix gushed. Beatrix's handshake was firm. "We have the whole week together. I'm sure we'll get to know each other."

Chapter Six

Samantha stepped out of the bath and wrapped herself in a towel. She often wished she had a bathtub in her apartment, it was the best place to think up plot ideas.

Sitting in the bath with the sun setting over the Teton Valley, a new idea came to her. Sloane Parker is between assignments and staying at a ski resort in Davos, Switzerland. She's relaxing in a hot tub at her chalet when she's approached by a striking redhead with wraparound sunglasses that hide her eyes. The redhead is wearing a white ski suit with a jeweled hood and holding the sweetest little Pomeranian dog.

The redhead introduces herself as Colette and says she found the dog shivering at the bottom of the ski lift. No one claimed it and she couldn't let it freeze to death. She's late for a photo shoot and they can't start without her.

Sloane offers to care for the dog and they go into Sloane's suite. Sloane enters the bathroom to get a towel, and when she comes out Colette is gone. Then she discovers that the red phone hidden under her pillow is also missing.

The woman isn't really a high-fashion model, and she isn't a redhead. The hair is a wig so that Sloane won't recognize her old nemesis, the impossibly beautiful blond agent Clarissa Cooper. Only Clarissa knows that Sloane can't resist stray dogs, and only Clarissa knows that British Intelligence makes all agents keep a secret cell phone underneath their pillows.

Sloane can't let Clarissa get away. She alerts the airport and train station. Then she arranges for the ski patrol to close the autobahn leading out of Davos. When she finally finds Clarissa hiding under a fur coat in the back of a Mercedes, she confiscates her passport and has her arrested for stealing property of the British government.

Samantha replaced the towel with a robe and sat at the dressing table. She didn't know why Beatrix had rubbed her the wrong way. They met so briefly and Beatrix was perfectly friendly.

Perhaps it was because Drew told Samantha about her ultimatum. Drew was a nice guy; she didn't want him to get hurt.

Samantha had the unsettling feeling that it was more than that. It had been so much fun snowmobiling with Drew this afternoon, and then drinking hot chocolates at the General Store. He had asked her to watch the Christmas parade after dinner.

She couldn't remember when she'd last enjoyed someone's company so much. And she thought Drew felt the same. But Beatrix acted as if she practically owned the ranch. The diamond ring sparkling on her left hand made it perfectly clear she still considered them to be engaged.

Samantha's phone buzzed and she answered.

"Mom!" Samantha said. "Why are you calling? It's one a.m. in Norway."

"We have a five a.m. flight to Zurich. I'm waiting for your father to get out of the shower," her mother replied.

"We're not in Norway, we spent Christmas Eve in Stockholm. We never went to bed, there was so much to see."

"You never went to bed?" Samantha asked nervously.

When she was growing up, her parents were both asleep by 9:00 P.M. Her mother said she couldn't expect her students to get the ten hours of sleep recommended for teenagers if she stood at the chalkboard yawning and desperate for coffee.

"Stockholm has the most wonderful Christmas traditions." Her mother kept talking. "On Christmas day, the whole city shuts down at three p.m. to watch old Disney cartoons on television. We learned that *Kalle Anka* means 'Donald Duck' in Swedish. Then we took a walking tour of Gamla Stan and ended up at Skeppsbron where they have the tallest Christmas tree in the world." Her mother reeled off the names as if she were a lifelong Swedish speaker. "You'll never guess who we had dinner with: Joyce and Paul Musselman. We haven't seen them for thirty years, but Paul started following me on Instagram. It's because of them that your father and I met. Paul was my first serious boyfriend, and your father and Joyce were dating."

"You had dinner with an old boyfriend?" Samantha said in alarm. "That must have been interesting."

"It's nothing like that," her mother scoffed. "Besides, Paul lost all his hair and developed a paunch. I suppose I never told you the story. We were all on spring break in Daytona Beach. We double dated at the Tiki Lounge. From the moment we sat down, I couldn't get over how attractive your father was. His eyes were so green and he had the best smile.

"Paul was sweet but he was an engineer and quite boring. And Joyce was getting a degree in fashion. Your father has no interest in clothes—he still thinks Sears only sells home goods. Well, Paul had indigestion and went to bed early, and Joyce and your father got into a fight. Your father was standing on the balcony of the Tiki Lounge and I joined him. We started talking and had so much in common: we both had a dog named Spot when we were children, and were thinking of joining the Peace Corps after college."

"You never told me you were in the Peace Corps," Samantha said, trying to imagine her parents at spring break where they played drinking games and held wet T-shirt contests.

"I never did. Everyone talked about joining the Peace Corps in those days, few people actually did it. It's like young people saying they want to 'go off the grid.' It sounds exciting but no one wants to live without the internet," her mother clucked. "Anyway, by the end of the night there was something between us. On the flight home, I broke up with Paul. Your father broke up with Joyce, and we have been together ever since."

"I'm surprised they wanted to have dinner with you tonight," Samantha said, laughing.

"Their lives turned out fine. Paul has a successful pool construction business and Joyce was a buyer at Bloomingdale's and they've been happily married for thirty years," her mother said matter-of-factly. "I want to hear about you. I read on a blog that Jackson Hole's male-to-female ratio is seven to one."

"I hadn't noticed," Samantha said with a smile. "I did go snowmobiling. Tonight, the ski patrol is going to ski down the mountain and there's a parade through town." She suddenly thought about Beatrix. "I'm not sure I'm going to go."

"You have to! I bet the ski patrol is full of great-looking men. If you dated one of them, you wouldn't have to be afraid of falling when you're skiing." Her voice became muffled. "I wish you had joined us. Being away from you on Christmas day still feels so strange. Next year, you have to come. We'll pick anywhere you want to go."

Samantha swallowed. The only place she wanted to be was in her own living room, with Socks curled up on the sofa beside her.

"You and Dad deserve to travel and I love hearing about your adventures." Samantha made her voice bright. "I couldn't have turned down Arthur's invitation anyway. I've never been invited to one of his Christmas parties before, it's quite an honor."

There was a honking sound on the other end of the phone. Samantha wondered if her mother had been crying and now, she was blowing her nose.

"Try to enjoy yourself, Samantha. I have to go," her mother said loudly. "I'll call you from Zurich. We'll be there in time to hear the Singing Christmas Tree at Werd-mühleplatz."

Samantha hung up, wondering how many languages her parents would speak by the time they arrived home. Her mind turned to Drew. They both had read *Lady Chat-terley's Lover*, and they never seemed to run out of things to talk about.

But she was being silly. Beatrix was here now, and Be-atrix and Drew were together. She had to stop thinking about Drew. He was just a friend.

Samantha walked to the closet to pick out a dress. Beatrix would probably be wearing some drop-dead de-signer outfit that wasn't yet in the stores. She silently thanked Emily for lending her so many clothes and she had something to wear other than sweatpants and old col-lege sweatshirts. Samantha might not be any competition for Beatrix, but at least she wasn't going to appear at Christmas dinner dressed like a professional dog walker.

Beatrix was talking to Arthur when Samantha entered the living room. The room was full of people but Samantha didn't see Drew.

"Samantha, come and join us," Arthur said, waving to her. "I sent Drew to the wine cellar for a bottle of champagne. Our first Christmas at the ranch deserves a real celebration. I had been looking for the perfect ranch to buy in Jackson Hole for years. But every ranch that came on the market was either subject to a bidding war between retired CEOs wanting to get back to nature or it was snatched up by some tech start-up entrepreneur who thought nothing of paying double the asking price. When I closed the deal on this place, I sent my Realtor a case of champagne to thank her."

"It was worth the wait. The ranch is spectacular and everything looks so lovely," Samantha commented.

A white Christmas tree with silver and blue ornaments stood near the fireplace, and a green fir tree decorated with lights twinkled at the window. Candles flickered on the side tables and there were platters of hors d'oeuvres.

"I was telling Beatrix this used to be a dude ranch." Arthur nursed his glass. "The barn has been there for fifty years. It was popular with Hollywood celebrities. They signed their names on the wall in the tack room. You can still see Jane Fonda's autograph, and there's a saddle used by Robert Redford."

"I loved horseback riding when I was in high school," Beatrix remarked. "I won so many trophies at gymkhanas, I ran out of space on my shelf."

Samantha had to admit that Beatrix looked stunning.

She wore a red velvet cocktail dress paired with black satin heels. Samantha was tempted to text Emily a photo of the dress. She'd love to find out the name of the designer. Perhaps she could buy a cheap copy for the publisher's Christmas party next year.

"I don't ride anymore," Beatrix was saying. She paused to take a ladylike sip of her cocktail. "Ever since my last horse, Gooseberry, died, I can't bring myself to get on a horse." Her perfect features were suddenly clouded with emotion. "We were together for so long; I'd feel as if I was betraying him."

Samantha breathed a sigh of relief. At least she didn't have to worry about running into Beatrix in the barn.

"You'll change your mind next summer when we all go riding." Arthur smiled at Beatrix. "Nothing makes you feel more fit than a day spent on horseback."

Drew appeared from the hallway. He held two champagne bottles and he looked handsome in a navy blazer and white shirt.

"There you are," Arthur said, beaming. "I hope you picked the best champagne. It's Christmas, and there's so much to be grateful for."

Arthur looked happier than he had since Samantha arrived. She felt a small tug at her heart. No wonder Drew felt guilty. Arthur was obviously very fond of Beatrix.

"Beatrix was telling me about her new project, now that you're both back in New York." Arthur addressed Drew. "I'm impressed, I may have to put a little money behind it myself."

"It's early stages yet. But I'm already in talks with a factory in Thailand, and I'm looking at a small retail space in lower Manhattan," Beatrix said modestly. "I'm going to manufacture sustainably made handbags. All the workers at the factory will get a living wage and a percentage of the profits will go to assist Thai rice farmers. Did you know that with climate change, the farmers have to radically alter the way they grow rice? I got the idea when Drew and I were living in the village near Chiang Mai. There's no point in building schools if the parents can't afford to keep the children there. I haven't thought of a name for the company yet." Beatrix turned to Samantha. "You must be creative. Maybe you can come up with one."

Samantha flushed. She was trying to process Beatrix's idea. It was quite brilliant. Like when Sloane Parker stopped Hans Becker from stealing ten million dollars' worth of gold from a gold mine in Mongolia. First, Sloane made Hans distribute a million dollars' worth of gold among the miners, then she turned the rest over to the Mongolian government. Mongolia had oodles of gold; the government wouldn't miss a few gold bricks. And the miners were grossly underpaid.

"Samantha is an author," Drew cut in. "She doesn't name brands."

"Arthur was telling me about the Sloane Parker books," Beatrix purred. "I'll have to read one. I mostly read biographies and memoirs. They're so inspiring."

Arthur took Beatrix to meet the other guests. Drew turned to Samantha.

"Beatrix didn't tell me she was coming. She just appeared."

Samantha tried to think of something to say.

"She's very beautiful," she said awkwardly. "You must be happy she's here."

Drew fiddled with his drink. "About the Christmas parade tonight—"

"Don't worry about me," Samantha cut in. Her face broke into a smile. "I'll probably drink too much champagne to go anyway. Suddenly, I'm very thirsty."

Samantha was relieved to be seated at the opposite end of the table from Drew and Beatrix. On her right was a woman in her forties named Gladys whose ten-year-old daughter was a budding author. Gladys's husband was an old fraternity brother of Arthur's and this was their first trip to Jackson Hole.

"Audrey's teacher says she has real talent," Gladys said to Samantha over a forkful of glazed ham. "Perhaps I could e-mail you her latest story. Audrey would love to get a professional opinion."

Arthur stood up before Samantha could answer. An open bottle of champagne stood in front of him.

"I'm thrilled you could all be in Jackson Hole this week," he began. "You've all been to enough of my house parties to know that the only drawback of coming is having to listen to my after-dinner speeches."

Everyone laughed and Arthur waited to continue.

"Tonight's speech might be even more grueling because you have to listen to me boast." He turned to Drew. "What father wouldn't make a fuss about his son and soon-to-be daughter-in-law back in New York at last. Men build their businesses for a number of reasons. Some want wealth, others are hungry for power, a few have wives who don't want them puttering around the house." Arthur paused among more laughter. "I've always had two goals: to share the joy of reading with as many people as possible, and to have something to pass on to my son." He raised his champagne glass. "The date and location of the wedding are up to the bride and groom, but I wanted to give them a special engagement present. What better time to announce it than at Christmastime, surrounded by friends?"

Samantha glanced at Drew. Drew's cheeks were pale and he was gripping his wineglass uncomfortably.

"Drew and Beatrix," Arthur said, nodding at them. "For the last five years, you've been crisscrossing the globe, making the world a better place. But even young love needs roots to flourish. I'm giving you my house in Connecticut. I hope it will be the scene of many happy occasions like this one. And don't worry about preparing a guest room for me." There was a twinkle in his eyes. "I already started moving my things into the apartment above the garage."

There were gasps around the table. Samantha knew from Charlie that the Connecticut house had won some kind of industry award for being completely green. It was decorated by a well-known designer and featured in *Fine Homes* magazine.

Beatrix jumped up and kissed Arthur briefly on the cheek. Drew shook his father's hand and gave him an awkward hug.

Samantha tried to concentrate on the conversation around her, but she couldn't help glancing at Drew. She couldn't tell what he was thinking. His head was down and he was pushing his mashed potatoes around his plate.

"Arthur says you're a writer," the woman across from her was saying. "I have this wonderful idea for a book. I know it would be a huge bestseller," she gushed to Samantha. "Perhaps we could discuss it over coffee."

Samantha pulled her eyes back to her plate. She wished more than anything she was in her own apartment. Socks would be nuzzling his Rudolph plush toy and "Last Christmas" would be playing on Spotify. But Arthur was the reason she was a published author and these people were his guests. If she wanted to afford her Spotify subscription and Socks's monthly order of extreme chew toys, she had to be polite.

She ate a bite of squash and smiled at the woman. "Of course, I can't wait to hear all about it."

After dinner, Arthur insisted everyone attend the torch parade in Teton Village. Samantha made sure she was in a different car than Drew and Beatrix. When they arrived, she slipped off by herself.

The village was more festive than Samantha had seen it yet. The ice-skating rink was lit up with colored lights, and giant candy canes were wrapped in red bows. Carolers dressed in pioneer costumes strolled around the square and children waited in line to sit on Santa's sleigh.

A woman sat by herself at one of the outdoor tables. She was in her late forties and wore a long overcoat and suede gloves. She took off her hood and Samantha recognized her. It was the woman from the gift store who had lent her the arrowhead necklace.

"Marigold." She walked over and joined her. "It's nice to see you."

Marigold glanced up. It took a moment for her to recognize Samantha. Then her face opened in a smile.

"It's nice to see you too, please sit down." Marigold waved at the bench. "I almost didn't come this year. It's beginning to feel like a snowy version of Main Street in Disneyland," she said. "It will be worth it when the ski patrol starts down the mountain. It's like watching a ballet."

"What a pretty coat." Samantha admired the bright colors and long fringes. "I've never seen anything like it."

"It was handmade by a Native American artisan, they sell them at Beaver Creek Hats and Leather," Marigold replied. "These days, we have down parkas and thermal underwear to stay warm. For centuries, Native Americans didn't have anything like that. They became very skillful at keeping out the cold," Marigold continued. "The men wore jackets and hats made from buffalo hide, and the women had deerskin leggings."

"I can't imagine anyone in Brooklyn walking around in deerskin leggings," Samantha said, laughing.

"I suppose not," Marigold agreed. She noticed Samantha's necklace. "You're wearing the arrowhead pendant."

"I've hardly taken it off," Samantha acknowledged. "The strangest thing happened yesterday. An icicle almost landed on my head. It missed me at the last minute. I couldn't help but wonder if . . ." Her voice trailed off.

Suddenly, she felt silly. The arrowhead didn't have magical powers. It had been a coincidence.

"There's nothing to wonder about," Marigold returned. "I told you the arrowhead protects the wearer from danger."

Samantha twisted the pendant. All day she had felt lighter. As if she was part of things, instead of standing anxiously on the sidelines. Perhaps the arrowhead was responsible for her new confidence.

"I don't know how to thank you," Samantha said.

"It's my pleasure. Even the strongest people sometimes need help." Marigold nodded. "It reminds me of one of my favorite legends. There was a farmer with a wife and two children. He worked very hard to give his family enough to eat. One year, there was an early frost and his crop was ruined. He made a small fire and offered tobacco to the Master of Life. He told him he'd always been grateful for his blessings, but now he was stuck.

"The Master of Life gave him special seeds and told him to plant them. The next morning, the frost had gone and the weather was as warm as summer. For the next few weeks, the weather stayed warm and the seeds grew into corn and beans. Then as quickly as the summer weather came, it disappeared and the long winter began. But the farmer and his family had enough to eat all winter," she finished. "You see, it's all right to ask for help. We can't always do everything alone."

Samantha recalled the hours she spent with her therapist after Roger left. Dr. Gruber counseled that Samantha had to learn to rely on herself. Maybe it was all right to love her career but want a marriage and a family too. To enjoy her nights watching Netflix with Socks, while still missing trying new Italian restaurants with Roger. She knew she could eat at a restaurant alone, but it wasn't the same as spending time in the company of someone she loved. The wine served by the glass was never as good as wines sold by the bottle, and she couldn't sample different types of pasta when she was by herself.

"I never thought about it like that," Samantha said slowly.

"Native Americans are very wise. They learned from watching the animals in the forest. Animals have to help each other to survive." She smiled at Samantha. "What better time for people to help one another than Christmas?"

"I would do anything for my dog, Socks, and sometimes I think he would do anything for me." Samantha nodded. "Last October, I took Socks apple picking. I told him to stay with me but he ran straight into a patch of poison oak. I carried him all the way to the car. By the time we got back to Manhattan, I was covered in itchy welts. And the other night, I had a terrible toothache. I think he knew I wasn't feeling great. He dragged the hot water bottle that he sleeps with onto my bed. I put it under my pillow and my tooth felt much better."

"There are many lessons we can learn"—Marigold smoothed her coat—"if only we're open to receiving them."

Music blared and Samantha turned her attention to the mountain. A dozen strobe lights illuminated the slopes and figures dressed in neon ski suits lined up on the ridge. The song changed to "All I Want for Christmas Is You" and the ski patrol started down the slope. Marigold was right, it was like a ballet. The torches turned the snow fluorescent colors and the whole mountain seemed to glow.

She turned back to Marigold but the bench was empty. She was about to go look for her when someone called her name.

It was Drew. He was walking toward her. He wore a green parka and navy après-ski boots.

"Drew," Samantha said awkwardly. She wondered if he noticed she was avoiding him. "Where's Beatrix?"

Drew waved at the mountain.

"She's with the ski patrol. She went night skiing."

"She's up there?" Samantha squinted into the lights. Clusters of skiers were following the ski patrol down the mountain.

"Beatrix has skied in Jackson Hole before, she knows the terrain well. And she's an excellent skier." Drew leaned against the bench. "She competed in the Junior Olympics."

Samantha wondered if there was anything Beatrix wasn't good at. She probably trained as a Cordon Bleu Chef and held an advanced degree in calligraphy or linguistics.

"I haven't skied since a field trip in high school," Samantha said. "It was a disaster. First, the bus broke down and we had to carry our skis the last half mile to the mountain. Then, it started snowing and our teacher made everyone come inside and sit in the lodge and play cards. I don't blame her now," Samantha said with a smile. "Who wants to chaperone a bunch of teenagers on a ski slope when you can sit by the fire and drink hot chocolate instead?"

"I'm not much of a night skier." Drew shrugged. He shuffled his feet. "To be honest, I'm happy to have time to think."

"What do you mean?" Samantha inquired.

"The scene at dinner, I felt like a jerk," Drew replied. "I accepted my father's gift when there may not even be a wedding. But I could hardly turn it down in front of his friends. And I didn't want to upset Beatrix."

"No, I suppose you couldn't," Samantha agreed.

"I wish Beatrix and I had a chance to talk first." Drew rubbed his gloved hands. "I've never seen my father so happy. Do you know the whole time I was growing up my father never brought women home? I always encouraged him, but he said he had me and his job. He didn't need anything else. He's done so much for me, I couldn't spoil his Christmas."

"It's a wonderful offer," Samantha said carefully. "Most couples would do anything for a house in Connecticut."

"It's a beautiful house, nothing like the penthouse in Manhattan," Drew sighed. "It's all oak floors and comfortable furniture and walls of books. The attic has a playroom, and there's a room off the kitchen just for wrapping paper."

No wonder Beatrix was still wearing her diamond ring. No single girl in New York was going to turn down a three-story house in Connecticut with its own wrapping paper room.

Drew kept talking. "At the publishing house, I'd have

a corner office and my own secretary. Expense account lunches with authors and agents, and book launches at trendy galleries. First, I'd be an assistant in marketing and publicity, then I'd learn production and distribution. I think I'd like marketing best; I enjoy problem solving and working on a team."

He dug his boots into the snow. His eyes clouded over and he hunched his shoulders.

"It's perfect unless what you want is to live in a tent in a Thai village," he continued. "In Thailand, I never slept past dawn. Some child always poked his head in to see if I had any more chocolate bars. And when I finished laying the foundation of the school, my hands were so caked in dirt, I couldn't see my fingers. But when I washed and sat down to a plate of pork with sweet chili and soy noodles, it tasted better than any steak frites I could eat in Manhattan."

Samantha took a deep breath. Drew had been so kind to her, she had to make him see the bright side.

"Beatrix's new company sounds really impressive," she said tentatively. "She could do a lot of good. And you could help schools in Manhattan. So many of them have no funding for libraries."

"Beatrix already has investors begging to see her prospectus," Drew acknowledged. "And I know all about the literacy problem at local schools. But it's just not where my passion is," he said. "My dream has always been to bring learning to children who've never seen the inside of a classroom."

Samantha understood. It was as if someone told her she had to write books about vampires instead of Sloane Parker books. There was nothing wrong with vampire books, she enjoyed reading them. But Sloane Parker was her passion.

She was about to answer when there was a popping sound. Big fizzy loops turned the sky pink and green, and shafts of gold sliced across the snow. Samantha craned her neck to see the silver pinwheels and the balls of bright orange diamonds. Suddenly one of the fireworks faltered and came tumbling down. She felt someone tugging her, and fell against Drew's chest.

"Are you all right?" Drew asked. "That firework almost landed on top of you."

Samantha glanced down at the ground. The firework was lying on the snow, giving off a faint acrid smell.

"I'm fine," Samantha said, realizing Drew still had his arm around her.

She hastily disentangled herself and brushed the snow from her jacket.

"That was a close one," Drew said, and whistled.

Samantha's hand went to the arrowhead pendant. She glanced around, wondering whether Marigold was still there. She had to tell her what happened.

"Drew, Samantha," a female voice called.

Samantha turned; it was Beatrix. She was dressed in head-to-toe pink. Her hood was rimmed with pink faux fur. Even her skis and boots were pink.

"Skiing was amazing, it reminded me how much I love skiing in Jackson Hole. You both should have come," Beatrix said, shaking out her hair. "I'm dying for a hot toddy. The bar at the Four Seasons is heavenly, will you join me?"

"I think I'll go back to the ranch," Samantha said.

"Do you want us to come with you? You had a bit of a scare," Drew wondered. He turned to Beatrix. "Samantha almost got hit by an unexploded firework."

The thought of sitting across from Beatrix while she

talked about the thrill of night skiing was more frightening than any firework.

Samantha set her face in a smile. "It's Beatrix's first night. You should stay and have fun."

Samantha sat on the bed in her guest room. She was going to change and take a bath. Charlie texted her a photo of Socks eating baked ham and turkey stuffing. At least one of them was enjoying Christmas night.

It wasn't that the entire evening was awful. Marigold had been fascinating to talk to, and the torch parade was dazzling. She hadn't even been afraid when the firework exploded; for some reason she'd known she'd be all right.

She tried to analyze why she was feeling unsettled. Was it because Drew kept his arm around her for an extra moment when she fell against him? Or how Beatrix managed to look gorgeous even when the only parts of her that were showing were her perfectly upturned nose and high cheekbones?

None of that mattered. Drew and Beatrix were engaged. No couple in New York gave up a six-figure income and a house in Connecticut. Especially not for sleeping bags and a tent infested with snakes in the mountains of Thailand.

Samantha glanced out the window at the fir trees blanketed in snow. The sky was black velvet and the stars were so bright and sparkly, they appeared to be made of tinsel. Suddenly she missed her apartment in Brooklyn. Christmas in Jackson Hole might resemble the inside of a snow globe, but there was no place like home.

Chapter Seven

It was midmorning the next day, and Samantha was taking Arthur's suggestion to borrow books from his library. It was the most spectacular space. She reached it by a spiral staircase, just like the staircase she once saw in a movie. In the movie, the staircase led up to a dusty old attic overflowing with books, and there was a secret manuscript that had been hidden for sixty years. It gave Samantha an idea for a Sloane Parker book. Sloane is in Rome, browsing at one of her favorite bookstores. A handsome dark-haired Italian enters and whispers something to the woman behind the counter. The dark-haired man glances around to make sure no one is watching, and climbs the circular staircase.

The man is Alfonso Bellini, the Italian computer hacker Sloane has been following for months. The bookstore is a front for a group of hackers who have infiltrated intelligence networks across Europe. The codes are stored in books and only the hackers can decipher them.

Alfonso is a known womanizer. Sloane is going to distract him with a little flirtation, then she's going to steal the code books.

Sloane is puzzled when Alfonso doesn't respond to her advances. It's only when she notices the manuscript on the desk that she discovers he isn't Alfonso. He's Alfonso's twin brother, Eduardo.

Eduardo is a struggling writer. Eduardo doesn't want his family to know about the manuscript because twenty-three publishers have already rejected it. He should be doing something worthwhile with his time, like working on his accounting certificate. Sloane feels sorry for him and puts him in touch with a publisher she knows in London. They end up having a discussion about Italian literature and Sloane leaves with a selection of books by writers she never heard of.

The spiral staircase in Arthur's library was the same dark wood, but the library itself was completely different. Two walls were floor-to-ceiling glass, and there was a coffee table and thick white carpet. Leather armchairs faced each other and the bookshelves were lined with books.

Samantha's phone buzzed and she answered.

"Samantha, it's Charlie," Charlie said when she answered. "I wanted to see if you're having a good Christmas."

"You mean you're checking up on me," Samantha replied, smiling. "I turned off the location tracker on my phone. I don't know why you insist on following me."

"I would never check your phone tracker," Charlie said indignantly. "And I already called Arthur to wish him a merry Christmas. He said you're having a wonderful time. You even went snowmobiling with everyone else."

Samantha wasn't going to tell Charlie about Marigold or the arrowhead pendant.

"Arthur is a great host, it's impossible not to have a good time," Samantha said truthfully. "I told you I wouldn't let you down."

"I'm glad." Charlie's voice grew serious. "I wanted to

warn you about something, in case you see it on social media. Arthur is in talks with Melody Minnow's agent for Melody to narrate a line of original audiobooks. Melody has a great voice; her agent is confident the audiobooks will be bestsellers."

Samantha heard Melody talk on a podcast once. She had one of those deep, throaty voices that some people found sexy but Samantha thought sounded as if Melody was recovering from a cold.

"Sloane Parker isn't available on audio," Samantha reminded Charlie. "So she won't be competition."

It was Samantha's decision to hold on to the audio rights for the Sloane Parker books so they wouldn't be produced. She was afraid that if the narrator gave Sloane the wrong accent—a Southern twang like Scarlett in *Gone with the Wind,* or something foreign like Anna Karenina—the reader wouldn't feel a connection with her. It was better to leave Sloane's voice to the reader's imagination.

"We should rethink that. Everyone listens to books on audio these days," Charlie suggested. "The marketing department is stepping up your campaign so you don't lose your edge. It's going to be called Extreme Sloane Parker, with images of you doing extreme sports: heli-skiing off a glacier in New Zealand, volcano surfing in Japan."

"Sloane would never surf in a volcano," Samantha protested. "Volcano ash is terrible for the skin."

"We could partner with a cosmetics company," Charlie offered. "Lancôme or Clinique might be interested."

Winter sun streamed on the bookshelf. Samantha recognized some of the books she loved: *Angels & Demons* by Dan Brown, *Gone Girl* by Gillian Flynn, a shelf devoted to John le Carré spy thrillers. She let out a sigh.

"Since when did reading stop being about checking

out your favorite books from the library and become about which heroine uses better moisturizer?"

"Publishers need to make a profit so we can all be paid," Charlie reminded her. "Thank god Emily's parents are taking care of the wedding, but I still need to come up with money for the honeymoon. Ever since we got engaged, Emily has dreamed of us going to Paris. Lately, she's been dropping hints. She made crepes for breakfast and there was a bottle of French cologne in my Christmas stocking."

Samantha and Roger used to talk about where they might go on a honeymoon. Samantha dreamed of visiting Tuscany and Roger wanted to ride in a gondola in Venice. Samantha teased him that he was a hopeless romantic. It was only when she scrolled through her Instagram that she noticed a partner at Roger's law firm posing in a gondola on the Grand Canal. Roger probably chose Venice so he could talk about it at the office.

Emily had been so good to Samantha. Emily chose the clothes to bring to Jackson Hole, and her parents were taking care of Socks over Christmas.

"I want Emily to have the perfect honeymoon," Samantha said. "I'll do whatever I need to keep book sales going."

"We'll talk about it later," Charlie replied cheerfully. "Just keep joining all the activities and making Arthur happy."

Samantha said goodbye and turned her attention to the bookshelf. Nothing would make her feel better than losing herself in the pages of a good book.

She pulled out a Vince Flynn thriller. The book next to it tipped over and she picked it up. It had a Japanese silk cover and was some kind of journal. She was about to put it back when she heard footsteps.

"Drew." She turned around. "I thought everyone was at breakfast."

"I already ate, I wanted to talk to you," Drew said, stepping off the staircase.

"Talk to me?" Samantha repeated, feeling slightly guilty. Arthur probably expected her to be at breakfast. But the thought of sitting across from Beatrix in one of her chic European parkas and hearing her talk about night skiing in Breuil-Cervinia, Italy, before Samantha even had her morning coffee was too much to bear.

"I wanted to thank you. I had a talk with Beatrix this morning," Drew said, sitting on an armchair. "It's because of something you said."

"Something I said?" Samantha racked her brain for anything she said about Drew and Beatrix.

"That Lady Chatterley gave up her grand estate to be with the gamekeeper," he continued. "When you're in love, you do anything for each other. An ultimatum is no way to solve things. Beatrix and I have to decide our future together."

"What about your father?" Samantha inquired. "He's counting on you to work with him and take over his position one day."

"My father could wait a few more years," Drew said pensively. "What's important is that Beatrix and I share the same goals. I want Beatrix to be happy more than anything, but she has to feel the same about me."

Drew looked so serious. His eyes seemed a darker blue, and his forehead knotted together.

"What did Beatrix say?" she asked.

"She didn't get a chance to say anything—my father knocked on the door and interrupted us," Drew sighed. "He didn't want us to miss Martha's maple pancakes." He knotted his hands. "We're going to discuss it after we all go dogsledding,"

"Dogsledding?" Samantha repeated, an uneasy feeling gripping her chest.

"Dogsledding is very popular in Jackson Hole. The guests have the opportunity to drive their own sled." Drew smiled. "Don't worry, the guide teaches us basic commands and the dogs are well trained. They're usually Samoyeds or Siberian Huskies."

Samantha pictured sled dogs as big and ferocious as wolves. A small animal would cross their path—a badger or a sweet little chipmunk—and the dogs would want to chase it. The sled would tip into deep, unplowed snow, and they'd all end up with soaked clothing and terrible cases of frostbite.

But Charlie had been insistent on the phone. She had to do whatever Arthur suggested.

Her hand went to the arrowhead pendant. She twirled it pensively and took a deep breath.

"I wouldn't miss it." She made her voice cheerful.

"Come down to the kitchen before we go." Drew stood up. "Martha saved you a stack of pancakes and there's a pot of fresh coffee."

The first part of the excursion went better than Samantha expected. Their guide had been a professional dogsledder for ten years and knew all there was to know about it. Guides were called mushers, and he led a team of 140 Alaskan racing tour dogs. The Alaskan racing dog was a descendant of the Siberian Huskies, but much gentler. Samantha immediately bonded with a dog called Alfie. Alfie had a white nose and his sad brown eyes reminded Samantha of Socks. She even took a photo of Alfie to send to Charlie to show Socks, but then deleted it from her phone. She didn't want Socks to become jealous because she was seeing other dogs.

The sky was a pale winter blue and the snow was as powdery as icing on a cake. Samantha didn't even mind the cold. She wore a red parka and a pair of waterproof boots she borrowed from the ranch's mudroom.

They stopped for lunch at the top of the trail. There were thermoses of hot soup, and they passed around bread and hunks of cheese. Perhaps next Christmas she could go dogsledding with her parents. She could even take Socks. She'd get him the doggy reindeer sweater she saw at the gift shop in Teton Village and a pair of booties.

After lunch, Beatrix insisted she wanted to drive the sled. Samantha tried to sit on a different one, but Beatrix's mouth formed a small pout.

"You have to come on my sled." Beatrix slipped her arm through Samantha's. "Drew is driving with his father; it would be more fun if you and I are together. I'm a great driver, I drove a sled in the Bavarian Alps." She gave a small laugh. "It was easy compared to steering the Porsche I rented in Munich. The Porsche was built for the racetrack, it had never been driven on the autobahn." Beatrix adjusted her mirrored sunglasses. "There's nothing to it. You simply trust your instincts."

Samantha reluctantly climbed on the sled and sat in the back. Beatrix gave the dogs a gentle pat and they set off down the trail. Samantha had to admit, Beatrix was a wonderful driver. She led the dogs with a combination of warmth and confidence that rivaled the professional mushers.

The calming motion of the sled combined with the familiar scent of the dogs' damp fur lulled Samantha into a new kind of happiness. Normally, in a situation like this, her fears of what could go wrong would consume her: she'd be bitten by a rabid dog and end up in the hospital, they'd be buried by an avalanche and no one would find them for days. Now those fears were strangely absent.

She was about to text a photo of the scenery to Charlie when the dogs started barking. Beatrix tried to quiet them. The lead dog was distracted by something in the distance. Suddenly, the sled lurched off the trail and careened down the hill.

Samantha watched anxiously as Beatrix leaned over the side and commanded the dogs to stop. They slowed and everyone sighed in relief. Then the dogs pulled free and the sled teetered and landed with a thud on its side.

Samantha brushed the snow from her jacket. She had fallen on soft snow and wasn't hurt. The other guests stood up and dusted off their parkas and boots. Only Beatrix remained on the ground. Her ankle was bent at a strange angle.

"Are you all right?" Samantha rushed over to her.

"A rabbit crossed the path. I should have known to avoid it." Beatrix's voice was muffled, as if she'd swallowed a mouthful of snow. "Some Alaskan racing dogs can't resist the smell of rabbit. It's like giving me a whiff of Chanel's Coco Mademoiselle."

"It wasn't your fault," Samantha assured her.

She wondered if Beatrix ever had to apologize for anything in her life. If Beatrix ever got so much as a parking ticket, the traffic cop would take one look at Beatrix's blond ponytail and full mouth and tear it up on the spot. This wasn't the time for petty jealousies. Beatrix was injured.

Samantha reached out her hand. "Try to get up."

Beatrix took Samantha's hand. Her face contorted into a grimace and she fell back on the snow.

"I can't, my ankle hurts," she said, wincing. "I'll have to wait until the other sled catches up."

Beatrix had been driving so fast, Drew's sled was far behind them. And Beatrix's parka was completely soaked. By the time the others arrived, Beatrix would be freezing.

Samantha unzipped her parka.

"Here, put on my parka." Samantha handed it to her. "And you can wear my gloves. Yours are ruined."

Beatrix glanced at her gloves, as if she'd just noticed the rip in the soft, Italian leather.

"You don't have to worry about me," Beatrix said firmly. "Once in St. Moritz, I cross-country skied from Corvatsch to Corviglia. The trail was closed due to bad weather and by the time I arrived, I had a terrible case of frostbite. All it took was a couple of Brandy Alexanders and an hour in front of the fireplace, and I was fine."

Samantha thought briefly that her publisher should hire Beatrix for the Extreme Sloane Parker campaign. Beatrix wasn't afraid of anything.

But Beatrix definitely wasn't fine now. Her voice came out in the wrong octave and she was shivering.

"You don't sound fine and I don't need my gloves." Samantha pulled off her gloves. She managed a smile. "I'll stand here and do jumping jacks until help arrives."

By the time the other sled appeared, Samantha's lips were blue with cold and she couldn't feel her fingers. Someone handed her a jacket and she was bundled onto the sled. Then she closed her eyes and didn't open them until the sled stopped in front of the ranch.

Hours later, Samantha stood in the hallway outside Beatrix's guest room. Arthur's doctor left and Drew came to find Samantha to tell her that Beatrix wanted to see her.

"Come in," Beatrix instructed when Samantha knocked.

Beatrix was propped against the headboard. Samantha had somehow expected her to resemble an invalid in a 1940s movie: The heroine's face would be perfectly made up with blond ringlets framing her cheeks like an angel. She'd be wearing some sexy silk camisole and be surrounded by bouquets of flowers sent by her admirers.

But Beatrix's skin was pale and there was a bruise under her eye. Her hair hung limply at her shoulders and Samantha couldn't help but notice the dark roots.

"Please sit." Beatrix waved at an ottoman. "I wanted to thank you."

"I didn't do anything," Samantha said, and shrugged. "Anyone would have given you their jacket."

"No one else did," Beatrix pointed out. She moved gingerly. "The doctor said it's a nasty sprain. A day in bed, and I'll be fine."

"When my father sprained his ankle, my mother applied hot compresses every two hours during the night," Samantha offered. "By the morning, the pain was almost gone."

"Drew and I aren't staying in the same room. Arthur is old-fashioned that way." Beatrix colored slightly. "Actually, I'm glad." She glanced at Samantha and her eyes seemed larger. "Drew and I are having a little communication problem. It's nothing serious. I wondered if you could talk to him."

"About what?" Samantha asked incredulously.

Samantha's voice sounded odd even to herself. As if she were Alice in Wonderland asking the rabbit which way she should go.

"Drew likes you," Beatrix continued. "He talks about you all the time. He might listen to you."

Samantha flashed over her private moments with Drew. When he told her a story on the plane so she wouldn't be nervous during takeoff. Drew offering to share his table at the Bunnery. Drinking hot chocolate together at the General Store. She pushed these thoughts away. This wasn't the closing montage of a romantic movie, and the diamond engagement ring was still securely on Beatrix's finger.

"What do you want me to talk to him about?" Samantha brought her mind back to Beatrix.

"Drew wants to keep traveling and building schools for the next few years. His father wouldn't support him, but it's not only about the money. My parents can be quite generous, they think Drew is the perfect son-in-law." She fiddled with the comforter. "I'm going to be thirty-one in March. I'll be thirty-five by the time we're living back in New York and can try for a baby. It might not happen."

"Thirty-five is young for getting pregnant these days," Samantha cut in.

"There are fertility issues in my family. Even if I got pregnant easily, how many children could we have before I'm forty?" Beatrix persisted, inspecting her nails anxiously. "I'm an only child and I've always dreamed of a big family. Pinkie Pie was my favorite My Little Pony because she had four siblings. And my mother bought me the whole range of American Girl dolls because I didn't want my first one, American Girl Courtney, to sit on the shelf alone."

Samantha's parents could never even afford one American Girl doll. Samantha had loved American Girl movies, but that was the closest she'd come to ever owning one.

Samantha had watched *Grace Stirs Up Success* after Roger left and she was feeling nostalgic, and almost moved to Paris herself to start a bakery. Recently she and Socks curled up and watched *Lea to the Rescue*.

Lea travels to the Brazilian rain forest to rescue her older brother and save exotic animals at the same time. Lea's character was a wonderful role model for young girls. And the movie plot gave her an idea for a Sloane Parker book.

"You and Drew need to decide on things together," Samantha suggested. "That's what a relationship is about."

Beatrix rolled her eyes. For a moment she was the old Beatrix, brash and full of confidence.

"You know what men are like. Deep down, they're all stubborn little boys." She twisted her diamond ring. "Drew needs to be pointed in the right direction. If I do it, I'm the nagging girlfriend. If you bring it up to him, you're a concerned friend."

"We're hardly friends," Samantha protested. "We met three days ago."

Beatrix's forehead creased. She really had wonderful skin for being thirty, and it must be natural. If she used Botox, she wouldn't be able to frown.

"Please, Samantha. I felt so close to you this afternoon, you practically saved my life. And I can't wait and I don't have anyone else to ask," Beatrix pleaded. "If Drew says anything to his father, well, there might not be any turning back."

Samantha took in Beatrix's pained expression. Everyone needed a friend. Without Charlie dragging her out of her endless rotation of James Bond movies mixed with the saddest romantic movies on Netflix—the ones where the hero or heroine has some terminal disease that isn't revealed until the final scene—Samantha may never have recovered after Roger left.

"All right," Samantha offered. "I'll do my best."

Beatrix reached for a glass of water.

"I don't know how to thank you," she gushed.

Beatrix flipped her hair over her shoulders and picked up the nail file on the bedside table.

"There's something special about you," she said knowingly. "From the moment I saw you, I knew we'd become friends."

Samantha sat at the dressing table in her room. It had been two hours since she and Beatrix talked. Dinner was in an hour, and she had to get dressed and do her makeup.

She still couldn't believe that Beatrix had confided in her and asked for her help with Drew. Yet, in a way she understood. Samantha had seen Beatrix at her most vulnerable; situations like that often created an instant bond. Samantha used a similar plot device in an upcoming Sloane Parker book.

Sloane gets bitten by a deadly snake at an ashram in India. While she's waiting for the medic to arrive with the antivenom medicine, she asks the female yogi she met only days earlier to tell Raj, the sexy computer programmer she's falling for, that they can't be together. Raj doesn't want children and Sloane's brush with death made her realize that one day, when she retires from British Intelligence, she'll want a family of her own. The female yogi suggests that Sloane wait until she's recovered and tell Raj herself, but Sloane insists he needs to know now. Raj is so handsome and charismatic, she's afraid she won't go through with it.

And Samantha understood how Beatrix felt. Having children was the most important thing in the world. Samantha couldn't imagine missing out on eventually getting married and starting a family.

But she had no idea what she was going to say to Drew,

or when she would find a moment to talk to him. Would he listen to her? What about her own growing feelings for him? She had been suppressing them because of the situation, but she couldn't deny the bolt of electricity when their arms touched, or how seeing him across the room made her happy.

Drew considered her merely a friend. And Marigold said Christmas was the perfect time to help others.

For the third night since she arrived, she wished she was home in Brooklyn with Socks. This time it was for a completely different reason.

Chapter Eight

The next morning, Samantha gazed out the window at the falling snow. The sky was a steel gray and a sharp wind rattled the branches. The minute anything appeared—a car heading up to the ski slopes, a deer crossing the field—it was obscured by a thick white curtain.

It was one of those mornings that were magical at a ski resort but would have been impossible in Brooklyn. At home, the sidewalks would be as slippery as a skating rink and taking Socks for his morning walk would mean digging out Samantha's proper boots from the hall closet. The moment she piled on her parka, her phone would ring and she'd get unbearably hot standing in the living room in so many layers. By the time she walked around the block, the snow would have turned to sleet, and her hands would be frozen from holding Socks's wet leash.

In Jackson Hole, the weather meant a lazy day tucked up in the ranch. Fires were lit in every fireplace and there was fresh coffee and hot chocolate in the kitchen. Dozens of movies were available in the home theater, and Samantha could see the steam rising from the outdoor hot tub.

She tapped on her computer and then snapped it

closed. Even with the cozy weather, she couldn't concentrate on her writing. She kept thinking about Beatrix's request and what she would say to Drew.

There wasn't a chance at dinner last night to bring it up, and Drew went skiing early this morning. It was Arthur's idea that Samantha and some of the guests who were less experienced skiers stay at the ranch. The conditions were precarious and he didn't want anyone getting hurt.

Samantha noticed the books she had borrowed from Arthur's library. She had slipped them in her purse when Drew came upstairs and forgot to return them.

The journal really was pretty with its Japanese silk cover.

She turned to the first page and was surprised to find it must have belonged to a young woman. It was written in red ink and the cursive had little hearts over the i's. The date on the first page was June 1991.

She closed it guiltily and placed it on the coffee table. Then she thought of the Nancy Drew books she devoured when she was a girl. Nancy Drew was the most capable sleuth in literature: more skilled than Agatha Christie's Hercule Poirot and Arthur Conan Doyle's Sherlock Holmes. At least, Sherlock Holmes had Watson to help solve crimes. Hercule Poirot was older and more experienced than Nancy Drew, but Nancy Drew was just as accomplished.

Nancy Drew was still in high school and she solved mysteries that baffled adults in River Heights. She wouldn't let a thirty-year-old journal go unread. She'd dive in and uncover something important: the solution to a decades-old feud or the answer to a riddle that had gone unsolved for years.

Samantha picked up the journal. It wouldn't hurt to

skim a few pages. It would distract her from deciding what to say to Drew, and she might get an idea for a new Sloane Parker book.

Dear Diary,

How many diaries are there that don't start with "I'm in love." Trust me, never have those words been truer. If you knew me better (and you will—I promise to write regularly), you'd know I don't fall in love easily. In fact, I'm against it. High school graduation was only a month ago and I have my whole life ahead of me. Why would I give in to something that takes up my time when I can concentrate on important things: one glorious summer working on the dude ranch and veterinary school in the fall.

But I couldn't help falling in love. Dutch is handsome and sophisticated; he makes the local Jackson Hole men seem like little boys. I didn't think that when we first met. He seemed like the most arrogant man ever. Dutch isn't even his name, it's his nickname. You'll laugh when I tell you how he got it.

I was standing in the ranch's kitchen, making breakfast. I can't face the day without three scrambled eggs, toast, and bacon. Dutch entered and sat at the long, wooden table.

"I'll take my eggs over easy, with four slices of bacon," he said to me. "And coffee would be nice. Two sugars, extra cream."

"The eggs are in the fridge." I pointed to the double fridge. "And you're welcome to some bacon. The stove is a bit tricky; you have to blow on it to turn on the gas."

He rubbed his forehead, perplexed.

"I thought you'd make it for me."

I turned around. I couldn't help but notice that he was good-looking. His light brown hair was cut short and his eyes were the color of honey. He had broad shoulders and an athlete's long legs.

"Why would you think that?" I questioned.

"I'm the new ranch hand. The woman in charge said a girl works here, so you're obviously the cook. A hot breakfast is provided."

"It is provided, Alice makes the meals. On Alice's day off, everyone makes their own breakfast," I explained. "I'm a tour guide, I lead the tourists on horseback rides."

He studied me critically.

"You couldn't possibly be a guide," he said. "The horses are twice as big as you."

I pulled myself up to my tallest height. 5'6" in my stocking feet.

"I'm tall for a girl," I said indignantly. "And I've known most of the horses since they were foals. We respect each other." I studied him right back. "You, on the other hand, have probably never worked on a dude ranch." I waved at his cowboy boots. "No experienced ranch hand would wear boots like that."

"These are handmade El Dorado boots." He stretched his legs. "I bought them at Jackson Bootery. They're the best boots they sell, the manager said they're made for working on a ranch."

I stifled a giggle. Then I put my hand over my mouth. It isn't nice to laugh at someone who just overpaid $200 for a pair of cowboy boots.

"I've known Jake, the manager, since he used to lead poker games in the high school parking lot," I replied. "He knows how to read people. He probably noticed the first-class plane ticket sticking out of your pocket and steered you straight to the El Dorados. If you had gone to Boot Barn, you could have had Stetson Outlaw Boots for half the price."

"How do you know I flew first-class?" he asked stiffly. "And you don't know what I paid for the boots." He smiled; his smile was really something. It made him resemble a movie star: wide and white and showing two dimples. "I'm good at looking out for myself."

I carried my plate to the table and sat beside him.

"I'm glad." I pointed at the stove. "Then you can fix your own breakfast. I have to eat and my first group arrives in thirty minutes."

He wanted to keep talking. At first, I was quiet. I like to get inside the head of the horses before the morning ride. He made bacon and offered me a piece. It was much better than mine. I tend to burn the edges and leave the middle soggy. His was crispy on the outside and juicy in the middle. So I asked him about himself. That way, I could keep eating.

He's from New York City and graduated from Columbia. He's working here for the summer and then starting business school. I told him I just graduated too; I didn't mention that it was from high school. His ego is already so big, if he knew he was talking to an eighteen-year-old girl who had never been east of the Teton River, it might explode.

"You haven't told me your name," he said, finishing his third cup of coffee.

"It's Diana," I replied. "You shouldn't drink so much coffee. It's bad for your heart, and the horses can tell if you're overstimulated. They respond better to calm direction."

He stirred a sugar cube into his coffee.

"Let me guess, you're studying to be a doctor," he said, raising his eyebrows.

I shook my head. "I'm going to be a veterinarian. Medical school takes too long, I don't want to start my life when I'm forty."

"We finally agree on something," he answered with a grin. "My parents wanted me to go to medical school. My father is a surgeon at Mount Sinai hospital. I refuse to be paying off school loans when I'm fifty. Two years of business school and then I'm starting my own company." He held out his hand formally. "My name is Dutch. Maybe we can have dinner tonight."

"No one is named Dutch." I giggled again. "Unless they're the male lead in a 1950s beach movie."

My mother says I have to stop giggling. Young women laugh, they don't giggle.

"It's my nickname, I got it freshman year." He shrugged. "I always made a girl pay for herself on a date."

"That's the most chauvinistic, self-centered thing I ever heard," I blurted out before I could stop myself.

"On the contrary, that way the girl knew where we stood," he countered. "There weren't any of those conversations about me being owed something because I bought her a burger." He went back to his plate of eggs. "You didn't answer my question. I don't know anyone else in Jackson Hole, but something tells me I've already met the prettiest, smartest girl in town. Will you have dinner with me?"

I couldn't help it. The way he looked at me was like no boy ever had. My knees went weak, there's no other way to describe it.

"Yes." I nodded solemnly. "I'll have dinner with you."

I took him to the Chuckwagon. He assumed I chose it because of its history. The Chuckwagon has been in business since 1948. The photos on the wall are of the original building with horses lined up outside, and not a car in sight.

But I picked it because Lianne, the hostess, promised me a free dinner in exchange for taking care of her cat when it had kittens. Dutch didn't have to know that. Let him believe I could afford the overpriced bison burgers.

"I have to admit, this looks delicious," he said, when the waiter set down our plates.

"It's buffalo meat, you won't find it anywhere but Wyoming," I answered, helping myself to a handful of onion rings. "It's better than those faddish dishes they serve at New York restaurants: focaccia with basil and pesto, and sun-dried tomato pizza."

"When were you in New York?" he asked curiously.

I flushed. How did I set myself up for that? Usually I controlled a conversation. He had a way of unmooring me, like a sailboat that slipped its anchor.

"Never. I haven't been out of the state," I admitted. "Tourists tell me about it. In Wyoming, people work too hard to exist on roots and vegetables; they need meat and potatoes."

"And onion rings." He smiled. "We didn't need to share a plate; you can order your own portion."

I dropped my hand from the plate.

"For some reason they taste better when they're shared," I said stiffly. It was time to change the subject. "Why are you in Jackson Hole?"

"I told you, to work at the ranch." He poured ketchup on his plate.

"Yes, but why?" I inquired. "Even without the cowboy boots, you don't look like you fit in."

He couldn't deny it. It was as if he'd walked straight out of an ad for men's cologne: white crewneck sweater, loafers without socks, blond streaks in his hair. His skin already had a new glow, he was going to tan easily.

He was quiet for a moment. Then he put down the ketchup bottle.

"The idea was to go somewhere I didn't fit in," he said. "Somewhere I could become someone new."

"What's wrong with who you are?" I wondered.

I scrunched my nose—another habit my mother doesn't approve of.

"Unless you're hiding something," I suggested. "You were expelled from university, or convicted of a felony."

He laughed. He had a nice laugh; it was confident, like everything about him.

"Neither of those things. I even donated part of my pay last summer to charity," he responded. "It's because of Thoreau."

"Thoreau?" I repeated, puzzled.

"Henry David Thoreau's experiment living on Walden Pond. He wanted to leave the overcivilized life and see if he could live off the land: 'I wanted to live deep and suck out all the marrow of life . . . to reduce it to its lowest terms, and publish its meaning to the world,'" Dutch recited. He looked at me carefully. "'Or if it were sublime, to know it by experience.'"

Until that I moment I thought he was the typical East Coast summer help. You know the type: he probably received a convertible at graduation, and his parents paid for his first apartment. He was here so he could talk about "horse wrangling" and "ironing a bull" to girls back in New York this fall.

But Dutch had a depth about him. I never read Thoreau but somehow, I knew what he was talking about.

"How do you find Jackson Hole so far?" I wondered. "Mean or sublime?"

Dutch looked at me with those brown eyes. From that moment I was completely lost.

"Sublime, of course," he said as if I should know his answer. "How could I not?"

We both ate silently. We followed the bison burger with Chuckwagon's famous deep-dish apple pie with buttercream topping.

"What about you?" he said, handing me a fork.

We had agreed to share the dessert. Not even I could finish off a piece of pie after the burger and onion rings.

"Where do you want to travel?" he asked me.

"Nowhere." I scooped up vanilla ice cream.

"All young people want to travel," he argued. "They want to visit cities like New York and Chicago. Or go to the West Coast and see the ocean. The sunset over the Pacific is like finding the treasure at the end of the rainbow. And there's a whole world outside of America: Paris and Rome for history, South America for music. Asia for thousands of years of knowledge."

"They sell postcards of cities, and I can read about history and music." I shrugged. "Where else can you wake up in the morning and see mountains and rivers? Where can you swim in glaciers in summer and ski on fresh powder during the winter? Not to mention the animals. You're as likely to run into a buffalo or deer in town as you are a friend," I finished. "Jackson Hole has everything I want. I'm happy here."

He started to say something and stopped. A smirk crossed my face and I glanced down at my plate. My mother said you never smirk in front of a boy, it was unladylike. For once, I was going to listen to her.

Dutch didn't argue with me. Who can argue with someone who's happy, when happiness is what people search for all their lives?

He took out his wallet and set down his credit card.

"What are you doing?" I asked.

He smiled that movie star smile again.

"I'm paying for your dinner. I'd like to see you again."

Samantha turned to the next page. There was a photo of a young woman on a horse. She had dark bangs and pigtails but Samantha could tell she was pretty. Her legs were long and shapely and she had a beautiful smile. There was something familiar about that smile.

The caption under the photo read: Grand Teton Dude Ranch, Summer 1991.

She closed the journal and placed it on the bedside table.

It was almost surprising to see the snow on the windowpane. She half expected to glance up and see Jackson Hole in the summer: green fields and forests thick with fir trees. Samantha always felt like that when she was immersed in writing. She'd hear Socks scratching to go out and think he was a baby leopard trapped in a hunter's cage. Or her phone would buzz and she expected the caller to be Phineas warning her that the take-out delivery guy was actually the errand boy for a sinister crime syndicate.

Who was Diana and how did her diary end up in Arthur's library? Nancy Drew would want to know more, and Nancy Drew would think of a way to find out.

Samantha had an idea. She grabbed a sweater and hurried downstairs to the mudroom to borrow a coat and boots.

Just crossing the driveway to the barn was colder than she had imagined. Inside, the air smelled of dry hay and the barn was pleasantly warm.

"Hello, Blixen." She reached into her pocket and took out four sugar cubes. "I brought you some sugar cubes, don't tell the other horses. If I took any more there wouldn't be enough for the guests' coffee. I promise to bring more tomorrow."

Blixen nuzzled her palm. He tipped his head back and swallowed the sugar.

"You really are a lucky horse, it's cozy in here," she said conversationally. "It's snowing so hard outside; you wouldn't be able to see your own nose."

Footsteps sounded behind her. She turned and Bruno stepped out of a stall.

"I thought I smelled perfume," Bruno said, smiling at her. "I didn't think anyone was brave enough to come out in this weather."

"I meant to bring Blixen some sugar for his birthday," Samantha replied. "I hope he doesn't mind that I'm late."

"Don't worry, my wife and I spoiled him." Bruno grinned. "I brought our Christmas leftovers: turkey and stuffing and apple pie for dessert. Blixen wasn't fond of the pie, but he loved the whipped cream topping."

Samantha laughed. She stroked Blixen's nose.

"I'm the same way. Every Christmas when I was growing up, my mother spent all day baking mince pies, but all I wanted was whipped cream in a bowl."

"It's too bad you aren't staying in Jackson Hole until the summer," Bruno mused. "You and Blixen would make a good pair. He loves having a rider who cares about him."

"That's the other reason I came out to the barn." Samantha warmed to her subject. "You said this used to be a dude ranch."

"For years," Bruno said, nodding. "It was called Snake Wheel Ranch."

Samantha was momentarily sidetracked from her questions. Why would anyone put the word "snake" in the name of a ranch? It was like an author using "spider" in a book title. It might attract a certain readership, but what about readers like Samantha who were afraid of spiders? They'd never pick it up.

"So, it wasn't the Grand Teton Dude Ranch?" Samantha inquired.

"The Grand Teton Dude Ranch was on the other side of town," Bruno recalled. "Dude ranches come and go. These days they're started by CEOs of tech start-ups who want to take their profits and try something different. Years ago, they were owned by the heads of movie studios who suddenly imagined themselves as cowboys. Most of them lasted one winter before deciding they'd rather run a sailing school in the Bahamas."

"Oh, I see." Samantha tried to keep the disappointment out of her voice. She had been sure that Arthur's ranch was once the Grand Teton Dude Ranch. "I thought this might have been the Grand Teton."

"Why the interest in dude ranches?" Bruno dragged his bucket to the next stall. "Are you going to set a book in Jackson Hole? Elaine tried to write a book about Jackson Hole once. She never got past the first chapter, she's not good at sitting for long periods."

"Writing is very mundane," Samantha agreed. "People think an author's life is riding around in limousines and preening on *Good Morning America*. Most writers spend their days in a bathrobe and slippers, glued to their computer."

Except for Melody Minnow. Melody mentioned in an interview that she slept naked. She probably didn't even own a bathrobe. Melody must dictate her books while riding a Peloton.

Setting a Sloane Parker book in Jackson Hole was a good idea. Samantha already had an idea for a plot. Sloane suspects that one of the guests at the dude ranch is Cliff Burbank, the head of a Ponzi scheme. She invites Cliff to play pool at Bull Moose Saloon. Cliff accepts and Sloane lets him win three straight games. She keeps plying him with Bull Moose vodka gimlets and he ends up boasting about separating unsuspecting senior citizens from their pensions. Sloane sends the phone recording to Phineas at British Intelligence and FBI agents are waiting for Cliff when he boards his private jet at Jackson Hole Airport.

Phineas is so pleased; he suggests Sloane spend an extra week at the ranch and enjoy herself. The only thing Sloane regrets is letting Cliff win at pool. Sloane became a champion billiard player while she was a Rhodes Scholar at Oxford and never lost a match.

"I'll consider it," Samantha responded, stroking Blixen's nose. "I came across something interesting, but it turns out it was merely a coincidence."

Bruno put down the bucket.

"I don't believe in coincidences, most things happen for a reason," Bruno reflected. "Like the way Elaine and I met. I was working over Christmas on the mountain. One night I asked a pretty blonde from California named

Suzy to go night skiing. At the last minute my mother called. She and my father had just driven into town and wanted me to have dinner with them." He smiled at his own story. "What would you do if you were a twenty-year-old male who was dying to share a chairlift with the girl of your dreams? But I could never say no to my mother, and they had driven two hundred miles to visit me. On the same night, the hostess at the Silver Dollar Grill was sick and her roommate, Elaine, filled in for her. Elaine was supposed to meet some guy to go night skiing too. But she couldn't let down her roommate. If Elaine and I had stuck with our plans, we wouldn't have ended up together." He picked up the bucket. "Coincidences don't exist. Everything important that happens in life is fate."

Or fate could string you along, giving little hints for three years that you found the person you're going to be happy with forever. Like when Roger stood Samantha up on their second date and she was determined to never see him again. It was only after she left Adrienne's Pizzabar in Midtown, where she had waited for an hour, and wandered into Joe's Pizza to get two pepperoni slices to go, one for her and one for Socks, that she found out what happened.

At first, she couldn't believe Roger was standing in line at Joe's Pizza in front of her. When she saw him, she almost walked out. But she was craving pizza, and she wasn't going to let some guy stop her from eating it twice in one night.

Then Roger noticed her. He quickly explained what happened. He'd lost Samantha's cell phone number. He called the receptionist at the PR firm to say that Adrienne's messed up his reservation and could they eat at

PizzArte instead. He waited at PizzArte for an hour and finally gave up. Now he was grabbing a pizza to go.

They marveled at how of all the take-out pizza places in Manhattan, they'd ended up in the same one. Then they took the pizza to her apartment and had a feast with Socks in front of the fireplace.

Or there were the years after Roger left. When she'd see a cute guy buying a John Grisham book at the bookstore or reaching for her favorite maple-syrup-flavored oatmeal at Trader Joe's and was positive they'd form an instant connection. There was always something wrong: the Grisham was a present for the guy's father, the oatmeal was on his girlfriend's shopping list. Samantha would continue her shopping and try not to feel disappointed. She didn't need love anyway, she had Socks and her writing.

Now Samantha brought her mind back to the present. The story she had built up in her head—that Arthur's ranch had been the Grand Teton Dude Ranch and the diary had sat here for thirty years—melted away. But who was Diana and why was her diary on Arthur's bookshelf?

"I wish that was true," Samantha said to Bruno.

Bruno opened the door of the next stall.

"It took me turning sixty to realize how little I knew when I was in my twenties," Bruno counseled with a smile. "The cowboys had it right. Life is an adventure, the best we can do is hang on and enjoy the ride."

Samantha stepped outside the barn as an SUV was pulling up in front of the ranch. Skiers piled out and she recognized Drew's green ski parka.

There wasn't time to mull over the diary. She had to

keep her promise to Beatrix and talk to Drew. The snow was coming down harder, and the wind sliced through her jacket. She instinctively touched the arrowhead pendant and crossed the courtyard to join him.

Chapter Nine

The ranch felt even warmer and more inviting now that the skiers had returned. The living room was full of guests. They sat around the fireplace in their snowflake sweaters, drinking mulled apple cider and recounting their adventures on the slopes.

Samantha was tempted to join them. Then she noticed Gladys, who at Christmas dinner wanted her to read her daughter Audrey's short story, and decided against it. She'd spend the afternoon hearing how Audrey's teacher said her writing was reminiscent of Louisa May Alcott, but with cell phones and social media.

Drew appeared from the kitchen. He was holding a mug and his eyes lit up when he noticed her.

"Samantha, I was hoping to find you," he said, and joined her. "Can we go somewhere and talk?"

"Somewhere to talk?" Samantha repeated.

She assumed Drew was going to tell her that he and Beatrix reached a compromise and already made up. Samantha felt an odd mixture of relief and disappointment. She told herself again that she was being silly. There was nothing between her and Drew. He considered her a friend.

She followed him into the game room. There was a

Ping-Pong table, a billiard table, and a table for chess and backgammon.

"My parents would love this room," she said, smiling. "My mother has to get out the folding table every week for their bridge games. Half the time, the legs don't open properly and she spends the next hour fixing it. Then she rolls her eyes and says she has to do everything: set up the table and prepare the snacks."

"Your mother sounds very capable," Drew said, and she could hear the envy in his voice.

"She always said girls can learn to do anything," Samantha said, nodding. "When I was twelve, she signed me up for a summer robotics camp because the boys in the robotics class at school were getting all the attention." Samantha laughed at the memory. "The teacher was surprised when I built a NAO humanoid robot before she explained it to the class."

"I don't even know what that is." Drew grinned. He looked at her appreciatively. "I wanted to thank you for giving Beatrix your jacket yesterday. If it weren't for you, she would have been in a lot worse shape."

"It was nothing." Samantha shrugged. "How is she?"

"I checked on her before I went skiing, she was asleep." Drew ran his fingers over the mug. "I haven't been upstairs yet." He looked at Samantha. "I just received an e-mail; I don't know what to do about it."

"What kind of e-mail?" Samantha wondered.

"From Kaman in the village near Chiang Mai." Drew took out his phone. He read out loud.

Dear Mr. Drew,
I apologize for interrupting your Christmas holiday with this e-mail. But before you left, you said

to reach out to you if I needed anything. At first, I didn't know how because there was a storm, and the village is without internet. So, I hitch-hiked to Chiang Mai and walked into the Four Seasons Hotel. The general manager was about to throw me out, even though I wore the slacks and sweater you gave me. I even washed my face with soap so I smelled good enough for a fancy hotel.

I told him that Mr. Drew and I had afternoon tea at the Four Seasons, and I needed to send you an urgent message. He must have taken pity on me because he let me use the computer. I have to write quickly, in case he changes his mind.

The plans for the school are not going forward. I heard my mother talking about it, and then the next day, all the workers were gone. Now the foundation sits there. By next year's monsoon season, all your hard work will be washed away.

I wouldn't say anything just for me, I'm thir-teen and soon I'll have to leave school and work. But I think about my younger brothers and sis-ter. They have a chance to learn in a classroom with a blackboard and books. I can't let that slip away.

My mother would be furious if she knew I contacted you. You are a rich, important Ameri-can, you have your own life to worry about. I know you better than she does. You would be disappointed if I didn't keep my promise to take my mother to afternoon tea at a fancy hotel when I grow up. I'll never be able to do that without go-ing to school.

I don't know if you can do anything from America, but I thought you'd want to know.

Please give my regards to your lovely girlfriend.

Warmest regards,
Kaman

Drew stopped reading. He placed his phone on the table.

"I taught Kaman how to write a letter," he said. "His punctuation is perfect."

Samantha realized there were tears in Drew's eyes.

"He's a lovely writer," she said, feeling a lump in her throat. "How can that happen to the school? There must be someone in charge."

Drew paced around the room. He slipped his hands in his pockets.

"All it takes is for someone to pocket the money and the whole thing shuts down." His brow creased together. "The only way to fix it is to go back to Thailand and supervise the construction myself. How can I do that if Beatrix refuses to come, and if my father is already picking out my office furniture?" He turned back to Samantha. "I can't disappoint Kaman when his future depends on it."

Drew reminded her of herself whenever she visited an animal shelter. She wanted to take home every dog: the beagle whose tail wagged faster than a windshield wiper, the golden retriever mix who was so big, his paws hung out of the cage.

"You said you were going to talk to Beatrix after you went dogsledding," she reminded him.

"We never did." He shrugged. "Now it's even worse. Don't you see? Yesterday, she really hurt herself. But a big black car whisked her back to the ranch, and an hour later the doctor made a house call. Now she's recovering in a soft bed with hot soup served on a silver tray and a cabinet of medicines to make her feel better. If the same thing happened in Thailand, she'd be shivering in a tent. Her ankle would hurt for days, and the only medicine would be some aspirin dug out of my suitcase that was probably expired because we'd been traveling for so long and I always forget to replace it."

"Yes, I see," Samantha said doubtfully. She thought about her promise to Beatrix.

"Someone must be able to take over the building of the school," Samantha tried again. "You can't take on all the responsibility yourself."

"It will simply become another failed attempt," he sighed. "I shouldn't take it personally. There are dozens of villages like it scattered over northern Thailand." He picked up his phone. "But this e-mail is personal. Kaman wrote to me; how can I ignore him?"

"Perhaps when Beatrix is better . . . ," Samantha said, and stopped.

This was harder than Samantha imagined. How could she keep her promise to Beatrix and counsel Drew at the same time?

Samantha believed in what Drew was doing. But Beatrix had a point. It was impossible to start a family while Beatrix and Drew were traipsing around the globe, cooking on a camp stove and washing their clothes in a river.

She tried to imagine facing a similar situation with Roger. There was a time when they would have solved it together. They'd sit in Central Park and hash out the pros and cons. Eventually they'd find a solution. Samantha would feel that familiar thrill of knowing they could do anything.

Roger hadn't even given her the chance to decide

their future. He simply sold his snow boots on eBay and moved to California.

"What would you do if you were me?" Drew asked.

Samantha pulled her mind from her thoughts. "It has nothing to do with me."

"Yes, but on the plane, you said you were afraid of everything," Drew persisted. "But you still flew to Jackson Hole. And you're doing things you don't want to do."

Samantha couldn't tell Drew about the arrowhead pendant. Somehow, she felt it would only keep working if she kept it private.

"I had to come, your father insisted," Samantha reminded him. "I didn't want Charlie's job to be in jeopardy."

"That's the thing," Drew said urgently. "You did it for other people, even though it made you uncomfortable."

Samantha shifted in her chair. She tried to think of what to say.

"Staying for a week at a luxurious ranch in Jackson Hole is different than spending years sleeping in a tent with snakes and spiders," she responded.

"Say you developed feelings for someone. It was completely unexpected, you thought you'd be single for ages and could live your life any way you pleased," Drew said slowly. "Then you meet this person who is so bright and lovely, almost overnight her happiness becomes as important to you as your own. Wouldn't that make a difference?"

"I don't know," Samantha said, and gulped. It was as if Drew was talking directly to her, and not discussing Beatrix at all.

He looked so handsome standing in front of the fireplace. His cheeks glowed from the day's skiing and his shoulders were broad under his ski sweater.

"That's how I felt when I met Beatrix," he continued, breaking the spell. "We met at the airport in Jakarta. She was so beautiful with that blond hair tumbling down her shoulders. She was wearing an orange dress that she bought at an outdoor market. Beatrix is very good at haggling with vendors. I remember thinking she probably wouldn't want anything to do with me. I hadn't bathed in days and I was wearing clothes that had been through two rainstorms and a ride in an open jeep.

"Our plane got delayed and the airline put us up at a hotel. We sat in the hotel bar, drinking rice wine called Tuak and talking about our travels. Beatrix had been in Bali. She wanted to introduce me to betutu—it's a Balinese dish that was the Balinese king's favorite meal. The hotel didn't serve it, so we found a rickshaw that would take us to a Balinese restaurant.

"I protested the whole way. We had to wake up early the next morning, we should eat at the hotel and go straight to bed. Beatrix laughed and said exploring the city was half the fun. The cab finally let us off at a diner. I was so hungry by then, I would have eaten the raw pork legs hanging in the window. I'm glad I listened to her. The betutu was the best thing I ever tasted: duck stuffed with peanuts and chili and spices. The duck takes eight hours to bake and it's served with perkedel, which is fried mashed potatoes."

Drew ran his hands through his hair. His eyes had a faraway look.

"I'd never met a woman like Beatrix. She was spirited and confident and up for anything," he finished. "Now her thirst for adventure has been replaced by a desire for one of those vacuum cleaners you command and it cleans your whole house."

Samantha felt a twinge of regret. She'd never drink

rice wine with a stranger in a hotel bar, or career through a foreign city in a rickshaw. Even if she believed the arrowhead pendant protected her, what if it failed and she was in another country, miles from home?

"My mother bought herself a Dyson vacuum cleaner last Christmas," Samantha said with a smile. "It changed her life."

Drew's expression was so anguished, Samantha felt bad for making a joke.

"Perhaps it's not a vacuum cleaner she wants, or even a house," Samantha said. "Maybe Beatrix wants a family. When you reach your thirties, you start wanting children more than anything. Sharing all the special moments with the man you love: the baby's first steps, hearing his first words, his first day of kindergarten."

Samantha bit her lip, wishing she could take back the words. Drew's mother left before he was old enough to start school.

"I'm sorry," she said, flustered. "I didn't mean—"

"No, you're right," Drew said heavily. "I want a family too. But I couldn't love a child more than I love Kaman and the other children in the village. How can I turn my back on him when he needs me? Isn't that what having children is about?"

Samantha was about to respond when the door opened.

"Samantha, Drew," Arthur said, entering the game room. "I was hoping I'd find you."

"I was telling Samantha about today's skiing," Drew improvised. "It was completely white out there, you couldn't see the tram."

Arthur walked over to the window.

"It's magical, isn't it?" Arthur glanced outside. "In Connecticut during a snowstorm, the snowplows come and by the following day the sidewalks are neat and orderly. In Jackson Hole, by tomorrow it will resemble a fairy tale. And it's so quiet, just us and the squirrels in the forest."

Samantha thought about the buffalo and the bears. But she didn't say anything. She didn't want to spoil Arthur's mood.

"I was going to take a tray up to Beatrix," Drew said, picking up his mug.

Arthur walked over to Drew.

"Would you mind doing it, Samantha?" he asked, patting Drew on the shoulder. "Drew and I have some business to discuss. I want to tell him about the spring book titles."

"Of course." Samantha stood up. She smiled at Drew and Arthur. "I'll see you at dinner."

Beatrix was reclining against the pillows when Samantha entered her guest room. Beatrix looked completely different than yesterday. The bruise on her cheek was concealed by makeup and she wore eye shadow and lipstick. Her hair had been washed and was back to its glorious shade of blond. Even her nails had fresh polish.

"Samantha!" Beatrix exclaimed, pleased to see her. "Angela just left and I feel much better. If it didn't hurt to stand up, I'd be good as new."

"Angela?" Samantha questioned, placing the tray on the bedside table.

"Arthur sent her, he's so thoughtful. Just like Drew." Beatrix beamed. "Angela works at a beauty salon in Jackson Hole. She did my hair and makeup and nails." Beatrix waved her hand in the air. "I told Arthur this morning that I didn't need pampering. He said it's impossible to be spoiled during Christmas, that's what the season is about." Her eyes seemed to become even larger. "Don't tell Arthur but I gave her an extra tip myself. Angela has a nine-year-old daughter, Penelope, who spends Christmas with her ex-husband in Utah. Now Angela will be able to afford the new snowboard that Penelope has been wanting when she returns home."

Beatrix continued to surprise her. Underneath that glamorous exterior, the hair that was now the color of butter with a hint of gold, the skin that was so smooth, it was almost sparkly, she genuinely cared about other people.

"Drew wanted to bring up the tray, but Arthur asked me to do it." Samantha pointed to the tray. "There's soup and bread and hot tea."

"That's wonderful, I'm ravenous." Beatrix sat up higher, her hair fanning out against the headboard. "First, I want to hear about Drew. Did you talk to him?"

Beatrix looked so much better. If Samantha told her about Kaman, she may feel bad all over again.

"I told Drew you wanted a family," Samantha said instead. "He wants a family too."

"I knew you'd get through to him." Beatrix's eyes shone. "I can't thank you enough."

"I didn't say much." Samantha's cheeks turned hot. "I just—"

"You don't have to say much, you have this way about you," Beatrix gushed. "You're so steady." Beatrix studied her fingernails. "I had a thought, it's the most wonderful idea in the world!"

"What kind of idea?" Samantha asked anxiously, hoping it didn't involve having to tell any more little white lies.

"I've always hated large weddings; it seems such a waste to have a big reception. The photographer is always pulling the bride and groom away and there's barely time to talk to the guests. You spend all that time choosing floral arrangements and sampling wedding cakes, then you don't have time to enjoy them."

Samantha was surprised. She expected women like Beatrix to dream of a wedding straight from the pages of *Vogue*. Beatrix would wear an elaborate gown with endless layers of chiffon, and there would be a twelve-piece orchestra and a cake that was so tall, it took six people to carry.

"I'm sure Drew won't insist on a big wedding," Samantha said. "Perhaps you could have it at the house in Connecticut."

"That's even worse." Beatrix rolled her eyes. "If you have the wedding at home, the plumbing could break, or the caterers could forget the wineglasses." She brightened. "I have a better idea. We'll have the wedding here at the ranch, on New Year's Eve!"

Samantha's jaw dropped in astonishment. What would Drew say?

"You couldn't possibly do that," Samantha protested. "That's in five days."

"I'm sure Arthur was planning some kind of New Year's Eve party. He'll be delighted." Beatrix warmed to her theme. "It will be so intimate, just Arthur and all the guests. What could be more romantic than a white wedding at a ranch in Wyoming?"

It would be terribly romantic. The ceremony would be in front of the stone fireplace in the living room. They could clear out the furniture for dancing, and the cake table would be next to the window. Snow would be falling softly outside; at midnight everyone would toast the bride and groom with champagne from Arthur's wine cellar.

Samantha shook herself. What was she thinking? Drew was worried about disappointing Kaman, while Samantha was helping Beatrix plan their wedding.

"It sounds wonderful, but what about your parents and friends?" Samantha asked.

"My parents won't mind," Beatrix insisted. "They'll throw us a big party when we're back in New York." Her voice caught, and for a moment she seemed less confident. "To be honest, I don't have many friends. I wondered if you would be my maid of honor."

Samantha's eyes widened.

"We've known each other for two days," Samantha protested. "You must have a best friend from high school or college who would be furious if I took her place."

"I didn't have a best friend in high school." Beatrix shrugged.

Beatrix was probably the head of the "mean girl squad," like Blair in *Gossip Girl*. Even Blair had Serena. There must have been someone who Beatrix was close to.

"Your roommate in college then," Samantha tried again.

"All the girls in high school and college were so cliquey," Beatrix said.

She reached into a drawer and took out a photo. She handed it to Samantha.

The photo was of a teenage girl with mouse-colored hair and braces.

"Who's this?" Samantha inquired.

"That's me at sixteen," Beatrix answered. "My first crush was on my orthodontist because he fixed my over-bite," she said with a smile. "I would have fallen in love with my mother's colorist too, but he was gay." She ticked off items on her fingers. "Then there was the personal trainer at my mother's gym, and the private shopper at Bloomingdale's. By the time I graduated from college, I had been worked on by New York's top beauty professionals."

Samantha tried to see something of Beatrix in the photo. It looked nothing like her.

"What about the gymkhanas and training for the winter Olympics?" Samantha asked, puzzled.

"Those were ways to become good at something my parents would approve of. None of them stuck," Beatrix sighed. "You and I are more similar than you think. I always loved writing, I wanted to major in journalism. I was going to be a war reporter—huddling in a foxhole to get as close to the story as possible. My parents wouldn't allow it. They said I could be anything I wanted as long as it was practical. So, I became a business major instead." Beatrix was thoughtful. "They were right in a way. Being a war reporter sounded exciting at the time. With a business degree I can build something of my own that helps others. There are so many people who need help out there, not just in war zones but everywhere. And I could have a family at the same time."

Samantha tried to picture Beatrix as a plain, insecure teenager. It seemed as unlikely as discovering that Socks came from a line of championship show dogs. But there was something about Beatrix that was too glossy.

Beatrix was so determined. Samantha was running out of ways to dissuade her.

"You don't have a wedding dress," Samantha urged. "Every bride deserves the dress of her dreams."

"My ankle is almost better, we'll go shopping tomorrow," Beatrix said eagerly. "We'll buy a maid of honor dress for you, and cowboy hats for Drew and Arthur."

"You have to discuss it with Drew first," Samantha said logically. "You can't just announce that you're getting married."

"We're engaged, and you said Drew wanted a family." Beatrix waved the large diamond on her finger. "We'll tell everyone at dinner tonight. Arthur will be thrilled, he's so proud of the ranch. The wedding will be our Christmas present to him."

Arthur would be thrilled. The only person who might not be happy was Drew.

Samantha sighed miserably. This was all her fault.

"Let's start planning the menu." Beatrix flipped open her laptop. "Bison of course, and there's a bakery in town. We can get one of those flaming cakes and maybe a cupcake tree."

A half hour later, Samantha was curled up on her bed and clicking through photos of Socks. She should be dressing for dinner, but she needed to do something comforting. If she was home, she'd heat up a bowl of noodles and sit on the sofa. Socks would jump in her lap and she'd tell him her problems.

There was no one at the ranch she could confide in. It had been easier when Beatrix seemed a grown-up Barbie doll come to life. This new Beatrix, with her past anguishes and future hopes and dreams, was much harder to dislike.

Beatrix was right: they were similar. Not in Beatrix's Wonder Woman figure and masses of blond hair, or her desire to be a war correspondent. Samantha never even considered writing a Sloane Parker book set in a war zone. The photos online of bombs ripping up residential neighborhoods and children with torn clothes running into the street were too heart-wrenching. She preferred writing about Sloane fighting the enemy from the helm of a sleek speedboat, or dropping out of a helicopter onto the deck of a luxury yacht.

But she and Beatrix wanted the same things: to build something of their own, and have love and a family. That didn't change Samantha's dilemma. She couldn't be the maid of honor when they'd just met, and when the groom was unsure about having a wedding. There was also the small detail that she believed she was falling for the groom herself.

Her phone buzzed and she answered.

"Samantha." Her mother's voice came down the line. "I'm glad I caught you. We're in Liechtenstein, it's a tiny country tucked between Austria and Switzerland. It has one of the highest wealth per capita in the world and it's still ruled by the royal family."

"Since when did you care about a country's wealth?" Samantha said with a smile. It felt good to have her mother on the other end of the phone.

"I always research a country's history. The most amazing thing happened." Her mother kept talking. "I posted a photo of your father and me in front of the royal palace and captioned it: 'You don't need to be royalty to enjoy Christmas holidays in Vaduz,'" she clucked. "The department of tourism reposted it and it's the most commented post on their site." She paused. "Apparently now we're influencers. We received a call from Prince Hans-Adam's personal secretary inviting us to a Christmas ball at the palace."

"You're going to a ball with the prince of Liechtenstein?" Samantha's jaw dropped.

"Heads of state from all over the world fly in for the ball. There's a private performance of *The Nutcracker* and the prince gives all the guests presents. Then everyone drinks champagne and takes to the dance floor." Her voice practically vibrated with excitement. "What if the prime minister of Canada is there and asks me to dance? I might faint."

Samantha's mother had a crush on Prime Minister

Justin Trudeau ever since she learned he had been a schoolteacher twenty years ago after he graduated from university. Samantha had to admit he was good-looking, with that mop of dark hair and sexy smile.

"You'll probably teach him a step or two," Samantha chuckled. "You've always been a good dancer."

"It's all about listening to the rhythm," her mother reflected. "Enough about us. I want to hear all about your holiday."

Samantha sighed. She fiddled with a pillow.

"There might actually be a wedding at the ranch on New Year's Eve."

"How romantic! I've always loved winter weddings," her mother gushed. "The wedding party always looks so elegant in photos with snow in the background. I bet you'll catch the bridal bouquet," she said encouragingly. "Your turn is coming soon."

"I haven't even met anyone, I'm hardly getting married," Samantha replied.

"You never know what life brings," her mother countered. "Who would have guessed that your father and I would celebrate the Christmas season in a proper castle with pages and footmen? Wait till I post the photos on Instagram, your aunt Phyllis won't believe it."

Samantha said goodbye and hung up. The snow had stopped and the forest was perfectly still.

She stood up and walked to the closet. The ranch may look like the setting for a fairy tale, but instead it felt like a bad dream.

There was nothing she could do but get dressed and go down to dinner.

Chapter Ten

Samantha stopped typing and glanced up absently from her laptop. Sloane Parker is at a Christmas ball at the InterContinental Carlton Cannes Hotel. Sloane knows she looks stunning: she's wearing a gown from Isabel Marant, the hot French designer. She isn't interested in the appraising glances from men. She's at the ball for one reason: to save her dear friend, the French agent Claire de Salle, from the clutches of a notorious arms dealer.

Sloane and Claire teamed up two years ago on the French Riviera. Together they infiltrated a terrorist cell that was operating out of a château in Cap Ferrat. It was only when the last terrorist had been deported, and Phineas and Yves Manon, the head of the French DGSE, called to congratulate them, that they relaxed.

Now Claire is in trouble and Sloane has to help her. The arms dealer, Baron Von Drusen, is making his way across the dance floor. Claire doesn't pay any attention. Instead, she gazes dreamily at the man she is dancing with: the handsome race car driver Oliver Stanton. Men are Claire's Achilles' heel and she can't help falling in love with every charismatic man she meets.

There is a Rolls-Royce and a driver downstairs waiting to whisk Claire to safety. Sloane notices the way

Claire is looking at Oliver and knows Claire won't leave without him. What Claire doesn't know is that Sloane and Oliver were recently lovers.

Sloane whispers in Claire's ear and Claire glances at the baron. Then Claire takes Oliver's hand and leads him off the dance floor. Sloane turns and purposely bumps into the baron, spilling champagne over his tuxedo. By the time the baron has mopped it up and Sloane has prettily insisted on getting him another glass, Claire and Oliver are in the car on the way to the nearest helicopter pad.

Samantha closed the laptop and sighed. That was the wonderful thing about Sloane, she never let romance control her life. Men came and went, but her work and her female friendships lasted forever. Samantha's closest friend from high school, Jessica, was a nurse in Philadelphia and the mother of twin girls, but they still found time to FaceTime once a month. And Whitney, her best friend from college, moved with her boyfriend to Oregon two years ago, but whenever Whitney visited New York, Samantha insisted Whitney stay at her apartment.

Last night's dinner had been almost impossible to sit through.

Beatrix had appeared at the dining table looking every inch the bride. She wore a glittering silver gown and her skin was burnished gold, as if she'd spent the day lying on the beach instead of recovering from a twisted ankle. Her hair was coiled into a braid and she didn't wear jewelry except for the diamond engagement ring.

When she made her announcement about the wedding, the whole table erupted into applause. Arthur looked happier than when the company had three books on *The New York Times* Best Seller list. Only Drew seemed dismayed. Samantha glanced at his pale cheeks, the way his jaw dropped, and was sure he was going to protest.

Then Beatrix kissed him deeply in front of everyone. By the time they parted, Drew's expression changed. A smile was fixed to his face and he made a speech saying how lucky he was that Beatrix didn't have her heart set on a wedding at the Plaza in New York. The guests laughed and the champagne started flowing. Samantha had more glasses than she could remember. There was no other way to get through the night without giving in to the pain in her own chest.

She couldn't ignore the way Drew made her feel any longer. All night she lay awake, trying to make excuses for herself. It was Christmas and it was normal to want to share it with someone. Drew was the only person besides Charlie who knew she wasn't like Sloane Parker. He had been so kind to her on the plane and she was grateful.

This was different. It felt as if she had known Drew forever, and yet there was a new kind of thrill. Like waiting for the review of her latest Sloane book when the reviewer already sent her publicist an e-mail thanking them for an advance copy, and saying it was the best thing she'd written.

In half an hour, Samantha was meeting Beatrix to go bridal shopping. There was nothing she could do except count the minutes until New Year's Eve. Then she'd pack her suitcase and board the flight back to New York. If she was lucky, she wouldn't run into Drew and Beatrix until next year's company Christmas party. Beatrix would probably be pregnant, and Samantha would stand at the bar with Charlie and Emily, getting drunk on eggnog. When Drew and Beatrix came over to say hello, she'd manage to congratulate them without it hurting her heart.

Samantha placed the laptop on the bedside table and slipped on her jacket.

Right now, she had to keep her promise to Beatrix. If Sloane Parker could give up Oliver Stanton without a backward glance, Samantha could put aside her feelings and be a good friend.

"I'm so glad we did this," Beatrix gushed, bouncing her shopping bags. "If we were in Manhattan, we'd be trampled at the after-Christmas sales, and it would be almost impossible to get an Uber. Shopping in Jackson Hole is much more fun. All the stores are on one street and the shopkeepers are so accommodating. Hank at the hat store was so sweet," she said happily to Samantha. "Usually it takes six weeks for a custom order, but Drew and Arthur's cowboy hats will be ready on New Year's Eve." Her eyes sparkled. "Drew is going to be surprised. This is so much better than a pair of cuff links or a gold watch as a gift."

Drew had been right. Beatrix was wonderful at negotiating with vendors. At Jackson Cake Company, she convinced the owner to make a huckleberry cupcake tree even though huckleberries were out of season. And at Teton Tailoring, she begged the seamstress to put aside her other work and alter the three-piece suit she'd found in Arthur's closet. Drew was taller than Arthur and the pants might be a little short, but the jacket and waist would fit perfectly.

Everything about Beatrix was bright and bouncy. Her smile was as blinding as the fresh snow, and her diamond ring glittered in the sun. Samantha couldn't help feeling like the wallflower at a school dance. But just when she wished she was back at the ranch, Beatrix declared she couldn't make a decision without her. Samantha was drawn in to a debate on whether Beatrix should wear opaque or sheer stockings, and by the time they left the store—with three pairs of the sexiest stockings Samantha had ever owned that Beatrix bought her as a thank-you—Samantha admitted she was having a good time.

"Look at those turquoise earrings." Beatrix pointed to a display in a gift shop window. "They'd be perfect as something blue."

It was only when they entered the store that Samantha realized they were in the souvenir shop where Marigold worked.

Marigold was standing behind the cash register. She smiled when she recognized Samantha.

"Samantha, what a lovely surprise." Marigold walked over to them.

"This is Beatrix," Samantha introduced them. "She's looking for a pair of earrings."

"I don't have to look any further," Beatrix announced. "I'm getting married on New Year's Eve and these are perfect."

"A winter wedding," Marigold said, taking the earrings from the window. "How lovely."

Samantha wondered grudgingly why everyone loved winter weddings. She'd always imagined getting married on a tropical beach. She'd be barefoot in a long white dress and the groom would wear all white, with the pants rolled up so they didn't get wet. The guests would drink out of hollowed-out coconuts and a canoe would be waiting to take them on their honeymoon.

"It's all last minute, we only started planning yesterday." Beatrix was still talking. "Samantha is my maid of honor. Without Samantha, there wouldn't even be a wedding."

Samantha put down the snow globe she was holding. She turned her attention to Beatrix.

"I didn't do anything," she declared.

"I wouldn't be standing here if it weren't for you," Beatrix said, and beamed. "I still can't believe we only met three days ago. I feel like we've been friends forever."

"You're the maid of honor and you only just met?" Marigold glanced from Samantha to Beatrix.

"It's a long story," Samantha mumbled, forcing herself to smile.

"With a fairy-tale ending." Beatrix gave a little laugh. She took out her credit card and handed it to Marigold.

"Could you please ring up the earrings?" she asked. Then she turned to Samantha. "Why don't you pick out a necklace or earrings for yourself. While you do that, I forgot to tell Hank the inscription for the cowboy hats. I'll meet you there when you're finished."

Beatrix hurried out of the store. Samantha was left standing awkwardly at the counter.

Marigold placed the earrings in a box and wrapped it in tissue paper.

"Your friend seems very generous," Marigold observed.

"Beatrix is like a strobe light at a rock concert." Samantha couldn't keep the bleakness out of her voice. "When she shines her light on you, it's impossible to look away."

Marigold studied Samantha carefully. She tied the box with a blue bow.

"You don't approve of this wedding," Marigold said.

Samantha barely knew Marigold. She couldn't share her feelings with a stranger.

"It happened so quickly," Samantha said instead. "I hope Beatrix doesn't regret not having a big wedding surrounded by all the people she loves."

"It's more than that," Marigold prodded. Her eyes lit

up in recognition. "Does it have something to do with the man you were sitting with at the fireworks display?"

"How did you know I was with anyone?" Samantha asked in surprise. "When I turned to the bench, you were gone."

"I went to get hot chocolates. When I came back, you were busy." Marigold smiled warmly. "I didn't see his face, but it seemed like you shouldn't be interrupted."

Samantha blushed furiously. She had to stop blushing. Sloane Parker never let her cheeks appear hot. It was the first rule of being a secret agent.

"He was just a friend." Samantha shrugged. She fiddled with a buffalo-shaped bottle opener. "Though he happens to be the groom."

"You and the groom have developed feelings for each other," Marigold said knowingly. "Deep down, Beatrix knows that and that's why she's rushing the wedding."

Samantha almost laughed. Beatrix never even asked Samantha about her love life. Beatrix probably assumed Samantha was the kind of woman who was promised to her high school sweetheart. She only saw him three times a year because he was doing legal pro bono work in Mississippi. They already agreed he would propose when he returned to New York, and they'd get married in her parents' house in New Jersey.

"The groom thinks of me as a friend, and I don't have feelings for him," Samantha insisted. "I just . . ." She put back the bottle opener. "I hope they're doing the right thing," she finished lamely. "Marriage is forever."

Marigold didn't answer. She rang up the earrings and handed them to Samantha.

"In Native American folklore, the arrowhead isn't merely used to ward off danger. It gives the wearer the courage to do all the things she's afraid of."

"What do you mean?" Samantha asked, frowning.

"Look inside yourself and see what you're searching for," Marigold instructed. "The answer might surprise you."

After Beatrix finished at the cowboy hat store, Samantha and Beatrix entered Jackson Hole's only bridal salon. From the minute they walked through the double-glazed doors, Samantha felt swept into a fantasy. The velvet wallpaper was petal pink and there were deep armchairs and a glass coffee table. A bottle of champagne sat in a bucket, and glass cases held pearl chokers and old-fashioned cameos.

Beatrix disappeared into a dressing room, and Samantha ran her fingers over a satin gown. She remembered how she used to scribble her and Roger's names on her notepad at the PR firm. Even after Roger left, she still believed weddings were the most magical thing in the world.

Was there another time in a woman's life when everything was about to change? When she was going to take a complete leap of faith and join her life to someone else's? And of all the millions of people, how was it possible to find each other? To discover the one person who made everything all right? The person who brings you hot chicken soup even though he has the same flu. The person you throw a surprise party for to celebrate his promotion, even when it falls on the same day you get fired.

What if Samantha never found that person again? Even Socks couldn't keep her company forever. And she could never get another dog to replace Socks.

Beatrix emerged from the dressing room.

At first, Samantha didn't recognize her. It wasn't the dress. Beatrix hadn't chosen a gown with a huge puffy skirt, or a slinky sheath slit to the thigh. The outfit she was wearing was simple: a pleated skirt that fell to her calf and a matching bolero jacket. It was Beatrix's expression that was different. Her eyes were misty and her mouth wobbled.

Beatrix had the look of a woman in love.

"What do you think?" Beatrix breathed.

Even Beatrix's voice was unfamiliar. The question came out almost as a whisper.

Samantha took in the soft cashmere. The color that was not quite white and not exactly pink. Tears came to Samantha's eyes and she blinked.

"Drew is lucky," Samantha said truthfully. "You're going to be the most beautiful bride."

They left the bridal salon and turned down Main Street. A man carrying a flat box strode toward them.

"Drew!" Beatrix stopped. She reached up and kissed him. "What are you doing here?"

"The same as you, a little wedding shopping," he replied, smiling at Beatrix and Samantha. "I was going to take the gondola to the top of the mountain and have lunch. You two should join me."

"I can't, I have an appointment with the florist at the ranch." Beatrix shook her head. She turned to Samantha. "You should go. It's past lunchtime, and we haven't had a bite. You must be hungry."

The last thing Samantha wanted was to be alone with Drew. And besides, the gondola ride seemed terrifying. She never understood how people could willingly shut themselves into a box the size of a Lego kit and dangle hundreds of feet from the ground. What if there was a strong wind and the wire snapped? It was too awful to think about.

"I should be there when you meet the florist," Samantha said. "I'll fix a sandwich at the ranch."

"You helped me enough this morning." Beatrix gently propelled Samantha toward Drew. "A restaurant on the mountain will be more fun. And you'll be doing me a favor." She smiled cheekily. "We don't want the groom to be alone so close to the wedding. He might have second thoughts and get cold feet."

Samantha glanced at Drew. She thought he would say they should all go back to the ranch. Instead he merely handed his box to Beatrix.

"Could you take this for me?" he asked. "Don't show it to my father. It's his best man present."

Samantha was silent on the gondola. Even with the arrowhead pendant around her neck, there was still a queasy feeling in her stomach. She kept her eyes on a little girl in a pink ski suit, holding a stuffed bunny. If the little girl could sit in the gondola without being afraid, so could Samantha.

"Are you all right?" Drew asked, when the gondola doors opened. "Your lips are white and you pulled the button off your jacket."

Samantha glanced down at her parka. She had pulled the button off. She'd have to find a needle and thread and restitch it.

"I'm fine," she said sheepishly. "Heights make me nauseous on an empty stomach."

Drew took her arm and led her toward the restaurant.

"Then we better feed you," he offered. "You won't be sorry you came. The Piste Mountain Bistro has the best views of anywhere in the valley."

The hostess seated them at a window table. The sky was a fierce blue, and snow-covered mountains stretched on forever. Far below, the shops in Teton Village huddled together, and in the distance, she could see the white expanse of the National Elk Refuge.

Drew ordered two plates of smoked chicken macaroni and cheese, with warm cheddar biscuits. There was a pot of honey butter and a green salad tossed with pine nuts.

"The cheddar biscuits are delicious," Samantha said, breathing in the scent of warm pastry and cheese.

Drew took a sip of hot apple cider. He wore a navy ski sweater that made his eyes even bluer.

"It's nice to have someone to talk to," Drew said truthfully.

Samantha put down her butter knife. She tried to appear nonchalant.

"So, you're not upset about the wedding?" she asked, keeping her voice casual.

"To be honest, I couldn't sleep last night. I went down to the home theater and flipped through the cable channels," Drew began. "I ended up watching the Australian Open. It made me start thinking. I played a lot of tennis in college, it's the only sport I really enjoy. Sometimes your opponent slices his serve over your head for the fourth straight game and you realize you don't have a chance of winning. Then the best thing to do is relax and enjoy the game," he pondered. "Beatrix and my father are incredibly well matched as double partners and I'm playing alone. I couldn't possibly win."

"I don't understand." Samantha frowned.

"Last night, I glanced around the table after Beatrix made her announcement. One of the guests is a reviewer for *The New York Times*. Another is the head buyer of a major bookstore chain," he continued. "How would it look to them if I called off the wedding and said I wasn't joining the company? It's time to put down my tennis racquet and shake hands across the net."

"What about Kaman and the school?" Samantha wondered.

"As soon as we get back to New York, I'm going to ask my father for an advance on my paycheck." He put down his mug. "I'll send that to Kaman. You were right. I can't take on all the responsibility myself." His shoulders sagged. "I have responsibilities here."

Samantha tried to swallow. Had she said that?

"You're talking about your future," she cut in. "Sitting in a corner office in Midtown instead of riding in a rickshaw in Jakarta. Attending budget meetings in an air-conditioned boardroom instead of getting your fingers caked in mud laying the foundation of a new school."

"You remember everything I told you," Drew said in surprise.

"I'm a writer, I always remember details," Samantha answered. "Beatrix and your father are important, but it's your life."

Drew turned his attention to the window.

"I've always loved being up high, the feeling of almost floating," he commented. "I don't remember much about my mother. A child psychologist told my father I'd heal faster if he removed her photos from the apartment. But I remember her taking me to the Empire State Building. I was four, it was a few months before she left," he said. "When we reached the observation deck, I ran up to the glass. I turned around and she was gone. It was so crowded, I started crying. A few minutes later she appeared. Her shoe had got caught in the pavement. She scooped me up and squeezed me tightly." He paused. "She said that even when I'm grown-up and far away, she'll be right next to me. Maybe not in person, but in her thoughts. That's what being a mother is about."

Drew smoothed the napkin in his lap.

"When I started traveling, I often dreamed of running into her. At an outdoor market in Bombay, or walking across a poppy field in Vietnam," he finished. "I never did, of course. I'm not a kid in my twenties anymore. Perhaps thirty-year-olds don't need mothers. It's time to grow up."

Drew was wrong. Samantha's mother turned every conversation into being about Samantha. She only wanted Samantha to be happy.

"We always need our parents," Samantha said quietly.

"I have my father. And now I'm getting married." Drew picked up his fork. "I'll get to be a parent myself one day, if I'm lucky."

They shared shortbread cookies for dessert and stepped onto the patio. It was like the Instagram videos Roger used to watch enviously when they couldn't afford ski vacations. Groups of young people lounged at long, wooden tables drinking lager and sharing plates of buffalo wings. Their goggles were pushed up to their foreheads and they chatted about black diamond runs and meeting up for après-ski drinks.

Samantha had never cared as much as Roger. She was perfectly happy eating Christmas lunch with her parents in New Jersey, while Roger celebrated with his family in Westchester. They'd meet on Christmas night and exchange presents. Samantha's kitchen was always filled with leftovers and they'd curl up on the sofa, playing with Socks and watching Christmas rom-coms.

"You seem far away," Drew interrupted her thoughts.

"I was thinking about Christmas." Samantha pulled her mind to the present. "I've never been away from New York at the holidays."

Drew leaned against the wooden railing. He smiled at her companionably.

"I'm glad my father invited you," he said to Samantha.

Samantha's whole body felt warm. She told herself it was the hot apple cider she drank, or the outdoor heat lamps. But the heat lamps weren't turned on, and she had been too full to drink more than a sip of hot apple cider.

"You are?" She turned to him.

"You have a way of looking at things that makes sense. You showed me that Beatrix only wants what every woman wants," he said with a grin. "Without you, I'd feel like a fox caught in a hunter's trap."

The gondola was almost empty on their descent. Samantha sat back in her seat and tried to not look out the window.

They were about halfway down when the gondola suddenly stalled. The motor hummed and it started briefly. There was a ragged lurch, and it stopped.

"What's wrong?" Samantha asked Drew.

He peered outside.

"I'm sure it's nothing," he assured her. "Probably a short delay."

"It has to be something." Samantha couldn't keep the panic out of her voice. "A three-feet-by-three-feet metal box doesn't dangle in midair for no reason."

Drew pointed to the loudspeaker built into the wall.

"They'll tell us," he promised. "These things have strict safety protocols; nothing can go wrong."

Samantha didn't bring up the article she'd read about the Pirates of the Caribbean ride at Disneyland. It was perfectly safe until one person almost got beheaded by a swashbuckling pirate and the ride had to be rerouted. Or the Tiki Twirl at Great America, where the riders get close to a giant flame. The flame was actually a halogen but it was so real, several riders complained of getting second-degree burns.

Instead, she fingered the arrowhead pendant and practiced the breathing she learned from a meditation app.

Finally, a voice came over the intercom. There was an electronic glitch that would be fixed momentarily.

"You see?" Drew said encouragingly. "We'll be at the base in no time."

"Would you tell me a story?" Samantha glanced up at Drew.

Drew rubbed his forehead.

"I have a better idea. You're the writer, you tell me a story." He thought for a moment. "Tell me the first time someone told you there wasn't a Santa Claus."

Samantha fiddled with the arrowhead pendant. She took a deep breath.

"It was a girl named Brittany in the fourth grade. Brittany had older sisters and was always whispering about tampons and sex-ed books. Two weeks before Christmas she announced that Santa Claus wasn't real. She claimed she had proof and would bring it to school.

"I was up all night. Even if I suspected she might be right, I didn't want to know. The next day in drama class, Brittany was about to take something out of her backpack. I stopped her and said she shouldn't be Mary in the Christmas pageant anymore. It was an Episcopal school and the Christmas pageant was the most important event of the year. The drama teacher overheard and assigned the role to another girl.

"Brittany demanded to know why. I said that Jesus's birth was a bigger miracle than Santa Claus. The audience would know if Brittany didn't believe in it, and it would spoil the pageant," Samantha finished. "Brittany zipped up her backpack and never said another word."

There was a purring sound and the motor sprung to life. The gondola jumped forward, and then moved smoothly on its tracks.

They were both silent until they reached the base. The doors opened and Samantha had never been so happy to step outside. She fleetingly thought of a Sloane Parker book where Sloane is held hostage on a Russian submarine. When Sloane is freed, she slips off her six-inch Bottega Veneta stilettos because she's been dreaming of feeling solid ground beneath her bare feet.

"Thank you for asking me to tell you a story," Samantha ventured. "It helped keep my mind occupied."

"It was a great story," Drew complimented her. "It reminded me why I've always loved Christmas." His eyes were soft and he had never looked so handsome. "It's the one time of year when it's all right to hang on to your dreams."

Samantha's phone buzzed as she entered her guest room.

"Samantha." Charlie's voice came down the line. "Arthur told me you're going to be the maid of honor at his son's wedding. He sounded thrilled."

Samantha unwound her scarf. She didn't want to talk about the wedding.

"I'm glad Arthur is happy." She sat cross-legged on the bed. "Tell me about Socks. Is he homesick?"

"Socks and Emily's parents' dog, Molly, have grown quite fond of each other," Charlie remarked. "They're going to have a doggy date on New Year's Eve."

"A doggy date?" Samantha inquired.

She should follow more dog Instagram accounts.

Doggy dating was probably a thing, with online dating sites and meetups at local dog parks.

"Emily's mother bought them matching party hats. They'll be in the den with TV dinner trays, watching *All Dogs Go to Heaven* and *Marley & Me*. At midnight, they'll tear open a doggy piñata. Inside are dog treats shaped like champagne bottles."

Samantha pictured Socks in a cone-shaped hat and black bow tie.

"Thank you for taking care of Socks," she said with a sigh. "I can't wait to see the photos."

"You should be proud of yourself. You're practically guaranteeing your next book contract," Charlie reminded her. "Who knows, maybe next we'll hear from the producer in Hollywood."

Samantha said goodbye and hung up.

Charlie was right, she should be proud of herself. It was obvious Drew didn't have feelings for Samantha. But at least she was helping people; that's what Christmas was about. Earlier that morning Beatrix practically floated from one shop to the next, and even Drew seemed content. The wedding décor was going to be stunning. Silver tablecloths and gold filigree chairs tied with gold and silver balloons. At midnight, the balloons would be released, and Drew and Beatrix would have their first dance.

Then why did Samantha wish she was spending New Year's Eve at home? Curled up with Socks, the only living being she needed in the world, and watching the ball drop on television.

Chapter Eleven

It was two hours until dinner, and Samantha had planned on returning the diary to Arthur's library. But if she went downstairs, she'd be drawn into a discussion with Beatrix about whether the place settings should have mistletoe or baby's breath. Being the maid of honor was exhausting, and Samantha needed a small break.

Instead, she flipped open the diary. It wouldn't hurt to read a little more and see if there were any clues on how it ended up in Arthur's library. Nancy Drew never solved a mystery on the first try. Like in *The Thirteenth Pearl*. Nancy's friend, Bess, went to the closet to borrow a scarf and the necklace fell out of Nancy's father's racoon coat pocket. The police accused Nancy's father of stealing the necklace. It turned out the real thief had gone around the neighborhood posing as the milkman. Her father was afraid he would catch cold and lent him the coat. Nancy proved her father was innocent by demonstrating that the racoon coat didn't fit him anymore, he'd outgrown it since college.

The next diary entry was dated July 1991.

Dear Diary,

Oh, diary, it's all over. The wonderful, glorious, magical time with Dutch is over. I can hear my twelfth-grade English teacher, Miss Stevens, saying adjectives are like exclamation marks. A sentence only needs one. She's probably never been properly in love. That feeling when the mountains seem more majestic, my morning coffee tastes better, and even the guests at the dude ranch are the most interesting, kindest people in the world.

Dutch said he has a surprise for me tonight. I asked for a clue and he gave me that smile—his incredible smile that can still melt me—and said I'd find out. We've already done so many fun things in the evenings. Last week, I took him to a covered wagon cookout. Everyone wears cowboy hats and sings western songs around a campfire.

I was afraid Dutch would think it was cheesy, but he loved it.

This morning, I overheard Dutch asking Alice whether someone could fill in for me on breakfast cleanup duty tomorrow. At first, I was furious that he changed my schedule without consulting me. Then I realized why he asked.

Dutch plans on spending the night together. Oh, diary, I can't sleep with him, I just can't.

We've never talked about sex. I'm not a virgin, of course. But I refuse to let what we have become a typical summer romance, spending our nights making out in some truck Dutch borrowed from another ranch hand. Now we actually talk to each other. Last night, we sat for hours on the porch, gazing up at the stars and talking about everything: why I want to be a vet, what he hopes to do with his business degree. When he kisses me good night, he kisses with his whole body. It's not a quick brushing of lips before he tries to unsnap my bra, like the other girls complain about.

And there's more. Dutch still doesn't know I'm only eighteen. I haven't lied, it just hasn't come up. When he finds out I just graduated from high school, he'll turn his attentions to Leila, the brunette cheerleader from Dallas. Or Mallory, who's twenty-seven and from Seattle. Mallory is an older woman and in law school. How could Dutch resist?

He's picking me up at 8:00 p.m. I'll go to dinner with him and then I'll tell him. At least we'll have one more meal together. Because after tonight, diary, I won't be able to eat for a week.

The next entry was dated a few days later.

Dear Diary,
The night started as I expected. Dutch took me to Handle Bar at the Four Seasons Hotel. All the other guests were so sophisticated. The women wore cocktail dresses and the men smelled of fancy cologne. They probably couldn't wait to get up to their rooms and feed each other chocolate-covered strawberries while they sat in their Jacuzzi bathtubs.

"Why are you smiling?" Dutch asked after the bartender brought our cocktails.

I've learned to drink a proper cocktail. Instead of wine in a box, or peach brandy straight from the bottle.

"This place." I waved at the plush carpeting, pinpoint lighting, and oak fireplace. "It's so predictable."

"What do you mean?" Dutch demanded. "The Four Seasons is the only five-star resort in Jackson Hole. The bartender came from the St. Regis in New York."

"How do you know where the bartender worked?" I asked sharply. "Have you brought other women here?"

I regretted it the minute I said it. We never talked about seeing other people. But it would have been almost impossible. We both worked from dawn until dinnertime. And we spent all our days off together.

Dutch didn't seem to mind. He's probably used to his date being jealous of other women.

"Of course I haven't." He leaned back in his chair. "I stopped in this afternoon. I wanted to make sure we got the best table."

We were seated next to the window. It was sunset and the sky seemed to be showing off: pinks and purples in giant brushstrokes against a milky white canvas.

"It's a perfect setting but it won't do any good," I said, sipping my Cosmopolitan.

"You're talking in riddles," Dutch said, frowning.

I fiddled with my glass. I didn't want to

bring it up yet, but I felt a little guilty. Dinner at the Four Seasons must cost a fortune. How would Dutch feel when I revealed I wasn't going to sleep with him after he'd paid for a three-course meal?

"You plan to seduce me. We'll move from here to the dining room. You'll order lobster for both of us because it's the most expensive thing on the menu. The waiter will insist we share a bottle of burgundy to go with our seafood, and you'll agree. I'll get quite drunk and then you'll . . ." I stopped midsentence.

The look of outrage on Dutch's face reminded me of the dude ranch manager when a guest insisted one of the horses tried to throw him.

"Go on," he prompted. "Let me guess. I'll take you upstairs to the suite I reserved. There will be a bottle of champagne and a box tied with a pink ribbon. You'll take off the tissue paper and discover a silk negligee from the hotel gift shop. You'll laugh and say you can't possibly accept it, and I'll reply that you're the most desirable woman I ever met. Then we'll fall into bed and make love for hours. In the morning, I'll soap your back in the shower and we'll laugh that we're both so sore, we won't be able to ride horses for a week." He took a sip of his cocktail and eyed me darkly. "But we'll be so besotted, we'll manage one more session before we go back to the ranch."

I gulped and closed my eyes. I couldn't help picturing Dutch kissing my breasts, his hands caressing my thighs. My eyes flew open and I blushed, as if he could tell what I was thinking.

"Something like that." I nodded.

"Firstly, if you think I'd spend that kind of money on a date, you're mistaken." He ticked items off on his fingers. "Secondly, I never buy lingerie for women. It's presumptuous and distasteful. Thirdly, I don't intend on deflowering a virgin." He looked at me carefully. "At least, not without a great deal of discussion first."

"What makes you think I'm a virgin!" I said angrily. I WAS angry. First, he treated this like it was a joke. Now he was furious at me for guessing the truth about his intentions.

"Everything," he responded. "The way you pull back when I kiss you good night, how you blush when other ranch hands talk about sex. Even the way you're sitting." He waved at me. "You're so rigid. Like a schoolteacher deciding whether my punishment should be expulsion or merely suspension."

"I can't help it if I sit up straight, I took dance lessons for years," I stormed back. "Just because I don't want to hear other people talking about sex doesn't mean I'm a prude. The only reasons I pull back when you kiss me is because . . ." My voice caught. My eyes dropped to the tablecloth.

I felt something brush my wrist. It was Dutch's hand.

"It's because what?" His voice was soft and buttery as fresh bread.

I glanced up at him.

"Because, if I let it go on longer, I'd never want you to stop."

"I don't want to stop," he said quietly. He removed his hand. "But that doesn't mean I'd do anything about it."

Then I told him everything. That I was eighteen. I wasn't a virgin; I went steady with a boy the last two months of high school. But I refused to be another girl Dutch had a fling with. I'd rather remember our summer as a wonderful interlude, full of interesting places and conversation.

When I finished, he didn't say anything. He merely signaled the waiter. I was afraid he was going to pay for our drinks and say we wouldn't be staying for dinner. Instead he handed me the menu.

"We're going to order from the bar menu," he said to the waiter. "The lady will order for both of us. She knows the local specialties better than I do."

I ordered elk chili and black bean burgers. I have to admit the food was delicious. If I ever have a lot of money, I'm going to celebrate my birthday at the Four Seasons.

"If you don't plan on seducing me, why did you ask Alice if I could have tomorrow morning off?" I asked when we were sipping espressos. It was still early and I wasn't worried about coffee keeping me awake.

"You'll see," he answered.

He stood up and asked the hostess for my coat. He's so tall. I can wear my highest heels and I only come up to his shoulders.

"Where are we going?" I wondered. We were walking through the lobby to the entrance.

"Do you trust me?" he asked.

"Yes." I nodded.

He took my hand and led me to the parking lot. "Then be quiet, and I'll show you."

We drove out of Jackson Hole toward Curtis Canyon Campground. It's next to Snake River and you can hear the rushing water when you're lying in your tent.

Dutch parked and jumped out of the car. He started unloading the trunk: two small tents, sleeping bags, and a camp stove.

"We're going camping?" I asked incredulously.

"Just because I grew up in Manhattan doesn't mean I never went camping," he answered, pitching the tents. "I was an Eagle Scout. I have eight merit badges, if you need proof."

"I don't need to see your merit badges," I said, laughing.

Even at the dude ranch, Dutch seemed different than the other ranch hands. His shirts were always pressed and he wore his cowboy hat at a different angle: low and over his forehead.

"Why didn't you tell me we were going camping?" I inquired.

"Because camping isn't the surprise. It's what we're going to do in the morning." He handed me a sleeping bag. He leaned close and kissed me. "Now, go to bed like a good girl. We have to get up early. I brought a camping radio with an alarm."

"How early?" I was used to getting up early, but Dutch was being so mysterious. For all I knew, we'd be up at four a.m.

"You'll find out when I wake you up." He dragged his sleeping bag into his tent. There was a twinkle in his eye. "Good night. If we stay out here any longer, I'll break all my resolutions."

I was afraid I'd lie awake for hours, but I went straight to sleep. Camping always does that to me. I love the fresh air. The way the stars feel so close, as if I could reach up and touch them.

The next morning, Dutch had to shake me awake. At first, I thought he was a bear rummaging through the tent. I almost threw my shoe at him. But then he said my name and I realized it was Dutch.

He had already made coffee and bacon. He only gave me a few minutes to eat until we hopped back in the car. We drove to an open field, and in front of us was a hot-air balloon.

"That's the surprise." He pointed at the balloon. "The balloon rides leave at six a.m. and I didn't want to be late."

"We're going on a hot-air balloon?" I asked in astonishment.

Hot-air balloon rides are popular with tourists, but they're expensive.

"Just you and me and the pilot." Dutch took my hand. "Alice prepared a picnic. Bread and cheese, and chocolate-covered strawberries." He smiled at me mischievously. "We can leave the picnic basket if you think I'm using it to seduce you."

"Are you kidding?" I demanded. "I've actually never tried a chocolate-covered strawberry, and I'm hungry. You wouldn't let me finish my bacon."

We sailed over the Teton River, past Teton National Park, and into Idaho. Dutch handed me binoculars and I saw elk and bison. And the colors! Waterfalls an impossibly pale shade of blue, fields greener than anything I've ever seen. Yellow poppies and marigolds. It seemed straight out of an animated Disney movie where everything is so bright and glittery, it can't be real.

Afterward, we sat in the field and finished our picnic. Neither of us wanted the morning to end.

"How did you think of it?" I asked. I felt like I was floating, as if the ground swayed gently beneath me.

"You've shown me Jackson Hole, I wanted to do something you hadn't experienced," Dutch said, slicing a wedge of cheddar cheese.

"You succeeded," I answered happily.

He handed me a piece of cheese. His expression was suddenly serious.

"There was another reason too. You say you're completely happy in Jackson Hole. If I showed you new places, you might change your mind and visit me in New York."

I almost responded that New York was different than Idaho. New York had tall buildings *and traffic and too many people. But Dutch was looking at me intently. Instead, I gulped.*

"I might." I nodded.

Then I had to do something to lighten the mood.

"You learned two things about me today," *I joked. "I'm eighteen and I'm not a virgin. You have to tell me two things about you."*

"Two things you don't know?" Dutch repeated. He chewed his bread thoughtfully. "I wasn't just an Eagle Scout in high school, I was also president of the debate society." He smiled. "In other words, I was a geek and didn't have a date until college."

I bit into a piece of cheese. "That's only one thing."

He thought about it. "In business school, I'm going back to using my real name. It's Arthur," he said. "Arthur Wentworth."

Samantha closed the diary. Dutch was Arthur! She couldn't believe she hadn't made that connection. She wondered if they had fallen in love, if Diana ever visited Arthur in New York.

It was great inspiration for a novel. Lately, Samantha longed to write something different. A book that wouldn't require her to pose for author photos riding a camel in the Gobi Desert or hanging out of a World War II fighter plane. The kind of book she always loved: boy meets girl, they fall in love, and are separated by fate. But she could hardly tell Arthur that she found the diary. It was private. Samantha shouldn't have read it in the first place.

She slipped the diary into her dressing table and got ready for dinner. She couldn't put off her maid of honor duties. Beatrix was probably waiting for her downstairs, trying to decide what the signature cocktail should be at the reception.

"Samantha, there you are." Beatrix approached her.

It was after dinner, and Samantha was curled up on a sofa in the living room. A few guests sat around the fireplace and the lights on the Christmas tree twinkled.

"I wanted to see if you'll come night tobogganing." Beatrix sat opposite her. "Bruno will drive us in the SUV."

"Tobogganing, now?" Samantha said, sipping her coffee with amaretto.

"They only offer it at night during Christmas," Beatrix said. "A magic carpet takes you up the hill, and you toboggan down to the bottom."

"I don't think so." Samantha held up her glass. "I've had a bit to drink and I'm so warm and cozy."

"We only go a small way up the mountain," Beatrix coaxed. "Afterward, we can have drinks in Teton Village and talk about girl stuff. Please, it's the closest thing I'll have to a bachelorette party."

Samantha inhaled the scent of amaretto. She had promised herself she would do whatever Beatrix asked.

"What about Drew?" Samantha tried again.

"He's playing poker with Arthur." Beatrix rolled her eyes. "I didn't want to interrupt; you know how men are about their poker games. No women allowed."

Samantha couldn't imagine Arthur saying that to Beatrix. But Beatrix was making a little pout. She wasn't going to take no for an answer.

"All right." Samantha nodded.

Samantha stood up, and Beatrix linked her arm through Samantha's.

"I don't have many more nights as a single woman," Beatrix said gaily. "I have to fit in all the fun I can."

Teton Village was bustling with tourists. Families toasted marshmallows at the outdoor firepits and children wearing ski sweaters did loops around the ice-skating rink.

"There are the snow tubes." Beatrix pointed to the mountain. Sleek black rubber tubes were lined up on the edge of the hill. An operator barked orders and rubbed them with a cloth, as if he were part of the pit crew getting a race car ready for the tracks.

The warm buzz of the amaretto had worn off and Samantha was nervous. She had expected the plastic toboggans she'd used as a child. They couldn't go fast, and if they tipped over and landed on top of you, they were light as a feather. Instead, these snow tubes resembled something that could qualify for the winter Olympics.

"You said we're going tobogganing." Samantha turned to Beatrix. "Those tubes are built for speed. And they look impossible to maneuver."

"Nonsense, children ride them." Beatrix guided Samantha to the line. "You point the tube down the hill and it practically drives itself."

Beatrix was right, children were lining up to take their turn. And anyway, Samantha was wearing the arrowhead pendant. Nothing bad would happen.

"All right," Samantha said, standing behind Beatrix. "You go first, I'll watch how you do it."

When it was Beatrix's turn, she stepped confidently into the tube. The operator pushed her off and she raised her arms over her head and waved. Samantha watched her whiz in circles down the mountain and tried to stop the sick feeling in her stomach.

Samantha was about to tell the operator she wasn't ready when he helped her into a tube. It launched into the air and she heard the whoops of other riders. Wind rushed around her ears and snowflakes flew into her eyes. The tube leapt over the moguls and she clung desperately to the sides.

Then all at once, the steep decline leveled off and she was at the top of a gentle slope. Pink lights illuminated the snow and the hill was filled with children on tubes. Samantha managed to smile at a little girl in a polka-dot ski suit who was waving at the other riders. The tube finally reached the bottom and Samantha stepped off.

"Wasn't that great?" Beatrix was beside her. "Let's go again."

Samantha was about to say once was enough, but then the little girl in the polka-dot ski suit marched confidently toward the line. Samantha remembered Bruno saying that Sloane Parker was a good influence on young women. Sloane made them believe they could do anything. Maybe the reverse was true. A six-year-old girl could show Samantha it was silly to be afraid.

"Why not?" Samantha followed Beatrix to the line. "It's early, and I'm not cold at all anymore."

Samantha and Beatrix sat in a booth at the Silver Dollar Grill. They had gone down the mountain four times. Samantha could still feel the adrenaline rush, the thrill of landing with one final whoosh at the bottom.

"I told you it would be fun," Beatrix said when they were both drinking Silver Dollar Coffees—Jameson whiskey and coffee topped with whipped cream. She grinned at Samantha. "Though it's nothing compared to the things you're used to doing."

"The things I'm used to?" Samantha repeated, puzzled.

"I started following you on Instagram," Beatrix confessed. "The photo of you climbing into a helicopter in the middle of a snowstorm. You're wearing that divine French ski suit, I googled the label so I could order it for myself." She sipped her coffee. "And the one of you swimming in a cage with sharks. I saved it to show to Drew. It would be a wonderful thing to do on a belated honeymoon."

The photo of Samantha getting into the helicopter had been taken at a photo studio in Queens. Samantha hadn't felt comfortable using it, but the art director insisted. It fit perfectly with the book she was promoting: Sloane Parker risks her life to rescue a group of refugees from a mountain top cabin in Afghanistan.

Samantha poked her whipped cream guiltily with her straw. She hated to lie to Beatrix. But if she told the truth, Beatrix might slip and mention it to Arthur.

"You did dangerous things for years," Samantha reminded her. "You took a boat down the Amazon River and lived in a village in Thailand."

"Before I met Drew, I only stayed in touristy places." Beatrix shrugged. "Sure, they were exotic locations. But there was always the internet and a place to plug in my hair dryer."

Samantha remembered Drew saying that Beatrix was like no woman he'd ever met. That she was up for anything.

"It's easy to be adventurous with someone you trust." Beatrix was still talking. "Drew is so calm and level-headed. Look at me now. I want the safe things in life: marriage, children, a family."

Samantha realized Beatrix was quite drunk. Her eyes were starry and there was a sheen to her complexion.

"Did I ever tell you how Drew proposed?" Beatrix leaned forward conspiratorially. "It was last Christmas in Paris. We spent the previous two months building a school in Vietnam. My father gave us three nights in Paris as a Christmas present." Beatrix smiled. "I spent the first twenty-fours in the bathtub. On the second day we went to a jewelry store on the Left Bank. Drew's father sent him a watch for Christmas and the band needed to be fixed. While he was talking to the jeweler, I tried on an engagement ring." Beatrix nursed her drink. "I didn't mean to. You know how it is, I was standing around and the most beautiful ring sat in the case: a round diamond flanked by the sweetest rubies. The salesclerk asked if I wanted to try it on and I couldn't resist.

"Drew and I had talked about marriage but only in the haziest way: something that might happen in the future. The minute I put it on, I felt like the French women you see at cafés sipping their café au laits with men whispering in their ear. The salesclerk started gushing that the ring was made for me. It was so tight on my finger, for a moment I couldn't get it off," she recalled. "Drew and the jeweler came over and I was so embarrassed."

Samantha flashed back to doing the same thing when she and Roger were together. It had been one of those perfect New York mornings when the air is clean and the streets are flooded with sunlight. She was walking past Tiffany's and decided to go inside.

Tiffany's was just as she imagined: mirrored walls and miles of pale robin's-egg blue carpet. There was a sweeping staircase to an upper level and cases of diamond pendants and bracelets. A salesgirl approached her and said she must try on the engagement rings. The salesgirl could tell just by looking at Samantha that she was in love.

Samantha slipped on the ring—a pear-shaped diamond on a platinum band—and felt like someone new: sophisticated and sexy and part of something. She quickly took it off but she practically floated through the day: she was living in Manhattan, with a great job and a loving boyfriend.

Now Samantha took a long sip of her coffee. She turned her attention back to Beatrix.

"The next night, we had dinner at a bistro in Montmartre," Beatrix was saying. "It was one of those places where the chef comes out and makes sure everything is to your liking. Except, he didn't leave. He served the dessert— some kind of flan—and stood there. Drew got down on one knee and pulled out the ring I had tried on at the jewelry store." Beatrix smiled at the memory. "Drew said later that he had been so nervous, he asked the owner to wait. He needed someone to give him courage.

"I sometimes wonder what would have happened if I hadn't tried on the ring, or if we had gone to a fancy restaurant where they left us alone," Beatrix finished uncertainly. "Maybe we wouldn't be engaged."

"Of course you'd be engaged," Samantha said, surprised. "Drew loves you. You're getting married in four days."

"If you're really in love, you don't need courage from someone else, it comes from inside," Beatrix reflected. "And I'm the one who's always pushing the relationship forward." She ran her fingers over her glass. "Sometimes it feels like Drew is along for the ride."

Samantha flashed on her conversations with Drew. On Samantha's own feelings for him. But Drew and Beatrix were getting married on New Year's Eve. Nothing was going to change that.

"Drew is a grown man," Samantha insisted. "He wouldn't agree to do something unless he wanted the same thing too."

Beatrix pushed her hair over her shoulders. She rubbed her lips together and laughed.

"You're right," she said, signaling to the waiter to refill their mugs. "All men are hopeless when it comes to weddings. My father was in his tennis whites an hour before their ceremony. He had a tennis match with his best man and forgot the time."

Samantha was sitting at the dressing table in her room getting ready for bed. Her phone buzzed and she answered.

"Darling, I'm glad I caught you," her mother began. "We just arrived in Monte Carlo; we're having the most wonderful time."

Samantha moved to the bed and curled up against the headboard. Her mother sounded a little tipsy. She almost never drank, but when she did, she talked for ages.

"I thought you were at the ball at the royal palace in Liechtenstein." Samantha frowned.

"That was last night, I posted the photos on Instagram," her mother continued. "A car picked us up at the airport and brought us to Hôtel Hermitage. You should see it! It looks like those meringue cakes they have on display at Kroger's supermarket. There were even gifts waiting in our room. A cravat for your father and *la pochette* for me." Her voice tinkled with laughter. "That's French for a necktie and clutch purse.

"This afternoon we toured the Exotic Garden and then

sat at the bar in the hotel. French women are so elegant and the men are terrible flirts. It's all perfectly innocent." She paused doubtfully. "Except for Victor. I told him, just because I agreed to an aperitif didn't mean he could ask for my room number."

"You had drinks with a strange man!" Samantha sat up straight.

"Your father went up to the room, he had an upset stomach from all the cheese he ate at lunch," her mother explained. "Victor was sitting next to me at the bar." She paused. "We had a lovely conversation until he suggested we go on to dinner. When I said no, he asked for my room number. Then he got quite huffy. Honestly, it was one Dubonnet. It couldn't have cost more than twenty Euros."

"What did you do?" Samantha inquired.

"I told the bartender to put both our drinks on my bill," she chuckled. "That will show him that women can take care of themselves. Then I said that my husband was waiting for me in our room, and he has close ties to the mafia. The French think everyone from New Jersey has ties to the mafia."

"I'm sure Victor won't bother you again," Samantha laughed.

"To be honest, it was quite flattering," her mother mused. "None of us are made to be alone, it's nice to feel attractive. That reminds me, a woman in the lobby was reading a Sloane Parker book. She said you must lead an exciting life." Her mother sighed. "We should spend Christmas in Monaco together next year. Trust me, it's much nicer wearing sandals rather than snow boots."

"I'll think about it," Samantha said with a smile.

"I sound like a broken record, but it's only because I love you." Her mother's voice wobbled. "Your father and I are lucky that we have our health and can travel, but that's not always the case. You should enjoy yourself while you're young."

Samantha recalled the flight to Jackson Hole. The sudden turbulence and the sinking feeling that they were all going to die. Asking Drew to tell her a story and then discovering they had landed.

"I have to go," her mother said. "We've been invited to the casino. I told your father not to let me near the roulette wheel. I can't be responsible for my actions when I have more than two drinks."

Samantha pressed End and leaned against the pillows. The heady rush from tobogganing was gone and she felt strangely deflated. Everyone thought being an author was glamorous. But her life consisted of getting the next book contract, and then hoping she'd turn the manuscript in on deadline. She still had an empty feeling inside. Beatrix and her mother were right: being in love was one of the most wonderful things in life.

Marigold said to look inside herself and see what she was missing. What was the point? Even if she knew what to wish for, that didn't mean it would come true.

Chapter Twelve

Samantha closed her notebook and placed it on the bedside table. It was midmorning the next day and she had barely slept. Finally, she did what she always did when she couldn't sleep. She slipped on fuzzy socks, took out her notebook, and scribbled the plot of a new Sloane Parker book.

Sloane is lying in bed in her room at the Pulitzer Hotel in Amsterdam when she receives a FaceTime call. She guesses it's the suave Dutch man, Drago, she met last night at the hotel bar. He wanted to continue their evening—drinking jenever chased with beer—in his room. But Sloane would never go to a man's hotel room. And besides, she's on an assignment. She'll respond to Drago's dinner invitation when it's over.

It's not Drago, it's Phineas. Sloane is shocked. Phineas never wants to FaceTime. Phineas has big news and he wants to see her reaction. The position of intelligence supervisor is available and Phineas recommended Sloane for the job.

At first, Sloane is thrilled. She'd have her own office at headquarters in London, with regular hours and an expense account. Perhaps she'd meet someone and they'd take long walks and hang out in bookshops in Notting Hill.

But she'd miss so many things about working in the field. The cab drivers who love to show off their cities, the hotel lounges filled with people with unique histories. There would be no more calls from Phineas, congratulating her on a completed mission and insisting she treat herself to a week's relaxation.

She tells Phineas she appreciates the offer but she's too young to sit in an office. When she hangs up, she wonders if she made the right decision. Would she gaze at her reflection in the mirror one day and see wrinkles and gray hair, and still be alone? A moment later, she gets a text from Drago saying he knows of a great Indian restaurant on the Prinsengracht canal. Sloane shoots back a text that she's busy, but maybe tomorrow. First, she has to break up the human trafficking ring, then she'll have dinner with Drago.

Samantha went to the closet and slipped on jeans and a sweater. What she needed was a cup of coffee from Arthur's fancy espresso machine. Then she'd plan the rest of the day.

Arthur and Drew were standing at the counter when she entered the kitchen.

"Samantha." Arthur beamed. "Come join us, we were talking about you."

"You were?" Samantha asked.

Drew was wearing a sweatshirt and shorts; a towel was draped around his neck.

"Drew and I just finished our morning workout." Arthur poured two cups of coffee and handed one to Samantha. "I was telling him about the sales and marketing team for Sloane Parker. They're doing a terrific job."

Samantha winced. She busied herself adding cream so Arthur didn't see her expression.

"I'm lucky to have them." She nodded.

"Nonsense, they're merely supporting a great writer. When I first started out in publishing, I worked in marketing. A great marketing plan can make the difference between a book becoming successful or fizzling out."

"I didn't know you worked in marketing," Samantha responded.

"I worked in every department, that's the only way to learn about the business. I was lucky, it was a small publishing company and I was given quite a bit of responsibility. I suppose that's why now I care so much. I could never sell the company to some huge conglomerate; it would be like giving away my own child." He sipped his coffee and his expression brightened. "Enough about me. Charlie told me about the movie interest from Hollywood. I hope you don't stop writing. Some authors get that first check from a film studio and put away their laptops. Life is more pleasant sitting by a swimming pool at the Beverly Hills Hotel."

"You don't have to worry. That won't happen with me." Samantha smiled. "I sunburn easily."

"I'm glad, I can't wait to see what the team comes up with next," Arthur rejoined. "I heard they want to do a photo shoot on one of Elon Musk's spaceships."

Samantha almost choked on her coffee. It was her own fault. She should never have mentioned to her publicist that she was thinking of setting a book in space. But it was a good idea. If Neil Armstrong could plant the first step for mankind on the moon, why couldn't Sloane Parker's Tory Burch pumps be the first footprint on Mars?

Arthur left, and Samantha and Drew sat at the kitchen table.

"My father has so many ideas," Drew said companionably. "He's creating marketing strategies while I'm shrugging off last night's dreams."

"Did you have a weird dream?" Samantha asked curiously.

"Last night I dreamed I was in Indonesia and came face-to-face with a Sumatran tiger." Drew grinned. "It's probably nerves. It's not every day that a guy gets married."

"Beatrix has the wedding details under control," Samantha assured him. "She's very capable. She could probably sew her own wedding dress and bake the cake if she had to."

Drew sipped his coffee. He ran his fingers over the rim of his cup.

"Beatrix is really happy to have you as a friend," he offered. "She's not the only one. My father thinks the world of you."

"As long as the Sloane Parker books keep selling," Samantha replied anxiously.

"It's more than that," Drew countered. "You turn in a book every year without asking for an extension. And you never complain. Some authors become prima donnas and want assistants for everything."

Drew was right. Samantha heard a rumor that Melody Minnow's assistant held the book Melody was reading when she ran on the treadmill.

"I love writing," Samantha said honestly. "I'm happiest when I'm sitting in front of my laptop."

Drew placed his cup on the table. His tone was casual.

"We might be working together when I assist in publicity and marketing," he commented.

Samantha hadn't thought about that: Drew sitting across from her at marketing meetings, working together on her publicity campaigns.

"I'm sure you'll be busy with lots of authors," she said hastily.

"I hope not." Drew looked at Samantha. "I hope I get to work with the ones I'm really excited about." His eyes were that deep, dark blue. "We'd make a great team."

Samantha walked around Teton Village. The other guests went cross-country skiing but she decided to go shopping instead. She spent an hour in a clothing store called Rodeo picking out something for her mother. At first, the salesgirl's suggestion of a fringed vest and faux-suede skirt seemed too outlandish. But then she scrolled through her mother's Instagram and saw the gown she wore to the royal ball in Liechtenstein—red satin with a gold velvet bodice—and decided the salesgirl's selection was perfect.

She was about to enter a cheese shop when she noticed a man about her age in a ski store. He was standing in front of the window, trying on pairs of gloves.

Her stomach dropped and she gripped her package. She must be imagining things. The man looked just like Roger.

The door to the ski shop opened and the man rushed out.

It was Roger. His hair had blond streaks and his cheeks were tan, but he looked exactly the same.

"Samantha." Roger approached her. "I can't believe it's you."

Samantha stood still in shock. All the things she dreamed of saying if she ever ran into Roger—how could he leave without any warning, didn't their promises to each other mean anything—stuck in her throat.

For a moment she was tempted to walk in the other

direction. Roger was the last person she wanted to see in Jackson Hole. But perhaps it was a coincidence. Maybe he had no idea she was here.

"What are you doing in Jackson Hole?" she gasped.

"I was hoping I'd find you. I'm staying with friends in Sun Valley, Idaho. Jeremy wanted to ski in Jackson Hole for a day and I decided to join him."

Roger looked so cocky and confident. His après-ski boots were the latest style and a pair of mirrored sunglasses hung around his neck. Even his shoulders seemed broader than she remembered. As if he spent most of his time at the gym or on a surfboard.

"You drove from Sun Valley?" she asked, surprised.

"It's only four hours. Jeremy has an Alfa Romeo SUV, it handles like a sports car."

Roger had always wanted to drive an Alfa Romeo. It was one of the things they were going to do in Italy.

"I saw your posts on Instagram about Jackson Hole." Roger was still talking. "I thought it would be nice to see you."

Samantha hadn't checked her Instagram. Charlie must have posted that she was in Jackson Hole.

Roger moved closer, as if he was afraid she was going to walk away.

"I like your hair longer," he commented. "Being a best-selling author agrees with you."

"I'm hardly that," Samantha said, and stiffened. Her mind flashed back to all the pain he had caused her. The weeks of lying on the sofa, watching sad movies and going through boxes of tissues.

The choking feeling rose up inside her and she forced herself to take deep breaths. Part of her wanted to lash out and tell him she had nothing to say to him. But there was something about seeing him, the familiarity in his tone, the way they could just pick up and start talking, that kept her rooted to the spot.

"You're being modest." He took her arm. "Why don't we have lunch and catch up."

Roger led her into a restaurant. For the first time since she arrived in Jackson Hole, Samantha didn't pay attention to the menu. She let Roger order for both of them. She wasn't the least bit hungry.

The waiter brought plates of bar food. There was a basket of buffalo wings and a pitcher of pale ale.

"I never expected you to be in a place like Jackson Hole," Roger said, sipping his beer. "You don't like to ski."

"I'm only here for a week and I'm staying with friends." Samantha bit into a wing and put it down.

This had been a bad idea. Just sitting across from Roger made her anxious.

Roger dipped a buffalo wing in ranch dressing. He leaned forward.

"I'm glad to see you, Samantha," he began. "I've missed you."

"It didn't seem that way," she returned sharply. "You left without telling me. You haven't called once to see how I am."

Roger rubbed his forehead. He placed his elbows on the table.

"I know now that was wrong," he ventured. "You were so entrenched in New York. You had a good job and you were so close to your parents; you wouldn't have come to California."

Samantha's head snapped up. Her eyes flashed.

"I'm an adult; you could have let me decide that for myself."

"Neither of us were grown-ups," Roger chuckled. "I

thought it was okay to heat up pizza for dinner and eat it on paper plates in front of the television."

Samantha flinched. She still heated up pizza when she was too tired to cook. Roger probably had one of those services that delivered healthy meals of quinoa and kale that he ate while he worked out his leg muscles.

Her initial anger at seeing him seemed to ebb in the restaurant. This wasn't New York, and they weren't going home to their respective apartments. Samantha was on vacation and Roger was just passing through.

There was no point in arguing. Roger was part of another life.

"None of it matters." Samantha shrugged. "It was a long time ago."

"It matters to me." Roger put down his fork. "It would have been my fault if you hated Los Angeles. I couldn't take the chance."

What Roger said made sense. But deep down, she knew there was something wrong with his reasoning. She just couldn't figure out what it was. Instead, she changed the subject.

"I'm sure you're enjoying it," she said, trying another bite of food.

"It's impossible to be unhappy in LA," Roger said expansively. "Everything that was difficult about New York is easy there. You can drive anywhere and you're never far from the ocean. There are so many hiking trails, and people wear running clothes to work." He grinned. "I even have my own parking space at the office."

He leaned forward and touched her hand.

"You should come and visit."

Samantha snatched her hand away. Suddenly his touch made her uncomfortable. She didn't want any of the old feelings to return.

"I can't leave Socks," she said quickly.

"Of course you can. Hire a dog sitter." He leaned back in his chair. His tone was clipped. "You're an author, you can write anywhere. Come for a couple of weeks. We could drive up the coast and see Big Sur."

"Dog sitters are expensive," Samantha replied. "And I don't have time to go on drives. I'm on deadline."

Roger took a large sip of beer. His face took on a wounded expression.

"That's not the real reason," he said evenly. "You don't want to see me."

Samantha's cheeks flushed. She fiddled with her napkin.

"It's been four years," she countered. "Why are you saying all this now?"

"I was seeing someone, a med student at UCLA, but it didn't work out," he conceded. "One of the associates at the firm showed me your Instagram account. His girlfriend is a fan of your books, he was impressed that I used to date you."

Samantha pictured Roger with some spunky medical student. She probably was one of those super achievers who trained for triathlons when she wasn't discovering the gene that was responsible for Alzheimer's.

"You looked me up because of my Instagram account?" Samantha repeated.

"Some of the places you've been are amazing. Don't you remember how we dreamed of visiting the Italian Alps?" he responded. "I bet the view from the mountain pass was incredible."

Samantha wasn't about to tell Roger she hadn't really been standing on an overpass above Cortina d'Ampezzo in the Italian Alps. The art department had Photoshopped Samantha into the picture.

"I have to go," Samantha announced, pushing away her plate.

Roger stood up. He ran his hands through his hair.

"Have drinks with me tonight," he urged. "Please, we still have so much to talk about."

Roger looked so earnest. Like when they first met at the animal shelter, and he insisted she take Socks because they belonged together. For a moment, her heart lifted and she wondered if she was being too hasty. Was it possible to recapture what they had?

But she couldn't let herself get hurt again. This time she might not survive.

"I'll think about it," she said tentatively.

Roger sat down. His easy manner returned.

"Text me and let me know. My phone number hasn't changed."

Samantha walked down the sidewalk. She wasn't ready to go back to the ranch. Before she could think about it, she entered the gift shop where Marigold worked.

"Samantha." Marigold glanced up from the cash register. "Are you all right? You look like you saw a ghost."

The years of being so angry at Roger and missing him at the same time welled up inside her. A tear rolled down her cheek and she brushed it away.

Samantha shook her head. "It's nothing."

"It's something, you're crying." Marigold frowned. "Why don't we go into the storeroom and you can tell me about it?"

"What about your customers?" Samantha asked.

Marigold turned the sign on the door to CLOSED. She motioned Samantha to follow her.

"I can take a break."

They sat on boxes in the storeroom. Marigold poured

two cups of tea, and Samantha told her about Roger. She hadn't heard from him in four years and he suddenly appeared in Jackson Hole.

"That's worse than seeing a ghost." Marigold grimaced.

"You don't think I'm overreacting?" Samantha wondered, sipping her tea.

"He broke your heart. Hearts don't mend easily," Marigold said matter-of-factly. "The question is, what do you want now?"

"For months after Roger left, I dreamed he'd show up at my door. He'd be holding a bunch of flowers, and doggy treats for Socks. I'd tell him that I couldn't go through that again and he'd apologize and say he'd changed. Then we'd curl up on the sofa and watch romantic movies, and it would be even better than before."

"And now?" Marigold prompted.

Samantha sighed. She placed her cup on the counter.

"His life seems so different," she debated. "Even if we got back together, I don't know if it would work. How could I trust him not to do the same thing again?"

Marigold added honey to her tea. She drank it thoughtfully.

"Native Americans have many legends about love. My Ojibwe friend taught me the story of a young girl named Dandelion. Her hair is the color of spun gold and she's so lovely, the South Wind and East Wind both fall in love with her. The South Wind is too shy to reveal his intentions, but the East Wind is very confident. He loves to hear himself talk, so when he courts her, he blows parts of her away. After a while, her golden hair is gone, and all that remains is her heart. Dandelion stops being a girl and becomes a flower instead.

"There's nothing more important than love when it's

nurturing, but love can also be the reverse. It can sap your energy and leave you with nothing," Marigold finished.

"I never heard anything like that," Samantha said.

"It wouldn't sell many Valentine's cards but it's a good lesson." Marigold gave a small smile. "You have to choose the kind of love that works for you."

Marigold stood up. She placed her cup in the little sink.

"I better open the store." Marigold walked to the door. "I wouldn't want customers going to Jackson Trading Company. They charge twice the price for their huckleberry jam."

"Thank you, you've been so kind." Samantha stood up and followed her.

"Kindness is what Christmas is about," Marigold offered. She touched Samantha's shoulder. "You're wiser than you think. You'll make the right decision."

Samantha slipped into the barn. She didn't feel like seeing anyone. First, she had to decide what to do about Roger.

"Hi, Blixen, it's nice to see you." She approached Blixen's stall. "I don't have any sugar cubes, but I brought you some huckleberry cereal. It tastes better than Froot Loops."

Samantha offered Blixen the cereal. He nuzzled her palm, and Samantha stroked his nose absently.

She was probably worrying for no reason. Roger asked her to visit, he didn't say anything about getting back together. He didn't really expect her to move to California. And he was hardly going to give up the sunshine and his new convertible to move back to New York. But he had come to Jackson Hole to see her.

Her phone buzzed with a new text. Emily had sent a

photo of Socks and Molly. They wore identical red knit sweaters and matching booties. The caption read: "Socks and Molly modeling their Christmas presents."

Samantha scrolled through old photos. Socks in his crate when he first came home from the animal shelter, Socks running in Fort Greene Park. When Samantha had left Socks to go on book tour, she was miserable from the moment she boarded the plane until she arrived back at her apartment. If Roger had feelings for her, it wouldn't have taken him four years to realize he missed her. He would have known right away.

The door opened. She thought it was Bruno, but it was Drew.

"Drew." She put away her phone. "I thought you were cross-country skiing."

"We just got back." Drew walked over to the stall. "I saw you go into the barn. I thought I'd join you."

Drew looked so handsome. His cheeks were raw from the cold and there were tan lines under his eyes from his goggles.

"I brought some cereal for Blixen." She held out her hand.

"I'm glad you're here." Drew moved beside her. "I wanted to talk to you about the wedding."

Samantha took a deep breath. She couldn't stand there and be happy for Drew and Beatrix when her stomach was tied in knots. She needed some time alone.

"I'm sorry, I can't right now." She stuffed the bag of cereal in her pocket and strode to the door.

Drew studied her curiously.

"Are you all right? You're very pale."

Samantha gulped. She hadn't meant to tell Drew about Roger. It made her sound vulnerable and insecure. But suddenly she couldn't keep it to herself. She told him how

Roger was following her on Instagram and drove all the way to Jackson Hole to see her. He'd asked her to meet him for a drink and she didn't know what to do.

When she finished, Drew's eyes darkened. His brow creased into a frown.

"He just expects you to pick up the way you were before?" he demanded.

"Not at all." Samantha shook her head. "New Yorkers love to visit California in the winter," she tried to joke. "After all, I can't wear shorts and flip-flops to look at the Christmas decorations on Fifth Avenue in December."

"Then you can wait until the summer and go out to the Hamptons." Drew's voice was tight. "After what he did to you, he doesn't deserve to be in the same state, let alone sit with you at a swimming pool." His tone turned softer. "You have to give yourself more credit. You're an amazing woman, Samantha, if . . ." He stopped.

Samantha froze, waiting for him to continue.

A text lit up the phone in his pocket. He took it out and read it quickly.

"I'm sorry, I have to go," he apologized. He seemed to shake himself. "We can talk more about this later if you like, and I did need your help with the wedding."

Samantha nodded. "I'll see you at dinner."

It was only when Drew left, when she heard his boots crunching on the snow, that she realized she had forgotten to exhale.

She let out her breath and pulled the phone from her pocket. What had Drew been about to say and why had he stopped?

"Roger," she texted. "I'm sorry, I can't make drinks tonight."

She stared at the phone, debating what else to say. It didn't matter. Roger was the East Wind in the legend. No matter what she wrote, her words would be drowned out by what Roger told himself about their relationship.

She pressed Send and slipped the phone back in her pocket. Then she trudged across the driveway and went upstairs to take a bath.

Chapter Thirteen

Samantha sat at one end of the long dining room table listening to Audrey's mother, Gladys, proclaim that Jane Austen was the greatest female writer of all time, and Samantha must see the latest adaption of *Pride and Prejudice*.

For once, Samantha was grateful to be seated beside Gladys. At least she was far away from Beatrix and Drew. Seeing them together reminded her of what she once shared with Roger.

She had checked her phone a dozen times to see if Roger responded to her text. She half expected him to reply that it was just one drink; he drove hours to see her. But her phone remained silent. Roger hadn't bothered to reply. She knew then that she had made the right decision.

It would have been nice to tell Arthur she had a headache and eat a sandwich in her room. But then she read Charlie's latest e-mail about Melody Minnow's new partnership with a juice company. Samantha had to make an appearance at dinner. She searched her closet for the perfect outfit—a pair of wool pants and the fisherman's sweater Emily said was all the rage this winter—and went downstairs to join the other guests.

Now, she had to admire Beatrix. Beatrix's blond hair was slicked back and diamond earrings glittered in her ears. Instead of discussing sorbet cups and honeymoon destinations, Beatrix acted as if she was already the hostess. She chatted with the reviewer from *The New York Times* about the latest bestsellers, and praised the buyer for the bookstore chain on his most recent book club selection.

Drew was strangely quiet during dinner. She wondered again what he had been going to say to her at the barn. It didn't matter. In four days, she'd be back in Brooklyn. She'd confide everything to Socks while Socks sat patiently, gnawing a peanut-butter-flavored bone. Soon Jackson Hole would become a Christmas memory, and Samantha and Socks would return to the routine of morning pee walks and monthly trips to Dog Wash N' Go to get Socks's nails clipped and his teeth brushed.

Arthur stood up and tapped his glass. He looked tan and fit in a dark blazer and turtleneck.

"I hope everyone is enjoying themselves," he began. "I'm going to go home a few pounds lighter and with excellent calf muscles. There's no sport like skiing for a tremendous workout."

A few people groaned in agreement. Arthur waited a moment to continue.

"Most cities have restaurants that are so iconic, tourists must experience them before they leave. In New York it's the Rainbow Room and the Russian Tea Room and, my favorite, Lombardi's on the Lower East Side. Lombardi's opened in 1905 and it still makes the best meatball pizza in Manhattan. In Jackson Hole, that place is Mangy Moose. Not only do they serve the tastiest baby back ribs, it's the true western experience. Every Thursday night, they host a mechanical-bull-riding contest."

There was a twinkle in his eye. "I've signed everyone up. The car leaves in half an hour."

Samantha tried to hide her grimace. She had researched mechanical bulls for the book where Sloane's fellow agent, Ricardo, masquerades as a bullfighter in Barcelona. A mechanical bull was also called a bucking machine, and injuries included bruised buttocks and saddle trauma. Ten percent of falls from mechanical bulls resulted in concussion and women were more prone to slip off the bull than men. At first, Samantha hadn't believe that statistic. But it was true. Women took their hands off the reins to fix their hair or adjust their top and were bucked off the saddle.

Samantha didn't have a choice. Arthur expected everyone to participate. And she was wearing the arrowhead pendant. Nothing bad would happen.

The interior of the Mangy Moose resembled the 1940s western movies her parents watched when Samantha was a child. Her father always loved the scene where the bad guy in the black hat steps out of the saloon, flanked by his menacing companions. The town belle is beside him and he's determined to marry her. Then the good guy rides up wearing a Stetson hat and shiny silver spurs. He orders the bad guy to get his hands off the girl, and threatens to run him and his evil buddies out of town. The bad guy slinks away on a black horse and the saloon owner buys a round of drinks for everyone in the bar.

Perhaps Samantha could write a western Sloane Parker book. Sloane, dressed in white pants and a white leather jacket, rides up on her trusty palomino. Clarissa Cooper is waiting for her. She's wearing a skintight black jumpsuit and sitting on a black horse twice as tall as Sloane's. Clarissa demands that Sloane leave town, but

Sloane doesn't move. Clarissa pulls out her pistol. In one swift move, Sloane lassos the pistol to the ground. Clarissa gallops off and the owner of the town's bakery brings out a chocolate cake to celebrate.

Samantha would share the idea with Charlie when she returned to New York.

Now, she slipped into the Mangy Moose's bathroom. Hopefully by the time she emerged, the tables in the front would be full. She'd sit in the back, and if she was lucky, the announcer wouldn't call on her.

But when she reappeared, Drew was hovering nearby. He walked over to her.

"Beatrix sent me to find you," Drew said. "She saved a table for us."

Samantha glanced at the stage. The bull was painted an angry red, with sharp pink horns. The announcer was speaking loudly into a microphone, while a puffy-faced man heaved himself into the saddle.

Drew followed her gaze. His face broke into a smile.

"I rode a mechanical bull once during college. It's not as bad as it looks," he said helpfully. "The trick is to hold on with your knees, then you can't fall off."

Samantha relaxed in spite of herself. She had missed talking to Drew. He made everything better.

"To be honest, I'm terrified," she admitted. "But your father expects everyone to participate."

"Don't worry, you'll be fine," he assured her. "You stared down a live elk. That bull is only metal and plastic."

Drew slipped his hands in his pockets. His expression changed.

"The thing I wanted to talk to you about earlier," he began. "This might not be the best place to start, but—"

Suddenly there was a break in the crowd. Beatrix appeared beside them.

"There you are, I've been looking for both of you," Beatrix cooed. "Apparently the bride is supposed to go next. I told Arthur I'm not riding that bull until you're both there to cheer me on."

Drew took his hands out of his pockets. He walked toward the bar.

"I was about to get us some drinks," he offered.

Beatrix linked her arms between Drew's and Samantha's.

"You better make them doubles," Beatrix said gaily. "The last rider lasted thirty seconds, I have to break his record."

Five minutes later, Beatrix climbed on the bull and made a mock salute to the crowd. The announcer handed her a long white veil and Beatrix fastened it over her hair. The bull purred to life and Beatrix slipped to the side. Then she righted herself and clasped the reins firmly with one hand, keeping the other hand in the air to maintain her balance.

Someone started chanting, and everyone else joined in. The bull kept bucking and Beatrix almost lost her balance. She managed to hang on and a few men near the stage whistled encouragement.

Finally, the bull slowed to a stop. The crowd clapped and Beatrix raised her hands in the air.

"Our new record holder at thirty-two seconds," the announcer proclaimed. "Ladies and gentlemen, who's going to try to beat the bride?"

Beatrix clambered off and joined their table.

"That wasn't so bad," Beatrix declared. Her cheeks were flushed and her eyes sparkled. "Samantha, you go next."

Samantha stood up and unwrapped her scarf. Their table was so close to the stage, she may as well get it over with. She touched her neck and froze. The arrowhead pendant necklace was gone. Her heart pounded and her hands felt clammy. She peered under the table, but the pendant wasn't there.

"I need to use the bathroom," she said quickly. "I'll be right back."

The pendant wasn't on the counter, or in the bathroom stall. She got down on her knees and searched the floor. It could have fallen off anywhere: in the parking lot, or somewhere in the bar. What was she going to do, and what would she say to Marigold if she couldn't find it?

A tightness formed in her chest, and she could barely swallow. The pendant had kept her safe. She couldn't ride the bull without it.

The door opened. Samantha was afraid it would be Beatrix, but it was Gladys.

"I was sent to find you," Gladys said to Samantha. She turned to the mirror and patted her helmetlike brown hair. "I told the announcer you're a famous author. He was impressed."

It was no use; Gladys wouldn't leave the bathroom without her. Samantha glanced in the mirror. Her cheeks were pale and her lips were almost blue.

"Do you want to borrow my lipstick?" Gladys offered, opening her purse. "Isn't this exciting? Though you must be used to it. Celebrities are always participating in odd charity events. Last week I watched a donkey basketball game on Facebook Live. A group of television chefs rode donkeys and played basketball at the same time."

Samantha handed back the lipstick and smoothed her hair. Gladys opened the door and Samantha followed her to the stage. The announcer was standing next to the bull, waving a flashlight at the crowd.

"There's our contestant." He pointed to Samantha.

"I've been told the next rider is a well-known author. Let's have some fun and change the setting to Most Challenging. It's a competition, folks, we have to keep it interesting."

The announcer helped Samantha onto the saddle, and she gingerly took the reins. Her pulse quickened and a pit formed in her stomach. Arthur's table was only half full; Drew and Beatrix were gone.

Before she could search the crowd, the announcer pressed the button. At first, the bull started slowly. Then it raised its head and pitched sideways. Samantha tried to hang on with her knees but the bull kept bucking. Suddenly the whole room tilted. The bull jerked so violently; the reins slipped out of her hands. She grabbed the saddle and then pitched forward and landed on her stomach in the middle of the stage.

"Send her home," a man bellowed from the back. "It's time for the men to have a turn."

"Now, Abe, that's not polite." The announcer shone his flashlight on Abe. "I say we give her another chance. We can't have her returning to New York and saying the locals aren't polite to tourists."

Samantha's side ached and there was a ringing in her ears. The announcer reached down to help her up, but she ignored him. She crept off the stage and edged down the back to the bathroom.

Her hands were shaking and she could barely turn on the tap. She leaned against the sink and blinked back tears. That was the most humiliating thing she had ever done.

Her cheeks were covered with dirt and straw stuck to her sweater. She waited until the chanting in the bar died down. Then she opened the door and slipped quietly out the entrance to the sidewalk.

The cold air hit her the minute she stepped outside. She had never felt such cold. Her jacket and scarf were in the bar and she couldn't go back inside. At least her wallet was in her pocket. She could pay for a taxi. She stumbled across the parking lot and noticed a taxi idling at the corner.

"The Wentworth Ranch, please," she said, climbing inside.

The driver put down the meter. He glanced in the rear-view mirror.

"You do realize it's minus fourteen outside?" he said, steering onto the road. "Tourists are lucky that Jackson Hole has taxis. All those big cities are overrun by Ubers." He kept talking. "If you had to wait for an Uber, you'd last ten minutes before you got pneumonia in that out-fit."

Samantha opened her mouth to answer, but closed it. It was none of the cab driver's business but she was too tired to argue.

The ranch was quiet when she arrived. The only light came from a bedroom on the second floor. Two figures stood by the window and Samantha realized it was Drew and Beatrix. They were standing close together and Drew's arms were around Beatrix.

She wondered what Drew had wanted to talk to her about. He probably wanted help with his speech for the reception. She couldn't face him tonight; she'd see him in the morning.

For a moment she imagined what it would be like to be Beatrix. To be held by someone you love, to always have someone to talk to. It was easy to tell Charlie that she didn't need anyone, she was perfectly happy with Socks for company. But that wasn't true. She couldn't have philosophical discussions with Socks, or talk about their future. All Socks cared about was getting his breakfast and dinner and that she took him for his evening walk.

She debated again if she had been too hasty with Roger. But it wouldn't have worked. Her feelings for Roger were somehow tainted, as if she had taken off her rose-colored glasses and viewed him in a new light. If she wanted excitement, she could always search the internet for a new setting for a Sloane Parker book. Sloane could go visit an aboriginal tribe in Australia or go on safari in Kenya. Some of those safaris were quite glamorous. Sloane would be dressed in a sexy cargo-style dress and the leopard skin boots that were so popular.

Samantha trudged upstairs to her room. Her ankles smarted and her knees were covered in bruises. She slipped off her shoes and spent half an hour applying hot towels to the bruises on her knees. Then she walked to the window to close the drapes.

A light was on in the barn. She peered more closely and noticed the light was flickering. Her heart began to hammer and she let out a gasp. It wasn't a light; it was a fire.

She grabbed a pair of slippers and dashed down the staircase. This time she didn't even notice the cold. She was moving too fast, racing over the slippery snow until the barn door was within reach.

Inside, the flames leapt from the corner with the Christmas tree. Smoke filled the air and the horses paced nervously in their stalls.

She couldn't get the horses to safety alone. Bruno lived in the apartment upstairs; he could help. She ran back outside and climbed the staircase. There was no answer to her knock and the lights weren't on inside.

What if Bruno was at the Mangy Moose, waiting to take the guests to the ranch?

She was about to go back to the barn when the door opened. Bruno stepped out. A robe was tied over his pajamas.

"The barn's on fire," she said before he could speak.

Bruno ran down the stairs and Samantha followed him. He grabbed a bucket while Samantha opened the first stall and led the horse outside. She heard the sizzling of water on flames and the air took on a pungent smell, like popcorn overcooked in the microwave.

"It's all right, the fire is out." Bruno's voice sounded behind her. He took the horse's reins and stroked him gently on the nose.

Fear and relief washed over her and she couldn't stop shaking. Bruno led her back into the barn and pulled out a stool.

"Sit down," he instructed. "You're in shock."

"I looked out my window and thought someone left the light on in the barn." Samantha sunk onto the stool. Her teeth chattered and she couldn't stop shivering. "Then, I realized there were flames."

Bruno stood near her. His cheeks were sooty and his silvery hair was covered in ash.

"It's my fault, I must have left on the Christmas tree lights," he said. "You were incredibly brave."

"I didn't do anything." Samantha shrugged. "I ran upstairs to find you."

"You opened the barn door without knowing what was inside," he insisted. "And you calmed the horses. A few more minutes, and the whole place could have gone up in flames."

Samantha glanced at the high ceilings, the wide stalls, the tall, graceful windows.

"I'm glad it didn't, it's such a beautiful structure."

"Arthur wouldn't care about the barn, but he'd care

very much if anything happened to you or his horses." Bruno's voice was tight. "Elaine is going to have my hide, and I don't blame her. I can't be trusted to turn off the damn lights on the Christmas tree."

"It's not your fault either," Samantha countered. "There might have been a fault in the wiring."

"I'm in charge of the horses," Bruno said, frowning. He studied Samantha closely. "I told you Blixen was smart. He knew the first time he met you that you were a true friend."

Bruno's wife, Elaine, clattered down the staircase and insisted on wrapping Samantha in blankets. Bruno found a bottle of scotch in the cupboard and Samantha drank some gratefully.

Elaine suggested Samantha come upstairs for a cup of hot chocolate, but Samantha wanted to go back to the main house.

"Are you sure you don't want to come inside?" Samantha asked Bruno when they reached the driveway.

"I need to take care of the horses." Bruno shook his head. He smiled thinly. "Elaine is already devising my punishment. She has years of practice; she was a very strict mother."

Samantha had barely opened the door when a figure came rushing toward her.

"Samantha, there you are." Arthur stood in front of her. "Bruno texted and told me what happened. I was about to come to the barn."

Arthur led her into the kitchen. Samantha sat at the table and told him everything that happened.

"I'll call the doctor to check you out." Arthur took his phone from his pocket.

"I don't need a doctor," she stopped him. "I'm perfectly fine."

Arthur walked to the coffee machine. He pressed the silver buttons and returned to the table with two steaming cups.

"It's warm milk and honey." He handed her one. "When you get to be my age, you can't sleep without it."

"I really didn't do anything. Bruno put out the fire," she said, accepting the cup. The hot milk smelled heavenly and the honey soothed her throat. For the first time since she saw the flames, she let herself relax.

"I don't know how to thank you," Arthur said, sipping his milk. His expression turned pensive and he resembled an older version of Drew. "When I was young, I thought I was so brave. But once I didn't act fast enough and lost the thing I loved most in the world." He paused as if he was bringing his mind back to the present. "I can see why your fans love you. You behaved exactly like Sloane Parker."

Later, Samantha leaned against the headboard in her room. It was midnight and she was exhausted. The other guests had returned from the bar and everyone stopped by to congratulate her. The only people who didn't appear were Drew and Beatrix. Perhaps they went to bed early and missed the commotion.

Her phone buzzed and she was tempted not to answer it. But it was her mother.

"Samantha," her mother's voice announced. "Did you see my Instagram story?"

How did her mother know about Instagram stories? Samantha had only discovered that feature a few months ago.

"We were at an outdoor market in Èze," her mother continued. "Èze dates back to medieval times, and the streets are made of cobblestones. Thank god I was wearing my new nonslip loafers those nice people from Amélie Pichard sent me. I would have broken my ankle in my sandals."

Samantha couldn't help but smile. Her mother had never owned a pair of designer shoes in her life.

"We were squeezing the melons and a thief grabbed my purse." Her mother was still talking. "Your father started chasing after him but I held him back. I didn't want him ending up in a French hospital, our insurance might not cover it."

Samantha held her breath, waiting for her mother to continue.

"I was sure the purse was gone," her mother said. "But this man approached us. He was quite old: he had that kind of wrinkly, parched skin you get from spending every day in the sun. A tan might look nice when you're young, but it really does age you."

"Did he retrieve the purse?" Samantha asked anxiously.

"Oh, yes, and the wallet was inside," her mother answered. "That wasn't the most exciting part. The real miracle was the man who brought back the purse. His name is Luc and he's lived in Èze his whole life. A year ago, Luc's wife died and he hasn't spoken to a single person since. Everyone in the village thought he'd become mute from the grief," she finished her story. "But he caught the thief and stayed with him until the gendarmes came."

"Are you and Dad all right?" Samantha questioned.

"We're fine," her mother replied. "The gendarme insisted on giving us a police escort back to Monte Carlo. He was worried we'd write about our experience on TripAdvisor and it would be bad for tourism."

Samantha let out a sigh of relief. "You must have been scared."

"I was at first. But look at the good that came out of it. Luc is a hero, it's a Christmas miracle." Her mother paused. "It made me remember that time when that new girl, Becky, was being bullied in high school and you stood up for her. It turned out that Becky's father was an independent movie producer. He gave you a walk-on part in his next movie and the mean girls were so envious. You were brave then, and you still are. You just have to believe in yourself."

Samantha was too tired and shaken to tell her mother about the fire in the barn. She said goodbye and hung up. She didn't feel like a hero tonight; she had been terribly scared. It was only the image of Blixen in his stall that allowed her to keep moving.

The fire didn't change anything. Drew and Beatrix were still getting married in three days.

She pulled the comforter over her cheeks and closed her eyes. Her own Christmas miracle seemed as unlikely as finding the turquoise arrowhead pendant.

Chapter Fourteen

Samantha sat up in bed the next morning and grimaced. The soreness in her ribs and pain in her calves were even worse. And she was coming down with a cold. Her head throbbed and her nose was stuffy.

She padded to the bathroom and stared bleakly at her refection. Her eyes were watery and a bruise had formed on her cheek. There were scratches on her arms and her hair needed brushing.

If only she could spend the day in bed, watching Christmas movies on her laptop. But she wanted to check on Blixen and tell Marigold about the lost pendant. And then there was Drew and Beatrix. Drew still wanted to talk to her, and Beatrix probably had something planned: getting their nails done or buying lingerie. Samantha pictured helping Beatrix choose lacy underwear and silk teddies for the honeymoon and let out a small groan.

There was a knock and Samantha opened the door.

Beatrix swept into the room. She wore pleated slacks and a belted jacket. A scarf was knotted around her neck and she wore suede gloves.

"Arthur told me what happened last night," Beatrix announced before Samantha could speak. "You saved the whole ranch from going up in flames."

"The fire was nowhere near the main house, and I didn't do anything," Samantha said, trying not to sneeze. "Bruno put out the flames and saved the horses."

"That's not what I heard. You're the hero of the hour," Beatrix replied. She settled onto the armchair. "I must have had too much moose punch at the bar, I can never handle rum. I practically fell asleep the minute I entered my room."

Beatrix couldn't have gone straight to bed. Samantha saw Drew and Beatrix together in Beatrix's room. Perhaps Drew slept there and they didn't want Arthur to know.

"I'm glad the horses weren't hurt," Samantha reflected. "I'm going to the barn to check on them."

"Arthur and Drew have been there all morning," Beatrix said. "Why don't we go into town and have breakfast instead."

It was almost noon and Samantha hadn't eaten a thing since dinner.

"I am hungry," Samantha wavered. "But I look awful and I think I'm coming down with a cold."

"Nonsense, you look lovely: like Joan of Arc when she returned from battle." Beatrix stood up. "A real cowboy breakfast is just what you need to make you feel better."

Beatrix borrowed Arthur's SUV and they drove into Teton Village.

Samantha sat across from Beatrix at Bubba's Bar-B-Que. Almost every booth was full. Waitresses carried old-fashioned coffeepots, and there was the smell of sausages and fresh-baked muffins.

"Aren't you eating anything?" Samantha asked when the waitress brought their plates.

They had ordered sausages, and biscuits with gravy,

and homemade granola. Beatrix was only toying with her food.

"I ate earlier." Beatrix shrugged. "All I want is coffee."

Samantha was beginning to feel better. The warm biscuits and hot coffee took away her chill.

"At least have granola," Samantha said, pushing the bowl across the table. "You're getting married tomorrow, you need to keep up your strength."

Beatrix opened a packet of sugar. She stirred it into her coffee.

"Actually, I have to go back to New York."

That's why Drew wanted to talk to Samantha. Drew and Beatrix were going back to New York.

"When are you and Drew leaving?" Samantha wondered.

Beatrix took a long sip of her coffee. She placed the cup on the table.

"Drew is staying here," Beatrix said. "There won't be a New Year's Eve wedding."

"It's a good idea to wait." Samantha nodded. "Arthur would love to host an engagement party, and you can plan a summer wedding. You can honeymoon somewhere warm and exotic: the Amalfi Coast or Costa Brava in Portugal."

Beatrix pulled off her gloves. The diamond ring was missing.

"There won't be a wedding," she confessed. "Drew and I aren't getting married."

Samantha put down her biscuit. Her heart beat uncomfortably and she looked at Beatrix.

"What do you mean, there won't be a wedding?"

"I've been doing a lot of thinking," Beatrix began. "Drew is handsome and intelligent and he's one of the kindest people I know." She sipped her coffee. "I'd have the life I always dreamed of, with a house in the country and a couple of children. They'd join the pony club and take sailing lessons in the summer. There would always be a few bicycles in the driveway and we'd have a cocker spaniel or a golden retriever. During the summers, we'd travel to Japan or South America to show them other cultures."

Samantha had an odd feeling in her chest. Those were the same things she had wanted for herself. Then Roger left, and she developed so many fears, she couldn't see past the double-bolt locks on her apartment door.

Perhaps Charlie was right. There was more to life than celebrating her latest book deal with a new pair of fuzzy socks and takeout from the Italian place nearby. But she couldn't imagine doing the things Beatrix described. The arrowhead pendant was gone, and the old feelings of anxiety had returned.

"A house and children really aren't important in a marriage," Beatrix was saying. "The important thing is to be happy without them."

"I don't understand." Samantha frowned. "Arthur is giving you a house, and Drew wants children. Isn't the point of marriage to find the person who wants the same things as you do?"

"That's what I thought too, but I was wrong."

Samantha had never seen Beatrix look so serious. Her perfectly smooth forehead was furrowed and she ran her long red fingernails over her coffee cup.

"It's like when I chose my gown last year for the Met Gala. The saleswoman at Saks wanted me to buy a Zac Posen. It was a straight white sheath; it would have looked gorgeous with a jeweled pendant or a tiara. I tried it on a few times, but I knew it wasn't right for me." Beatrix paused. "I finally chose the dreamiest Alexander McQueen instead.

The fabric had this whimsical fruit pattern and the skirt was tiered with a small train."

"I didn't know you and Drew attended the Met Gala," Samantha said.

The Met Gala was one of Samantha's favorite events in New York. She studied the photos every year to get inspiration for Sloane Parker's gowns. In her latest manuscript, Sloane wears a stunning fuchsia Versace like the one Amal Clooney wore a few years ago.

"I was so excited; it was the first time I'd been invited. Did you know that all the money goes to charity? The year before they raised nineteen million dollars for the Met Museum's Art Institute," Beatrix continued. "But we didn't go. We were in Vietnam and there was a delay in construction. Drew couldn't leave and I wouldn't go without him," she sighed. "The night of the ball, I sat in a tent, putting chamomile lotion on Drew's mosquito bites.

"My point is that the Met Gala is a once-in-a-lifetime experience. If I was going to invest all that money and time in a dress, I wanted it to be stunning without jewelry," Beatrix finished. "It's the same with marriage. You have to marry the person who makes you happy just being together, even if you never have anything else. Drew and I get along but I want so much more. That's not the way to start a marriage."

Samantha had never compared marriage to a ball gown. But somehow, she understood.

"What did Arthur say?" Samantha asked.

"We haven't told him, we'll tell him later," Beatrix admitted. "Drew couldn't leave, of course. So, we decided I should go back to New York." She smiled at Samantha. "I hope you and I remain friends. Getting to know you has been one of the best parts about my engagement."

Strangely, Samantha felt the same. Beatrix wasn't

anything like she expected when she first saw the cool, collected blonde across the living room. Beatrix had a way of looking at things that was unique, and yet came from the heart. And Beatrix genuinely cared about helping others.

"Of course we will," Samantha agreed. "Though you may have to come out to Brooklyn. I don't get into Manhattan often."

"Actually, I might not stay in New York." Beatrix's voice was casual. "I'm thinking of going back to school."

"You're starting your new company!" Samantha protested.

"That's really more Drew's kind of thing." Beatrix waved her hand. "I ran into my orthodontist's son recently in New York. He took over his father's practice. I may go to dental school and become a pediatric orthodontist," she said with a grin. "I told you I had a crush on my orthodontist when I was sixteen, he changed my life."

After they finished breakfast, Samantha drove Beatrix to Jackson Hole's airport. Beatrix took her suitcase from the trunk and hugged Samantha.

"I meant what I said about getting together," Beatrix said. "You have to tell me what happens in the next Sloane Parker book. In the one I'm reading now, Sloane saves Pedro from a Mexican drug cartel. Sloane pretends to be a local by drinking the worm in the bottom of the Mezcal bottle. Then she drives through the jungle to stop the drug lord from reaching the border."

That was a difficult plot to write. Samantha decided to eat the worm in a bottle of tequila to make the writing authentic. But she couldn't do it. Just seeing the worm floating in the bottle made her queasy.

"You're reading a Sloane Parker book?" Samantha asked in surprise.

Beatrix swung her purse over her shoulder.

"I downloaded it for the plane," she replied. "I started it this morning and couldn't put it down."

Samantha drove back into Teton Village. Her throat was sore and she couldn't stop sniffling. She'd pick up some cough medicine and then see Marigold.

A familiar-looking man stood in line at the pharmacy. He turned around and Samantha realized it was Drew. Before he could see her, she ducked behind the aisle. Drew just broke up with one of the most beautiful women in Manhattan. Samantha couldn't run into him with blotchy skin and a red nose.

Drew paid for his purchases and left. Samantha breathed a sigh of relief. She put the cough medicine in her basket. Suddenly the pharmacy door opened and Drew walked toward her.

"Samantha?" He approached her. "What are you doing here?"

Samantha grabbed an item off the shelf. She pretended to read the directions on the packaging.

"Drew! I thought you were at the barn," she said, feigning surprise. "I came in to get a few things."

Drew glanced at the package.

"You're buying a chin strap?"

Samantha glanced down at the box. What was a chin strap, and what was it doing in the cough syrup aisle?

"I'm coming down with a cold," she said quickly. "You wear the chin strap at night and it opens your nasal passages."

Drew took a box from the shelf.

"It sounds interesting. I'll get one for myself," he said. "I'm glad I ran into you; I need to talk to you."

Samantha wanted to see Marigold. But she couldn't keep putting Drew off.

"I'll finish shopping and meet you at the ranch," Samantha suggested.

"Actually, I'd rather we talk in the village," he replied. "You do look pale. Why don't we sit by the fireplace in Grand Teton Lodge? It will be quiet, and we can order hot tea with honey."

The lobby of Grand Teton Lodge seemed straight out of a postcard. Moose heads hung on the walls and there were black-and-white photos of the Old West. Tall columns were made from giant tree trunks and a Christmas tree reached all the way to the ceiling.

"I was with my father all morning," Drew said when the waiter brought their tea. "He's very grateful to you."

"I didn't do anything," Samantha said. "Bruno put out the fire."

"You alerted Bruno and soothed the horses," Drew insisted. "I told you that you're braver than you think."

Samantha wanted to tell Drew about the arrowhead pendant. How it made her feel so confident. Now it was gone and she didn't know what to do. But this wasn't the time, Drew obviously had something on his mind.

"I just took Beatrix to the airport." Samantha changed the subject. "She's going back to New York."

Drew looked up from his teacup. "She told you?"

Samantha told him everything that Beatrix said at breakfast.

Drew fiddled with his cup. He placed it on the saucer.

"I'm glad that Beatrix is happy," he ventured. "It wasn't quite like that."

"What do you mean?" Samantha inquired.

Drew stretched his legs in front of him.

"Beatrix is like the lights on the Christmas tree. She's bright and sparkly and fun. When we met, it was impossible not to fall in love with her. After a while I stopped thinking about our love. There was so much else to concentrate on: having enough medicine for the children, making sure the workers got decent meals. Love was something that was there, like a familiar pair of shoes you wear every day." He stopped to think. "Then life changed and I thought about our love all over again. All week, I've debated whether I love Beatrix enough. Do I love her enough to give up my work, do I love her enough to stay in New York?" He rubbed his hands together. "Love isn't like that. You either love someone or you don't."

"But you said you're in love with Beatrix," Samantha reminded him. "And your father is counting on you to join the publishing house."

"I might join him, we haven't discussed it," Drew reflected. "Just considering it made me realize my feelings for Beatrix. I don't love her enough to make that decision."

"So, canceling the wedding wasn't Beatrix's idea?" Samantha asked.

"Perhaps we were both trying too hard and realized it at the same time," Drew offered. "I'd been wanting to say something to her for a few days." He gazed at Samantha steadily. "Ever since the gondola got stuck on the mountain."

Samantha's pulse quickened. She glanced down at her hands.

"I don't understand," she cut in.

There was something about the way Drew was gazing at her that made her flustered.

"I wanted to talk to you. Things got in the way, and we didn't have a moment together."

"You said you wanted to talk about the wedding."

"I did. I wanted to say I couldn't go through with it because—" Drew stopped. He looked at Samantha and his eyes were the most brilliant shade of blue. "Because no matter how much I tried to fight them, I was developing feelings for you."

Samantha felt like she was swimming underwater. Her eyes were misty and a chill ran down her spine.

"That's what you wanted to say?" she gasped.

"It started the moment I met you on the plane," he ruminated. "You asked me to tell you a story, and I told you about Kaman and the school in Thailand. Even then, I could see that you understood. Then we shared waffles at the Bunnery and strolled around the village. There was something about you that made me feel like I'd known you forever."

Samantha was completely still. She had felt exactly the same way.

"And you were so nice to Beatrix. Many women are jealous of Beatrix. You saw her good sides." He grinned. "Beatrix said this week hasn't been a disaster—at least she got you as a friend.

"I kept telling myself that none of it mattered. Beatrix and I were engaged." Drew kept talking. "Then the gondola got stuck. You were so lovely with your dark hair and those big brown eyes. I could have looked at you forever. I knew that if I never had anything in the world except you beside me, I'd be completely happy."

"Last night, I came home from the bar and saw you and Beatrix next to the window. I thought, I thought . . . ," Samantha blurted out.

"We were saying goodbye," Drew acknowledged. "Beatrix was embarrassed about having to tell my father the news. He's a grown man, though. We can't get married to please him."

Samantha put down her teacup. She wanted to say something but her head was throbbing. She was having trouble concentrating.

She'd go to the bathroom and splash warm water on her face. Then she'd come back and finish their conversation.

She stood up, but her head was foggy and her stomach ached. She put out her hand to steady herself. Then the lobby with its glorious Christmas tree and colored lights seemed to tilt. Her knees buckled and everything went black.

Samantha blinked and opened her eyes. She was lying in her bed at the ranch. There was a mug of hot cocoa, and the bedside table was scattered with cough medicine and a box of tissues.

The last few hours were hazy. She remembered Drew piling her into the car and driving to the ranch. He carried her upstairs and then she had a succession of visitors: Arthur and the doctor, and Bruno with a plate of Elaine's biscuits.

She tried to tell everyone she was fine but she kept drifting in and out of sleep. Now she was awake, but her head pounded and it was hard to open her eyes.

"You're awake," a male voice said.

Samantha opened her eyes wider. Drew sat beside the bed. He put down the magazine he'd been reading.

"How long have you been sitting there?" she wondered.

"Long enough to learn everything about the bison population in Jackson Hole," he said with a grin.

Samantha tried to sit up. She winced and fell back against the pillows.

"You didn't have to stay with me. It's just a cold."

"Combined with delayed shock from the fire, and a few bruises from riding the mechanical bull," Drew confirmed. "Dr. Parr said you're not to get out of bed. He'll come back and check on you in the morning."

"We only have two more days at the ranch," Samantha protested. Her body felt shivery and her throat hurt.

"That's why you have to follow his instructions," Drew commented. "My father is mortified. He wanted you to know he'll do anything: ask the cook to prepare special meals, lease a private jet to fly you home."

Samantha cringed; she'd never fly in a private jet. They were so small; how could one feel safe in a plane the size of a mini cereal box? And you never knew who was the pilot. It could be an ex–Air Force pilot who thought nothing of doing tricks in the air.

"That's very kind of him. But I'm not hungry and I'm quite happy to fly back commercial."

"You had us all very worried," Drew reflected. "Me, especially." He spread out his hands. "To be honest, I was so nervous telling you my feelings. I didn't expect that kind of reaction."

Samantha started to laugh. But Drew looked so serious. She bit her lip and covered her face with her hands.

"It had nothing to do with what you said," she began. "Actually I . . ." Her throat was parched and she reached for a glass of water.

Drew handed her the glass.

"Why don't we talk about it tomorrow," he offered. "Dr. Parr is downstairs. If you pass out again, it will be my fault."

Samantha nodded in agreement. She was too tired to talk about anything.

"If you don't mind," she ventured.

Drew stood up. He kissed her softly on the cheek.

"I'm going to go and check on the chicken soup," Drew said. "Just because you're not hungry doesn't mean you shouldn't eat."

He walked to the door and turned around.

"Samantha, I want you to know I meant everything I said," he began. "Just looking at you while you were sleeping made me realize again that you're the loveliest woman I've ever met."

Samantha wanted to say he couldn't mean it. Her cheeks were pale and she hadn't brushed her hair. But she didn't have the strength to argue.

She waited until Drew closed the door. Then she pulled the covers over her cheeks and closed her eyes. Tomorrow she'd wake up and worry about the future. Right now, it felt like a Christmas miracle.

Chapter Fifteen

Samantha sat against the headboard and sipped a glass of orange juice. She was so tired of drinking liquids: hot tea, and warm milk with honey, and soup that was nothing more than broth with a few vegetables. But Dr. Parr gave her a lecture on getting adequate nutrition. So, she dutifully nibbled everything on her tray this morning: toast and fruit, and a soft-boiled egg that reminded her of being sick when she was a child.

Drew had already stopped by twice. The first time she was barely awake; she saw him peering through the door. The warmth of his expression brought back everything from the day before: Beatrix's surprise announcement and Drew telling her his feelings and then her fainting in the lodge.

It was such an unlikely series of events she wanted to use it for a future Sloane Parker book: Sloane is relaxing at a ski chalet in Vaud, Switzerland, when she spies a familiar-looking man at the bar. It's Oliver Stanton, the handsome race car driver she gave up to protect her friend, the French agent Claire de Salle. Oliver offers to buy her a drink. Sloane declines, she would never go behind Claire's back. But the bartender sets down her favorite après-ski cocktail: Frangelico and Grand Marnier drizzled with chocolate. Oliver sits beside her and tells his story.

He and Claire spent a month in Nice, France, while Oliver prepared to race in the Grand Prix. At first it was magical: they sailed in the bay and took long drives into the hills. Then they started having fights. Claire hated his superstitions before a race, and they didn't enjoy the same movies. One night, there was a note on Oliver's pillow. Claire had accepted an assignment in New York and would be gone for six months. It was better they end things now; long-distance relationships never worked.

After Sloane finishes her cocktail, Sloane and Oliver move to the outdoor hot tub. They stay up all night talking and it's the best night of Sloane's life. She turns her phone off; it's Christmas and she's on holiday. Phineas at British Intelligence can wait until tomorrow to contact her.

The second time Drew appeared, Samantha gently told him to come back later. She wanted to take a bath and put on makeup. It was fine to see each other in pajamas and with a runny nose after six months of dating. But she was hardly going to discuss their future in the robe and faded slippers she usually wore to take Socks on his morning walk.

Even if Samantha and Drew shared the same feelings, how could Samantha know it would last? Samantha thought she had loved Roger. And Drew and Beatrix had been engaged. What if it was a rebound relationship for both of them? Then she recalled how being with Drew made her feel excited and secure at the same time. And Drew seemed to light up around her. As if he'd unwrapped the most wonderful Christmas present.

Then there was Arthur. Samantha knew that Arthur

adored Beatrix; he might blame Samantha for the breakup. Samantha wouldn't be able to write Sloane Parker books anymore, and Charlie could lose his job without her on his list.

Samantha remembered something Arthur said after the fire: he praised Samantha for saving the barn, and said once he moved too slowly and lost something terribly important. She couldn't help but wonder if he was talking about Diana.

Drew was helping the electrician in the barn; he'd be gone for ages. Samantha had time to read a few pages of Diana's diary before she took a bath.

She took out the diary and flipped to the next entry.

September 1991

Dear Diary,
You'll never guess where I am. Every morning, I have to open the curtains to make sure it's all still there: taxicabs idling on the pavement instead of cows trudging across a field, young people riding skateboards and blaring their boom boxes. A tattoo parlor next to a pet store with puppies in the window. And the smells! Greek food and spicy noodles and incense from a shop that sells enamel jewelry.
I'm sure you figured it out, I'm in New York! I'll tell you how it happened.
It was late August and Arthur was leaving the following week. Yes, I call him Arthur, though it took some getting used to. Anyway, we'd been having the best time. Arthur is a wonderful horseback rider. We explored Teton Valley: up Kodak Hill and over Little Pulpit

and through Whetstone Trail. I'll never forget seeing it through Arthur's eyes: creeks flanked by seagrass, wildflowers prettier than any painting, and miles of fields that reached the horizon.

We ate so many picnics, and we camped at every campground between Jackson Hole and Yellowstone Park. The camping was really a way to have privacy when we made love. It was wonderful going to bed with the owls and waking to the smell of Arthur brewing coffee and cooking sausage on the little camp stove.

Yes, diary, after the hot-air balloon ride, we couldn't keep our hands off each other. I can't believe how good sex is. The first time didn't go exactly as planned. I decided to cook dinner. It was Alice's night off and we had the kitchen to ourselves.

I cut my finger slicing cucumber for the salad. By the time I rinsed it and found a bandage, the baked chicken was overdone and the mashed potatoes were burnt. Arthur disappeared and I thought he wasn't coming back. Then he appeared with a shopping bag. He had gone to the market and bought makings for pizza: meatballs and cherry tomatoes and ricotta cheese. There's a restaurant in New York called Lombardi's that uses the same ingredients on their pizza. It's Arthur's favorite food.

After we ate, we sat on the porch for ages. By the time we went to his cabin, his roommate was there. We couldn't have any privacy so we went to my cabin instead. My bed is so narrow, it was like making love on a child's cot. It's hard to be passionate when Arthur's legs were sticking off the bed and we practically had to lie on our sides. But he was slow and gentle and we made it work.

After that, we found all sorts of places to make love. Beside streams when we went fishing. In the loft above the barn. Then one night, Arthur handed me an envelope. I couldn't imagine what was inside.

It was an acceptance letter from NYU's pre-veterinarian program.

My eyes widened and I gasped.

"I don't understand." I frowned. "I never applied to NYU."

Arthur toyed with his coffee cup. We were sitting at the kitchen table.

"I applied for you," he answered, as if it was the most natural thing in the world.

"You did what!" I exclaimed. "I don't want to go to university in New York. It's dirty and crowded and everything costs a fortune."

"You've never been to New York," he said indignantly. "Central Park is 840 acres of grass and lakes. It even has horseback riding trails. And not all of New York is expensive. Subways are cheap and Yankee Stadium sells the best cheeseburgers for $1.99 each."

I had seen photos of Central Park, but I never imagined it was so big. And hamburgers in Jackson Hole cost at least three dollars.

"That's not the point." I refused to be swayed. "I never considered college in New York. I can't afford the tuition."

"You don't have to." He turned the page of the acceptance letter. "You received a full scholarship including room and board."

Even if I went to school in Wyoming, I'd have to pay for housing and food. I couldn't live at home; the university is four hours from Jackson Hole.

"How could I qualify for a scholarship when they don't know anything about me?"

Arthur sipped his coffee.

"I got the name of your guidance counselor from your parents. The counselor sent your transcripts and teacher recommendations." He smiled. Oh diary, that smile. It never fails to win me over. "You never told me you were president of the honor society and head of the committee to save hawks from extinction."

I shrugged. It's silly to boast about one's high school accomplishments after graduation.

"NYU has one of the best pre-vet programs," he continued. "From there, you're bound to get accepted to Cornell."

Cornell's veterinarian school is the best in America. I've dreamed of attending, but I never thought it was possible.

Outside the window, it was a typical Jackson Hole sunset. The sky was a burnt orange and the tops of the mountains were tipped with pink and yellow. How could I leave Wyoming when it's so beautiful?

"I've never lived anywhere else," I wavered. "I couldn't survive without the mountains."

He leaned forward and kissed me.

"New York has something more important than mountains," he whispered. "It would have us, together. And I'm in love with you."

Arthur had told me he loved me before. But only in bed, in the afterglow of sex.

I stirred my coffee.

"It's a big decision," I said. "I'll give you my answer tomorrow."

"Which part are you unsure about?" he wanted to know. "Accepting the scholarship or having feelings for me?"

Arthur is over six feet tall, with the ease and confidence of a movie star. For once he seemed unsure of himself. I leaned forward and kissed him.

"Only the first part," I whispered back. "I'm falling in love with you too."

The next entry was dated October 1991.

Dear Diary,

Everyone says autumn is the best season in New York. There are things I love about it: my dorm room looks out on Union Square and there are so many different types of people. And nothing is better than gelato on late summer days. But I miss Wyoming. The only animals I see are my roommate's ferret and the cat that hangs out on the front steps. The buildings are so close together, sometimes I can't see the sky. And it's never as brilliant a blue as the sky in Jackson Hole.

Arthur is attending business school at Columbia and we don't see each other every day.

When we do, it's as good as it's always been. We explore the city and he insists on paying for everything. But that doesn't stop me from feeling like one of the horses at the dude ranch last summer. It was an Irish Hunter imported from Ireland, and I could tell it was homesick.

I've had the flu for the last few days, and that's made it worse. It's hard to get better with sirens screaming outside my window. Tomorrow night, Arthur wants me to have dinner with his parents. How am I going to put on a dress and heels when I can hardly get out of bed?

The next entry was dated a week later.

Dear Diary,

Arthur's parents live in one of those doorman buildings on the Upper West Side. You should have seen it: floor-to-ceiling windows, silk upholstery, and a kitchen with all the latest gadgets.

I squeezed Arthur's hand so tightly when we arrived, his fingers turned blue. Then his father offered me a cocktail and I felt better. His mother is quite lovely. She's a part-time professor and involved in New York charities. His father is an older version of Arthur, without Arthur's gentle sense of humor.

They asked me the usual questions—how do I like college, what are my goals—and they were impressed with my answers. Even Arthur seemed pleased.

Then we sat down to dinner and it went

downhill. Arthur's father opened a bottle of red wine and I spilled some on the tablecloth. It wasn't exactly my fault. The housekeeper was juggling three plates and I jumped up to help her. Arthur's mother said not to worry, but I could tell that his father was upset.

Arthur's mother asked what I missed about Jackson Hole. I started listing things: swimming in the hot springs and fishing at Emily's Pond, cross-country skiing in the winter. All of a sudden, I started crying. Arthur was furious.

I couldn't tell him why I was really crying. That came later, in his apartment. After we left his parents, he said he wanted to go somewhere quiet for a nightcap. I knew he really wanted to have a fight without my roommate eavesdropping.

"What were you thinking, trying to serve dinner?" Arthur demanded. He was pacing around his living room, clutching a shot glass.

"I couldn't just sit there," I returned. "I'm used to helping Alice at the ranch."

"My parents' housekeeper has been with them for twenty years. She knows how to carry a few dinner plates," Arthur said. "You embarrassed everyone and ruined a fine tablecloth."

"I'll pay for a new one," I said through gritted teeth.

"It's not about the money," Arthur said. "It was your attitude. Then you started crying, as if you're not living in one of the most exciting cities in the world. My parents are both lifelong New Yorkers, how do you think that made them feel?"

"I'll write your mother an apology," I said guiltily. "She was nice. I like her very much."

"Why shouldn't my mother be nice?" he asked. He was only half listening to my answers. And he didn't look at me. I wondered if he was going to break up with me.

He set his glass on the coffee table.

"I didn't only take you there to meet my parents," he said, sitting across from me. "My mother wanted to give me something."

He took a velvet box from his pocket. Inside was the most beautiful diamond ring. An emerald-cut diamond on a platinum band.

I was so surprised; I didn't know what to say.

"It's my mother's engagement ring," he said, filling the silence. "I told my parents I was going to propose."

"You want to get married?" I said in shock.

"That's what two people do when they're in love."

"We're both in school," I protested. "We hardly know each other."

Arthur's serious expression was replaced by a cheeky grin.

"I believe I know you quite well." His eyes traveled over my body. "And I've received an exciting offer. A friend of my father's wants me to join his publishing house. He doesn't have any children, and he wants me to take it over."

"I'm in college. I have years ahead of me."

"There's no reason why you can't continue

once we're married," he said. "We'll get an apartment in Midtown. It will be much more convenient. We can meet for lunch and take walks in Central Park. We can even go riding on the weekends."

It sounded lovely. To be honest, I'm not a fan of the dorms. And my favorite part of New York is Central Park.

But I couldn't marry Arthur.

"I'm sorry, but the answer is no." I shook my head. "Your parents would think I'm marrying you for the wrong reasons."

Arthur's face contorted. He jumped up.

"If you think they'll say you married me for my money, you're wrong," he declared. "I would never take money from my parents. We'll live modestly in the beginning."

My heart pounded and I took a deep breath. My stomach was tied in knots and I was beginning to shake.

"It's not about money. It's because I'm pregnant."

He dropped into a chair. "You're what?"

"I thought I had the flu. It wouldn't go away, so I took a pregnancy test." I still couldn't look at him. "That's why I was crying. I cry about everything: because I expected an A on a test and got a B plus, when the cat that lives next door got stuck outside in the rain. If we got married, your parents would think I was trying to trap you."

"I was raised Catholic; I won't let you—"

"I thought about it, I'm not going to have an abortion," I assured him. "I'll live with my parents in Jackson Hole. Eventually I'll go back to school, but for now I'll take care of the baby."

Arthur got up and paced around the room.

"Is that what you want? To live in Jackson Hole your whole life? Your old high school boyfriend will still be in town and your parents will invite him to dinner. You'll start sleeping together and he'll ask you to marry him. He'll get a job in a ski shop and you'll go back to the dude ranch and spend your life kissing up to tourists."

"For your information, my high school boyfriend is studying pre-med at Notre Dame," I snapped. "And what's wrong with working at the dude ranch? I'd be with people who like the same things as I do. And I wouldn't have to apologize for helping to serve dinner. In Wyoming it's called good manners."

It felt good to get angry. Since I arrived in New York, I haven't had the confidence to get angry about anything.

Arthur sat across from me. He leaned forward.

"You and I like the same things. We both love horses and reading." He took my hand. "I'd know why you agreed to marry me, that has to count for something. I'd marry you if you were nine months pregnant and had to stand at the altar naked because you couldn't fit into a dress. I love you and I can't be without you."

Oh, diary. I couldn't imagine a life without Arthur's smile. Never kissing him again or having his body pressed against mine.

CHRISTMAS AT THE RANCH | 241

"I don't think the priest would marry us if I was naked," I said with a grin.

He sensed the change in my mood. He picked up the box and took out the diamond ring.

"Diana, I've loved you since the moment we met." He got down on his knee. *"I promise to spend my life making you happy. Will you marry me?"*

What choice did I have, diary?

I said yes.

Samantha stopped reading. She went back and flipped through the pages.

She wanted to be mistaken, but the dates matched up. Arthur and Diana got married and had a baby. The diary could have belonged to Drew's mother.

How did it end up in Arthur's library? Perhaps Arthur didn't know it was there. When he furnished the ranch, he probably brought books from his apartment in New York. The journal sat unnoticed until Samantha found it behind a Vince Flynn thriller.

The door opened and Drew poked his head in.

"You're up!" he said, entering the room.

"Drew." Samantha slipped the diary behind her back. "I was about to take a bath."

"The electrician didn't need me, so I went into the village," Drew said. "I have a surprise for you."

"What kind of surprise?" she asked, shifting the diary into her other hand.

"Don't worry, it was approved by Dr. Parr," he said with a smile. "It does mean leaving this room. Dress warmly, you'll need a hat and gloves."

"Where are we going?" she wondered.

"You'll see," he said, his eyes as bright as the fire in the fireplace. "I'll wait for you downstairs."

When Samantha appeared, a white Rolls-Royce stood in the driveway. A man in a gray uniform jumped out.

"Good afternoon, Miss Morgan, Mr. Wentworth," he greeted them. "I'm Adam; I'll be your guide. There's hot chocolate in a thermos or coffee if you prefer."

Drew took her hand and led her to the car.

"Dr. Parr said it would be good for you to get fresh air. But you have to stay warm," Drew said when they were seated. The upholstery was buttery leather and there were lace curtains and thick white carpet. A glass partition separated the seats and there were blankets to put over their knees.

"The car is called a snow coach and it does tours of the valley," Drew said. "In the trunk there's a picnic basket with sandwiches and dessert."

Samantha recalled Arthur taking Diana on a hot-air balloon ride. She couldn't think about the diary, she had to concentrate on Drew.

"You didn't have to do this." She turned to him. "I would have been happy eating a bowl of soup in the kitchen."

"We only have two more days and there's still so much to see." He paused. He squeezed her hand. "Plus, I wanted to spend some time together."

Samantha impulsively leaned forward and kissed him on the cheek.

"I'm glad you did," she agreed. Her whole body tingled and she felt happy. "It's a perfect Christmas treat."

They kept the partition down so Adam could describe the scenery. Adam pointed out the snowshoers on Taggart

Lake and the hiking trail that led up to Delicate Arch. In the summer, you could stand beneath the arch and watch the sun rise over the Tetons.

The car drove into Bridger-Teton National Forest. The road had been cleared by snowplows. On either side of them, the fir trees were thick with fresh powder, and the sun made rainbow-colored patterns on the icicles.

Adam stopped the car in front of a clearing. The air was fresh and clear, and smelled of winter blooms. The Elk Refuge stretched below them, and above were the snow-covered domes of the Teton mountains.

"I've never seen anything so beautiful," Samantha gushed.

It was impossible to know where to look first. She didn't want to miss any of it: the deer that came so close to the car that she could see their wet noses, the tiny footprints in the snow that must be squirrels and chipmunks.

Adam brought out the picnic basket. Samantha and Drew ate thick sandwiches and éclairs, and washed it down with hot chocolate.

"There's so much beauty in the world. That's what's wonderful about traveling to new places," Drew mused, biting into his sandwich. "This is so different than the fields of Thailand or the jungles in the Amazon, but it's just as spectacular."

Samantha put her sandwich on the little tray. Drew spent his life going to places she couldn't imagine. How could she even contemplate traveling to Thailand to help build schools when something as simple as finding a new dentist after her old one retired made her break out in hives? When Trader Joe's ran out of her favorite oatmeal, she ate cold cereal for a week because she was afraid to shop at a different grocery store.

It was time to tell Drew about the arrowhead pendant.

She told him about meeting Marigold at the gift shop and that she lent her the arrowhead pendant and it gave her the confidence to ride in the snowmobile and go snow tubing. Now she'd lost it.

Drew waited until she finished. He set down his sandwich.

"When I was in second grade, our teacher taught us to write letters. I was so excited; I wrote a letter to my mother. I told her that I won the spelling bee and my favorite subject was geography. But I didn't know where to send it. I couldn't ask my father, he refused to talk about her." He paused. "Stanley, the doorman in our building, could tell I was upset. He asked what was wrong and I explained. He told me to leave the letters with him, he'd make sure they reached my mother. I asked how he knew her address and he admitted he didn't.

"He said children wrote to the Tooth Fairy and Santa Claus and the Easter Bunny. Somehow, the letters arrived. Or Santa Claus wouldn't know where to deliver presents.

"I didn't argue. It made sense. Every Friday I gave Stanley a stack of letters. After about a year, Stanley left and we got a new doorman. I stopped writing the letters but somehow, it didn't matter anymore. I was enjoying life and the things I was doing enough without having to share them," he finished. "Perhaps the pendant went missing because you don't need it anymore."

Samantha pictured Drew as a child, transcribing the events in his life. But this was different. Samantha was a grown woman and her fears weren't dismissed so easily. What if she joined Drew at some exotic destination and was paralyzed with fear? She'd spoil things for him too.

"I don't know," she wavered.

Drew leaned forward and kissed her. The kiss was warm and sweet, and she kissed him back.

There was a coughing sound from Adam standing outside of the car.

Drew grinned. He closed the curtains and pushed the button that raised the partition.

"I believe in you," he whispered, kissing her again. "You're the brightest, loveliest woman I know."

Samantha sat at the dressing table in her room. The rest of the drive had been so romantic. The car wound through the valley, and they talked about books and movies.

Now, Drew went to talk to his father and Samantha came upstairs to rest.

Her phone buzzed and she answered.

"Samantha," her mother said. "We've had the most thrilling day; you won't believe what happened."

"I'm sure you'll tell me," Samantha chuckled. Her mother was so full of energy. Ever since her parents left for Europe, her mother seemed ten years younger.

"Tomorrow is the New Year's Eve ball, so we wanted to do more sightseeing," her mother was saying. "We drove to Villefranche-sur-Mer. It's a tiny village above Monte Carlo with views of the Mediterranean.

"After lunch, we walked around town and I noticed a hotel called Chez Hughuette. That's my grandmother's middle name, I always found it strange. The owner told us the most tragic story. The hotel was built by Count Alfonse du Lapin for his bride, Countess Hughuette du Lapin. The countess lived at the château alone while Alfonse fought in the Napoleonic Wars. On the day he arrived home, he was so excited to see her, he ran in front of a horse. He was trampled to death while Hughuette watched from the window.

"Countess Hughuette's great-niece married an American and settled in New York. I think that was my great-grandmother! She died before I was born. After all, how many girls from New Jersey end up with the middle name 'Hughuette'?

"Can you believe it? I'm related to a countess! I've always thought I must be French. I adore crepes and I can't resist French chocolates, although, who can? I had to promise your father I wasn't going to start putting on airs," she finished. "I think he was jealous. When we came back to the hotel, he went online and ordered a DNA kit for himself."

"I'll have to buy you a beret instead of a cowboy hat," Samantha said with a smile.

"I would love a beret," her mother answered brightly. "Preferably in red. I look good in red." She paused. "Buy a cowboy hat for yourself instead. So that when you're back in Brooklyn, you can remind yourself that you flew to Jackson Hole. You can do anything you want, Samantha. You just have to trust in yourself."

Samantha said goodbye and hung up.

Her mind returned to Diana's diary. It was as if she had been given some huge secret that she didn't want to know. Then she thought about Drew and their wonderful kisses. It had been so long since she'd felt like this about anyone. It was impossible to know what came next but she didn't want it to end.

Outside the window, a soft snow began to fall. Samantha picked up her hairbrush. If only Christmas week would last forever.

Chapter Sixteen

Samantha looked up from her notebook and gazed out the window. She had been resting in her room for an hour but it was impossible to relax. She kept thinking about the diary and whether Diana was Drew's mother. What would Drew say if she told him? How could she keep it to herself? It wasn't her place to know and she wished she never read the diary in the first place.

And then there were her feelings for Drew. The snow coach tour had been so romantic. She could have sat beside him listening to the whoosh of the wheels on the freshly plowed roads forever. What would happen when the week was over and they had to go back to their own lives?

It had given her an idea for a Sloane Parker book. The plot came to her so quickly, she had to write it down. Sloane has just delivered supplies to a convent high in the Himalayas. She is on the way back down the treacherous mountain path on her donkey, Socrates, when the donkey stumbles and falls. Socrates's ankle is broken and it can't continue.

It would take hours to reach the bottom on foot and a snowstorm is approaching. Sloane gave all her food to the nuns, except for a chocolate bar and a bag of granola. She'll freeze to death or starve before anyone finds her.

The wind begins to blow and she clings to the rocks, stroking the poor donkey's head. Her lips turn blue and she is about to give up hope when she hears a voice. A man riding a donkey emerges from the path below. It's Damien, one of her recruits at British Intelligence.

Damien makes a splint for Socrates's ankle. Then he and Sloane climb on Damien's donkey, while Socrates trails behind them. It's only later when they're safely at base camp that Sloane is able to thank Damien. If it weren't for him, she would have frozen to death. Damien says she should really thank herself. Sloane left a trail of carrots on the trail, and that's how Damien was able to find her.

Sloane is surprised and pleased that he remembered. The first thing she teaches new recruits is to mark their paths in case they get lost. The bright orange of the carrots is impossible to miss and carrots wouldn't get eaten by hawks. Hawks are meat eaters; they don't touch vegetables.

Sloane and Damien snuggle together in the sleeping bag to stay warm. In the morning, the snowstorm is over and Sloane wakes up to a fresh, new world. She can't wait to tell Phineas that the classes for new recruits really work.

Samantha closed the notebook and pulled on jeans and a sweater. She couldn't put off seeing Marigold any longer. She grabbed her jacket and hurried down the staircase.

The keys to the SUV that Beatrix had borrowed were sitting on a table in the entry. Samantha tucked them in her pocket and slipped outside. She'd drive herself into town. She wouldn't be gone long, and she didn't want Arthur or Drew asking where she was going.

The gift shop was quiet when Samantha entered. Marigold stood at the counter, arranging postcards.

"Samantha," Marigold said, turning around. "How nice to see you. I've hardly had any customers all day. Most families go home on New Year's Day and they want to get in as much skiing as possible."

"I didn't come to buy anything," Samantha said guiltily. "I wanted to talk to you."

Marigold smiled her radiant smile.

"That's even better," Marigold answered. "I've hardly spoken to anyone besides a little boy who kept touching the glass jars," she chuckled. "I had to ask him to stop. His hands were covered in sticky icing from his cinnamon bun."

Samantha had so much to tell Marigold. She didn't know where to start.

"Last time I saw you, was just after you had run into your old boyfriend," Marigold prompted. "I gather you told him you didn't want to see him."

"How did you know?" Samantha asked in surprise.

"There's something different about you." Marigold studied her. "When you came in last time, you carried a certain heaviness. It's gone now. There's an openness you didn't have before."

Samantha recalled her kisses with Drew. Just thinking about them made her happy.

"Roger didn't seem too upset." Samantha shrugged. "He left without texting goodbye."

"He's probably embarrassed. Men wound more easily than we think," Marigold acknowledged. "Tell me, what else has been going on? How is the wedding coming along?"

Marigold had said that Samantha and the groom were developing feelings for each other. That was why Beatrix was rushing the wedding.

"Beatrix left. There isn't going to be a wedding," Samantha told her. "You predicted it; how did you know?"

"I don't have any secret powers, I simply listened to you," Marigold said with a little laugh. "Everyone is so busy with their own opinions these days; they don't listen to each other. A Native American friend who belongs to one of the Plains tribes taught me differently. They believe that hundreds of years ago when they started hunting buffalo, they called on the Great Spirit to guide them. The Great Spirit instructed them to only kill what they needed to survive, and to let the rest of the herd roam free. That way Native Americans formed a connection with the animals, and they learned to live together. That belief continues with some tribes today. The Great Spirit guides them to do the right thing for each other and for all creatures; it's the only way the Earth will survive. It takes concentration to hear the Great Spirit. It's easy for personal desires to get in the way. It's the same with hearing people around us. If we really listen, there's so much we can learn."

Samantha thought about people she knew who spent all their time posting on social media. No one really listened to each other. The only thing they were interested in was how many likes they got.

"I never thought about it like that, but I understand." Samantha nodded. "Though that's not the reason I came to see you." She fiddled with a postcard. "I feel terrible. I lost the arrowhead pendant."

"Is that what you're worried about?" Marigold asked dismissively. "You didn't lose it. I'm sure it will turn up when it's ready."

"What do you mean?" Samantha wondered.

"If you kept the arrowhead pendant with you always, you wouldn't recognize your own strengths," Marigold offered. "How could a caterpillar become a butterfly if it stayed in its cocoon?"

"You said the arrowhead protects the wearer from harm, and it was true." Samantha's voice became urgent. "After I lost it, I fell off the mechanical bull at the bar; I've never been so humiliated. And the barn caught fire. Everyone said I was brave, but they're wrong. I had to save the horses, but I've never been so frightened in my life. Now all the fears have returned. I've started checking the weather forecast for New Year's Day," she continued in a rush. "I do that before I have to fly. If the weather app says it's going to be bad weather, I panic. Once I postponed an important trip and the app was wrong. I caused a lot of trouble for nothing."

"It couldn't have been too terrible," Marigold said wisely. "Most things aren't as important as we think."

Samantha had been scheduled to sign books and do an interview at a small bookstore in Ohio. The weather app said there were going to be severe thunderstorms, so Samantha canceled her flight. It worked out in the end. She did the interview over Zoom and the bookstore was flooded with orders. The following year they invited her back. Still, she felt awful at the time.

"I don't know," Samantha wavered.

Her hands felt clammy and her stomach was doing little flips. She had to tell Marigold about Drew. There was no one else she could talk to, and she didn't know what to do.

"I'm developing feelings for someone. But I'm afraid it won't work," Samantha began. "Our lifestyles are so different and I don't want to disappoint him."

"Is it the man you were sitting with on the bench?" Marigold wondered.

"He and Beatrix were supposed to get married," Samantha said and nodded, feeling guilty all over again. "He has feelings for me too, but what if they don't last? He just broke off their engagement and I wasn't completely over Roger until recently. What if this is a rebound relationship for both of us?"

Marigold arranged a stack of postcards.

"Love is scary for everyone. You're giving yourself to the person you care about most in the world. Love can also make you more fulfilled than anything else in life. We all need to belong to something." Marigold waved out the store window. "I belong to this town. For me, visiting the Elk Refuge and seeing the deer and buffalo are all I need to be content. None of us were made to be alone."

"That's why I never thought Roger would leave New York," Samantha said grimly. "He couldn't live without baseball and the hot dogs from Yankee Stadium."

"New Yorkers are passionate about their food," Marigold agreed, smiling. "They insist their pizza is better than in Italy. I doubt the people in Naples would agree." Her tone grew serious. "You'll know what you belong to when you find it. It's like coming home."

"Since Roger left, I believed having my dog, Socks, was enough." Samantha pulled out her phone. She found the photos of Socks and Molly in their Christmas sweaters and handed it to Marigold. "Socks is spending Christmas with my boss and he's already made a new friend."

Marigold flicked through the recent photos. She stopped at a photo of Samantha and Drew in front of the Rolls-Royce.

"That's quite a car," she commented.

"It's called a snow coach," Samantha said happily,

remembering their morning. "Drew arranged it and we had so much fun."

Marigold studied the photo for a long time. She handed the phone back to Samantha.

"Is Drew the one who was supposed to be getting married?" Marigold asked.

"Yes," Samantha said with a sigh. All the problems came rushing back. "Being with Drew makes me so happy. I don't know what to do."

"You don't have to decide now," Marigold counseled. "My Native Americans friends have taught me that patience is one thing that separates humans from animals. With the internet, we've lost that virtue. You can get it back."

When Samantha returned to the ranch, Arthur was sitting in the living room. A fire crackled in the fireplace and the lights on the Christmas tree twinkled in the afternoon light.

"Samantha." Arthur looked up from the book he was reading. "Please join me."

She hung up her jacket and sat across from him on the sofa.

"I'd offer you a cocktail but I don't drink before six p.m.," Arthur said with a smile. "I'm a little old-fashioned."

"I don't want anything." Samantha shook her head. She turned to the window. "It's so pretty, I never tire of the view."

"I agree, it's better than all the galleries in New York." Arthur placed the book on the coffee table. "Drew told me the wedding is postponed. Beatrix had to go back to New York."

Drew hadn't told Arthur the engagement was over. Beatrix and Drew wanted to do it together.

"Drew thought I'd be upset, but all I care about is that he's happy." Arthur was still talking. "When you first have a baby it's like being given a blank notebook. You fill the pages any way you like. If you're a good parent, you spend the next eighteen years attending their events, overseeing their homework, and making so many bowls of cereal you consider buying stock in General Mills." He smiled. "Then it's over. The kid goes off to college and starts a career. There isn't an extra set of car keys in the entry or a jar of peanut butter in the pantry. If they're fairly happy, they assume they owe you something for everything you did. Parenting isn't like that," he finished. "The only reward we need is knowing that we gave our child enough love and attention, so they want to do the same for their children."

"My parents are the same," Samantha acknowledged. "They only want me to be happy."

"Of course, one doesn't always see it that way when one is young," Arthur chuckled. "When I was a boy, I was certain my mother made me eat broccoli to punish me. And I was furious at my father for not wanting me to major in underwater photography in college. I saw a documentary on Jacques Cousteau and thought it would be thrilling. It wouldn't have suited me, I'm not a good swimmer."

"It can take a while to find what we love to do," Samantha said. "I'm lucky that I get to write books for a living."

"We're lucky to have you." Arthur sat up straighter. "I shouldn't take up your time. Dr. Parr wants you to rest."

"If I rest any more, I'll be like the bears that hibernate all winter." Samantha grinned, standing up. "I'll go upstairs and freshen up."

"One more thing," Arthur said.

Samantha turned around pensively. Maybe Drew had told him after all.

"I decided we're going to have a New Year's Eve party anyway." His eyes danced. "We can't let six bottles of vintage champagne go to waste."

Samantha paced around her room. Marigold had made her feel better, but there were still things troubling her. She and Drew hadn't discussed what would happen when they left the ranch. If he went back to Thailand, she might never see him again. It was easy for Marigold to say Samantha would find her courage. But she was like the lion in *The Wizard of Oz*. The moment she thought about it, it completely deserted her.

And there was the diary. She couldn't keep it secret from Drew forever. What if she was wrong? Perhaps Diana and Arthur called the engagement off, like Beatrix and Drew. Diana raised her baby in Jackson Hole, and Arthur married another woman.

Samantha took the diary out of the bedside table. She'd read a few more entries to find out for sure if Diana was Drew's mother. Then she'd figure what to tell Drew.

December 1995

Dear Diary,
I haven't written to you in four years, I'm a terrible correspondent. To be fair, I lost you for ages. I only discovered you last week when I was cleaning out the nursery. You'd been beneath a pile of blankets all this time!
I read my entries from the beginning and almost didn't recognize myself. How I miss the confident young woman who made breakfast

for ten hungry cowboys on the dude ranch, who thought nothing of horseback riding over Glacier Gulch in the pouring rain.

I've had the most terrible time. Even as I write that, I feel guilty. You see, I have everything I could dream of. A husband who loves me, a wonderful little boy, and enough money to be comfortable. But that makes it worse. I want to be happy. Happiness comes from within, and I've never been so miserable in my life.

It started after Drew was born. Looking back, I see I had postpartum depression. Even if I had recognized it, Arthur wouldn't have allowed me to see a therapist. He's old-fashioned that way. He would think it reflected badly on our marriage.

After six months I felt better, but it was still difficult. Drew cried all the time as a baby and I refused to hire a nanny. I can be stubborn too! I wasn't working or going to school, so felt I should raise my own child. And I was afraid of being lonely without Drew to take care of.

You can't have a conversation with a baby, and Arthur worked late almost every night. He said he was doing it for us. And it was true. He bought pretty things for the apartment: a painting, new dishes, and silverware. Sometimes he'd surprise me by taking me out to dinner. But that didn't fill the hours of the day.

It was all right when Arthur's parents lived in New York. I like his mother, and she visited fairly often. Two years ago, his father had a heart attack and they moved to Palm Beach.

After that, I tried to join a mothers' group and attend meetups, but the other mothers are different. They either have important careers or they're members of charity boards. They aren't interested in a former ranch hand from Jackson Hole, Wyoming.

I thought it would get easier when Drew was older. And I adore him. He's sweet and bright and everything I could ask for. But I'm not a good mother. I'm always nervous something will happen to him: he'll get sick; we'll get into an accident in a taxi. When he's away from me—at preschool, or with a little friend—I worry about him even more.

I often wonder if it would be different if we lived in Jackson Hole. I never worried about anything before. It's as if being in New York doesn't provide me enough oxygen. I can't tell you how much I miss the mountains and the fields. Every morning before I open my eyes, I hope for one small second that I'll see buffalo crossing a field. When I do open them, all I see is Mrs. Abernathy's laundry hanging in her kitchen window.

Thank goodness I have one friend. Arthur doesn't approve. Ellery is our building doorman; I don't know what I'd do without him. He lets Drew push his little trucks around the floor in the lobby and we chat. Ellery is Irish, he moved to New York to be close to his daughter after his wife died. He lived on a farm his whole life; he misses horses as much as I do.

Arthur is coming home early; he has a surprise for me. Maybe it will be tickets to Jackson Hole for Christmas. We usually go to Palm Beach. I'd happily give up seeing Santa Claus on a boat from Arthur's parents' marina and visit Santa under the antlers in Teton Village instead.

The next entry was dated a week later.

Dear Diary,

Arthur and I are in a terrible fight. He hasn't talked to me for days and he's sleeping in the study.

It started the day he had a surprise. He insisted I hire a babysitter, even though I get anxious leaving Drew with anyone. So I called an agency. We left Drew with an older woman named Beth and climbed into a cab.

"You complain that you don't have anyone to talk to, but you haven't said a word," Arthur said, when we were sitting in traffic on Lexington Avenue.

"You asked about my morning and I told you I hadn't done anything," I said matter-of-factly.

"I know what you're saying even when you don't say it." Arthur folded his arms. "It's usually that there isn't a single person in Manhattan to talk to."

Arthur has become so touchy. And he's always rearranging my words. Sometimes I feel like we're playing a complicated game of snakes and ladders.

"That isn't true. I love to talk to you." I fiddled with my hemline. "I was thinking about

Drew. What if he wakes from his nap and thinks something's happened to me?"

"Beth will tell him you've gone to lunch." Arthur sounded exasperated. His tone softened and he took my hand. "I've cleared my work calendar for the next two hours; can we please try to enjoy ourselves?"

Oh diary, I still love him! I love his eyes and his smile and even the way he hunches over when he's upset. But we can't seem to get along.

"I promise," I agreed solemnly. "You still haven't told me where we're going. I didn't know how to dress."

Arthur turned to me. His eyes were warm.

"Do you remember years ago when I said I'd meet you at the altar even if you were naked, because I couldn't live without you?" he asked. "I still feel the same. It doesn't matter what you wear, you'll always be the most beautiful woman in New York."

We kissed. For a moment I thought everything would be all right.

The taxi pulled up in front of one of those fancy co-op buildings on the Upper East Side.

"I thought we were going to lunch." I frowned.

"We are, I have to drop off a manuscript first." Arthur stepped out of the cab and opened my door. "It will only take a minute. Come with me."

The lobby was elegant with plush white carpet and crystal chandeliers. I guessed that the apartment probably belonged to a famous author. Arthur's company is doing very well.

He's signing well-known authors and getting their new books onto bestseller lists.

Arthur knocked but there was no answer. He turned the handle and the door was unlocked.

"He probably stepped out for a minute," Arthur said. "Let's wait inside."

The living room was beautifully furnished with modern sofas and bright rugs. The walls were practically all glass. It was so high up, I looked down on Central Park and the East River.

The front door opened and a man entered. He wore a pin-striped suit and carried a briefcase.

"You must be the author," I introduced myself. "I'm Diana Wentworth, Arthur's wife."

The man shook my hand. "I'm not an author, I'm the Realtor."

I turned to Arthur, who had just reappeared from the study.

"Diana, this is Martin Manning, he's handling the sale for us," Arthur said, joining us. There was a smug expression on his face.

"What sale?" I asked.

"The purchase, actually." Martin turned to me, smiling. "Congratulations, Mrs. Wentworth. You're the new owner of apartment 36C in one of the most coveted co-op buildings in New York."

I glanced from Martin to Arthur.

"We're not looking for a new place," I insisted.

Arthur and I have gotten into arguments

about our apartment. Now that he's doing well financially, he wants us to move. But I refuse. Our apartment is only two bedrooms and the neighborhood isn't ideal, but I couldn't survive without Ellery. And I like the location. It isn't as snooty as other parts of Manhattan and it's close to the park.

"We're not looking anymore," Arthur corrected. He smiled at me grandly. "Merry Christmas, Diana. This is your early Christmas present."

I tried to conceal my concern. It wasn't the kind of home in which to raise a small child. Drew would leave fingerprints on the windows. And it's so high up, it would take ages to get down the elevator.

"You were finding it hard to move. So, I decided to keep looking," Arthur continued. "Martin found this before it was on the market. We're lucky, it's almost impossible to get approved. One of my authors is on the board."

I can only imagine what kind of people lived there. Probably not ones who'll welcome a young woman from Wyoming and a three-year-old boy.

"Is it big enough?" I asked, trying to think of a reason why we shouldn't take it.

"The apartment next door might become available soon." Martin turned to me. "You and Arthur will be the first to know."

"We'd practically have the floor to ourselves." Arthur squeezed my hand. "You al-

ways say the thing you don't like about New York is not being able to see the sky." He waved at the window. "It's right there."

How could Arthur not understand? I don't want to live in the sky, I only want to see it from the ground.

After we signed the papers, we went to lunch at Le Cirque to celebrate. I could hardly eat a bite. I kept thinking about Christmastime in Jackson Hole. Eating cinnamon rolls at the Bunnery and singing Christmas carols in Teton Village. Oh diary, is it possible to miss a place so much, it makes it hard to breathe?

After lunch, Arthur went back to the office and Drew and I spent the afternoon making a puzzle. I was so upset; I didn't pick up anything for dinner. Now it's snowing—not the powdery snow we get in Wyoming. Snow that turns to sleet and makes the sidewalks slippery. I'll order pizza from Lombardi's for dinner. It's still Arthur's favorite food. At least there's one thing that I'll get right!

Samantha closed the diary. Suddenly everything clicked into place. Downstairs, the living room was empty. She grabbed the car keys from the table in the entryway and drove into the village.

It was after 5:00 P.M. when she reached the gift shop. She was afraid it might be closed. But Marigold was standing behind the counter when she entered.

"Samantha." Marigold glanced up from the cash register. "What are you doing back? I was about to close but

I had a last-minute flurry of customers." She smiled. "A woman refused to return to Michigan without an 'I left my heart in Jackson Hole' pillow."

"I'm glad I caught you," Samantha said.

Now that she was here, she didn't know what to say. Maybe this was a bad idea. She should go back to the ranch and spend the evening with Drew.

"Did something happen?" Marigold prompted.

Samantha brought her mind back to Marigold. She couldn't walk away. Drew was too important to her.

"How could you leave Arthur and Drew and come back to Jackson Hole?" Samantha blurted out before she could stop herself. "Drew was only four years old. He's missed you so much."

In all the time Samantha had spent with Marigold, she always seemed so sure of herself. Now her face fell and her hands trembled.

"What are you talking about?" Marigold asked, closing the cash register.

Samantha took the journal from her purse.

"I found your diary. Arthur said I could borrow some books from his library. It fell off the shelf and I picked it up." She handed it to Marigold. "I shouldn't have read it; I wish I never had. But I'm in love with Drew and you hurt him so much. I don't know what to do."

Marigold took the journal cautiously. She turned it over in her hand.

"Does Drew know about this?" She looked up at Samantha.

Samantha shook her head. "No one has seen it. I came here as soon as I figured it out."

"How did you know it was mine?"

"It all fell into place. This afternoon you mentioned that New Yorkers are passionate about their pizza. In the diary, you wrote that Lombardi's pizza is Arthur's favorite food," Samantha began. "There were other things. When I showed you the photos of Socks on my phone, you stared at the photo of Drew for so long. There was something different in your expression. Then, I remembered you left Jackson Hole when you were young. When you returned, you changed your name.'"

Samantha stopped to take a breath.

"I see why you're a good writer," Marigold said quietly. "You don't forget any details."

"It doesn't make sense." Samantha's voice was plaintive. "You loved Drew, you even said you still loved Arthur. How could you leave? You never tried to contact Drew. He grew up believing you didn't love him."

Marigold walked around the counter. She motioned for Samantha to sit on a stool.

"All right, I'll tell you." Marigold sat beside her. "I loved Drew more than anything. But I was a terrible mother. I refused to get a nanny, but I became too afraid to take Drew anywhere. I don't know why; it happened gradually. I was afraid to go to the playground in case he got hurt, or to the park in case he got abducted by a stranger. I wanted to see a therapist but Arthur wouldn't hear of it." Marigold twisted her hands. "He believed that would make him a failure too.

"It grew worse in our last year of marriage. We moved into the apartment on the Upper East Side and I was so lonely. I missed our old doorman, Ellery, and Drew missed his friends in the neighborhood. The people in the new building were very standoffish. When I told them I was from Wyoming, the women slipped their Chanel sunglasses over their perfectly upturned noses and ignored me. The building had a doorman but we weren't really friends. I was too afraid what the other residents would say if I talked to him. Drew didn't have any friends nearby and we couldn't even get a dog. How could we take a dog for walks when we lived on the thirty-sixth floor?

"I tried to talk to Arthur, but he was always at work. Sometimes he was gone all week at conferences. When he was in New York, he never seemed to leave the office." Marigold sighed. "I missed Wyoming so much. I missed the sky and the mountains and the air.

"It was the Christmas after we moved to the Upper East Side, Drew was four years old. I took him to Macy's to meet Santa Claus. Christmas was my favorite season; I was determined Drew wouldn't miss out. The line to see Santa Claus stretched on forever. It was so hot in the store. We'd been standing there for ages, when I started to feel faint.

"I looked for someone to watch Drew, but the other mothers were preoccupied. Before I knew what I was doing, I ducked out of the store. I was only going to stand outside long enough to get some air. But it had started snowing. The snowflakes felt so good against my skin, I was gone longer than I planned.

"When I returned, Drew was missing. I ran up and down the aisles, calling his name," she fretted. "Finally, security escorted me to the office. They brought Drew in a while later. He'd gotten on the escalator to find me. They discovered him crying behind a rack of coats."

Samantha wanted to say how terrible that must have been. But Marigold kept talking.

"The security guard drove us to our apartment; Arthur was waiting. He wouldn't listen to my apologies. He hired a nanny; I was hardly allowed near Drew. I wanted to take Drew to Jackson Hole, or to Palm Beach to stay with Arthur's parents. Arthur refused." She shrugged. "He thought I'd run away with Drew and not return.

"For months, I carried on. I taught myself to cook, I even took up painting. But the only talent I ever had was for horseback riding," she finished. "I barely saw Drew except for dinnertime and before he went to bed. One day, I packed a bag and flew to Jackson Hole. I imagined I'd be gone a few weeks. The longer I was here, the more I realized I could finally breathe."

"Why didn't you tell Arthur you were in Jackson Hole?" Samantha cut in.

"Arthur was so angry, I needed to find myself first," Marigold said doubtfully. "Then I couldn't leave. I even booked a ticket, but I came down with the flu and was in bed for a week. Finally, I wrote to Arthur. I begged him to send Drew. He didn't answer. His attorney sent a letter saying Arthur had started divorce proceedings. After that, I wrote to Drew every month. I never got a reply. Eventually I gave up."

"Drew wrote you letters when he was older," Samantha interrupted. "He didn't know where to send them."

"I had no idea that Arthur recently bought the ranch." Marigold looked at Samantha. "You mustn't tell Drew that I'm here. It would only hurt him."

"You're his mother," Samantha urged. "And it was so long ago."

Marigold's confidence seemed to return. She smoothed her slacks.

"I've spent the last twenty years learning from Native Americans. Some of my most valued friends are part of their communities. They believe the world has a certain balance. When someone loses something important, other things move in to take its place. Drew has many wonderful things in his life: work that he enjoys, his relationship with Arthur, and now he's found love. There's no room for me."

"What about Arthur?" Samantha asked. "He might forgive you."

Marigold gazed out the window. Snow fell on the pavement, and a light mist shrouded the village.

"Arthur wasn't that kind of man." Marigold shook her head. "I can't blame him. What I did was unforgivable."

Chapter Seventeen

Samantha turned into the ranch's driveway and switched off the engine. She had driven straight from the gift shop, but she wasn't ready to go inside. There was so much to think about.

The main house looked beautiful in the moonlight. The outdoor Christmas lights flickered and she could see the glow of the fireplace in the living room. Drew and Arthur were probably sitting with the other guests, drinking buttered rum and talking about tomorrow's ski conditions.

She recalled when she first arrived in Jackson Hole. The ranch resembled a holiday postcard with its slanted wooden roof and views of the valley. The mountains rose behind it and there was a forest of fir trees.

She had entered the living room, and Drew had been standing at the bar. She was so worried he would reveal her secrets to Arthur: she wasn't anything like Sloane Parker, her Instagram posts were fake. He merely smiled that impish smile and said he already knew what Samantha wanted to drink: Kahlúa with a dash of cream.

This was different. The diary wasn't her secret, it was Marigold's. And Marigold made Samantha promise she wouldn't say anything to Drew. But how could Samantha stay silent when Drew had been longing for his mother for years?

There was more. Love was built on trust. If Samantha wanted a relationship with Drew, she couldn't keep the diary to herself. Every time Drew looked at Samantha, she'd know she was hiding something.

The lights in the barn were on. She slipped the car keys into her pocket and started across the gravel.

"Blixen," she greeted the horse. "I'm sorry I didn't bring you anything, I'll make up for it tomorrow. You look warm and fed." She stroked his nose. "Bruno was so upset about the fire, I'm sure he's been spoiling you rotten."

She found a brush and started brushing Blixen's mane.

"It must be easy being a horse, you don't have doubts and fears," she continued. "I've gotten myself into a mess and I don't know what to do. I thought the only things to be afraid of were a plane crash, or an elk charging toward me, but I was wrong. You can be just as afraid of doing the wrong thing and losing something so precious, you'll never experience anything like it again."

There was the sound of footsteps. She turned and Bruno appeared in the doorway.

"I thought I heard someone." Bruno approached her. "I was in the tack room. The electrician left a bit of a mess, but at least he's finished. The wiring is perfect. Not that it matters," he said glumly. "Elaine said she'd let me have a Christmas tree in the barn again when hell freezes over."

"That doesn't sound like Elaine," Samantha said with a smile.

"Maybe not the last part, but she didn't have to." Bruno grimaced. "She says it with the way she looks at me. And what she serves me for dinner. For the last two nights it's been turkey and brussels sprouts. I hate brussels sprouts. That's why they're left over to begin with."

"Elaine will come around." Samantha grinned. "Brussels sprouts don't last forever."

"I didn't mean to eavesdrop, but I couldn't help overhearing you." Bruno's tone grew serious. "Is this something to do with Drew?"

Samantha glanced at Bruno in surprise.

"How did you know?" she wondered.

"He's been helping in the barn; he can't stop talking about you. Other people might not notice, he probably doesn't realize it himself. He kept squeezing your name in: 'Samantha was so brave in the fire; Samantha says Blixen loves huckleberry cereal.' I was young once; I can tell when a man is stuck on a girl."

"Please don't say anything," Samantha urged. "It's all so new, and he and Beatrix just broke up . . ."

"I raised two daughters, I know when to keep quiet." Bruno nodded. "Whatever is bothering you, it sounds like it's not something you can keep to yourself."

Samantha sighed. She put down the brush.

"I don't know what to do," she admitted. "I don't want to hurt Drew, but we need to be able to trust each other. You can't keep secrets in a relationship."

"Elaine says you can learn everything from books. I remember reading *Black Beauty* to our daughter. Black Beauty goes from being a happy foal raised on a farm to a difficult life pulling cabs in London. No one taught him how to pull a carriage, he had to learn by instinct to survive. Horses trust their instincts to overcome all sorts of obstacles," he counseled. "Let your instincts guide you. You can't do the wrong thing, as long as it comes from your heart."

"*Black Beauty* was one of my favorite books," Samantha said fondly. "I read it so many times, I wore out my copy."

Bruno smiled at her. He picked up the brush. "Go up to the main house and talk to Drew. Blixen has been receiving so much attention. If you keep brushing him, he'll think he's some kind of movie star."

Samantha stood at the kitchen counter pouring warm milk into a cup. Drew wasn't downstairs when she entered the ranch. She decided to make two mugs of hot chocolate.

The kitchen door opened. Drew stood in the hallway.

"Drew." Samantha looked up. Just seeing him made her feel better. "It's so cold outside, I was going to bring you a cup of hot chocolate."

Drew entered the kitchen. He perched on a chair.

"I saw you drive up; I came out to say hello. You went straight to the barn."

"I wanted to check on the horses," she said awkwardly.

"You dropped this." He took something out of his pocket. "It fell out of the car onto the driveway."

Drew handed her a silk-covered journal. Samantha turned it over and gasped. It was the diary. Samantha had planned on returning it to Arthur's library.

"When I picked it up, it fell open." Drew's brow furrowed. "I recognized my mother's name, so I read the first few entries. I had no idea my mother kept a diary. I've never seen it before and my father never mentioned it. Where did you get it and why didn't you tell me?"

Samantha eyes met Drew's. She had never seen him look so hurt.

Her stomach turned and she put down the mug.

"I don't think your father knows. It was hidden in the bookshelf, behind some other books. I was going to tell you," she faltered. "I didn't mean to find it. It just happened."

"You better tell me now." His tone was brusque. "Because I can't understand why you have something that was my mother's, and why you kept it a secret."

Samantha told him everything: about finding the journal in Arthur's bookshelf, taking it up to her room by accident. Her suspicions that Diana was his mother, wanting to know for sure before she said anything.

"You should never have started reading it in the first place," Drew said when she finished. "When you suspected that Diana was my mother, you should have told me. How could I ever trust you when you kept such a huge secret from me?"

"I only found out for sure this afternoon," Samantha said plaintively. "And it wasn't my secret. Diana calls herself Marigold now. She changed her name when she moved back to Jackson Hole. She works at the gift shop and we became friends, I had no idea she had anything to do with you. Then I read the diaries and realized who she was. She made me promise not to tell you. She's afraid of hurting you all over again."

"You think this doesn't hurt me?" He picked up the journal. "You should have come to me the moment you had any idea. We could have figured it out together."

"I'm sorry." She took a deep breath. "What I did was wrong. But you should meet Marigold. She's wise and kind. She gave me all sorts of advice before I knew who she was. She loves you, she only wanted to protect you."

"She abandoned me and my father." Drew's face grew hot. "And now she's hiding out in Jackson Hole. Even if I can't expect more from her, I did from you." He glowered. "I have feelings for you and thought you felt the same."

"I do have feelings for you," Samantha tried again. "I was going to bring you hot chocolate and tell you everything."

"When you care about someone, you don't pick and choose what to reveal and when to reveal it. You trust each other enough to tell the truth." He stood up. "I'm going out, I'll see you later."

Samantha sat on the bed and gazed out the window. She told Arthur she wasn't hungry for dinner and would make something for herself later.

For a moment, she wondered what it would be like to be at home. She and Socks would be getting ready to celebrate New Year's Eve with their annual traditions: Socks would eat wet food instead of his usual kibble. Samantha would drink sparkling apple cider while they watched the ball drop at Rockefeller Center on Samantha's laptop. She never drank champagne alone, and somehow watching the festivities on a proper television made her lonely. It was better to have it playing on the thirteen-inch screen of her computer.

For the first time, she didn't long to be in her apartment. And Socks was having a good time with Molly. Instead, Samantha wanted to spend New Year's Eve with Drew. They'd dance and mingle with the other guests. At midnight Arthur would make a toast. She and Drew would find a quiet spot to kiss and she'd never want the night to end.

The chance of that happening now was as likely as Santa Claus appearing with late Christmas presents.

The time on her phone said 9:00 P.M. There were twenty-four hours until the party. She had no idea how she could change Drew's mind, but she had to think of something.

Chapter Eighteen

The next morning, Samantha woke to a feeling of pressure in her chest. She'd barely slept all night. Every time she closed her eyes, she pictured Drew standing in the ranch's kitchen, holding the diary. He was so hurt and angry. And she couldn't blame him.

In the middle of the night she took out her notebook and scribbled down a plot for a Sloane Parker book. It's the first week of January and Sloane receives a letter from Phineas that she's been fired. Her old nemesis, Clarissa Cooper, is taking over her missions. She immediately calls Phineas and demands to know why. Phineas won't tell her. British Intelligence information is classified and Sloane has lost her intelligence clearance.

Sloane's phone rings. It's Miss Mulberry, Phineas's longtime secretary. Sloane and Miss Mulberry have been friends for years. Sloane never misses sending Miss Mulberry a Christmas fruitcake.

Miss Mulberry knows why Sloane was fired. Phineas was on his way to Christmas Eve lunch at his club when he saw Sloane at the Savoy with the Russian agent Boris Popov. Phineas assumed that Sloane was giving away British Intelligence secrets and had Miss Mulberry draft the letter the next day.

Miss Mulberry did some sleuthing and discovered the truth. Clarissa Cooper was at the Savoy with Boris. Clarissa arranged to meet Boris at the same time as Phineas's lunch, knowing Phineas would walk by the restaurant on the way to the club. Phineas would never come inside—he couldn't be seen talking to a Russian agent. Clarissa positioned herself with her back to the window. She wore the exact same Burberry trench coat that Sloane had for years. She even dyed her hair to be the same color as Sloane's glossy chestnut.

Sloane asks how Miss Mulberry can be sure. Miss Mulberry and Clarissa go to the same hair salon. Clarissa told her stylist and swore her to secrecy. One can never trust a stylist, they live for gossip.

Sloane calls Clarissa and insists Clarissa turn down the position. Then Sloane calls a friend at Immigration and alerts him that Boris is staying at the Savoy. Boris is deported and Sloane gets her job back, plus a 20 percent raise for the new year.

But writing out the plot didn't make Samantha feel better. Sloane would never get herself into a mess for love. And Sloane and Phineas have a history. Phineas believes in her.

Samantha idly opened her laptop. She could search for a flight and leave today. But Beatrix had already gone back to New York. Samantha couldn't disappoint Arthur by leaving before the party.

Her phone buzzed and she answered another call from her mother.

"Samantha, how are you?" her mother asked. "Did you see my photos on Instagram?"

"I haven't checked my feed this morning," Samantha replied.

"The New Year's Eve ball is tonight and the royal palace treated me to a complimentary visit at the beauty salon," her mother continued. "I have French nails plus a new hairstyle. The stylist wanted me to get extensions but I wasn't ready to try that." She paused. "I was calling to ask how it's going with your new man."

Samantha sat up against the headboard. She hadn't mentioned Drew to her mother.

"How do you know I met someone?"

"I had a feeling," her mother clucked. "Your father and I visited a fortune-teller this afternoon. It's all the rage in Monaco and perfectly legitimate. Madame LeFevre read my palm and saw church bells in my future. Your father says she meant the bells at the cathedral that ring at midnight on New Year's Eve, but he's wrong. I have my own intuition and I predict wedding bells in the near future."

Samantha was about to say wedding bells were as likely as snow in Monte Carlo. But there was no one else she could talk to. Perhaps her mother had some advice.

"I did meet someone," Samantha conceded. "He's warm and kind and handsome. But I did something stupid, and I'm afraid he won't forgive me."

"We all do foolish things sometimes," her mother said. "When your father and I were on the Alaskan cruise last year, he dressed up as a polar bear on Halloween. It was one of the most embarrassing nights of my life. And he won't let me forget how I sobbed during the first dance at Aunt Phyllis's wedding. I've never been good at drinking straight tequila, and 'At Last' always makes me cry."

Samantha took a deep breath. "This is a little bit different. I kept a secret from him. It wasn't my secret to share, but I should have told him anyway."

"I'm not sure one should share everything in a relationship," her mother countered. "When your father turned fifty, he wanted a toupee. He looked like a French mime but I never said anything. He decided against it, but I couldn't hurt his feelings by telling him the truth."

"This is a bit more serious than that," Samantha said. "He's hurt and I don't know if he'll forgive me."

"Do you really care about him?" her mother wondered.

"I've never felt like this before," Samantha admitted.

"Do you remember the book report you wrote in the fifth grade? It was for *My Friend Flicka*. The book is about a ten-year-old boy named Ken who lives on a ranch in Wyoming. Ken receives a filly named Flicka and it's Ken's job to care for her. Ken loves Flicka more than anything. Flicka is wounded and Ken's father might have to put her down. The day before she's supposed to be shot, Flicka wades into a stream and gets stuck. Ken goes in after her, but he can't release her. He spends the night in the stream comforting her. In the morning, Ken's father finds them. Ken has developed a fever but Flicka's wound is better. Ken almost dies from pneumonia, but Flicka improves. By the end of the book, Ken and Flicka both recover.

"In the report, you wrote that there was nothing more important than standing by the things you love. You got an A+ and I was so proud of you," her mother finished. "If you have feelings for this man, you can't let him go. It may not happen immediately, but eventually he'll get over it. Love is more powerful than you think." Her voice cracked. "If it wasn't, your father and I would never have made it to our thirtieth anniversary."

"You and Dad are special," Samantha said. For some reason, tears formed in her eyes. "Not every couple has a happy marriage and are good role models to their children."

"You're the one who's special, Samantha," her mother responded. "It was a delight to raise you, and nothing has changed since you became an adult. Though, I do worry about your wedding day."

"What do you mean?" Samantha wondered.

"Your father and I will cry so much, we'll run out of Kleenex," she chuckled. "Just think how the head table at the reception will look if it's littered with tissues."

Samantha laughed a little too, and her mother said goodbye. Samantha hung up.

Outside the window, the ground was coated with fresh snow. The sun nestled between the mountains and a family of deer darted across the field.

Jackson Hole was so beautiful and so many wonderful things had happened in such a short period of time, Samantha couldn't just give up now.

She jumped up and walked to the closet. She slipped on a pair of suede pants and a cashmere sweater. First, she'd do her hair and makeup and then she'd go downstairs. Drew had to appear sometime, and she'd be waiting for him.

Samantha spent the whole day curled up in an armchair in the living room. Every time the front door opened, she was certain it was Drew. But it never was.

By afternoon, she grew restless and walked out to the barn. No one was there, and she fed the horses and went back inside. She checked her phone a dozen times, but there was no call or text. She wanted to ask Arthur whether he'd seen Drew, but Arthur had gone into the village and hadn't returned.

There was nothing to do except get ready for the party.

She trudged upstairs and tried to get excited about her dress. Emily had packed it, and it was lovely: a Marchesa ruffled-silk cocktail dress and silver stilettos. When she first unpacked the shoes, she texted Emily and said she couldn't possibly walk in them, they were like something Sloane Parker would wear. Emily texted back that there would be no need for her to walk at a New Year's Eve party. All Samantha had to do was stand in them, holding a glass of champagne.

Now, Samantha took them out of the box. There didn't seem any point in wearing them when the only people who would notice were Arthur and perhaps Gladys. But she had promised she'd send Emily a photo.

She took a bath and fixed her hair and makeup. Then she spritzed her wrists with perfume and went downstairs to join the party.

In the few hours she'd been in her room, the living room had been completely transformed. The sofas were moved against the wall and there was a dance floor and a long bar. The rugs were rolled up and the wood floor was so polished, Samantha could see her reflection. Black and gold balloons hung from the ceiling, and the lights on the Christmas tree sparkled in the low light.

Round tables were scattered around the space. Each table held a floating lily and there were glass bowls of brightly colored jelly beans.

Arthur stood in the corner. He looked handsome in a black tuxedo and white bow tie.

"It looks like a fairy tale," Samantha said, joining him.

"It came out well, didn't it?" Arthur beamed. "Drew texted and said he got held up, he'd be here later." He glanced at Samantha. "You're not drinking champagne. Can I get you a glass?"

"It's a little early, I'll never make it to midnight if I start now." Samantha shook her head. "I'll walk around and say hello to the other guests."

Samantha moved away and stood by the window.

Drew had texted his father but he hadn't tried to contact Samantha. The feeling of desperation washed over her and her heart contracted. He obviously didn't want to talk to her and she was overwhelmed by how much knowing that hurt her.

"Samantha," a male voice said. "I need you in the barn."

Samantha turned around. It was Bruno. He wore his chauffer's uniform and his forehead was furrowed in a frown.

"Are the horses all right?" she asked anxiously.

"This isn't the place to discuss it." Bruno glanced around the room. "It's better if I show you."

It was freezing outside and Samantha only wore a thin dress. She grabbed a coat from the downstairs closet and followed Bruno.

The barn was dark when they entered.

"In the tack room," Bruno said, turning on some lights.

Samantha opened the door to the tack room. A figure stood in the corner. His back was to her.

"Drew," she said, when he turned around.

Drew wore a navy jacket and corduroy slacks. His boots were dusted with snow and there were snowflakes in his hair.

"Samantha. I wanted to talk to you before I went into the party," he said uncertainly.

Samantha's stomach dropped. Drew didn't want to embarrass her in front of everyone. He brought her out here to say he didn't think they should continue their relationship.

"I need to say something first," she blurted out before she could stop herself. "I know what I did was wrong. There's nothing more important than trust in a relationship; telling the truth comes before anything. I'm sorry and I didn't mean to hurt you." She fiddled with her jacket. "I know I said those things before. If I keep saying them, maybe at some point, you'll hear them."

Drew looked stone-faced and she was afraid she wasn't getting through to him. She took a deep breath and started again.

"When Marigold gave me the arrowhead pendant, I believed it kept me safe. I had the confidence to try things I wouldn't have before. But I was wrong. It wasn't the arrowhead; it was my feelings for you. When you fall in love, you care about the other person more than yourself. Every morning you wake up, and there's nothing you can't accomplish. It's the most wonderful feeling and it doesn't go away." She looked up at him. "Because you know the other person feels the same about you. Love gave me strength. Now that I found it, I won't let it slip away. It might take weeks or even months, but one day you'll see it too."

Drew remained silent. Samantha wrapped her jacket around her.

"I should go," she said awkwardly. "I'll tell Arthur I'm not feeling well and go up to my room. You enjoy the rest of the party."

She walked toward the door, but Drew called out.

"Samantha, wait," he stopped her. "You didn't let me say anything."

She turned around. "I didn't think you were going to."

"I was collecting my thoughts," he said somberly. He walked toward her.

"You're right, I was upset and angry. I even considered going back to New York today. Bruno found me in the kitchen, eating the crust off my sandwich." He smiled thinly. "It's a thing I used to do when I was a kid. He told me I was acting like a five-year-old, and I better snap out of it."

"Bruno?" Samantha repeated.

Drew nodded. He ran his hands through his hair.

"He couldn't stand by and watch me lose the best thing that will ever happen to me," he continued. "It took me a while to come around, but he was right. We all make mistakes. It would have been a much bigger mistake to let you go.

"I'm falling in love with you and I'll never feel like this again. I wanted to come and tell you right away. But there was something I had to do first. Bruno drove me into the village." He paused. "I spent the afternoon with my mother."

Samantha gasped.

"You were with Marigold?"

"We had a lot of things to talk about," Drew confirmed. "She wrote to me for years. I guess my father received the letters and never told me." He shifted his feet. "It doesn't excuse her for leaving, but holding on to a grudge doesn't help. She loves me and wants a relationship. We're going to try to start again."

Tears welled up in Samantha's eyes.

"I'm glad. She's a special person."

"She's upstairs having a cup of tea with Elaine," Drew said. He somehow looked lighter, as if a weight had been lifted from his shoulders. "She wants to come to the party, but I needed to talk to you first."

Drew took Samantha's hand. His palm was warm on top of hers. She remembered the first time their hands touched on the plane. She had asked him to tell her a story.

"What are you thinking about?" he asked, noticing her expression.

"If I hadn't been afraid of takeoff, we never would have started talking," Samantha said, smiling up at him.

"You are beautiful. I would have thought of some reason to talk to you," Drew said knowingly.

"I doubt that!" Samantha laughed. The worry and fear dissolved and she felt bright and happy. "You only asked me to move my books from your seat."

"It was a lot of books," he conceded. "We'll have to take that into consideration. Most women need a whole closet for their clothes; you'll need a whole room for your books."

"We have plenty of time to figure it out," Samantha replied. "Right now, we better go back to the house before Arthur sends a search party."

Drew lifted his hand and touched her cheek. "There's something I want to do first."

"What is it?"

He wrapped his arms around her and kissed her. The kiss was long and deep, and she kissed him back.

"I wanted to do that all afternoon," he said, when they parted. He leaned forward to kiss her again. "Now that I have, I don't want to stop."

Samantha stood in the living room, sipping a glass of champagne. Drew had gone upstairs to change. The party was in full swing. Jazz played over the speakers and couples danced on the dance floor. A waiter passed around platters of hors d'oeuvres, and crystal champagne flutes lined the bar.

The door to the kitchen opened. A woman stood in the hallway.

Samantha almost didn't recognize Marigold. She wore a black velvet cocktail dress and pearl earrings. Her hair was twisted into a knot, and there was the shimmer of lipstick on her mouth.

Samantha glanced across the room at Arthur. His brow furrowed and he clenched his glass. Marigold caught his eye and gave him a little wave.

Arthur crossed the room and joined her.

"Diana," he said. "What are you doing here?"

Marigold held out her hand.

"Bruno told me about the party," she replied. "I hope you don't mind me inviting myself. I felt like dancing."

"Like dancing?" Arthur repeated, puzzled.

Marigold's eyes twinkled and she smiled.

"I haven't danced in twenty-five years and I've missed it so much." She glanced up at Arthur. Her face was bright and expectant. "Would you dance with me?"

Arthur's expression changed. Samantha recognized that look. It was the way her parents sometimes looked at each other when no one else was in the room. It was the way Drew had looked at Samantha in the barn before he kissed her.

Arthur tucked Marigold's arms into his. He led her to the dance floor.

"I'd be delighted."

Chapter Nineteen

It was midmorning the next day, and Samantha stood in the ranch's kitchen. After the party, she and Drew stayed up talking for hours. This morning, Drew went for a run and Samantha was desperate for a cup of coffee.

Everything about last night had been magical. They danced and drank champagne and ate plates of quail eggs and king crab legs. Every now and then, they slipped away and stole kisses in the pantry.

At midnight, Arthur had arranged for a surprise fireworks display. The guests stood at the window while pink and silver-pink lights soared across the sky. Samantha had never felt so lucky. She was with Drew on New Year's Eve in one of the most beautiful places in the world.

This afternoon they were booked on the same flight to New York. Before they left, Samantha had to send some e-mails and finish packing.

Arthur stood at the kitchen door. He wore jogging sweats and a towel was draped around his neck.

"Samantha, good morning." He joined her at the espresso machine. "Would you like help with that?"

"Yes, please," she answered. "I'm still not sure how to use it. I'd have to stay an extra month to figure out all the buttons."

"It's not just you." Arthur placed two cups on the metal grill. "When they delivered it, they sent a guy whose only job is teach customers how to make a cappuccino."

Arthur waited for the milk to foam. He added it to the espresso and brought the cups to the table.

"I'm glad you're here. I wanted to talk to you." He sat down. "Drew and I went for a run this morning. We talked about everything. He's not ready to settle down and work at the publishing house. I don't mind at all." Arthur's eyes twinkled and he smiled. "It might be the fresh mountain air, but I'm feeling quite young myself. I'm not ready to turn it over to someone else."

"I'm glad." Samantha nodded. "The authors are lucky to have you."

"He also told me the wedding was canceled, he and Beatrix broke up. They were going to tell me together, but he couldn't wait. He called Beatrix this morning and got her approval." Arthur stirred a sugar cube into his coffee. "I suspected something like that. No bride leaves town one day before her wedding without a good reason."

Samantha concentrated on her cup. She was afraid to look at Arthur.

"Then he told me about you," Arthur continued. "He didn't have to say much, I already knew."

Samantha's eyes flew up to meet Arthur's.

"You knew?"

"Anyone could tell there was something between you," he chuckled. "You both have that certain glow." His voice became serious. "He's very taken with you, Samantha. I've never seen him like that before."

"I feel the same," Samantha said. "It's as if we've known each other forever."

"Feeling like that only happens once. When you find it, it's the best thing in the world. The problem is that everyday life gets in the way, and you forget what you have." He ran his fingers over the rim of his cup. "Then it can slip away before you realize what you lost."

Samantha's mind went to Diana. Arthur and Diana danced for hours last night, but Samantha hadn't seen Diana this morning.

"Of course, in some ways, life is easier these days," he reflected. "There are so many opportunities and many people work remotely." He gazed out the window. "I've been thinking of spending more time in Jackson Hole. I bought this ranch; I should enjoy it." He paused. "I wanted to talk to you about something else too. I didn't know that Diana was still in Jackson Hole until last night. I never answered the letters she wrote twenty-five years ago, and I didn't think she'd stay here forever. But perhaps subconsciously I thought it was possible. Why else would I have picked Jackson Hole rather than somewhere else?" he admitted, almost to himself. "I wanted to thank you."

"To thank me?" Samantha questioned.

"For bringing Diana to the party. Her journals must have sat on the bookshelf in New York for years. I never knew they were there, and everything was boxed and brought to Jackson Hole. Diana and I sat up all night and read them together." He looked at Samantha. "I learned more about her in a few hours than I did during our entire marriage, and it's thanks to you."

Samantha shook her head guiltily. "I should never have read it in the first place. I already apologized to Drew and Marigold."

"Sometimes we don't do things exactly right." Arthur shrugged. "In publishing it's called instinct. How many books do other editors turn down that an editor feels so strongly about, he insists I buy it? It ends up becoming a bestseller and everyone is thrilled. Something led you to read that diary and I'm grateful. You reunited the most important people in my life."

For a moment, Samantha was tempted to tell Arthur the truth about Sloane Parker's marketing campaign. But this wasn't the time and it wasn't only her decision. Charlie would have to agree to tell Arthur.

Besides, Samantha had an even better idea. She was going to write a different type of novel as well as writing the next Sloane Parker book.

She was going to write a love story.

The door opened and footsteps sounded in the hall-way.

"Samantha, Arthur." Marigold appeared. She wore tight-fitting slacks and a quilted jacket. "Bruno was introducing me to the horses in the barn. Blixen and I got along very well. He is a big fan of huckleberry cereal."

"Marigold," Samantha greeted her. "It's nice to see you."

Marigold joined them at the table. She glanced from Samantha to Arthur.

"Why don't you call me Diana. Arthur reminded me that it's such a pretty name."

Arthur touched Diana's hand. He leaned forward in his chair.

"I always thought it suited you," he said to Diana fondly. "It means 'goddess of the hunt.'"

"Bruno asked if I wanted to ride in the spring when the snow melts," Diana continued. "The horses will need to be exercised."

"Only if I can come too," Arthur answered. "Blixen can be a difficult horse to ride. He has a mind of his own."

Diana turned to Arthur. Her voice was firm but a smile played around her mouth.

"I've been riding for forty years," she reminded him. "I'm quite sure I can handle him."

Arthur's eyes crinkled at the corners. He leaned over and kissed her.

"I know you can," he chuckled. "I want to be there to watch."

Arthur sipped his coffee and turned to Samantha. "Perhaps next summer you and Drew can join us. There's nowhere as beautiful as Wyoming in the summer."

Samantha glanced out the window at the snow-covered mountains. She imagined what it would be like in the summer, when the fields were the brightest green and the forests were thick with fir trees.

She finished her coffee and nodded.

"I can't think of anything I'd like more."

Samantha sat at the dressing table in her room and took out her phone. She had promised her mother she'd look at the photos on Instagram of the royal ball. There was a picture of her parents on the steps of the palace. Her mother wore a green satin gown with a voluminous skirt. Her father was dashing in a white tuxedo, and they were being greeted by a page in a wig and breeches. She flicked through photos of them dancing, and being introduced to a woman wearing a jeweled tiara.

There was a direct message on Samantha's feed. It was from Beatrix, wishing her a happy new year. Underneath were an emoji of colored streamers and a handful of xox's.

Samantha flipped through Beatrix's feed. There was a photo of Beatrix stepping into a limousine. She wore the kind of dress only Beatrix could pull off: a skintight gold lamé sheath with a slit up the side. Her hair was held back to showcase her slender neck and she wore diamond earrings. Beside her was a man with dark hair and green eyes. The caption read, "On the way to the Society of Orthodontists Holiday Party at the Plaza. Are my teeth white enough?"

Samantha smiled and wondered if the man was the son of Beatrix's orthodontist.

Her phone buzzed and she answered.

"Samantha. It's Charlie." Charlie's voice came over the line. "I called to say happy new year, and to give you some news. The Hollywood producer called. Zach loves Sloane, he's going to give the book to his boss."

"I'm glad," Samantha said.

"I can already imagine Sloane on the big screen. Arthur will be over the moon," Charlie continued. "That reminds me, I have more good news. Emily got you the invitation of the year: a ticket to the Met Ball in May." His voice was full of enthusiasm. "You'll have to get the kind of dress that Sloane Parker would wear. It will time perfectly with the release of your next paperback. It will be great for your image."

Samantha fiddled with the phone.

"I can't go; I won't be in New York in May."

"What do you mean you won't be in New York? You hardly ever leave your apartment."

"I'm writing a new Sloane Parker book set in Thailand," she explained. "I'm going to spend a few months there doing research."

Charlie was silent. Samantha thought they had been cut off but his voice came over the phone's speaker.

"You do all your research on the internet," he protested. "I can't even get you to go out to Queens to try a new Thai restaurant."

"This book is very important to me; I want to get the details right."

"What will you do with Socks while you're gone?" he wondered.

"I was hoping he could stay with Emily's parents," Samantha ventured. "It seems like Socks made some new friends."

"I'm sure Emily's parents would be delighted," Charlie replied. There was a smile in his voice. "I told you Jackson Hole would be good for you. You sound like a new woman."

Samantha said goodbye and hung up. She opened the drawer to take out her hairbrush and something fell to the floor. It was the arrowhead pendant. It must have fallen off when she was getting ready to ride the mechanical bull.

There was a knock at the door. Drew poked his head inside.

"Are you ready? Bruno is waiting to drive us to the airport."

"I'm all packed," she said and nodded, slipping the pendant into her pocket. "I need to return something to Diana first."

"She's waiting downstairs with my father to say goodbye," Drew replied. He picked up Samantha's suitcase. "There's one more thing. I e-mailed Kaman and said we're coming to Thailand. He wants to give you a welcome present. I didn't know what you'd want."

Samantha glanced around the room to make sure she hadn't forgotten anything. A stack of fluffy white towels stood on the dresser, and there were fresh flowers in the vase on the bedside table.

"I can't think of anything," she answered, taking Drew's hand.

Her heart was full, and she felt warm and happy.

"I have everything I ever wanted."

Acknowledgments

Thank you to my wonderful agent, Johanna Castillo, and to my fantastic editor, Sallie Lotz at St. Martin's Press. And as always, thank you to my children for making every Christmas special: Alex, Andrew, Heather, Madeleine, and Thomas. And to Sarah and Lily.

Read on for a look ahead to

CHRISTMAS AT THE LAKE —

the next heartwarming Christmas novel
by Anita Hughes, now available in
trade paperback from St. Martin's Griffin!

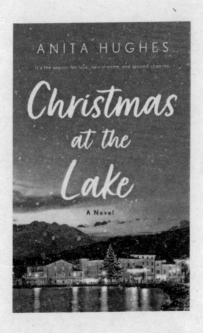

Chapter One

It was Christmas Eve and in six hours, Rebecca Huntley was going to marry her college sweetheart, and the love of her life, Ben Cole. They had planned for the ceremony to be held in the small chapel at Grace Cathedral with its mosaic tile floor and stained-glass windows, where Rebecca had listened to the San Francisco Boys Chorus sing Christmas carols every year since she could remember, followed by an intimate yet lavish reception at the Four Seasons Hotel. After their send-off, Rebecca and Ben planned to climb into the vintage car she had rented from a local film company for the three-hour drive to Christmas Cove Lodge in the quaint village of Christmas Cove on the shores of Lake Tahoe.

Rebecca was looking forward to the honeymoon more than anything. More than cutting the strawberry-infused wedding cake with lemon-buttercream frosting ordered from their favorite bakery on Fillmore Street. Even more than seeing the expression on Ben's face when she walked down the aisle in her oyster-colored silk Mikado gown. The honeymoon was going to be seven days of ice-skating, exploring the Christmas market, and strolling along the lakefront. Rebecca had even booked a sleigh ride with real reindeer.

The best part about the honeymoon was that it would be just her and Ben together. They had both agreed on a strict no-work policy. No phones, no laptops, and no late meetings that started at 5:00 p.m. and somehow lasted so long that when they arrived home at 10:00 p.m., they ate whatever they could find in the fridge, standing up at the counter, before falling into bed.

They had been working too hard lately. The company they started eight years ago when they were students at UC Berkeley, a dating app called Dealbreakers .com that matched up couples by the things they hated, instead of what they had in common, was about to go public. Their days were filled with meetings with venture capitalists.

It hadn't helped that Rebecca decided not to hire a wedding planner. She didn't want to simply show up at the church in her gown and have some woman in a severe black dress point her down the aisle when the organ music started. And she loved choosing the decor for the reception. She loved seeing the flower arrangements she had sketched for the florist become vases filled with crimson and white pansies. She had painstakingly picked out the party favors: small jars filled with coffee beans at each place setting.

All the weekends spent designing place cards, deciding on lighting and tablecloths, had been worth it. It was their wedding day, and they were going to remember it forever.

There was a knock at the door. The makeup artist wasn't due for two hours. It was probably the bellboy delivering more wedding presents to be stacked on the dining table and delivered to their apartment after the wedding.

Rebecca opened the door, and Ben stood in the hallway. He had spent the night at their apartment, while she stayed in the Four Seasons bridal suite. It had been odd waking up alone, and she wasn't used to staying somewhere so luxurious. The few times they'd allowed themselves proper vacations since founding their company, it was more fun to stay at Airbnbs or quaint hotels where they could soak up the local culture.

But Rebecca had made herself give in and enjoy the beauty and luxury of the bridal suite decorated for Christmas. The walls were paneled wood, and the carpet was a thick wool, the seafoam green of the San Francisco Bay. A white grand piano stood next to the window and there was a Christmas tree strung with colored lights. Linen sofas faced each other and the stone fireplace was hung with stockings. Vases of red and white Christmas roses stood everywhere: on the bar, in the bedroom, and on the giant coffee table carved from the base of a redwood tree. How often would she have the chance to stay in a place this beautiful?

"Ben." Rebecca ushered him inside. "Are you all right? You look terrible."

Ben had left the rehearsal dinner early, saying he felt a migraine coming on and that he didn't want it to get worse. A sheen of perspiration stuck to his forehead, and his blue eyes, usually as bright as the bay on a clear day, were tired and missing their usual shine.

"I didn't sleep," he admitted.

He followed her inside and sat down on the sofa. Even when he was sick, he was still incredibly handsome. His light brown hair was parted to the side and he had a dimple on his cheek.

Ben had been the captain of the soccer team at UC Berkeley. When they'd first met—standing at the counter of a burger place near campus—the first thing Rebecca noticed was how muscular and athletic he was, with broad shoulders and strong thighs.

They'd both put in their order at the same time. Cheeseburgers with steak fries and mayonnaise instead of ketchup.

The waitress had picked up her notepad and glanced from Rebecca to Ben.

"Is this together?"

"No, we've never met." Rebecca shook her head and turned to Ben. "I hate ketchup. It's always too watery and the fries get soggy."

"Ketchup is the worst," Ben agreed solemnly. "I've lost an entire burger to ketchup that pools on the bottom of the plate."

The waitress finished scribbling on her notepad.

"Well, perhaps you should eat together."

That's when Rebecca glanced over at Ben and noticed his radiant smile. She knew right away that something important had happened. That she'd met someone who would change her life.

Ben almost never got sick. In all the years of building the company, he only had the flu once. Even then, he kept working until Rebecca threatened to call his mother to come and take care of him unless he put away his laptop. But this was different. He couldn't stand at the altar in his tuxedo if he was about to faint.

"Rebecca, we need to talk," he began.

He twisted his watchband, the way he did before having a difficult conversation. Rebecca used to think it was odd that Ben wore a watch when everything he did was on his phone. The watch wasn't about telling the time, it was like one of those rubber stress balls many CEOs kept on their desk.

He pushed his hair over his forehead. "I can't get married."

"I'll call Kimi. She invented this drink for when she's coming down with something before an important presentation. A seaweed and cauliflower-rice smoothie, with a spoonful of cocoa powder. It sounds awful, but it works." Rebecca rushed to find her phone.

Kimi had been Rebecca's best friend ever since Kimi was hired as a senior programmer at Dealbreakers.com. Rebecca and Kimi bonded over a love of shopping at the Anthropologie outlet store and drinking cold-brew coffee. Over the years they had shared everything. Kimi's nine-month-old daughter, Leila, had just started day care two days a week, and Kimi wanted to make sure she and her husband, Andy, stayed healthy.

"I mean I can't marry you ever." Ben looked up at her. His mouth sagged at the corners and his expression was anguished. "You must have seen it coming, Rebecca. We've both changed. We couldn't even agree on the number of guests to invite to our wedding."

Ben had wanted to get married in Grace Cathedral's main sanctuary followed by a reception for three hundred in the Four Seasons' grand ballroom. They were one of Silicon Valley's power couples, so it was expected that they have an over-the-top celebration. Rebecca had no problem with large groups; she had given countless speeches at tech conventions. But this wasn't an industry event, as it was their wedding. Finally, they agreed on fifty guests, but with a surprise musical guest. Adam Levine from Maroon 5 was scheduled to perform.

But Ben was right, they hadn't agreed on many things recently. For years, they lived frugally and poured all their money into the company. Lately, Ben was more interested in the trappings of success. He had ordered one of those German cars you built out online, and then took months to arrive. He wanted to put down a deposit on a penthouse in the newest skyscraper being built South of Market. Rebecca longed to buy a house near the water in Sausalito. Luckily, they both fell in love with a Bernadoodle puppy named Oliver, and it was impossible to have a dog when you lived thirty floors up in the sky. They compromised and made an offer on a sweet Victorian house in the Castro district.

Rebecca had always appreciated the simple things. Her bedside table held a forever-growing stack of books she was reading. Her favorite activity on the weekends was simply walking with Ben along the pier. And she was most excited about moving into a house because they could have a garden. But Ben hadn't minded before. It was only in the past few months that the things she enjoyed weren't enough for him.

They'd been together for most of their twenties. Of course they had changed. That didn't mean they'd stopped loving each other, Rebecca thought.

The words tried to register in her brain. Whatever Ben was going through could be fixed. As long as they faced it together.

"We can postpone the wedding and go to therapy. Kimi and Andy went through a rough period a year ago, and now they're happier than ever."

"You know I don't believe in therapy," Ben said. "And this isn't the kind of thing that can be fixed. I am sorry, Rebecca."

Rebecca was alarmed by the change in his voice. It was stern and almost businesslike. A heavy feeling settled on her chest. Once, she read that long-term relationships based on mutual love and respect didn't break up. Unless one of the couple fell in love. With someone else.

Ben had developed feelings for another woman. Rebecca knew exactly who.

"It's Natalie, isn't it?" she breathed.

Natalie Gordon was the head of legal. She had only been at the company less than a year, and even Rebecca was intimidated by her. Natalie had graduated from Duke undergrad and Columbia Law School. She'd even won Miss Teenage Louisiana, which she'd only entered so she could donate the prize money to charity.

Natalie was instrumental in their public offering, so it made sense that Natalie and Ben spent so much time together. Rebecca had noticed the proprietary air Natalie assumed about Ben when they were all in the conference room together. And there had been late meetings that Rebecca didn't attend. She had her own work, and there was often some wedding detail that she had to take care of.

She tried to think of any times when Ben and Natalie had been alone. There were a few Saturday mornings that Ben met Natalie at a café to talk strategy. Ben went jogging first, and he always invited Rebecca to join them. Rebecca declined; she was happy to spend the extra hours in bed and make her own leisurely coffee when she got up.

And there was one Friday night a couple of weeks ago, when Ben skipped their cherished Friday-night ritual of eating takeout and watching a cheesy movie on Netflix and worked late at the office. He had been so stressed, Rebecca hadn't said anything even though she was disappointed. Should Rebecca have volunteered to pick up the takeout and bring it to the office?

Had Natalie been with him then?

Why hadn't Rebecca noticed the cracks forming in their relationship, the differences in their goals, like hairline fractures in a piece of pottery? If she had, she could have tried to smooth them over before Natalie filled them in herself.

A thought flashed through her mind, and she pushed it away. If she hadn't insisted on doing the planning herself, would this wedding have gotten as far as it did?

Ben looked at her guiltily.

"It's nothing either of us planned. Natalie almost quit because she didn't want to come between us." He spread his hands in his lap. "I convinced her to stay. It wouldn't have helped." He hung his head. "The kind of thing Natalie and I have, it doesn't go away."

Suddenly, Rebecca was so angry, she could barely breathe.

"Of course you fell for Natalie. It's a chapter in a psychology textbook." Her eyes flamed. "The hotshot attorney who pushes a computer screen across the table promising you the payoff for all the years of twelve-hour days. It doesn't hurt that she looks like Hailee Steinfeld."

Rebecca hated commenting on another woman's looks. And she adored Hailee Steinfeld; she was a gifted actress. But she had to say something—Natalie had stolen her fiancé.

"It's not like that," Ben said quietly. "I thought you more than anyone would understand. Haven't we always said that the only thing we care about is each other's happiness?"

Rebecca felt as if she had been punched in the stomach. When they'd first started dating, Rebecca had confided her nervousness about getting serious. Her parents had divorced when she was ten. Her parents almost never fought, so it was a surprise to Rebecca. Later her father explained they got married too young. Her mother was in her last year in art school and her father was a newly graduated engineer. They grew apart until her mother fell in love and moved to a cattle farm in Argentina. It was just Rebecca and her father for a long time and Rebecca often felt lonely. It took years to repair her relationship with her mother and they still weren't close. When she was in her senior year of high school, her father remarried and now he lived in Seattle with his new wife and twin sons. Rebecca visited twice a year, but her father was usually too busy to spend quality time together.

Ben had simply kissed her and said he would never hurt her. She believed him, and for the last eight years he had been her family.

They had solved so many crises together. There was the time when Dealbreakers.com was about to go under and they finally secured an investor. They had been about to sign the deal when they discovered a company in the investor's portfolio with questionable ethics. They spent two sleepless nights and went through six bags of Trader Joe's plantain chips, trying to decide what to do. Eventually, they decided to turn down the investor. It was better to let Dealbreakers fail than to be part of anything they didn't approve of.

And there had been crises outside the office too. Like when their beloved Biggles, the beagle mix they rescued from an animal shelter, had to be put down. They held each other so tightly, Rebecca thought she'd suffocate and choke on her own tears at the same time. It had taken until recently for either of them to be ready to get another dog.

This wasn't something they could solve together. Now it was Rebecca who was standing between Ben and what he wanted.

"How could you wait until today?" Rebecca demanded. "We're supposed to get married in six hours."

"I thought if I ignored my feelings, eventually they might go away," Ben sighed. "I finally came to terms with the fact that it was impossible at the rehearsal." He rubbed his chin. "I couldn't start our marriage by living a lie. I didn't want to tell you at the rehearsal dinner, I thought it would be better if we were alone."

Did that mean Ben was with Natalie last night? Had he gone home, or had he stayed at her place instead?

"Natalie and I are going to leave tonight for three weeks in St. Barts," Ben said, as if he could read her mind. "Her parents rent a villa at a resort there every Christmas, and I found a last-minute flight. I'll e-mail the guests before we go. They all signed nondisclosure agreements about the wedding. None of this will leak out and affect the public offering. When we return, we can all get on with our lives."

Rebecca wanted to say she couldn't care less about the public offering. But it wouldn't help.

"We still haven't closed on the new house, I'm sure we can get out of it." Ben kept talking. "And you can have Oliver. Natalie doesn't like big dogs, and I know how much he already means to you."

They were supposed to pick up the new puppy when they returned from the honeymoon. Rebecca had pictures of him on her phone. His adorable black-and-white face, the white tip on his tail. Every time she looked at it, she felt happy. How would she look after a dog who would one day grow to be sixty pounds in their eight-hundred-square-foot apartment? She didn't care, it was love at first sight.

Ben stood up and walked to the door.

"I should go." He stuffed his hands in his pockets.

"I'm really sorry, Rebecca. One day you'll see that it was the right thing to do."

And then he left, closing the door behind him.

The suite was completely quiet. The lights on the Christmas tree twinkled and Rebecca could smell pine needles and roses. She stood up and walked uncertainly into the bedroom. Her lace veil sat on the dressing table, and her shoes—the most romantic shoes she'd ever owned, satin sling-back heels with pearl-encrusted bows—stood next to the bed.

She sank down onto the floor and hugged the shoes to her chest. Then she let the tears come, until her shoulders shook, her T-shirt was wet, and she thought she'd never stop sobbing.

An hour later, Kimi arrived. Rebecca had sent her a flurry of texts.

"So many men get cold feet before their wedding," Kimi said when Rebecca had repeated the whole story.

They sat in the suite's living room, drinking vodka and orange juice from the minibar. For once, Rebecca didn't care what the minibar cost. She only wanted something to numb the pain.

"And all couples disagree on things," Kimi continued. "You know how I felt about having a baby. Now I'd walk on hot coals to get Leila's favorite teddy bear if she dropped it."

Kimi's husband, Andy, was thirty-four and anxious to start a family. Kimi wanted children too, but she preferred to wait a few years. Her parents had emigrated from South Korea when Kimi was a baby so she could have every opportunity. Kimi had worked hard to get into UCLA, and then went to Stanford for her master's degree in computer science before accepting the position at Deal breakers.com.

She didn't want to put a child in day care full-time, but she loved her job and cherished her time with Andy. They went to therapy and came to an agreement. Andy would work from home three days a week, and they'd leave Leila with Kimi's parents every Friday evening so they never missed a date night.

"You would not risk third-degree burns to give Leila her stuffed animal." Rebecca smiled for the first time since she'd spoken to Ben. "And Ben won't go to therapy. You work with Natalie every day; I can't compete with her."

In the magazine profiles about Ben and Rebecca, the writer usually described Rebecca as "attractive" and "engaging." She had inherited her mother's fine light brown hair and her father's brown eyes. Her body was lean from years of running. But she couldn't compare to Natalie's beauty and charisma.

"Looks have nothing to do with love. I loved Andy even when he went to that barber in the Mission District and got a haircut that embarrassed his own mother."

"It's not just Natalie's looks, it's the way she carries herself," Rebecca reflected. "As if she knows how special she is, and everyone in the room should be grateful to be around her."

"That sounds exhausting," Kimi said sullenly. "Marriage isn't about winning some sort of prize. It's about doing the hard work together. The week after Leila was born, my boobs stuck to anything I was wearing, and I made coffee in the Instant Pot instead of the coffeemaker. We ate coffee-infused chicken and rice for days, neither of us could sleep because we were loaded up with caffeine. Finally, Andy insisted we order takeout and send our clothes to the cleaners. We spent the whole week holding Leila and watching *The Bachelor*. It was the best week of my life."

A pain shot through Rebecca's shoulders. She and Ben had wanted children. A girl and a boy, and a third baby if the first two were the same sex.

"I'm sorry." Kimi noticed Rebecca's expression. "Being a parent isn't all about those adorable winter jackets with ears, and cute booties with matching scarves in the Christmas windows at Macy's. Leila is teething. She's like a little beaver, I have bite marks on my shoulder."

Rebecca set her glass on the coffee table. Getting drunk would only delay the pain. It was better to feel it and get it over with.

"I don't want to be married to someone who doesn't love me," Rebecca conceded. "But you can't imagine how it feels. In a few hours, the Four Seasons' white Rolls-Royce was supposed to take us to the church. The window would mist up because it's so cold outside, and I'd keep rubbing it with my glove because I wouldn't want to miss seeing the eighty-foot Christmas tree in Union Square or City Hall lit up for Christmas on my wedding day. At the reception, Ben was supposed to give a toast"—her eyes filled with tears—"and after the reception, we were to go down to the parking garage and get into the car for our honeymoon. The car was going to be a surprise for Ben. A silver 1963 Corvette that was used in a *Fast and Furious* movie. It took me ages to track it down." Rebecca kept talking, as if it was the only way to stop the images of her wedding day from disappearing forever. "It would be so late when we arrive at Christmas Cove Lodge that we'd both be tempted to crawl into bed. But when we were escorted to our suite, and we saw the crackling fire in the fireplace, and the tray of champagne, hot chocolate, and pumpkin bread on the coffee table, we would decide to stay up all night and talk about the wedding instead." She gulped. "By the time the fire would go out and we'd eaten the last bite of pumpkin bread, we'd fall asleep together on the sofa. I'd still be in my going-away outfit and Ben would be wearing his tuxedo. Except without the tie," she finished bravely. "Ben hates wearing a tie. He'd probably take it off the minute the reception ended."

Kimi ran her fingernails over the rim of her glass.

"You can still go on the honeymoon. There's no point staying in San Francisco," Kimi suggested. "Instead of listening to tourists ring the bells of the cable cars all day, you can relax in an indoor Jacuzzi overlooking the lake."

"I can't go on my honeymoon alone," Rebecca objected.

Kimi jumped up. Her sleek black hair swayed at her shoulders and she paced around the room.

"I'll go with you. Andy is off all week, he can take care of Leila." Her tone grew excited. "We'll go snowshoeing and eat at those funky little diners where they don't even have a menu, and the cook serves whatever he likes."

"The suite only has one bed," Rebecca said doubtfully.

But deep down, she knew it was a good idea. She wasn't ready to go back to the apartment. And she didn't want to be alone in San Francisco at Christmas. Her mother hadn't even come for the wedding. She was going to watch it on FaceTime from Argentina. Rebecca had been upset; she'd even offered to buy plane tickets for her mother and her husband, Carlos. Her mother explained it wasn't the cost. Carlos had injured his back and couldn't sit in a plane for so many hours. Carlos was in a lot of pain, and her mother didn't want to leave him. Her father and his family had come for the wedding, but they were treating it like a Christmas vacation. They were so busy sightseeing, she had barely seen them. In the morning they were leaving to spend a few days in Carmel before returning to Seattle.

"I'd be happy to share the bed, or I can take the sofa," Kimi said cheerfully. "Anything will be better than sleeping with a bit of drool on the sheets and waking up with a crick in my neck because I fell asleep while I was nursing."

Why shouldn't Rebecca use their reservation for a vacation? Lake Tahoe was her favorite place in the world. It had been her idea to spend their honeymoon there. Ben had wanted to go skiing in the French Alps, or rent an overwater bungalow in Tahiti with a Plexiglas floor, so you could see all the fish.

Rebecca didn't want to do something so extravagant when they were buying a house and paying off Ben's new car, and also had all the expenses of a new puppy. And Lake Tahoe was special to them. It was where they'd gotten engaged two summers ago.

It had been the Fourth of July weekend. They'd spent three nights at a charming Airbnb. On the last evening, Ben packed a picnic and they ate it on the shores of the lake. He chose all their favorite foods: focaccia and tomatoes and mozzarella with pesto.

"We don't have the time or money to go to Lake Como in Italy, so I thought we could have an Italian picnic instead," he'd said, filling two glasses with cabernet.

It was almost sunset, and the lake was infused with a pink-and-gold light. A layer of fog settled on the water, and the air smelled of primroses and pansies.

"I can't think of anyplace I'd rather be," Rebecca said as she stretched her legs.

They had spent the whole day bicycling around the lake. Her calves ached, her shoulders were slightly sunburned, and she'd never felt so happy.

"You have to try the dessert." Ben handed her a white ceramic cup. "It's tiramisu. The bakery on Main Street uses all local ingredients."

Rebecca ate the tiramisu. At the bottom of the cup were the words "Will you marry me?"

She put her hand over her mouth and gasped. They had talked about getting married for a while, but there was always so much to do.

"I know we said we wouldn't think about getting married until we felt the company was stable"—Ben was kneeling on the picnic blanket—"but I don't care if we never travel farther than here, or if we live in the same one-bedroom apartment for the rest of our lives. All I want and need is right in front of me." He took a velvet box out of his pocket. "You make me happier than I ever thought possible. Rebecca Huntley, will you marry me?"

Rebecca nodded yes, and Ben slipped the diamond solitaire ring on her finger. Then they kissed for so long, her lips were numb. They only parted when a pigeon came dangerously close and threatened to eat the leftover pesto.

How had Ben gone from arranging something so simple and sweet to wanting products and experiences that were promoted by influencers with millions of followers? And how had he fallen in love with Natalie? Most importantly, how had she missed the signs?

"You can spend the whole week crying on my shoulder," Kimi said, interrupting her thoughts. "That's what a mother's shoulder is for." She grinned.

Rebecca stood up and hugged her friend.

"I'd love to go together, and I promise I won't cry." She wiped her eyes deliberately. "How can I, when I'm lucky enough to spend Christmas week with my best friend in Christmas Cove?"